circa 2000

circa 2000

gay fiction at the millennium

edited by

Robert Drake & Terry Wolverton

 alyson books

los angeles | new york

MANUFACTURED IN THE UNITED STATES OF AMERICA.

THIS TRADE PAPERBACK ORIGINAL IS PUBLISHED BY
ALYSON PUBLICATIONS,
P.O. BOX 4371, LOS ANGELES, CA 90078-4371.
DISTRIBUTION IN THE UNITED KINGDOM BY
TURNAROUND PUBLISHER SERVICES LTD.,
UNIT 3, OLYMPIA TRADING ESTATE, COBURG ROAD, WOOD GREEN,
LONDON N22 6TZ ENGLAND.

FIRST EDITION: SEPTEMBER 2000

00 01 02 03 04 **a** 10 9 8 7 6 5 4 3 2 1

ISBN: 1-55583-517-1

LIBRARY OF CONGRESS CATALOGING-IN-PUBLICATION DATA
CIRCA 2000 : GAY FICTION AT THE MILLENNIUM / EDITED BY
ROBERT DRAKE AND TERRY WOLVERTON—1ST ED.
    ISBN 1-55583-517-1 (PBK)
    1. GAY MEN—FICTION. 2. GAY MEN'S WRITINGS, AMERICAN.
3. AMERICAN FICTION—20TH CENTURY. 4. AMERICAN FICTION—
MALE AUTHORS. I. DRAKE, ROBERT. II. WOLVERTON, TERRY.
PS648.H57 C57 2000
813'.540809206642—DC21   00-032773

CREDITS
COVER PHOTOGRAPHY AND DESIGN BY PHILIP PIROLO.

Contents

Introduction

It's a hazy, white-sky afternoon in Los Angeles, in that slow surreal week between Christmas and New Year's when everything seems in a state of suspension, and I am talking on the phone to Robert Drake. It's midnight in Dublin, where he takes the call. Robert is my friend and colleague; for the past decade, he and I have worked together editing nine literary anthologies of work by lesbians and gay men.

We don't talk on the phone as much since he moved to Ireland the summer of 1998; we rely mostly on frequent but terse E-mails detailing the tasks outstanding for these millennial anthologies—endlessly revised contributors' lists, promotional strategies, the nightmare of obtaining permissions to reprint.

Our conversation today has been more personal—the status of my ongoing heartbreak over a failed love affair, his missing the longtime partner he left behind in the States despite his happiness with his new young Irish lover. Inevitably, though, our conversation strays back to work, the strongest thread that connects us.

"Do you realize," he says pensively, "that these are probably the last anthologies we'll do together?"

The afternoon is blueing toward darkness, and as he asks this, I feel a pang. Of course I had known it—my burnout with editing and his relocation to Ireland had virtually assured it—but his articulation brings home the pathos of this milestone.

I never aspired to be an editor. When I first met Robert in the summer of 1989, I was working on a novel and teaching creative writing classes at the Los Angeles Gay and Lesbian Center. My students were giving a reading, and Robert came because he'd read about it in the paper.

Afterward he introduced himself to me, a tall, dark-haired man whose wire-rimmed glasses called attention to a distinctive profile. He was an agent, he explained, interested in representing gay and lesbian writers. He talked too fast, the way agents do, but with more sincerity. "I'm really impressed with a lot of what I've heard today," he told me, "and I wonder if you'd like to work with me."

His idea was to produce a volume of new fiction by West Coast gay and lesbian writers. "Several editors have told me that California is where the hot new writing is coming from." Robert believed I could help him locate some of that "hot new writing," and I agreed to try.

That first volume, *Indivisible* (Plume, 1991), expressed a value that was central to our work together: that the gay and lesbian literary communities could benefit from cross-pollination, that we need to be reading each other's work. This stance confounded the segregated marketing structures of gay and lesbian publishing. When we approached publishers about a second volume, everyone refused us, not because they hadn't liked or respected the first volume, but because no one could figure out how to market it.

We then proposed a series of companion volumes, *His* and *Hers*, coedited by both of us, released simultaneously. In 1998 *His*[2] received a Lambda Literary Award, but Robert was in Ireland, so I accepted it on his behalf.

An inveterate fan of *The X-Files*, Robert used to joke that he and I were the Scully and Mulder of gay and lesbian letters; he is the true believer, writing of the gay community as the "mother ship," while I am the hard-eyed pragmatist, worrying about deadlines and systems. What we share is a passion for and commitment to the craft of fiction; over the ten years we've worked together, we've striven to establish and fulfill high standards of literary merit, publishing work that stretches its readers from the standpoints of both form and content.

The anthology you hold now was not my idea. The day Robert

called me to propose *Circa 2000: Gay Fiction at the Millennium* and its companion volume for lesbians, I was cranky and burned out. Although I felt proud of the seven books we had already produced, the sacrificial nature of the enterprise was beginning to wear on me. Reading hundreds of manuscripts, negotiating with authors and agents who seemed to believe we were making a whole lot more money on these books than we ever have (the compensation works out to slightly less than 10 cents per manuscript we read), confronting the seemingly insurmountable difficulty of upping our sales figures with only a minuscule marketing budget—these things were taking their toll on my time, my spirit, and my own writing.

Robert listened to me vent and never disagreed. I knew he was lying when he assured me this would be a project on which we would make a bundle (we didn't); I similarly doubted him when he claimed this process would be so much easier because we wouldn't need to invite open submissions (it wasn't). He still talked too fast, but I let his persuasions wash over me until I gave in. I enjoyed our working process, the way our sensibilities differed—I drawn to more experimental, craft-based work; he to classical stories and historical settings, more popular themes—yet we still retained respect for one another. I liked the way he'd give in to me when I really wanted a story or fiercely argued against one. We both gave each other that latitude, didn't insist on consensus, allowed one another to include those works about which we felt passionate.

Our process underwent a change when Robert moved to Ireland the summer of 1998. He'd met a young man, fallen in love, was willing to uproot his entire life to pursue the relationship. I questioned the wisdom of this path, but when he said to me, "If I don't do this, I'll regret it for the rest of my life," I could only wish him well.

On this day in late December, when he reminds me that our work together is about to come to an end, I know I will miss it. I'll miss the great enthusiasm he brings to each project, the irreverence with which he regards the sacred cows of gay and lesbian politics; I'll even miss scolding him for missed deadlines and lame excuses.

What neither of us can know, as the tumult of 1998 draws to a merciful close, is that our work together will be halted by a much more ominous event. That on January 31, 1999, in Sligo, Ireland, Robert will be gay-bashed, beaten unconscious in his own home by two men with whom he'd been earlier seen drinking in a pub. That these men would later claim to police they'd been "victims of a homosexual pass" (a ridiculous claim to any of us who know Robert). That Robert would be in a coma for two months, eventually Medivac'd home to Philadelphia, still unconscious. Or that I would visit him in the hospital in early May, witness my friend and colleague wizened, unable to speak or control his movements. Witness him struggle to lift a baseball cap from his head—each brain function summoned by will, each movement separate as stop-time photography—and to put it on again. That he would cry when I tell him, "I love you."

Neither of us can know how it will fall to me to finish alone our last projects, months behind schedule, coaxed but never pressured by my understanding editor. The book you hold now is the product of Robert's vision, our combined selections, and finally my efforts. We sought to feature works by those writers we believe will be influential in the new millennium. There are authors included here who have been prominent in the closing decades of the 20th century: M. Shayne Bell, Bernard Cooper, Scott Heim, David Leavitt, Michael Lowenthal, William J. Mann, Christian McLaughlin, Frank Ronan, and Colm Tóibín. There are authors whose influence is just beginning to be felt: Mitch Cullin, Jameson Currier, David Ebershoff, Thomas Glave, Russell Leong, Jaime Manrique, David Newman, and David Vernon. And we've included a few of writers who are at the beginning of their publishing careers—Eitan Alexander, Andy Quan, and Keith Ridgway—whose voices promise that we will be hearing a lot more from them in the decades to come.

It's an idiosyncratic roster of writers, heavily dependent on Robert's and my own tastes. It is not entirely faithful to the list Robert had sworn was final just prior to his attack; one writer declined to be included, two writers I could never locate. There are many outstanding writers who could have easily substituted for the ones who are included here with no diminution of the overall product. Our intention is not to anoint these writers above others but to say simply, here are some writers worth paying attention to; here are some voices that will continue to have resonance.

I'm not much given to fixed categories. Novel excerpts bump up against short stories; science fiction jostles beside literary fiction; punk sensibility elbows its way next to high camp and classically constructed stories. The end of the 20th century has been about the breaking down of fixed categories—of art forms, of culture, of gender, of sexual orientation—the blurring of borders to allow an infinite variety of options for identity and expression. This dissolution brings excitement and possibility but also confusion, frustration, a certain anxiety. My students, for example, want me to tell them definitively how a short story is different from a personal essay; their foreheads pucker with worry when I say that those forms are moving closer and closer together. Especially in the United States, we want to *know,* and fixed categories allow us the illusion—however false—that we do.

How long we can float in this sea of suspended definitions is difficult to predict, and in part dependent on the culture's tolerance for ambiguity. Will the millennium see a move back to rigid definitions and the certainty they promise, or will we continue to dissolve categories until we humans understand ourselves quite differently, until sexual orientation as identity seems a quaint and archaic notion?

If we live long enough, we may discover answers to these questions. Until then, let's revel in art, with all its ambiguities. What this anthology aims to do is introduce you to, or remind you about, a selection of writers whose intelligence, style, and heart may ease our passage into the next millennium.

It is with humility, ever more mindful of the frailty, the ephemeral nature of all things, that I, on behalf of Robert and myself, offer you this book.

—Terry Wolverton

Beneath the Planet of the Compulsives

Eitan Alexander

"I have never made but one prayer to God, a very short one: 'O Lord, make my enemies ridiculous.' And God granted it." —Voltaire

I have this problem. And one of the things I'm doing about it is going to these meetings. I'm in this program called Coitus and Anal Compulsive Addicts Anonymous. That makes the acronym for it C.A.A.C.A.A. At first I never even used to mention that name to anyone outside the group. It doesn't bother me that much anymore. Still, some people in the program are really hyper about the "anonymous" part, so don't tell anyone else about this.

I guess it would help if I gave you some background on what C.A.A.C.A.A. is all about. Basically, it's a program to get you sober. Not from drugs—at least, not from what most people think of as drugs, like alcohol, cocaine, or heroin. It's for people who are addicted to sex or love. Or drama. Until recently, if I was with another homosexual, it was mostly stuff like jacking off in a car or giving a blow job in a porno booth or getting reamed, bent over a trash can in an alley. It's hard to break the habits you develop as a child. About three years ago, I got arrested by an undercover transit cop. The big ape came on to me in an empty Metro Line car at 3 A.M. It was either jail time or a fine, community service, and mandatory attendance at a twelve-step group for sexual recovery. There are actually a lot of different programs that deal with this issue, but I picked C.A.A.C.A.A. because it's almost all gay men that are involved with it, and that's a big part of my problem. Being involved with gay men.

I fulfilled my debt to society after a year, but I'm still showing up.

At some meetings we read from *Redemption and Healing;* it's the main piece of literature for the group. We pick a chapter, then one person reads the first paragraph and passes it to the person on his left, who has to stop squirming in his metal folding chair long enough to read it before passing it on again. After the chapter is finished, we discuss it. It's kind of like Bible study, although it's not supposed to be religious at all, it's supposed to be "spiritual." But all the references to God and prayer make that a little difficult to figure out. Some people in the program still haven't or don't want to.

Like this guy from the program that I dated once. C.A.A.C.A.A. doesn't encourage dating between members, but it's acceptable if you've been in the program for a while; you're just supposed to discuss it reasonably first. His idea of a date turned out to be a service at this "nondenominational" church. It wasn't an ideal first date, but it was OK. There was an incredible choir. I was really enjoying them, and then they got to a song where they had choreographed these little movements. The choir was singing about new beginnings. Every time they sang about the sunrise in the chorus, they raised their arms in big circles above their heads, and when they sang about turning your life around, they made a 360-degree turn where they were standing, holding their arms up, and wiggling their fingers. It reminded me of a third-grade recital. I said so to my date while we were swaying back and forth and clapping, and he smiled back at me.

After the service we went for a walk on the beach. I saw some people I knew and made introductions. My date told them about the church service, all teeth and enthusiasm. While he talked my friends kept on turning to me and squinting. When he started talking about the choir, I kind of nudged him with my elbow and imitated the choir's choreography, making a little circular trail in the sand. My friends giggled a little. The guy I was with turned around and walked away.

So I spent the rest of the day with my friends. One of them had just bought the complete collection of *The Simpsons* on disc. We were all laughing as we talked about our favorite episodes and moments. I gave my flawless vocal impersonation of Grandpa Simpson after the minimum of prodding. Then I told everyone the details of my afternoon, and we laughed some more.

The next night I was at a meeting, my church date came in late and almost immediately shared about the whole incident, no names mentioned, and thanked God for letting him love himself enough to take care of himself and set boundaries. I still see him at almost every meeting I go to. Especially at the study meetings, the ones where we read from *Redemption and Healing*.

It's this study meeting that I went to a short while ago that I want to tell you about. It was pretty crowded. I got there in time to grab the last available seat. The chairs were arranged in concentric circles, and there was an empty one in the small circle in the middle. Sitting across from me was this guy that I've never seen in the group before. Another ape. I'm no specist; I know the correct term is Simian-American. It's just that this monkey was really fine, a lot better looking than that cop on the bus. I started looking around the room, I didn't want to just sit there and gape at him. In the meetings guys will share about how they sexualize the other men that are in the room with them. They're always thanked for their honesty afterward, but you don't want to be caught in the act. Besides, I didn't want to make my monkey uncomfortable. He was the only simian in the room. I saw some familiar faces and nodded hello. I didn't see my church date anywhere. Wherever I looked though, my eyes always came back to that ape.

He was big. Huge, really; he obviously spent a lot of time at the gym. You know how those guys get once they start pumping iron, they look like superheroes. I can't believe people ever thought they could impose some sort of control over that. I remember the pictures I would load down from the Grid when I was about ten. Shots of street arrests, three or four cops hauling off a domestic, usually a chimp or an orang, some scattered groceries or dry cleaning on the ground. If Animal Control had cornered a worker, an ape or a gorilla, there were usually a dozen or more officers circled around them, pointing their stun rods toward the center. I didn't realize until later, after I had seen the documentaries they made for Public Mandate Videolink, that the simians always had their mouths closed. You can see it in all the pictures. Their lips are pressed tight and drawn to their ears from clenching their teeth. They had decided in their underground meetings not to make any noise if they were arrested. They thought sapiens would think of them as wild animals if they heard them yelling or screeching. I guess they were right, some people still do. There were also pictures of the camps: chimps, apes, baboons mixed into small barracks and warehouses. The government thought they would kill each other off if they crammed all the different species together. The riot shots were my favorites. I printed up hard copies of the ones where they were using high pressure hoses for crowd control. All those wet hairy bodies, I used to lock the door to the bathroom and masturbate to them. I finally burned those pictures, to commemorate one of the times when I had 30 days of sexual sobriety.

The ape sitting across from me was wearing a really tight white T-shirt, and I could see how incredibly defined his abs were. You know, a lot of simians do those stomach exercises, mostly to straighten their spine. That's why in all those infomercials for home ab machines and tapes, there's always a bunch of chimps and apes in the audience standing up and testifying about their posture. Well, this guy's spine was as straight as it can get for a monkey. It almost negated his Neanderthal hunch. Almost, but not quite. He had on a pair of gray sweat shorts and some white Converse high-tops. They must've been about size 19.

The meeting began, and after some announcements this guy a couple of seats to my left started reading the chapter. He was hunched over, his right elbow on his right knee, the fist of that arm supporting his chin. He held the copy of *Redemption and Healing* open in his left palm, resting on the other knee. He looked like Rodin's *Thinker,* and when he read the text, he made it sound like he was seeing it for the first time, even though I'd seen him in meetings since I started coming three years ago.

"Some of us did not want to believe in God, in fact, some of us still don't. And that's all right, this program is open to all who have a desire to be cured of their compulsion. If, for example, a newcomer is firm in his faith of science and cannot see how God or a higher power can fit in the plan, we can offer him a scientific approach. We can show him that C.A.A.C.A.A. has evidenced prodigious results. In the recovery equation then, the newcomer could then substitute the group itself for the higher power. How often have we heard, perhaps from ourselves even, 'But that's so easy, will that really work?' 'Yes,' we can answer. 'It can, and it has…'"

It was the chapter about accepting your higher power. Not only is this chapter as boring as the rest of the book, it's the longest one. It's not that I don't appreciate the recovery I've gained since I've been in these rooms. Since I'm not jacking off and cruising so much anymore, I have a lot more free time on my hands and more stuff to fill it with. Like hiking and writing and holding down a job, things you can't get arrested for. But it doesn't make this stuff any more palatable. I couldn't be bothered to concentrate on the text, and I was already really distracted by the monkey sitting across from me. I didn't want to spent the meeting obsessing on the ape; then again, I wouldn't have been in that room if that sort of thing was within my control or, better yet, not even an issue in the first place.

One topic that the guys in program always talk about are the sexual thoughts that constantly fill their minds, triggered by a look, a movement, a drop in the humidity level. Among the confessions of sexual thought crimes, there's a lot of talk about how fast they fall in love. I think I've heard the phrase "I was already picking out china patterns" in the last three years more than I heard "What are you into" in the fifteen before that. But I've never heard anyone mention one of the things I fantasize about. If I'm fiending on someone, I start imagining that I'm at their funeral, that I'm the bereaved lover.

So, at this meeting I was creating this scenario where I'm sitting graveside watching the large ebony casket containing my beloved monkey's remains being lowered into the ground. They usually die a few years after I meet them too, so they still look the same. I see myself sitting rigid and silent, wet eyes concealed behind tortoise-shell Vuarnets. My grieving friends surround me. They clasp my hand, squeeze my shoulder. And even within my fantasy, I'm reminiscing. Remembering the sensation of his leathery ape lips pressed against mine; he was such a good hard kisser. Remembering the way he would pick at his fur while we were watching TV; he would never do that when other people were around. Even with all his talk about moving beyond tolerance to appreciation, he was so vigilant about fit-ting in, but I understood. How he loved to fuck in the shower and he knew the taste of his freshly scrubbed monkey asshole drove me wild.

I stopped daydreaming when the book was finally passed to my ape. He started reading.

> "Some of us believed in God once. We may have
> lost our faith for many reasons. We may have been
> disgusted by the acts we witnessed 'religious' people
> committing like hypocrisy or bigotry. We could
> quote the numbers of people killed in the name of
> 'God' and supply you with the dates. But to the
> disenchanted we can say, 'We too felt superior, but
> God is God, no matter who prays to him...'."

What I noticed most of all was that every time he said God or reli-gion, his top lip would turn up at the left. It was the beginning of that feral snarl that I can't imagine being suppressed by any amount of socialization. Right at that moment, I knew my monkey was an atheist.

It's one of the central issues of the simian value system. Mostly I learned about it from TV. When I was a little kid there was this thing on Sean Lennon's talk show, "Simians: Savior vs. Science." And there was the Cody Gifford special for Public Mandate, *God,*

Darwin, and the Species Next Door. It's a real touchy subject for most monkeys, what with all the churches treating them as everything from devil's spawn to ignorant savages in need of salvation.

I guess my obsession about simians has made me a little more knowledgeable about them than the majority of sapiens, but I hardly knew any until a few years ago. One night some of us were downtown looking for this new club, but we didn't have the address. We saw a couple of gorillas assuming that familiar bouncer stance outside an unmarked door. At the time the latest clubs were just starting to use simians for doormen and bouncers, so we thought we were at the right place. It turned out to be the "Monkey Bar." It was pretty underground then; even apes hardly knew about it. And sapiens, forget it. They weren't going to let us in at first, but there was this chimp working the door and he said it was OK. It turned out he was totally queer. Some of the monkey population was just starting to get really retro about the homo thing; it looked like it was going to get nasty, and I think he was just surrounding himself with comrades. I realized I'd never seen simians socialize away from sapien influence. Most of the younger simians were fed up with the "tame yourself" attitude of their parents. That club was wild, and it was loud. We had a blast, though honestly I was really intimidated at first. Later that night, me and the chimp that had let us in, we had gotten really drunk and were dancing together and that's when he told me about "Hollywood Jungle."

"Hollywood Jungle" is kind of an infamous bathhouse. And the thing it's infamous for is that it caters to the interspecies crowd. Back then, it had just opened up. Sometimes I tell the story like I went there on some sexual multicultural goodwill mission. But by that time I was already hitting the baths whenever I could get away from my job or my friends.

I was at the "Hollywood Jungle" the night after "Monkey Bar." The first thing that blew me away about the place was how it looked inside. I've been to a lot of baths and sex clubs, and at the best they were kind of industrial and depressing. They always make them look like a warehouse or an abandoned building. I've had sex in warehouses and abandoned buildings. There's no cover charge. This place looked organic, all curved and layered.

I was standing there taking in the architecture, and this big chimpanzee came up and started talking to me, you know, "I haven't seen you here before," the usual. He offered to show me around, and when we got to this one room on the top level, I followed him inside and he shut the door behind him and he started handling me and kissing me. Pretty soon we were down on the ground and he started nailing me. My first monkey. After a couple of strokes, he started howling and his whole body started shaking like a clothes dryer with a pair of sneakers inside.

When I've talked to other recovering addicts, a lot of them have said that the most potent drug for them was adrenaline. I know it's true for me, I would get most excited when the hunt was on, when I was at a bar and it looked like someone was going to come on to me, my heart would pound and my whole body would tingle. Nothing else mattered then, I felt so focused, kind of hyperaware. It was the same if someone was skulking around the door to my room in a bathhouse or following me around in a park. But when we got to the sex, after a while I'd have to really work my imagination to keep up that level of intoxication. Usually I'd just make some lame excuse, if that, to get away and start looking for it again. But monkey sex is different. The noise and the physical frenzy, it's kind of unpredictable. From what I've seen, sex is one of two things that makes simians totally lose control. And I know all about being out of control, which I guess brings me back to the meeting.

When my monkey turned to the person on the left to pass the book, I could see that my boundary-setting church date was sitting right behind him. Up until then the huge form of the simian had completely blocked him from my view. But when I saw him sitting back in the second row, with his eyes closed and a half smile on his face, I got this idea.

While the next few people read, I kept my face toward the floor, but I rolled my eyes up as far as I could so I could see the bottom half of my monkey's head. Every time one of the readers would mention

God or faith or a higher power, his lip would curl and quiver. I just waited for the copy of *Redemption and Healing* to be passed to me.

When the person on my right was finished, I looked up at him, smiled, took the book, put it in my lap, and bowed my head toward the text.

> "Some of us came to the program with our faith still
> intact. But we were confused, frustrated, because
> we didn't know how our compulsion and addictions fit
> into God's plan for us. Why wasn't our higher power
> helping us, giving us some sign. But it wasn't
> faith in God that was the problem, it was our
> approach to it, the quality and the honesty of it...."

That part I read as it was written in the book in front of me. But some of what I was about to say next wasn't in *Redemption and Healing*. I had thought of it while I was watching my monkey man's mouth, rehearsed it silently while the last few people had read. I was a little worried that I wouldn't be able to make it sound enough like the original text. There were a few people there that night that I was pretty sure would know the chapter almost verbatim. And there's a tradition in the program that if someone speaking during a meeting says anything inappropriate, something too suggestive sexually or something that disrupts the format of the meeting, that you can knock, on a chair or a wall or a table, to alert them, and anyone else who didn't catch it, to their transgression. I didn't think what I was going to say would take long enough for one of them to react if they wanted to, but you never know.

> "We were just waiting, often inactive, other than
> the activity spurred by our compulsions, waiting for
> Redemption to find us. It could have been right
> outside our door...."

I rolled my eyes up again so I could see my ape. I was wishing I

could see my church date too. I wanted to see if he still had that con-
tented grin on his face.

> "We wouldn't have noticed it even if Jesus Christ
> himself came to our door, held out three nails in
> his hand and said..."

And then I broke out my trusty Grandpa Simpson voice.

> "'Hey, can you put me up for the night?'"

I stopped talking, and there was a moment of silence. Then the
ape started cracking up. I'm not sure, maybe he'd had a real stressful day. Maybe he was a big *Simpsons* fan. Or maybe he actually
thought that old joke was really funny. Whatever the reason, he started laughing. At first it was that startled bark that just flies out of you
when you're not expecting something funny. I remember thinking
Perfect! because that was exactly what I was hoping for. I was already
imagining that during the break he would come over to speak to me;
we would get along so well we might even skip the rest of the meeting and go out for coffee or a walk. But I had forgotten one thing:
that besides sex, the other thing simians have trouble keeping under
control is laughter.
  All of a sudden my ape doubled over and shook silently for a second or two. Then he snapped upright in his chair, threw back his
head, and started howling. Tears were streaming from his eyes and
his mouth was pointed at the ceiling and it just kept on snapping
open and those screeches kept on coming out of it. The other guys
in the room, a lot of them had been at least chuckling before; now
they were all just staring at my monkey. Most of them had this look
on their face like they were in a zoo or at a circus. I should have
known better. A lot of people haven't been around this before. I just
forgot, that's all. And the ape, he was still laughing. It seemed like a
long time before he stopped screeching. Before his body stopped
shaking and jerking. By then most of the other guys had stopped

staring at him, they were just staring at the floor. I was still smiling, even though I didn't much feel like it. I just didn't want him to think I thought he was some freak.

When the ape noticed everyone staring at the floor, he tried to keep the rest of the laughter inside and nearly choked in the process. He looked at me for a second and then bent forward to rest his head between his hands. I caught sight of my church date then. He looked at me briefly too and then closed his eyes and turned his head to the floor, shaking it slowly from side to side. I looked away as he started to put the palms of his hands together as if in prayer.

I didn't know what else to do, so I started to reread the paragraph as written. When I finished I passed the book to the guy on my left, and I looked at that beautiful monkey. He was staring at the floor just like everyone else, and I watched his chest heave up and down as he tried to control his breathing. The skin under his eyes was really damp, and I wasn't sure it was all from his laughing fit anymore. So I looked at the floor too, but no matter what part of it I focused on, I could always see that big pair of Converse high-tops. I gave up and let them fill my vision until the spaces between the treads of the soles were big enough for at least one metal folding chair and a large ebony casket.

Mrs. Lincoln's China

M. Shayne Bell

So I stayed in the crowd across the street from the east gates to the White House. My son Cyril, he'd said to me, "Mama, I know how bad you want a cup of Mrs. Lincoln's to drink your coffee from, but stay back from those gates. If you're pressed up next to them, you're liable to get crushed before they give way. You don't have to be the first one in the White House to get a cup. You just come along when you can."

I figured there was some truth to his words. Three years before, my daughter Lydia Ann, who was just sixteen years old at the time, went early to the AC/DC reunion concert because the seating was open and she wanted to sit up close. She liked the drummer, and if you sit up close and take binoculars you can see everything there is to see about a man sitting on stage in front of you, down to the kind of socks he's wearing, but a crowd formed up behind her and started shoving forward and my Lydia Ann thought she was going to suffocate in the press of people before security opened the gates, and even then six people got trampled to death when everybody rushed forward, so I looked at the crowd outside the White House gates and thought to myself, Georgia May, you want a cup of Mrs. Lincoln's because you love her husband and a cup of theirs would make you remember all the good he did, but there's no sense in risking your life, even for a cup President Lincoln might have drank coffee out of, so I took my Cyril's advice and hung back.

Besides, I figured I had the advantage over most folks in that crowd: Most of them had come just to take whatever they could get because they'd gone without for so long, and to maybe in the process scare the folks in power into running this country like it was meant to be, a place where people could live a decent life. But me, I was going in with a plan. I knew just what I wanted to take from the White House. I'd toured the White House two years before and seen the China Room, and I'd looked and looked at Mrs. Lincoln's china and thought how she and the president I loved had eaten off those dishes, and when I started to see how things were going to go in this city and what was likely to take place with or without my blessing, I made up my mind to be in the crowd that would sweep into the White House and pick it clean, but I'd go there looking for one thing: a cup from Mrs. Lincoln's china—oh, that and maybe the saucer to go with it and a plate or two if I could get them, which explains the two sacks I'd brought along to carry the dishes in and the old dish towels I'd brought to wrap them in to keep them from chipping, but I would have truly settled for just one coffee cup.

It was a hot late-August day, and about noon the crowd quieted down. It was hard to keep up the yelling and screaming when you were so hot you could hardly stand it and sweat was making wet tracks down the front and back of your blouse and all you could think of was how you wanted a cold drink of some kind, maybe a Coke with lots of ice.

Some people tried to keep up the screaming and meant to rouse the rest of us to it, but it wasn't working. Only a few people yelled along with them, and I certainly didn't, not then. I started to wonder if we'd get in the White House at all or if we'd give up in that heat and go home, then try again in the evening or later at night, but I hoped we wouldn't have to rush the White House at night, because I didn't want to rush it in the dark. Storming a place like the White House seemed scary enough without adding darkness on top of it, when suddenly the marines guarding the gates just walked away and disappeared inside the East Wing. Everybody in the crowd was trying to see what was happening, standing on tiptoes and looking, and suddenly it made sense to me: They were giving up. They were opening the place up to us without bloodshed. We were going to get in the White House after all, and in the broad daylight. The president and everybody inside were probably gone already, out tunnels in the basement, whisked off to Camp David or who cares where.

The gates were locked, so people started climbing over the gates and the fence and walking a little warily up to the White House, almost like they were going to buy tickets and take a tour. Two nice young girls gave me a hand up to the top of the fence, and we all three jumped down together onto the grass on the other side and made our way up the lawn toward the doors of the East Wing Lobby. The doors were swung wide when I got to them and shoved my way inside, but some folks were already trying to shove their way outside, their arms full of figurines and paintings and the like, no dishes yet. I saw a lot of people just standing around looking at the rooms and the things in them and at each other, amazed that we were inside like this and that nobody was trying to stop us.

For a minute it seemed as if the spirit of the place settled over us: Here we were in the mansion where the great and powerful presidents of this land had lived, some of them good people, and it didn't seem right, somehow, to just tear into the place and start taking things or breaking them right away. But somebody outside threw a rock and busted out one of the front windows, and somebody inside started yanking down the drapes, and I knew the craziness was starting. I made a beeline for the China Room.

And who should I find standing in the doorway but my own son Cyril.

"What kept you, Mama?" he asked.

I was about to explain the fence I'd climbed, which I didn't find as easy a thing to do as I used to, when he grinned at me and held up a cup of Mrs. Lincoln's: white china with a gold edge around the top and a purple border below and the eagle that represented this country. The cup looked so regal yet fragile in Cyril's hand while the breaking and the shouting grew and grew all around us. Cyril put the cup in my hands. It felt cool and clean. It wasn't dusty at all. Someone had taken good care of this cup.

"I want a saucer too," I said, while I wrapped the cup in a dish towel and put it in my sack. "Wasn't there one with it?"

Cyril stepped back so I could walk past him into the room, which was empty of people. Cyril's friends Randy Lewis and Vincent Henry were standing in the other doorway, and they grinned at me—they were holding back all the people to give me first chance at what I wanted.

"We can't hold back these people long, Mama," Cyril said. "You've got to hurry."

So hurry I did. I went straight to the Lincoln china on display in its china cabinet. I knew right where it was. All the china was displayed in order of the president, starting at the right of the fireplace with pieces from the Washington's personal china and stretching around the room to a place setting from the present president's set. In the spot for the Lincolns' china was a display of just eleven pieces from Mrs. Lincoln's first set, including the saucer that went with my cup. Most of the 175 pieces of Lincoln china left were kept up in the president's private quarters or down in a basement storage area, which I wouldn't have time to find. I opened the cabinet door, took out the saucer, wrapped it quick, and put it in my sack.

That's when the lights went out. It being the middle of the day, plenty of light still came in from the windows, but the riot was clearly getting worse. I started wrapping and packing as quick as I could: a dinner plate, an ice cream plate, a teacup and saucer. I'd pretty well finished wrapping the Lincoln display—water mug, three fruit baskets, custard cup, and everything—when the shooting started, a way off by the East Wing Lobby. Cyril ran up and took my arm. "You've got to go, Mama," he said.

People had rushed into the China Room once Cyril left the doorway, and they started smashing the dishes in the cabinets and tearing at the paintings on the walls and breaking out the windows. I grabbed up a few more dishes and shoved them in my sack. I decided to chance the chipping, since I didn't have time to wrap them. It wasn't safe to stay here any longer. Cyril took my other sack and ran around the room shoving dishes into it, I didn't know then from what services, and he came back and pulled me toward the door. I kicked the cabinet door shut behind me on the off chance of saving what we left behind.

The crowd was going wild, breaking and tearing at anything they could. "Stop it!" I wanted to shout. "These are good dishes—take them home and use them." But nobody would have listened— nobody could have heard me in that noise. Some fat man tried to kick my sack of china, but I swung it out of the way, and Cyril punched the man's face.

"Come on, Mama!" Cyril shouted.

"I'm coming!" I shouted back.

But I couldn't help it. I picked up an unbroken bowl thrown down on the rug and two wine goblets from I didn't know which services on the way out of the China Room and stuffed them in my sack. Cyril helped me out of the White House through a back door and across the lawn to the fence, which surprised me. I thought he'd spend all his time in the White House having the fun he'd come to have with his friends. But he helped me over the fence, then handed me my sack of Lincoln china and his sack of odds and ends. I ran off down the street toward my apartment, and he ran off back toward the White House. I didn't see Cyril again for three days.

I lugged my china home and got it up the dark stairs to my door. The lights were out in the stairwell. I still managed to get my key out of my pocket in the front of my skirt and open the door by feel without having to set down the china and chance chipping it any more. I carried the sacks into the bedroom and carefully set them down on the bed. Then I opened the drapes to let in the sunlight and looked out the window.

There were fires everywhere in the city, and smoke rising up from one point of the horizon to the other, not to mention the shooting and the deeper sound of what must have been cannons over by Annapolis. Seeing and hearing all that made me sick at heart. I started to wonder, what if they come to burn the building I live in? I thought maybe I shouldn't unpack the china in my sacks. If I had to run, I could pick up those sacks and run with them.

So I spent the evening getting ready to run. I locked the doors to keep people out till I was ready to go. Then I tried to call Lydia Ann, but the phones were dead. So I wrapped the Lincoln china I hadn't had time to wrap, this time in my good dish towels, and—when I ran out of those—in my good pillowcases, which I'd want to take if I had to abandon everything else. I didn't bother with Cyril's sack of odds-and-ends china because I didn't even know what was in there and I wasn't sure I had time. Once I'd squared away the Lincoln china and packed up some food and an extra change of clothes and took out the money I'd hid behind the fridge and stuffed it into the box of Shredded Wheat cereal I planned to take, I sat by the window in the bedroom and watched and listened to the riot and worried about Lydia Ann and Cyril.

When night came, the city was lit up by fire. The shooting never stopped till 3 in the morning, when it stopped all of a sudden for about twenty minutes, all over the city. I stood by the window then, looking out and wondering if the craziness was over so soon, but of course it wasn't. It started up again. I sat by my bedroom window all the rest of that night and into the morning, watching.

By noon, since I hadn't had to run yet, I figured I might not have to. So I pulled all the drapes and dragged chairs in front of the door to block it and took a nap on the couch. I didn't want to move the china unless I had to, considering the pieces I hadn't wrapped in the second sack and the chipping I'd cause, so I left it all on the bed.

When I woke up, it was dark. I tried the lights, but the power was still off. I felt my way into the black kitchen and pulled matches out of a drawer and lit a candle. I tried the phone to call Lydia Ann again and Cyril, but the phone was still dead. I tried to cook some supper, but the water was off, so I just made sandwiches out of the cheese and tomatoes in the fridge before they spoiled and drank some of the water I had left in a pitcher. Then I carried my candle into the bedroom so I could take a look at the china in Cyril's sack of odds and ends and wrap it.

I reached in and pulled out a plate with a blue border and gold stems of wheat painted in that border. The American eagle was pictured in the white middle of the plate. I didn't know which president and his wife had had such a plate. I reached in and pulled out a dessert plate that had a pretty white flower in the middle. The back of the plate said Syringa, and below that Idaho. I figured the Syringa must have been Idaho's state flower, but I didn't know which president's wife had ordered this plate either. I pulled out the two crystal wine goblets that were the last things I'd taken. They were simple in design but lovely.

I took the candle and went after the Margaret Brown Klapthor book, *Official White House China: 1789 to the Present,* which I'd bought after the White House tour I'd taken two years before, and carried the book into the bedroom. I put the candle on the nightstand and knelt by the bed and started leafing through the book looking for pictures of china that matched the china and goblets I had on my bed.

The plate with gold wheat and the blue border turned out to be President Harrison's. Mrs. Caroline Harrison had painted the wheat herself, the guidebook said, back in the days when women did that sort of thing. I picked up the plate and looked at it again. The wheat was beautifully painted, and I realized that Caroline Harrison had been a real artist. Her work looked professionally done, to me.

The plate with the flower in the middle was the Johnsons'. The guidebook said Lady Bird had ordered a service of china that pictured wildflowers, not the state flowers, of all fifty states and D.C. People used to go on tours hoping to see the wildflower from their state on display in a place setting from Lady Bird's china. I pulled two more plates from that service out of Cyril's sack. They pictured the California poppy and the Oregon grape, which meant I'd ended up with plates of the western states. I wished Cyril had picked out the plate with D.C.'s flower on it. I didn't even know D.C. had an official flower, let alone a wildflower. Maybe they'd used the dandelion or some other weed that grew up between cracks in sidewalks.

I started looking to see if I could match a picture to the wine goblets, when there was a burst of gunfire just up the street from my building. I blew out the candle and didn't move in the sudden darkness. I heard shouting and more firing, then running in the alleyway below my window. I was glad I'd pulled the drapes so no one could have seen my light before it was gone altogether. I knelt there next to my bed and smelled the smoke from the candle and listened to the shouting and the shots and thought of my Cyril and Lydia Ann, wondering what was happening to them. When things had quieted down outside, I reached out and touched the smooth china of one of the Johnson's dessert plates: The people who'd ordered these plates were the people who'd dreamed of a great society. It hadn't lasted long. It hadn't even been many years before the ugly billboards Mrs. Johnson had had torn down all over the country were put back up and you couldn't walk down a street or take a bus ride anywhere without having gaudy billboards scream at you to buy this or that bit of nonsense. It was all tacky and cheap. Tacky and cheap was what too many people tried to make all of our lives and the world around us. But Mrs. Johnson had tried to fight that trend, and she and her husband had dreamed dreams, and worked as if they could make a difference in the world, and ordered china with delicate wildflowers on them. It had been a time when grace and beauty had stood a chance.

Over the next two days, I cataloged the china I'd taken: of the Lincoln china, one dinner plate, one custard cup, one fish platter, one regular platter, one water jug, one ice cream plate, three fruit baskets, a teacup and saucer, and a coffee cup and saucer; of the Johnson china, one plate, three dessert plates; of the Harrison china, one plate, one coffee cup and saucer; and in addition, two Kennedy wine goblets and one Hayes soup bowl with a crab painted on it. I wrapped everything in my best pillowcases and dish towels and kept them in sacks at the foot of my bed, ready for me to pick up and run with if I had to. I also wrapped two green Depression-glass plates of my mother's and put them in the sacks. I'd want them too if I had to leave everything else.

Three days after we'd stormed the White House, Cyril came knocking on my door. I recognized his voice, of course, so I dared drag away the chairs and unlock the door, and there stood Cyril with sacks of food in his arms.

"I thought you might be needing a few things, Mama," he said.

I hugged him and cried a little, and asked him if he'd seen or heard from Lydia Ann, which he hadn't. I'd already decided I had to go and find her and help her if she needed it, but I decided to tell Cyril about that decision a little later. I asked him to tell me where he'd gotten the food, but he wouldn't say much about that. I made him stay while I cooked supper for us both. The gas was still on, and I'd dipped out all the clean water from the toilet reservoir, so I had water to boil with and drink. Cyril had brought me potatoes and a canned ham and all kinds of other canned things, soups and green peas, and even a jar of instant Taster's Choice coffee. I put the ham in the oven to heat through and set the potatoes to boil and decided to set the table with the Lincoln china.

I brought out my nicest white tablecloth and spread it over the table. The tablecloth had been my mama's, and it was way too big for any table I'd ever had, but I thought it was the tablecloth I should use with the Lincoln china. It hung down low, nearly to the floor, but it looked fine even so. I set the lit candle in the middle of the table. Then I unwrapped the Lincoln dinner plate for me and the fish platter for Cyril and set them out. They looked so pretty on my table, the dark purple of the border set off by my white tablecloth. The candlelight glistened off the china. I could imagine the president and Mrs. Lincoln hosting a state dinner, maybe for the ambassador from Japan, who would have come dressed in a kimono for men or whatever it was men wore in Japan back then, and all of them eating in just the kind of light Cyril and I were going to eat in. I unwrapped and polished the coffee cup and the teacup and their saucers and set them out for the coffee. My shoddy old flatware looked sad beside all the presidential finery, but it would have to do.

Cyril stacked the furniture back in front of the door, then just sat at the table while I cooked, he was so tired. He told me he'd gone to talk to Randy Lewis, who had a shortwave radio and batteries to run it on, and that Randy had heard there was fighting and rioting all over the country. None of the networks were on, so we couldn't have gotten any news even if we'd had power to run a TV or radio.

The potatoes finished cooking, and I whipped them by hand with butter that hadn't quite spoiled yet and canned Sego milk, which works in potatoes when you don't have anything else. The whipping took a while, but Cyril and I both like our potatoes whipped, so I stuck with the whipping till it was done. I opened the canned peas and boiled them, then set water to boil for the coffee. When the ham was heated, I sliced it and made a gravy, and we sat down to eat.

The food looked so good, and it smelled so good, and in the candlelight it seemed the shooting and the screams were far off, somehow, though of course they really weren't. It struck me as a rare blessing that a mother and her son could sit down to a decent supper in times like these, and I was grateful to Cyril for his thoughtfulness to me.

I dished myself some potatoes and handed Cyril the bowl. "I'm going to walk over to Lydia Ann's apartment tomorrow when it's light and try to find her," I said.

Cyril looked up at me and took the potatoes.

"I'll go look for her after supper," he said. "Don't you go out yet, not even in the day. It will be safer for me to go in the dark."

I covered my potatoes with gravy and handed Cyril the gravy bowl. "If you go tonight to look for your sister, I'm going with you. I can't stand this not knowing about Lydia Ann."

He took the gravy and shook his head.

"Don't tell me no," I said, serving myself a slice of ham. "I'm her mama, and I have to know if she's all right. If you say the darkness is safer, I'll go tonight in the dark, and I'll go alone if I have to."

He took the ham and didn't say anything. I'd told him about my decision to search for Lydia Ann in the same tone of voice I always used with my children to tell them the discussion was over and that trying to convince me to change my mind was a waste of time. He still recognized that tone of mine. We dished up some green peas and started eating.

"Is the water ready for the coffee?" Cyril asked.

I'd left it boiling on the stove. Cyril got up to get it and the jar of coffee, but the shoelace hooks in his boots caught the tablecloth and Cyril stumbled and jerked the tablecloth forward and the candle fell over and went out and I heard Cyril hit the floor and dishes shattering around him.

I couldn't move. I just sat there in the dark till I heard Cyril start getting up. I went for the matches then and another candle and bumped into Cyril and told him to stand still and asked if he was hurt and got a match and struck it and lit the candle and held it up. Cyril and I looked at each other, then at the table.

"Oh, Cyril," I said, but he didn't say anything, not I'm sorry or even, Well, look at that. He seemed too stunned to say anything to me, then. The fish platter was on the floor and busted, together with the teacup and saucer and my old bowl I'd put the peas in—all busted. But the ham and the potatoes and my plate of food and the coffee cup and saucer were still on the table. He hadn't pulled off the whole tablecloth. I got the broom and dustpan and started sweeping up the pieces, and the sound of that china tinkling into my dustpan sounded like a judgment on us all and I started to cry, and Cyril said he'd finish sweeping, so I handed him the broom, but I got out rags and tried to wipe up the mess off the floor, which wasn't easy considering how little water I had, and all the while I was crying. Everything was just too much for me then. When the mess was cleaned up and the tablecloth straightened, I sat back in my chair and just looked at my food sitting on a Lincoln plate while Cyril dished himself some more food onto a regular melmac plate out of my cupboard.

"What have we done, Cyril?" I said.

"The dishes would have all been broken anyway if we'd left them sitting in the White House, Mama."

But that was not the point.

"Eat, Mama, if you want to feel up to going for a walk with me to Lydia Ann's," he said.

"Don't patronize me," I said.

I stopped my crying and stood up and got myself a melmac plate out of the cupboard and scraped my food onto it off of the Lincoln plate. Then I ever so carefully washed the Lincoln plate and didn't begrudge it the water. I wrapped it up in a fine dish towel and put it and the unbroken cup and saucer back with the other dishes in their sacks. Then I hid the sacks in the broom closet, where thieves wouldn't spend much time looking, I thought, if they came in here.

The china I'd taken was a duty I had assumed. I realized that now. It represented a heritage not mine alone. The day would come when other people besides me would want to take a look at Mrs. Lincoln's china, and Mrs. Johnson's and Mrs. Harrison's. They'd want to look and remember the dreams we'd once had in this country and the kind of lives folks had once led. Till that time, I had a duty to safe-guard what had become my charge. Wouldn't the people in power someday be surprised when I walked up and handed them the china and said, Look here at what I've saved for all of us.

And I got other ideas. I sat back down to eat my cold food and told Cyril what I was thinking. "The minute it starts to look safe," I said, "I want to walk back to the White House and take a look around. I'll bet there's a cup or two that didn't get busted and maybe a saucer thrown on the rug that didn't break or get trampled. There will be things here and there that I can pick up and bring back to save and take care of. Maybe I'm being called to do this, Cyril, or maybe I'm calling myself. It's folks like me, I guess, who will have to make ourselves responsible for saving some of our heritage through this time."

He looked at me for a while, then finally started eating again. "I'll go with you to the White House," he said. "I don't want you going up there alone."

"I'd be glad for your help," I said, and I thought how saving things like a president's china would give us a purpose to get us through the troubled days ahead.

While I cleared off the table, Cyril told me how Randy Lewis had heard on his shortwave that they were talking about setting up a temporary capital in either Denver or St. Paul. "I imagine they'll fight now over which one of those cities gets to be capital for a while," I said.

Meanwhile, we had the living to take care of and a job to do after that. Little by little, we'd put the world back right.

I sent Cyril to pull the furniture away from the door again, while I dressed in my black dress so I'd look inconspicuous out on the streets. Then I set matches and a candle by the door for when I got back, blew out the candle, and locked the door behind me. Mrs. Lincoln's china was safe, for now, in my broom closet. I set out with Cyril to find my Lydia Ann.

Hunters and Gatherers

Bernard Cooper

Rick had been searching for the Pillings' address for over twenty minutes, and the hungrier he became, the harder it was to concentrate on the dimly lit street signs, the six-digit numbers stenciled on curbs. Westgate Village was a planned community an hour away from the downtown loft where Rick lived, and its street names were an endless rearrangement of the same bucolic phrase: Valley Vista Circle, Village Road, Valley View Court. Each one-story ranch house looked nearly the same except for the color of its garage door, and Rick, who'd skipped lunch, began to wonder if the entire suburb was a hunger-induced hallucination. Jerry Pilling, giddy as a kid at the prospect of throwing a party, had given Rick hasty directions over the phone so many weeks ago that Rick now had a hard time deciphering his own scrawl. He pulled over to the curb, squinted at what he'd written on a scrap of paper, and tried to retrace his turns. All the while, digestive juices sluiced through his stomach and a dull ache came and went.

Rick was about to give up and head for a phone booth when a Mustang crept past, the driver peering this way and that, on the prowl for an address. Jerry had described the party as a chance for his wife, Meg, to meet a group of his gay friends, and after much wrangling she'd finally agreed, but only on the condition that she could invite her hairdresser, the one "avowed" homosexual she knew. Rick had a hunch that the man driving the Mustang was Mrs. Pilling's hairdresser—the skin of his face was shiny and taut, his silver hair moussed—and decided to follow him. "Avowed" had about it a quaint, anachronistic ring, and Rick pictured a dandy in an ascot, hand raised as he swore some sort of oath. Sure enough, the

Mustang pulled up to the right address within minutes. A house with double doors and deep eaves, it sat at the end of a cul-de-sac. PILLING was chiseled on a wooden sign, the front lawn glowing greenly in the dusk.

Rick had met Jerry Pilling on a midnight flight from New York to Los Angeles. Returning home from his one-man show at a Soho gallery, Rick was solvent and optimistic for the first time in a year. Seatmates in the back of the plane, the two of them struck up a conversation, or rather, Rick listened across the dark heartlands of America as tiny bottles of Smirnoff's accumulated on Jerry's tray table. "Meg and I are Mormons," Jerry told him, shaking the last drops of alcohol into his plastic tumbler, "so we aren't allowed to drink. But I bend the rules depending on the altitude." He touched Rick's arm and his breath, as pungent as jet fuel, sterilized the air between them. "I'm terrified of flying." This was the first of Jerry's confessions; soon they came with escalating candor, the consonants softened by booze. "Do you know any Mormons?" asked Jerry. "Personally, I mean."

"Only impersonally," laughed Rick.

"Well, take it from me, not all of us are polygamists who bathe in our holy undergarments. There's lots of ways to be a Mormon; at least, that's the way *I* see it."

"There's a Mormon guy at my gym," ventured Rick, "who wears the garments under his workout clothes, even in summer."

"Or proselytize on our bicycles."

"I'm sorry?"

"Not all of us proselytize on our bicycles."

Rick pictured Jerry listing from a Schwinn.

"Listen," said Jerry, giving Rick a let's-lay-our-cards-on-the-tray-table look. "Are you by any chance...I don't mean to be presumptuous, so forgive me if I'm wrong, but you haven't said anything about a wife, and I was wondering if you're..."

"Gay?"

"I knew it!" blurted Jerry, slapping his armrest. "I have a sick sense—sixth sense—about these things. I am too!"

To Rick's way of thinking, Jerry was unduly excited by this coincidence, as if he'd discovered they shared the same mother. Still, he
found something ingenuous about the portly, balding stranger
beside him. He eyed Jerry's wedding ring, and with no prompting
whatsoever, Jerry launched into the story of his marriage. "I only
recently told Meg that I fooled around with men in college. Groping
a housebrother, that sort of thing." This piqued Rick's interest, and
he had to steer Jerry back to the subject when, trying to recall the
name of his fraternity, he was sidetracked into a muddled pronunciation of Greek letters. "The point," continued Jerry, "is that I wanted to write off my college flings as trial and error, youthful confusion. But after six children and twenty years of marriage, I couldn't
ignore my thing for guys. College men especially. Studious types.
Blond. With glasses." Jerry sighed. "The more I tried to pray it away,
the stronger it got."

The plane hit a patch of turbulence over Kansas. Snug in his seat
and buffered by vodka, Jerry didn't seem to notice. A few passengers
shifted beneath their blankets. A baby bawled in the forward cabin.
"We counseled with the church elders, Meg and me, and they
thought that male companionship—strictly platonic of course—
would help me 'scratch the itch,' as they put it. So we decided to stay
married and faithful, and I'm going to make some homosexual
friends." Jerry brightened. "We'll have to have you over for dinner."

"The church *wants* you to have gay friends?"

"Hey," said Jerry, shifting in his seat. "They didn't say homosexual or not. But 'male companionship' is open to interpretation, don't
you think?" He stirred his drink with an index finger, then sucked his
finger and took a swig. "According to the church, if me and Meg get
divorced, old Jerry here wanders around heaven for time immemo-
rial, a soul without a family."

It was delicate: Rick didn't want to mock Jerry's religious beliefs,
but he found this punishment cruel and unusual. Not to mention
superstitious. "Do you really believe that's what would happen?"

"The idea scares me whether I believe in it or not. An outcast even
after I'm dead. Lifelong bonds coming to nothing. Estranged from

my very own kids." He chewed an ice cube and shivered. "I joined Affirmation, a group of gay Mormons, and they say the church is run by humans, and humans don't know everything there is to know about the creator's plan; only one judgment matters in the end, and at least He'll know what made me tick and how I tried to do what's right. But Rick," said Jerry, leaning close, "here's where I part company with the folks at Affirmation: They're skeptical about a man staying married."

"You mean, about a gay man staying married?"

"Isn't that what I said? Anyway, living in a family makes me happy. My kids are turning into people I like, and the little ones shriek and swamp me every time I walk through the door. Chalk it up to my having been an only child, but even when they're fighting and crying, the chaos is kind of cozy, you know?"

"What about your wife?"

"I'd tried to tell her when we were dating, but she'd shush me and say the past didn't matter. It probably didn't occur to her I was messing with men. She wanted a husband, and I wanted to be normal; in that respect we were meant for each other. And here I am." Jerry looked around, then whispered, "I'm the only man Meg has ever slept with. And let me tell you something: I've never pretended. I've always loved her, and I always will. In the bedroom too. Love must count for something, right?" The seat belt signs were turned off and a low, electronic bell rang throughout the cabin. "Sorry if I talked your ear off," said Jerry. "I should really keep my big mouth shut. But keeping quiet wears me out a lot more than talking." His head lolled toward the oval window. Rick leaned forward and gazed out too. Beads of condensation gathered on the glass. Below them, as far as the eye could see, dawn tinted the rim of the earth; roads and rooftops and plowed fields—tiny hints of human habitation—were just becoming visible through thin, drifting layers of clouds.

The double doors swung open, and there stood Mrs. Pilling. Her tight auburn curls were a miracle of modern cosmetology, their true color and texture unguessable. She glanced back and forth between

Rick and her hairdresser, smiling nervously. "Did you and Oscar come together?" she asked. Perhaps she assumed that Rick and Oscar had crossed paths in the small province of their "lifestyle." Rick felt a pang of sympathy for Meg; she's trying to hold up the walls, he thought, just like the rest of us. Dressed in slinky blue culottes, eyelids dusted with matching shadow, Meg appeared every inch the camera-ready hostess; the only thing missing, lamented Rick, was a platter of canapés. He felt certain her stylish outfit was meant to show her husband's unconventional friends that she was a woman with flair, not the stodgy, narrow-minded matron they might have expected.

"It's serendipity," Oscar told her, handing over a bouquet laced with baby's breath. "We met tonight on this very doorstep."

"Oscar treats me like a queen," said Meg, plunging her powdered nose into the flowers.

Jerry Pilling darted out the door. "Gentlemen," he bellowed, "welcome to the hinterlands!" His hail voice and viselike handshake were far more manly than Rick remembered. Dressed in loose black linen, Oscar rippled as Jerry pumped his hand. "Meg's raved about you," he told Oscar. "Says you're the only man who can give her hair volume."

"Noblesse oblige," said Oscar. He turned toward Mrs. Pilling. "Meg, dear, you'd better get that nosegay into some water."

Rick and Oscar followed the Pillings into a spacious living room, as ornate, thought Rick, as a rococo salon. Overstuffed sofas and chairs were piled with tasseled pillows. Stripes and plaids and herringbones collided, vying for attention. One wall was an archive of framed family photographs. Jerry and Meg pointed to the pictures and boasted about their kids in unison—a long, overlapping roll call—and it sounded to Rick like they'd given birth to a happy hive, several more than the half-dozen children Jerry mentioned on the plane. Snapshots in which the whole family posed together had the voluminous look of class pictures. Rick imagined the Pillings' grocery cart loaded to the brim with potato chip bags, Cheerios boxes as big as luggage, six-packs of soda, gallons of milk. While the Pillings, as verbose as docents, led him along the wall, Rick searched every tabletop for a bowl of peanuts or a wedge of cheese, finding instead an endless array of ceramic animals, dried flowers, and colorful blown-glass clowns. The clowns looked as though they were molded out of hard candy, and Rick could almost taste their antic faces.

"Where *is* your brood?" asked Oscar.

"Simon's at debating. Mandy's at ballet. The rest of the kids have already eaten. They're in their rooms doing who knows what." Jerry nodded toward a hallway that burrowed deep into one wing of the house. Light seeped from beneath its row of doors.

"I'll check on the kids," said Meg.

"How 'bout I show you the grounds," said Jerry, slapping them both on the back.

The yard was a vast expanse of concrete with a kidney-shaped swimming pool in the center. Lit from within, the pool threw woozy refractions onto the surrounding cinder-block walls. Pool toys bobbed atop the water like flotsam from a shipwreck. An inflatable shark, bleached by the sun, floated belly-up. Jerry bent down at the edge of the pool and fiddled with the water filter, which made a shrill sucking noise; from behind, it looked as if he were trying to drink the pool through a straw. Blood sugar plummeting, Rick wondered if it would be impolite to ask for a Coke or whether he should wait until something was offered. He scolded himself for being a recluse; if he got out of the studio more often, he might know how to behave in these situations.

The sliding glass doors rumbled open and Meg ushered the remaining guests into the warm night. Mitchell Coply was Jerry's dentist. A man in his early forties, he had the slim, diminutive build of a schoolboy. A lock of hair sprang onto his forehead no matter how often he brushed it away. His puckish appearance was contradicted by tired, melancholy eyes behind his gold-rimmed glasses. During the round of introductions, Mitchell was soft-spoken and shy about eye contact, the kind of man incapable of concealing his sadness. Jan Kirby was an agent who worked with Jerry at a real estate office that specialized in new housing developments throughout the

San Fernando Valley. Tall and broad-shouldered, Jan wore a pin-striped pantsuit and running shoes. After meeting the other guests, she stood perilously close to the edge of the pool and faced the deep end, hands on her hips. Lit from below by the pool light, she looked to Rick like a deity about to part, or walk across, the water. "After dessert," she said in her husky voice, "let's go skinny-dipping." It took everyone a second to realize she was joking. Mrs. Pilling wagged a finger at Jan—naughty, naughty—and gave a fair imitation of laughter.

By the time the guests reassembled indoors to see the Pillings' remodeled kitchen, Rick was actively praying for snack food. The thought of salty pretzels possessed him, though he'd have happily settled for Triscuits, Cheese Nips, anything with weight and flavor. Meg Pilling ran her manicured hand across the width of a new refrigerator, like one of those models who stroke appliances on game shows. The built-in ice maker suddenly dumped a few chiming ice cubes into a tumbler. Mitchell nodded thoughtfully. Oscar applauded and said, "Brava!" Jan asked if the refrigerator could heel or play dead. Only after the demonstration did Rick notice the absence of cooking odors. The windows of the double ovens were dark, the granite countertops barren. Copper pots hung above the electric range in descending size, mere decoration. Rick tried to fight his hangdog expression; hadn't Jerry said there'd be dinner?

"Folks," announced Jerry, after corralling everyone into the living room. "Have a seat. The wife and I have a little surprise." The four guests squeezed among an avalanche of tasseled pillows and sank, side by side, into the plaid couch. "Honey," Jerry said to Meg, "you've got the floor."

Meg Pilling walked to the center of the room and faced the couch, hands clasped before her. She taught at Westgate Elementary, which explained her exemplary posture and the lilting, patient cadence of her voice. Rick had no trouble envisioning a troupe of mesmerized second-graders following her every order. He wondered if she was about to ask them to make their dinner out of paste and construction paper.

Meg cleared her throat and gazed into the upturned faces of her guests. "Jerry and I wanted to do something fun and unusual, so we've planned a really outlandish night." She grinned and shot a look at her husband. Jerry beamed back. "I bet you're all just itching to know what it is." As if on cue, everyone suddenly nodded and mumbled and shifted about. "Well..." she said, milking the suspense, "we're going to give you each five dollars and let you go to the store on your own—there are several excellent supermarkets in the area—so you can buy something to fix for a potluck!"

No one stirred or spoke. Rick wasn't sure he'd heard her correctly.

"We have all the cooking utensils you'll need," said Meg. "And that brand-new kitchen is just sitting there, waiting! The only rules are that you don't go over your five-dollar limit, and that you're back here within half an hour."

"Do we have to actually cook what we buy?" asked Mitchell. The idea of culinary effort seemed to depress him. "Can't we buy something frozen or from the deli section?"

Meg's smile wavered. Through the crack in her composure, Rick thought he glimpsed a hint of misery. "Now, that wouldn't be very creative, would it?" She looked at her husband as if to say, You've got to prod some people into the party spirit.

"I get it," rasped Jan. "Hunters and gatherers!"

"How primitive," said Oscar.

"I used to love scavenger hunts," said Mitchell. "Of course, those were the days when a kid could knock on a stranger's door without being molested or kidnapped." He pushed his glasses up the bridge of his nose.

"Well," said Meg, reviving her smile, "you're safe in Westgate."

"She's absolutely right," said Jerry. "If you're not back in half an hour, we'll file a report with the Bureau of Missing Persons." He removed a wallet from his back pocket and dealt out five-dollar bills. Peering up from a sitting position, reaching out for what amounted to his allowance, Rick had to admit that, fiscally speaking, Jerry fit the paternal role, confident and ceremonious as he handled money.

"Largess!" exclaimed Oscar. He took his five and winked at Rick.

"I ironed them," said Meg, to explain the crisp, unblemished bills. "Are there any more questions?"

Rick was going to ask the Pillings to give him explicit directions back to the house so he wouldn't get lost again, but he was nearly moved to tears by the thought that he could not only buy food for the potluck, but also something to eat right away, even before he got to the cash register. Rick was first to rise to his feet, a move which, considering the plush upholstery, took some leverage. The others straggled after him. Meg and Jerry each grabbed a knob of the double doors and swung them open. "I wish I had a starting gun," said Jerry.

Mitchell paused in the doorway and asked, "Aren't you coming too?"

From the way the Pillings looked at each other, it was clear this possibility hadn't crossed their minds. "We'll keep the home fires burning," said Jerry.

"Your best bet is to head back to the freeway exit," said Meg. "Toward the commercial district. You can't miss it." She watched her guests scatter across the front lawn, trudging toward their cars.

"Just look for signs of life," yelled Jerry.

Once inside his car, Rick noticed Jan in a Mercedes parked across the street, her face lit by the glow of a cigarette lighter, eyes rolling back as she took the first, languorous drag. Parked behind her, Mitchell furrowed his brow and squinted at a road map, disappearing within its folds. Oscar barreled by in his Mustang, shrugging at Rick and honking his horn. Jerry and Meg stood beside each other in the wide bright doorway of their sprawling home. They waved at Rick as he revved his engine, one fluttering arm per spouse.

Anyone who saw the Pillings in their doorway that night would probably take their happiness and compatibility for granted. Rick wondered what, if anything, Jan and Oscar and Mitchell knew about the couple's compromised marriage. He wouldn't have been surprised to learn that Meg and Jerry had let their secrets slip; it's easy, thought Rick, to confide in someone you see at work, or to someone who runs his fingers through your hair or probes them into your open mouth.

As he pulled away from the curb, he couldn't help but marvel at the Pillings' elaborate domesticity: offspring, swimming pool, blown-glass clowns. While touring their home, Rick sensed that Meg and Jerry meant to impress each other more than their visitors: *See what we have. See what we've done. Our life together is no illusion, no mistake.*

Since Oscar seemed to know where he was going, Rick tried to catch up with the Mustang's taillights, but they shot away like comets near a street named Valley Court. Checking his rearview mirror for Mitchell and Jan, he saw nothing but the empty road behind him. Once again, Rick found himself navigating the maze of Westgate, its lawns trimmed, its houses all alike. He aimed his car toward a concentration of hazy light, a distant promise of people and commerce.

It had been so long since Rick cooked a meal, he was worried he'd forgotten how. Working in his studio till dinnertime, light-headed from paint fumes, he'd usually stand before the open refrigerator and nibble at scraps of food or jump into his car and head for Casa Carnitas, the local taco stand. Dinners had been different when Eric was alive. The two of them had sometimes dedicated entire nights to the alchemy of cooking; gas jets thumped when lit by a match, the raw becoming tender, the cold becoming hot. Chopping and stirring and sautéing not only took time but seemed to prolong it, the minutes enriched with their arguments and gossip. When their studio grew warm and fragrant with the vapor of sauces, stews, and soups, Rick found himself believing Eric might never succumb to the virus. Not if he could be tempted by food. Not if he gained weight.

"I wouldn't be so worried if I could put on a few pounds," Eric told him one night, peering down at himself as if over the edge of a cliff. The more elusive Eric's appetite became, the more time he and Rick spent planning and preparing meals. They began to visit ethnic groceries, farmers' markets, carnicerias, bakeries. At a restaurant supply store near Chinatown, they bought a garlic press, a set of wire whisks, and what they decided was their most frivolous purchase to date: a lemon zester. Although he often couldn't finish a meal, Eric insisted that cooking gave him pleasure, distracted him from the neuropathy that numbed his lips and hands and feet. They had sex less often now that Eric was home all day, groggy from medication, and Rick suspected that their libido, rerouted, had given birth to lavish repasts.

In the early evenings Rick cleaned his brushes, climbed the stairs to the sleeping loft, and crawled into bed beside Eric. The mattress lay on the floor, surrounded by issues of *Art In America,* bottles of AZT, and crumpled clothes. Rick would reach beneath Eric's sweat-shirt and rub his back while they watched cooking shows on television, both of them soothed by the warmth and give of skin. On channel 13, Madeleine Duprey might fricassee a game hen or make a sumptuous ratatouille, rolling her Rs with such panache, they began to doubt she was really French. Next came Our Man Masami, a chef who dismembered vegetables with a glinting cleaver and, laughing a high, delirious laugh, tossed them into a hissing a wok. At 6 o'clock, a pale and almost inaudible woman on a cable station cooked entrees on a wobbling hot plate, her ingredients spilling on her clothes or the floor. Such clumsiness belied her excitement; she closed her eyes when tasting the food, chewing fast, a happy rabbit. They took notes while they watched, salivating. They cheered and grumbled like football fans, shouting out comments like "Needs something crunchy!" or "Too much cumin!"

Over time, however, it was Rick who grew padded with fat, his trousers tight around the waist, while Eric, whittled by the blade of AIDS, could barely bring himself to eat; cheeks hollow, eyes indifferent, he'd prod the food with a fork.

Alarmed by Eric's weight loss, Dr. Santos started him on a regimen of Oxandrin tablets, steroid injections, and cans of a rich nutritional drink. His weight finally stabilized, but his already pale skin continued to grow translucent. Rick began to notice thin blue veins beneath Eric's temples, wrists, and groin, a glimpse into the tributaries, the secret depths of his lover's flesh. Still, Rick held on to the hope that he was only imagining Eric's fragility, making it into something more ominous than it really was. Until one Sunday at the farmers' market.

They were walking back to their car, both of them carrying bags of fresh food. Eric had been in good spirits that morning, eager for an outing. Enormous clouds raced overhead, their shadows strafing the city streets. Taking a shortcut, they turned down an alley, and a blustery wind funneled toward them. Eric's jacket blew open—the bright red lining flared for an instant, as disconcerting as the sight of blood—and he toppled backward, landing on his back. Apples and onions spilled from the bags, scattering among the trash and broken glass that littered the alley. Sprawled on the asphalt, Eric couldn't move his arm, and Rick knelt down to cradle his head. "Is this happening?" Eric asked. An eerie calm tempered Eric's voice, as if he'd observed, from far away, the fall of some frail, unlucky stranger.

In the emergency room, while Eric was being x-rayed, Rick told the attending physician that Eric must have tripped on a crack in the asphalt and lost his footing. But later, sitting alone in the waiting room, he couldn't stop repeating to himself, *A gust of wind knocked Eric over.*

AZT, it turned out, had made his bones brittle, and so Dr. Santos discontinued Eric's antivirals while his fractured arm had time to heal. This caused a sequence of illnesses that worsened Eric's weight loss. The most dire was an inability to absorb nutrients, a condition difficult to treat because the battery of sophisticated lab tests could find nothing wrong. Now and then he managed sips of broth, cubes of Jell-O, diluted juice, but nothing he ate or drank sustained him. Eric was eventually admitted to the hospital for observation and tethered to an IV unit. Rick offered to smuggle into the hospital the heavy, soporific dishes Eric had loved as a child: biscuits with gravy, chicken-fried steak, icebox cake. But the foods he'd once loved revolted him now, and Rick's offer made him feel like a finicky child. "Honey," he told Rick, "it's better if you don't try to feed me." For days Rick sat by the bed while Eric faded in and out of sleep, his meals growing cold. Nurses swept through the room and changed the IV bag that dripped into Eric's arm, a clear solution that bypassed the tongue, his body unburdened by texture or taste.

Despite daily infusions and the few bites of food he forced himself to eat, Eric was dying of starvation. "AIDS-related wasting," Dr. Santos told Rick in the corridor, "remains one of our most difficult battles." The doctor spoke in a solicitous whisper, but Rick heard surrender ring through the ward, drowning out authority and hope. "Do you understand," asked Dr. Santos, "how wasting works?" Rick knew very well how wasting worked: Lips papery, eyes puzzled, forehead hot, Eric retreated into the stillness and solitude of his body. No wish or prayer or entreaty could restore him. "What more," he asked the doctor, "do I need to know?"

Looming above the smaller shops and strip malls that surrounded it, the Westgate Safeway had the glaring, imperious presence of an oil refinery or a power plant. Rick parked his car at the far end of the lot. He'd given little thought to what he might fix for the potluck. On the drive here, struck by a fresh a sense of Eric's absence, he'd had to remind himself that a year had passed since his death. Except for teaching two graduate seminars at a local art school, Rick had spent most of that year in his studio, working on paintings of slender, disconnected bones glowing against a black background. Now that the paintings were being shown in New York, Rick had accepted Jerry's invitation as part of a plan to end his isolation and revive his flagging social life. He didn't know anyone like Meg and Jerry, which accounted for the evening's strain and also its sense of adventure. Tonight anything sounded better than returning to an empty studio.

The second he stepped through the supermarket's automatic doors, Rick heard a tune he recognized but couldn't identify, its perky, repetitive rhythms urging him down the aisles. Wandering past shelves stocked with eye-catching cans and packages, Rick became one big, indiscriminate craving. Everything looked appetizing. In the Pet Food section, basted dog bones seemed like the perfect complement to a sharp Stilton or a salmon pate. In Household Cleaning Products, pastel kitchen sponges had the fanciful, minty appeal of petits fours. The linoleum throughout the store was creamy white and speckled like spumoni. "Your eyes are bigger than your stomach," he remembered his mother saying when he'd heaped his plate with more than he could eat. Once, he'd learned about the world by putting its pretty objects in his mouth—the dusty taste of a wooden block, a bitter waxy bite of Crayola—and tonight he'd reclaimed, without even trying, this long-lost, infant wisdom.

When he rounded the corner, he caught a glimpse of Jan, in her pinstriped suit, jogging toward Gourmet Foods. With his head turned, Rick almost ran into a man who was handing out samples of Inferno Chili. Standing behind a folding table, he wore a white apron and stirred a pot that was heated from beneath by Sterno. Peering inside the pot, Rick saw kidney beans, chunks of tomato, and bits of ruddy onion. The concoction bubbled like lava, small eruptions burping from its surface. "Try some?" asked the man. He held out a plastic spoon, a dollop of chili steaming at its tip, the smell robust and peppery.

Before Rick even began to chew, chili lit the wick of his tongue, his taste buds scorched by exhilarating flame. His eyes watered, nose ran. Perspiration beaded on his skin. He wrenched the spoon out of his mouth and grabbed a can of the stuff, as if reading the ingredients might explain the unearthly surge of heat. "A taste of hell in every bite!" exclaimed the devil on the label, grinning maliciously. Rick opened his mouth, half expecting to exhale fire and torch the store. The man in the apron handed him a tiny paper cup filled with Gatorade. "Only thing that cuts the burn," he said. "That cayenne's got a kick." When he smiled, wrinkles radiated from his brown eyes. His black mustache was waxed at the ends, his jaw shaped like a horseshoe. Rick wanted to thank him, but his throat had closed, leaving him speechless. "Here's one for the road," said the man, offering Rick another shot. At first, Rick wasn't sure if his gallant, folksy manners were real, or his languorous twang authentic. He studied the man through tearing eyes. His name tag read EARL. Dazed in the aftermath of chili, cool air wafting from the dairy case, Rick couldn't stop staring.

Ordinarily, Rick wasn't attracted to dark-haired men or to men with mustaches, especially waxed. Any guy who reminded him of potbellied stoves and tooled-leather belts had always struck him as so remote from his own tastes and sympathies as to be practically extra-terrestrial. In the past year, though, every man seemed alien to Rick because he didn't look or smell like Eric. He'd dated two men since Eric's death, but neither involvement lasted long. In the middle of an intimate dinner, he found himself staring across the table at mas-ticating teeth, tufts of hair on the knuckles of a hand, and though he was glad his companions were mammals, these features were vividly physical without being the least erotic. The one time he did have sex, it was to prove to himself that he could excite someone besides Eric. While flailing naked, he'd inventory the way he and his new partner made love: *Now he's plunging his tongue into my mouth, now I'm lick-ing the inside of his thigh.* He might as well have brought a clipboard to bed. After sex was over, Rick knew he'd been a lousy lover, mired in the past, hopelessly distracted, as spontaneous as a windup toy. And now, at the Westgate Safeway, of all places, while Muzak tinkled in the glaring air, Rick's desire awoke from hibernation. Earl returned Rick's gaze—there was no mistaking—with the same flirta-tious curiosity. "What brings you to the Safeway?" Earl asked as he slowly stirred the Inferno.

Coated with dust, its brown enamel faded by the sun, Earl's ancient station wagon looked like a boulder that had rolled into the parking lot. Rick carried the folding table and cooking equipment while Earl gripped a cardboard box filled with cans of Inferno. Now that Earl had taken off his apron, Rick could better see the outline of his body and the motion of his ropy limbs. Earl propped the boxes on the roof of the car and fished in his jeans' pocket for keys. The Golden State freeway roared in the distance. "By the way," said Earl, "you can keep your five bucks; there's no finer way to promote a product than feeding it directly to the people.'"

"It isn't my money," Rick reminded him. "And besides, Inferno will be the bargain of the party." They lifted the tailgate, loaded the car. As they slid inside and slammed their doors, the station wagon creaked on its springs. "Just throw that crap in the back," said Earl. "I wasn't expecting company." Rick reached down and chucked cans of Sterno, a box of plastic spoons, and a stack of paper cups into the back seat. Crumpled McDonald's bags and a few empty soft-drink cans littered the floor. Rick told Earl that the station wagon reminded him of his studio when he was too steeped in work to think about cleaning, to give order to anything but art; the disarray was industrious. "I guess I can see that," said Earl, nodding at the compliment and idling the engine. "It's in me to give a thing my all. Before selling Inferno, I did a stint at a pitiful little radio station in Buford. My spot was called *The Classical Half Hour,* but it was more like a fancy fifteen minutes. I'll tell you, though, this gig's as solitary as being a DJ. During long hauls, I've been known to interrogate myself just to have a conversation." Earl laughed and shook his head. "The things you'll confess, alone on the road." He twisted a knob on the dashboard and a tape deck sputtered to life. "Johann Sebastian Bach," said Earl, upping the volume. "Best antidote I know to a day of Muzak." He threw the station wagon into reverse.

"Do you know your way around Westgate?" asked Rick.

"All I know these days are supermarkets. Anyplace in between is just gas stations and motels. If it doesn't have a checkout stand, it's not on my map. Don't you know where we're headed?"

The directions were locked in Rick's car back at the lot, and after convincing Earl to keep him company, he wasn't about to suggest they turn around. Rick peered through the bird droppings and insect remains that splattered the windshield, doing his best to guess the way back to Meg and Jerry's. He couldn't help but interpret the windshield as a good omen: Earl had traveled numberless gritty miles to meet him, and even if they only spent one night together, the unlikelihood of their having met, combined with the tape deck's welling arpeggios, made their impromptu date seem predestined. "It's funny," said Earl, "to have a passenger." As Rick leaned toward the dash and squinted at street signs, he told Earl about his conversation with Jerry on the plane. All the while, he could sense Earl staring. Lack of subtlety was one of Earl's most appealing traits, and Rick had to use every ounce of restraint and concentration to keep his mind on the road. But when Earl rested his hand on Rick's thigh, impulse ordered Rick to pounce. He dove headfirst into the driver's seat, yanked Earl's shirt from his jeans, and kissed his stomach, the flesh warm, taut, and salty. Earl gasped and arched his back, allowing Rick to lift his shirt higher. Rick pulled his head back far enough to see Earl's stomach in the emerald light of the dashboard. Wind from the open windows ruffled Rick's hair and blew into his shirt. The velocity of the car, the rumble of the engine, the bumps in the road felt metabolic. "That," he said, peering up from Earl's lap, "is one beautiful belly button." Rick couldn't help noticing that the things he said and did that night were unlike him, or at least unlike the recluse he'd become, and his audacity, like a file baked in a cake, freed him from the cell of himself. He circled and probed Earl's navel with his tongue.

"Yikes," heaved Earl. "You *are* an artist!" He steered the car to the side of the road with one hand and gripped a hank of Rick's hair with the other, pressing him against his stomach. The station wagon grazed the curb and lurched to a stop, its cargo rolling and clattering in the back.

Earl's mouth was wet and generous, his hard jaw covered with stubble. When he moaned, his bony chest rattled with pleasure, an erection tenting his jeans. The more they kissed, the more Rick realized how alone he'd been, and the more alone he realized he'd been, the deeper and greedier his kisses became. The restless pressure of Earl's hands had the power to cause and alleviate need. Finally the two of them pulled apart long enough to catch their breath and make a plan: an appearance at the potluck, back to the Safeway for condoms and Rick's car, then on to Earl's motel.

After ringing the doorbell, the two of them waited on the front stoop, cooking equipment in tow. As Rick reached out to squeeze Earl's shoulder, he remembered reaching beneath Eric's sweatshirt and rubbing the supple muscles of his back. The memory, blunt and unbidden, lingered in his hands.

When no one answered the door, they snuck inside the house as quietly as thieves. In the living room, Earl's eyes widened. "Holy Moly," he whispered, appraising the place. "Beats the rooms at Best Western." The guests had gathered in the dining room, where sliding glass doors opened onto the backyard and the luminous pool. Everyone stood around the table and added to the hum of conversation. Even from a distance, Rick could hear the strain of people trying to keep the ball of small talk aloft. A surprised hush greeted Rick as he walked into the room with a stranger. Oscar looked at them quizzically. Rick introduced Earl all around, counting on the possibility that the Pillings were too bent on being "outlandish" and too restrained by good manners to object to an uninvited guest. Earl dipped his head and repeated each name. "I sure appreciate the invitation," he said to Meg. There had been no invitation, of course, but Earl's gratitude disarmed Mrs. Pilling and prompted her to chime, "We're glad you could come."

Meg had set the table in anticipation of a buffet. The white tablecloth matched the napkins fanned atop it. Empty china bowls and plates waited to be filled with food. The crystal chandelier cast a faceted light. Rick had to admit that Earl made a scruffy addition to the pristine room and the well-dressed guests; as a result of their feverish making out, his hair was mussed, his mustache frayed. A stew pot dangled from the end his arm and he stood there with the dreamy, limp demeanor of a kid who'd just awoken from a nap. Rick didn't dare imagine what *he* looked like, though he suspected a hickey was imprinted on his neck. Propped against Rick's chest was a cardboard box. He set it on the table and explained that, for a mere five dollars, Earl was going to treat them to an up-and-coming American meal.

"Up-and-coming, indeed," repeated Oscar, who could skew any phrase toward innuendo.

Rick shot Oscar a warning glance.

Earl cleared his throat, straightened up, and mustered all the salesmanship he had left. "This is just about the most savory pot of chili you'll ever taste," he said, in his polished, disc-jockey modulations. "Inferno's aiming for a three-year growth plan with a product-recognition goal along the lines of, say, your Dinty Moore or Del Monte." He lit a fire beneath the pot and began stacking cans of Inferno into a pyramid, display-style. "We've got quite a few backers in South Dallas, the kind of ranchers who're all wallet and no cows."

Mitchell smiled for the first time that night, and Rick was sure he found Earl attractive. Jerry saw Mitchell smiling at Earl, and his body tensed. It occurred to Rick that Jerry might harbor a secret crush; didn't Mitchell possess the collegiate look, glasses and all, that had made the airborne Jerry rhapsodic? Noticing the devil on the cans, Meg folded her arms and turned to share a look of consternation with her husband. When Meg saw Jerry staring at his dentist, the same hunch that occurred to Rick seemed to cross her mind. Her arms slipped loose and fell to her sides.

This was the aspect of parties that Rick found most wondrous and suffocating: One suddenly became entangled in the invisible lines of lust or envy or resentment that stretched between the guests, a web of intrigue whose threads are so elusive they only exist in the realm of speculation. Suddenly, Rick was walloped by an idea: a diagram of the party would be his next painting. He imagined, stretching across a wash of muddy color, filaments of strong, unspoken feeling.

Once Earl had completed his pitch, the others took turns presenting their purchases. Jan dredged from a Safeway bag, one by one, a can of baby corncobs, a tin of Norwegian sardines, and a glass jar crammed with tiny white cocktail onions that, even beneath the flattering light of the chandelier, looked haplessly subterranean. She placed the offerings on the table. Everyone eyed the foreign labels. "It's gor-may," she enunciated. "I once had a girlfriend who lived for pickled foods." Meg blushed, as if "pickled foods" were a euphemism. Jerry began to struggle with the jar of onions, huffing and gritting his teeth until Jan grabbed it from his hand and twisted off the lid with a flick of her wrist. "You loosened it for me," she told him, and Rick imagined that she'd had to say that, or something equally reassuring, to many men in order to downplay her prowess and spare them embarrassment. She dumped the onions into a bowl.

Mitchell contributed three boxes of Munchables, a packaged assortment of lunch meats, crackers, and processed cheese spreads that could be served in various combinations. He ripped open the boxes and, shoulders hunched in an occupational posture, prepared a plate of meticulous hors d'oeuvres.

Oscar proffered a one-pound box of Marzipan from Heidi's Kandy Kitchen, a concession he'd found tucked away in a strip mall. Everyone o-o-ohed at the replicas of plump strawberries, ripe bananas, and sanguine apples. Each fruit exuded an oily sheen, a sweet almond odor. Meg said, "They're precious," and gingerly nibbled a miniature orange. What happened next was something that Rick, who considered himself visually sophisticated, if not downright jaded, had never conceived of, let alone seen. Meg let loose a warble of horror, and her right eyelid began to widen and contract, the eyeball rolling languidly in its socket. Her otherwise mild and maternal presence gave way to a kind of lascivious rapture, and if Meg weren't mortified into silence, Rick would have expected her to purr with delight, lick her own shoulder, or nip at the air. The instant Jerry became aware that his wife was seized by a fit of involuntary blinking, he pulled out a chair into which Meg plummeted. With one hand she applied pressure to her tremulous brow, and with the other held her eyelid closed by the lashes. While trying without success to control of the upper half of her face, her jaw went lax and revealed a nasty mash of marzipan. When Meg realized she was flashing food at her stunned guests, she shut her mouth with such force, her teeth snapped like the clasp of a purse.

"Oh, my God," yelped Mitchell. "I read about it in dental school, but I've never seen it happen firsthand!"

"What is it?" barked Jan. She stood erect and ready, as though prepared to pin Mrs. Pilling to the floor if the spasms worsened.

Meg waved her hand as if to say, *Don't look at me, please.* Everyone crowded closer.

Rick tried not to gape, but from this vantage point he could see

Mrs. Pilling's pupil dilating and contracting in an effort to adjust to the changing light, an ocular phenomenon whose helplessness he found hypnotic. The body is such a mystery, he thought; you forget that your eyes are apertures, that your skin is a huge and vulnerable organ, that your muscles have a will of their own.

Mitchell cut through the huddled crowd and bent over Meg. "Is it Marcus Gunn Reflex?" he asked.

Meg nodded.

"You've heard of it?" marveled Jerry. "I'm very impressed." He dashed through the swinging door and retrieved a glass of water from the kitchen. While Meg took a couple of grateful gulps, Jerry rested his hands on her shoulders, his wedding band catching the light. "It hasn't happened in years, has it, darling?"

Meg poked and kneaded her own cheek as if putting the finishing touches on a clay bust. "I think it's stopped," she said. She tilted her face toward the light, eager for confirmation. Motionless and circumspect, the party gazed at Mrs. Pilling and waited to see if the twitching returned. A warm breeze blew through the screen doors. A swing set clanked in the backyard. Crickets throbbed on the lawns of Westgate. At last, Mitchell pronounced the episode over, and there came a collective murmur of relief.

"Marcus Gunn Reflex is rare," explained Mitchell. "It's caused when the chewing muscles and salivary glands are connected to the muscles that control the eyes. Anything can set it off: certain kinds of food, emotional stress, even novocaine injected into the wrong spot."

"It's painless," said Meg, "but unpredictable and terribly embarrassing."

"And congenital," added Jerry. "Her mother first noticed it when she was nursing Meg in the hospital. 'It made my baby look like a little sucking glutton,' she used to tell me. 'So blissful at the teat.' "

Meg twisted around and glared at Jerry. "Thank you," she said. She took a deep breath and hoisted herself out of the chair. "Will you all excuse me?" Meg fled into the kitchen, indignant and liquid in her blue silk culottes. Jerry hurried after her. No sooner had the swinging door stilled than there arose the angry clank of pots, a furious blast of tap water. The Pillings must not have been familiar with the acoustics of their new kitchen because all that decoy noise did little to mask their voices. "I'm embarrassed enough as it is, Jerry, without you regaling your friends with stories about my breast-feeding. They don't have to know everything about me."

"What do you mean, 'embarrassed enough as it is'?"

"I can't look at those people without thinking about what they do with each other in bed."

Oscar sighed a breathy, facetious sigh. "One look at me and people think of sex."

"They don't do anything with each other," said Jerry. "They didn't even know each other until tonight."

Jan peeled the lid from the tin of Sardines, releasing a briny reek. A regiment of fish stared back, darkly iridescent. "What are these marinated in anyway?" she asked. "Motor oil?"

Earl surveyed the buffet. "This," he said, "is one cockamamie potluck." He hummed under his breath and dished chili into the bowls.

"Luck is the operative word in potluck," mused Oscar. "On the groaning board before you, what looks like mere food is actually the manifestation of chance." He waved a hand over the table. "Things come together in ways you'd never expect."

"And fall apart in ways you'd never expect," added Mitchell.

"Then don't think about what they do in bed, Meg."

"I can't be around them and *not* think about it. That's the problem with homosexuals."

"But this party was your idea as much as mine."

"No, Jerry. It was *your* idea. I agreed to this party because after consulting with the elders I was ready to do whatever it took to live up to our vows, to keep you happy and faithful. But you know what I found out tonight, Jerry? I found out I'm old-fashioned. And I'm tired of being polite. Men lying with men, women with women: It's a sin, period. And you condone it." Silverware clanked like scrap metal. "I saw you looking at that Mitchell."

Mitchell took a bite of chili and his eyes began to water. "Even if I were attracted to Jerry," he said, "I'd never date a patient.

Especially not a heterosexual. It's hard enough to find someone compatible; why would I want to make the odds impossible by going after a straight man? Besides, abscesses and gum recession don't exactly fan the flames of lust." He sniffed, removed a handkerchief from his back pocket, and blew his nose. "This is delicious," he said to Earl.

"Jerry was cruising the pants off you," said Oscar. "The man could use a few lessons in the art of the clandestine glance. Especially if he plans to stay married." He plucked a tiny pineapple from the table, turning it this way and that to admire its diamond-ed rind. "Meg is a lovely woman when she's not besieged by queers."

"Besieged?" said Rick. "I seem to recall being invited."

"In Texas," said Earl, "the married ones go to another town when they want to fool around. They'll do everything with another man but kiss him on the lips, and they think that makes them—"

"Pure as the driven snow," said Oscar. "It's amazing, all the intimate things you can do with another human being and still remain a virgin." No sooner had he popped the marzipan into his mouth than he seemed, for a split second, tangible yet absent, lost in the confection's density and sweetness.

"Don't tell me you weren't ogling him," said Meg. "I have eyes."

"That's an understatement," said Oscar.

Jan fished a baby corncob from a bowl. "Hold on, you guys. I don't blame her for being upset. It's another case of the wife getting the short end of the stick. I'm awfully fond of Jerry, but at the office he's one of the boys when he's with gay men and one of the men when he's with straight women." She poked the cob—a pale, extraneous finger—into the air for emphasis. "Jerry wants it both ways," she continued, "which would be harmless, I guess, unless you were married to him and had a horde of kids to take care of. None of us would want to be in Meg's position."

"Of course not," said Rick, "But the way Jerry explained it…"

Meg hissed, "You twist things around till they suit you."

"I'm trying to do what's best for…"

"...me and the kids? Spare me the piety, Jerry."

"For all of us, I was going to say. Don't second-guess me. So I think a man is handsome; what's that have to do with how I feel about you?"

"Nothing," said Meg. "And it hurts."

"I know what Jerry's going through," said Mitchell. "My ex-wife is still furious because I told her I was gay. And because I didn't tell her sooner."

"In other words," said Rick, "she's mad at you for failing at the marriage *and* for trying to make it work."

A glass broke in the kitchen. "Look what you made me do," shrilled Meg.

Mitchell gazed into his plate. "Do you think we should leave?"

"Not me," said Rick. "I don't care if they start throwing knives. I've waited all night to eat, and I'm not going anywhere until I'm full." He loaded his bowl, took Earl by the hand, and walked outside. At the pool's edge, Rick yanked off his shoes and socks, rolled up his pants, and dangled his legs in the tepid water. Earl sat behind him, knees against Rick's back. The two of them gazed into the night sky hovering weightlessly above the suburbs. "Sure would be nice to stay in one place for a while," lamented Earl. "Tomorrow I've got a gig at a Market Basket in Placerville." The bass notes of his voice vibrated in Rick's rib cage, like the rumble of a truck passing in the distance. Rick might have felt a pang of sadness about Earl's leaving, but the temperate air, the plentiful stars, and the pool as bright and fathomless as daylight fortified him against despair. Compared to losing Eric, he thought, all my future losses are bound to be bearable. But the moment he heard Earl speak again, he knew this wasn't true. "I wish I lived here," said Earl. His words were so plaintive, so burdened with yearning, that Rick laughed when Earl added, "But then I'd probably be in the kitchen scrapping with my wife."

Oscar and Mitchell and Jan walked toward the pool, a talkative trio. Each of them held a china plate filled with incongruous food. Rick recognized in their speech and gestures small flourishes of goodwill—a stray touch, a teasing retort—that a stranger might mis-take for flirtation. When Jan delivered the punch line of a joke—"And the priest says, 'Young lady, when you get to heaven, Saint Finger is going to wag his Peter at you' "—laughter displaced the silence of the night. Somehow a party had sprouted in the Pillings' backyard like a dandelion through a crack in the sidewalk. Rick leaned against Earl's knees, eating and swinging his legs until waves slapped at the sides of the pool, sending rafts and lifesavers drifting on choppy turquoise currents.

The sound of churning water drew two of the Pillings' children from their rooms. They materialized from behind the swing set at far end of the house. The youngest, a barefoot girl in an oversized T-shirt—Rick guessed her to be about ten—sauntered toward the strangers. She plunked herself down by the water and tried to gar-ner, without seeming to, as much attention as possible. When the inflatable shark drifted toward her, she flung out a leg and kicked it in the snout. The shark wheezed and sailed away. "I'm Yvonne," she announced.

"That's not her real name," said the boy from the opposite side of the pool, hands thrust in his pockets. Rick had no trouble imagining him as a grown man who inhabited the periphery of parties, lobbing skeptical remarks into the crowd, eyes animated by the same watch-fulness that shone in them tonight.

"I'm the governess," announced the girl.

"She's my little sister," said the boy. "She likes to act bratty and pretend she's things she's not."

The girl went on, undaunted. "Are you friends of Mr. and Mrs. Pilling?"

The guests paused, considering her question.

"Excuse us," came the voices of Meg and Jerry from inside the dining room. Everyone turned to face them. Jerry stared forlornly into the backyard, as if he were outside the house looking in. "I'm afraid it's late," he said, pointing to his watch. Meg said, "We hate to be party poopers." Their voices, strained through the wire mesh of the screen doors, were timid and thin.

Oscar bent over and lifted Rick, then Earl, to their feet. Rick brushed off his jeans and glanced at Earl with such overt, erotic promise, Oscar clicked his tongue.

Jan and Mitchell hurried their conversation, determined to fit in a few remarks before parting. "I bet your ex-wife will be more forgiving when she finds another husband," said Jan. "If I knew more heterosexual men, I'd set her up on a blind date." Mitchell agreed that things would be easier once she was coupled, but behind the gold-rimmed glasses, his eyes conveyed their native doubt.

The little girl and her brother bolted across the concrete, flung open the screen doors, and ran into the dining room. Yvonne nearly collided with her father, embracing his leg, and Rick wondered what it would be like to be grabbed by your brash and affectionate child just when love seemed the most far-fetched. The boy gravitated toward his mother but remained aloof. He peered into the yard, waiting to see what would happen next. Ever the considerate hostess, Meg reached over and flicked a wall switch; an outdoor light suddenly blazed beneath the eaves, a magnet drawing moths from the night, their shadows churning against the house.

"Shall we take our leave?" asked Oscar. And the visitors headed inside.

☐   ☐   ☐

Rick received a postcard from Arizona that depicted a jackelope, the imaginary offspring of an antelope and a jackrabbit. A postcard from Florida showed a freight train's flatcar loaded with an orange the size of a house. Earl sent the most surreal cards he could find, either because he favored them or thought they'd appeal to the artist in Rick. They arrived every few weeks, a reminder that the world's oddities were inexhaustible.

Eventually, however, the cards stopped coming, as Rick knew they would. He often chided himself for not writing back, but Earl never asked for a reply or included a return address. Besides, Rick was at work on a new painting, and apart from a nagging set of technical and aesthetic preoccupations, he had little to talk about. He'd come to think of his encounter with Earl as a thing completed, an improvised composition that one more brush stroke would ruin.

And then, just as Rick was about to relegate his evening in Westgate to the past, a letter arrived from Meg and Jerry. It was one of those Xeroxed family newsletters sent out at Christmas. Rick thought of them as artifacts from his parents' generation, a form of braggadocio in the guise of a greeting, its gossip purged of secrets and upheavals. The Pillings' newsletter was printed on red paper decorated with sprigs of holly—Meg's choice, Rick was certain. Itemized in alphabetical order were the academic and athletic victories of their six children. Rick noted with amusement that nowhere was there mention of a girl named Yvonne. Other than parental hyperbole, the highlights of Meg's and Jerry's year were reserved for the last two sentences: *We visited the big island of Hawaii in September, where we glimpsed the fury of a live volcano. Upon our return, Jerry assumed a position on the church's high council.*

Rick turned the letter over, searching for a salutation scrawled in the margins, or for some note that would say what became of Jerry and whether his equivocations persisted. But the margins were empty, and even the signatures were photocopied. Rick slid the Pillings' letter into the rolltop desk he'd inherited from Eric and swiveled around to face his latest painting. The cavernous studio contained a homey commotion of paintbrushes, drop cloths, and old coffee cans encrusted with acrylics. Outside the windows, sunlight burned through the clouds and ignited random patches of the city— a glass high-rise, a peeling billboard—then quickly faded away. The fluid, moody light animated his painting. Its imagery was based on his recollection of the Saturday morning cartoons in which trails of enticing odor wafted from hot pies, freshly baked bread, and juicy pot roasts; then, as now, he loved how those long ghostly arms rippled through a room and caressed a face, burrowed into nostrils, and beckoned to the hungry with curling fingers. Follow. Taste. Be sated.

Rick leaned forward. Thanks to hours spent feathering wet paint with a small brush, tendrils of scent reached across the canvas. One moment they seemed to float closer. The next they seemed to recede.

Excerpt from The Cosmology of Bing

Mitch Cullin

Thank god for the dry Martini served during lunch.

Thank god for the whiskey sour once the plates were removed from the table, and a second whiskey sour before escaping, thank you very much.

Then how lovely the world seemed to Bing when he exited Eric's Rotisserie and began walking across campus, not at all drunk, no, not even tipsy. At last the fall faculty luncheon was finished, so now he ambled forward, already late for his Thursday afternoon class, leaving the others behind—his associates in the astronomy department, that cloistered threesome of Dr. Richards, Dr. Hershfield, Dr. McDouglas, or, as he often denounced them to his wife, that Holy Trinity of Rot: "The faggot, Jew, and royal cunt." The summer break hadn't changed their minds one bit; they despised him for no other reason, he imagined, than for just being himself—surely outspoken (yes, yes, after a couple of drinks it was hard to stop talking), sometimes irreverent (a few humorous remarks here and there at his colleagues' expense), a cosmologist obsessed by the apocalyptic possibility of vacuum decay (the annihilation of everything, instant crunch, space-time reduced to a sudden singularity)—but, with oaks branching out overhead, shading the sidewalk, he could care less. Why bother? He had tenure, a book on supernovas in its third printing, the respect of three or four graduate students, the admiration of earnest undergraduates. The Holy Trinity couldn't disgrace him even if they tried. And did they try? Had they?

Almost a year ago Dr. Richards, the department head, had mentioned complaints received from several students—one ludicrous charge involving flatulence and sexist jokes, another depicting Bing, disheveled and seemingly intoxicated, staggering about a classroom, making sloppy notations on the chalkboard.

"All fabrications," Bing insisted. "Lies of the worst kind."

He knew damn well that he never behaved in such ways.

"If I had, believe me, I'd remember."

Nonetheless, he was warned.

"Put your house in order," Dr. Richards said, that contemptible queen. "This reflects badly on all of us, and you'd better pray I don't catch you plastered on campus."

The following spring, a potentially damaging complaint was filed. But it didn't come from a student. Joy Vanderhoof, the administrative secretary for the department, claimed Bing called in the middle of night, twice in March, and screamed obscenities at her: "You vile cow! Repugnant excrement! Judas lover!"

"He was obviously drunk," her written grievance stated. "To be honest, I had a difficult time understanding him. He said I was evil. He said I should be ashamed of myself. When I asked why, he started yelling. So I hung up. When he called two weeks later, our conversation was pretty much the same, except I hung up quickly rather than allow him the opportunity to yell."

Once again, Bing protested his innocence in Dr. Richards' office. He rose from his chair and paced, saying, "Where's the evidence? There isn't any, right? The woman was most likely dreaming, or under the influence. Or both. She's deluded, Mike. And she's vicious. She has it in for me. I think you do too."

"That's nonsense. You know it. But come on, Bing, you can't help wondering why she'd lie about this. Frankly, I don't think she would. Do you?"

"I have no idea. I really don't."

But, in reality, he understood everything. Joy Vanderhoof hated him because Dr. McDouglas hated him. Dr. McDouglas hated him because, as she put it, "He lacked professionalism and style." When he said hello, she ignored him. When he spoke in meetings, she frowned. So did Joy. How cozy those two hens were, with their wide hips and cups of coffee, gossiping in the lounge like catty schoolgirls. He'd overheard them, stood outside the lounge and eavesdropped. They were talking about him, whispering and laughing. And what had Joy said about his wife? What was it again?

"Pitiful thing, she belongs in that movie, you know, *What Ever Happened to Baby Jane?*"

"But she's scarier."

"Oh, that's awful. We're bad."

Then Joy laughed. She laughed so loudly that it startled Bing.

Evil, he thought. I hope you die pleading.

And for a moment he considered surprising them. He'd stride into the lounge, pointing a shaky finger, saying nothing—leveling them with an accusatory glare. Instead, he turned and walked away, mumbling, "Rotten bitches, rotten—"

So perhaps he did call Joy. Perhaps he wanted to put her straight, to wake her from her smug sleep and rattle her. Anyway, she couldn't prove it. She never did. Still, Bing was warned, though less sternly than before ("If you didn't call her, I'm truly sorry. If you did and it comes to light, there'll be serious consequences."), and he wore his indignation for weeks afterward, shaking his head and scowling when Joy was nearby. In some small sense, he figured, it was a victory.

But now, this fall, the Holy Trinity struck back. He was assigned only one section to teach, a simple overview class for undergrads— Origins of the Universe, Tuesdays and Thursdays, 1:20–2:35 P.M., ASTR 305G; a demotion of sorts, no doubt pursued by fat-ass McDouglas, agreed upon by Hershfield, OK'ed by Richards. Ignoring past protocol, he hadn't been consulted on the decision. Furthermore, he had always worked with both the brightest graduates and smartest undergraduates, had taught two co-convening courses each semester (Cosmology and Astrophysics in the fall, Theoretical Astrophysics and Theories of Space-Time in the spring).

"It's unfair, Mike. I might as well be a part-time lecturer."

"That's ridiculous. You're getting more freedom than the rest of us and your salary is the same. Christ, you go on and on about never having enough hours in the week for research—so you've finally got it. I'm envious. Who wouldn't be?"

"That's not the point."

So what was?

He wouldn't say.

But Dr. Richards knew—Hershfield was teaching Astrophysics, McDouglas was doing Cosmology. And Bing, paranoid and worried Bing, his lot was the Origins of the Universe and restless undergrads and attendance taken at every lecture and extensive homework assignments and sloppy term papers and quizzes and exams and boring office hours when he had better things to do. Naturally, a man of Bing's position would feel somewhat slighted, a man who had spent sixteen years engaging intense undergrads from the Honors Program and often brilliant graduate students. But there was a drinking problem to contend with, complicated by increasingly erratic behavior (public flatulence being one thing, harassing phone calls being quite another). Poor Bing, he really wasn't the envy of anyone.

"You're taking this too personally."

"Exactly how should I take it then?"

"I suppose, well, as a gift."

A gift. That was funny.

No matter, Bing thought. You can't humiliate me so easily. I'll take your gift and make the most of it. You'll see.

And here on a humid August afternoon, while the city of Houston waited for autumn, Bing found himself smiling. Moss University was teeming with fresh faces, and he felt uncanny and sharp, as new and alive as the young people passing him on the sidewalk. With his thinning gray hair combed neatly, swept over the bald spot on his shiny scalp, his bow tie pressing at his throat, he strode without haste—the very vision of a self-assured and purposeful academic—studying those who came toward him, on their way to and from classes.

The undergrads were obvious. Backpack straps pulled around shoulders, hands in pockets or arms cradling books. Such serious expressions. Boys with baseball caps, T-shirts and ridiculous baggy jeans. Girls in jeans and T-shirts, not so different in attire from the boys. All crossing the open quad, moving beneath Herbert R. Moss' stern statue, a towering monument to the university founder whose grave existed below the marble cowboy boots of his likeness.

Moss, Bing thought, you look miserable. Buck up, old man, there they are, enriching themselves at the finest private university in Texas; the future you wrote so passionately about: "Souls not yet born, let them be free to consider everything when they come here, where no possibility or dream shall be denied." Indeed. But times change, of course, and your pastoral institution is hardly pastoral anymore, flourishing instead amongst skyscrapers and traffic. And, yes, sidewalks weren't part of your grand plan, just grass and trees, a mingling of nature and stately halls. Unfortunate, I know, that a few souls not yet born would come into this world needing wheelchairs and easy access. Oh, well. Anyway, I think your misery is really disdain; something about the young women traversing what was never meant to be theirs in the first place, denying a major part of your dream. You had no idea, did you?

Still, the young men remained plentiful. How perfect each one appeared, how contained; the best of them were lanky and immature, with their short hair and earrings, boxers showing past the waistline (casualness and vogue, that odd charm). They roamed in various directions, off to the library, heading for walkways that ran alongside red-brick, ivy-covered buildings, a few pausing in the shade of oaks. Smooth skin and tanned necks sheltered under clustered leaves. Bing gazed at them as if he were staring through a telescope, aroused by a unique and revelatory discovery.

Was I ever like that?

The sun cast his shadow in front of him, giving his chubby and stunted limbs the illusion of wiry length. Forty years earlier, he was sprightly and vigorous, a swimmer for his college. Young men were his closest friends then. He showered in the locker room with them, got drunk with them, stayed awake until dawn smoking Lucky Strikes and listening to jazz records or reading poetry with them. And, how strange it seemed to him now, he was actually one of those handsome boys.

Except he was a Bing. He had always been. The name was a bad investment, bestowed upon him when Bing Crosby embodied American suaveness. His mother felt positive that Bings would someday rival Mikes. Only later, during his graduate years in the '60s, did the name become a joke, though he took any chiding in stride. To at least three professors he was The Big Bing, a student of infinite ideas and inexhaustible energy. To several peers, he was Bing No-thing—one who couldn't be stirred by student protests and politics and rock 'n' roll, not while stars exploded in supernovas and dispersed into space.

But these days, to his students and colleagues, what was he? A runty man, aged fifty-eight, who could easily pass for sixty-eight. And what did the mirror reveal? Someone far removed from the slender swimmer and his long dead namesake. More like W.C. Fields—the round face, fleshy and pale, the gin blossom nose and squinting eyes. Yes, he was The Bigger Bing, expanding at a steady rate, intrinsically the same, unbridled by time.

He checked his wristwatch.

Almost ten minutes late. And shit, he'd forgotten the course notes in his office. No problem. The Origins of the Universe could be addressed without written aid.

And taking a deep breath, he continued forward, bringing a palm to his scalp, patting down renegade hairs. There would be no more stories of a disarranged and drunken Bing. He'd surprise those cryptos—damnable Richards, Hershfield, McDouglas. Sneaky Joy Vanderhoof.

That's right, he thought. You can't humble me that easy. I'm bigger than you think.

2.

Damn notes. Should've kept them in a pocket.

And where had they left off? What was said? Bing couldn't recall having even lectured. The syllabuses were passed out, surely. Introductions were made, of course. But today—where to begin? He had no idea.

"Well, let me see. Perhaps I should ask you. I suspect some fledgling astronomers in the room have a few thoughts on how to proceed."

This was the Thursday class, supposedly the same students as from the Tuesday class, yet Bing found himself standing in front of quiet strangers—sixty-eight blank faces staring at him, slouched bodies occupying seats in the Thompson Planetarium, not a single person worth remembering. But the first weeks always seemed awkward, a required adjustment period while minds were being made up (some students would drop the course, latecomers would appear). And sometimes a month passed before a class formed its own distinct personality—morose, cheerful, maybe chatty—and from that collective one or two promising individuals usually emerged.

"Professor Owen, can I ask a question?"

A young woman's voice, very deep and loud. But she hadn't raised her hand. So Bing peered forward, looking for her, and said, "You just did. Ask another if you wish."

No one smiled or laughed. A tough crowd.

"Stand up please. I don't know where you are."

She cleared her throat and then stood, a solitary soul in the back row.

"There you are," he said.

Yes, there she was. Bleached hair as white as milk, cropped close to her scalp. Black tank top. Fingers fidgeting with the loops of her blue jeans.

"This might be off the subject, but I was wondering if you believed in alien life, as in extraterrestrial beings visiting us. Because I do. I mean, if you consider that we all come from the same source, it doesn't seem so impossible that equally intelligent beings or even smarter-than-us beings might actually be here from another galaxy. Because when I was fourteen my brother and me actually saw what was obviously an alien craft one night at my grandparents' house in Virginia. There's no other explanation, really. So I'm not surprised at all."

Sit down, he thought. Go away. Die.

Blank faces turned to see her. Then, as if on cue, the very same faces returned to Bing, who was rubbing his chin. Chewing absently on the cap of his pen, a boy sitting in the front row smirked and shook his head. Bing liked that kid.

"There was a question somewhere in there, I think."

"Yes."

"Seems you want to know if I believe extraterrestrials visit the earth?"

She nodded.

"Something like that, yeah."

"But you already know they do. I'll just take your word for it."

He glanced at the boy in the front row, giving him a wink.

"Well, I guess I was wondering if you feel our government has been lying to us about—"

He knew her. He had known her for years and years. Sometimes she was male, sometimes black, sometimes Latino or Asian, more often than not she was female and white and young. And she had to be heard. He had never taught a class in which she didn't exist. And when her peers grew tired of her rambling—her inane questions and comments—she would still fail to sense the complete meaningless of her own words and thoughts. White-girl disease, he called it. How she talked talked talked, blathering with authority. He hated her with every inch of his flesh.

"Hitler's mother," Bing said, interrupting her.

That got their attention.

One hundred and thirty-six eyes gazed at him beneath the starless planetarium sky, indifference now tinged with curiosity. This was Origins of the Universe? No Big Bang. No expansion of space. Wasn't Professor Owen supposed to inflate a balloon—a balloon that represents galaxy clusters—explaining that the space between the clusters increases, but the size of the clusters doesn't.

"Hitler's mother had a saying. She'd go, 'If you believe it, it is so.' Unfortunately, her son took that to heart. Anyway—and what I suppose I'm trying to say is—if you believe it, dear, it is so. Frankly, this whole extraterrestrial thing leaves me limp."

And that was that.

"OK."

She shrugged, sinking into her seat.

But what I want to tell you is that the universe is rich with tangible mysteries. Honestly, no aliens need apply. And in our galaxy— where vast storms rotate counter-clockwise on Neptune, and ice volcanoes shoot frigid geysers on Triton, and the sun's magnetic activity inexplicably wanes and intensifies again every eleven years—there is profound violence and beauty. That's what I should tell you, but I won't. I'm bored and restless and I don't want to be here anymore than the rest of you do. So I'm sorry. My notes are in my office; that's where I'll be going. I thought we could manage without them. I guess not. Some days are better than others, I suppose.

What now?

He consulted his watch.

Over ten minutes late in arriving. Then about ten minutes of engaging zombie children, a brief discussion concerning aliens in Virginia and government cover-ups. Approximately fifty minutes remaining.

Class dismissed.

"Do your reading or readings. Do whatever the syllabus says to do. Be ready on Tuesday, all right? Have a great weekend. Do yourself a favor—have a super weekend!"

And Bing watched them all rise from their seats en masse, gathering books and backpacks. The pen-chewing boy shuffled by without as much as a nod. No one said a word, at least not to him; they filed out through the side doors, making a hasty escape—quiet as church mice, just the sounds of big jeans swooshing, sneakers clomping, the doors opening and shutting.

Then he was alone.

How long had it taken? Thirty seconds? Maybe fifteen? He hadn't noticed White-Girl Disease leaving, but, alas, she was nowhere to be seen.

You keep haunting me, he thought. You're a ghost. Good riddance.

And just then, how peaceful the planetarium felt; this was the only decent place in Houston for watching the stars. At night the city glowed, eclipsing the heavens. But in here—with the flip of a switch, the twisting of a few knobs—the city disappeared, the Milky Way shone clear and perfect; one could almost imagine sitting in the countryside after nightfall, an unclouded sky above, the constellations revealing themselves.

As a college student, Bing had worked at a similar place, though it was smaller and in disrepair. He ran the Star Show for high school field trips, putting on elaborate displays while selections from Holst's *The Planets* played through a single loudspeaker. The ceiling leaked, the dome interior was streaked with water damage. But when the lights dimmed and the stars faded in, the ruin became invisible.

"This is where you find your spot in the galaxy," he explained to his audience. "My role is to guide you along."

At eighteen, he wasn't much older than most of the field trippers. Still, he sensed that he was further along, that he'd digested vast amounts of knowledge in a short period of time. He ate textbooks.

"I'm probably a genius," he often said to his mother.

"You're a genius of something," she'd reply, "except I don't know what."

It was 1958, and he studied under Professor Graham Wilmot, a teacher whose lectures made Bing fall in love with the universe.

"That's why you're here," Wilmot told his students, "to find your place in the universe. My function is to help you."

And he did; it was Wilmot who offered Bing the job of running the Star Show, and it was Wilmot who wrote him a flattering recommendation when it came time to apply for graduate school. But the Star Show—listening to Holst, running the projector, speaking to a group of high schoolers as if he were a professor—that was the best. He couldn't thank Wilmot enough.

And some evenings, after swimming practice, he unlocked the planetarium, snuck inside, and performed a Star Show for his own enjoyment. And more than once, when the occasion presented itself, he brought someone along with him in the middle of the night, a man he'd met at a bar near campus. A stranger. Romantic, not sleazy, he reasoned. A discreet encounter, a mutual exchange. The chance of discovery was slim. Forget that he never knew the man's name, or that he felt miserable for days afterward. How many ended up going with him? As a freshman, six. As a sophomore, nine. None as a junior—that's when he began dating his future wife. Never again, he promised himself. I'm a new man, I'm changed.

That was forty years ago.

3.

The course notes—or, in the very least, the syllabus. One or the other would be helpful.

"Dammit, where are you?"

Bing leaned forward in his seat and began rummaging through the papers on his desk, exploring a mess of unread memos, forgotten letters, a year's worth of university bulletins that he was supposed to give students.

Not there.

He lifted books.

He checked inside his briefcase, twice.

Nothing.

Think.

He propped his elbows among the papers, cupping his face in his hands.

Let's see, let's see. That's right, yes. Must be at home. Somewhere on his desk at home. Of course.

"Hey, did you get Tong's E-mail?"

Who's that?

His hands parted as if fastened to hinges. Peekaboo.

There was Scott, filling the office doorway with his girth, his Metallica concert shirt, his bushy topknot of hair (an obscene tuft that sprouted from his crown like a pom-pom); he grinned within his woolly beard. "Dr. Spacey Casey," Bing sometimes called him, but only after several rounds at their favorite pub, The Stag's Horn.

"Haven't checked my E-mail today," Bing said. "I'll do it later."

"Well, I suggest you do it sooner rather than later. He's got big news."

"I know that. He woke me with the news, so I know. I knew before the rest of you bastards did. Tong and me are like this—"

Bing crossed his fingers—left hand, right hand—holding them up for Scott to see.

"Yeah, yeah, whatever—pretty interesting, no?"

"Yes," Bing said, "it's amazing."

It was worth envy; on sabbatical in the Sonoran desert of southern Arizona, atop a mountain peak, Professor Tong had left his night watch at the Goldwater Observatory and walked outside. He was hoping to confirm with his eyes what had already been revealed by a freshly developed photograph—a photograph taken through the telescope two hours previously. And while searching the sky, he spotted the luminous object, an anomaly that hadn't existed earlier that evening, glowing amid a satellite galaxy of the Milky Way. Making sure astronomers worldwide would know, Tong reported the sighting to the International Astronomical Union. Then he called Bing the following morning, waking him with the words, "A supernova. Ostensibly it is, but I'm positive. Without a doubt in my mind, a fifth-magnitude object. I saw it. Didn't even need the telescope. It was there, plain as day."

Plain as night, Bing thought. Lucky sonofabitch.

"The little guy sounded loopy," he told Scott. "Thought he was drunk at first."

"Hell, I'd be drunk," said Scott. "I'd start drinking at dawn and keep going. I mean, Jesus, you remember the last time a supernova got seen with the naked eye?"

"Not in my lifetime."

"For certain. And you know it ain't happening again while either of us is still breathing. Tong just made the books."

The books, history, being in the right place at the right time—what did it matter?

"I'm happy for him," Bing said.

Scott flexed his shoulders. "I'd love to say the same."

I'm sure you would, Scott. But all's fair, and you're a part-time lecturer. Men like you don't make the books. Men like Tong and me do. That's why we're professors, that's why we get sabbaticals and research grants—so we can make the books, son. So we can write them too. And why exactly weren't you at the faculty luncheon anyway? I could've used your company. No one talked to me. Well, almost no one. The Holy Trinity sure didn't. Not for a second. They think they've got me beat. Perhaps you think that too, that they got me beat. But if you and Tong had been there with me, we could've had our own trinity—then we could've walked out together into this fine afternoon, laughing and talking like great friends. There are some things more important than supernovas, you know, and friendship is one of them. And love. And a good joke. Which reminds me. Did you hear McDouglas is getting liposuction? The operation takes place May, June, July, August, September, October, November, and December. That's a good one. I need to tell you that sometime. I think you'd like it. Tong would.

Bing motioned for Scott to enter. Then he pointed at the chair in front of his desk.

"Come and sit a spell. I've got office hours soon, don't think anyone will show up, though."

"Would like to," said Scott, scratching the tip of his nose with a finger, "except my three o'clock class would probably miss me. How about drinks later? The Stag's Horn and happy hour?"

"Can't tonight. Tomorrow's better. Is that good for you?"

"Sure. I'll call you at home."

"Sounds good."

Bing nodded. A resolute nod, like a firm handshake. And after Scott wandered away into the corridor, he went to the door and closed it, locked it, tested the handle making certain.

Just for a moment, he thought. Just while I get a nip.

The nip. Ten High bourbon. A half-pint bottle, half full, in the bottom drawer of his file cabinet. Then a quick swig. One more. Go easy. That's enough, that's good. He returned the bottle, hiding it between manila folders, filing it under the letter T.

The drawer slid shut.

Bing sighed as he stood. He wiped his lips with the back of his hand. Then he straightened his bow tie, smoothed his hair, checked his zipper.

Ready.

He unlocked the door and pulled it open.

And waiting in the corridor, standing before the doorway, a green backpack hanging from a shoulder, was the pen-chewing boy; with a fist raised, poised for knocking, his presence startled Bing.

"What're you doing?"

"Sorry," the boy said, lowering his fist. "I was about to knock. You're having office hours, right?"

Bing's face revealed nothing.

"These are my office hours, yes."

The boy let the backpack slip; in one deft move the strap went from his shoulder to his hand, where the backpack then dangled at his side.

"There's this article you wrote. It interested me a lot."

Article? What article?

Bing glanced at the boy's slim, tanned neck. Then he glanced at his shoes, then at his brown eyes.

"You're in my class, correct?"

"Yes. I read an article you published in *Scientific Foundations*."

"Which one?"

" 'Vacuum Decay and Cosmic Locality.' "

"You read that? Really?"

Bing couldn't believe it—this child reading and understanding that article.

"Yes."

"You're an undergraduate?"

"Yes."

What an attractive boy he was too: tall and lanky, a born basket-ball player, with sandy hair parted in the middle, hair that fell into place after a hand ran through it. And how clean he seemed; his skin looked scrubbed and ruddy, his big swooshy jeans were pressed, his black tennis shoes unblemished. Yes, the hoop earring in his left nos-tril was silly, but, Bing reasoned, he's young. And smart. And hand-some—the kind of boy who must be beautiful and toned and smooth without his clothing on. Perhaps a swimmer.

"Come in, please."

Then the door shut behind them, and Bing found himself seated at his desk, the boy sitting across from him. Between them the dis-array of papers. And Bing wondered if the boy would like a pen to chew, but decided it might be an inappropriate suggestion, even if mentioned in jest. Anyway, this was business.

Name?

Nick. Nick Nicols. A sophomore.

Major?

Undecided.

Except he loved reading, especially Whitman and Salinger. So maybe an English degree.

Bing wanted to know more about him. But not yet. Not today.

"And what exactly did you think of my article?"

Bing felt the Ten High in his throat, a residual sensation, warming.

Nick's face brightened. How thin his lips were, how red.

There are some things more important than supernovas, Tong. There are other worlds to explore with the naked eye, you know.

4.

Ms. Bunny was late. And Bing was worried.

"She's dead."

He'd braved a rainy evening and slick streets, had arrived early so he could get a stool beside the baby grand. Now he waited, sipping his second pink lady, wondering if Ms. Bunny met with tragedy en route to the piano bar. Maybe her car skidded from the wet road, crashing into a tree, the impact killing her. He imagined her fake eyelashes knocked askew, her bones cracking, her powder-blue wig flying through the windshield amid shattering glass, and then the confused expressions of the paramedics as they discovered that the enchanting Ms. Bunny was, in reality, a man.

No more tacky jokes and sad songs, Bing thought. No more "Stormy Weather." No more "That Old Black Magic." Ms. Bunny is no more.

The announcement of her death would create an astonished silence, shocking all the other men seated around the piano, the regulars for Torch Song Thursday at Edward's, those chatty old queens with their dyed hair and silk shirts and cocktails; there wasn't a jowly face among them worthy of consoling Bing. Only Damien. But Damien was different. He was younger than the rest—thirty-three, a psychology graduate student, favored as a research assistant—and cute in a compact elfish way: He'd made a living as a jockey before pursuing a doctorate.

And it pleased Bing to be seen in Damien's company. The pair turned heads when arriving together, aroused whispers when settling next to one another near the piano. They traded rounds like close friends, talked intimately like lovers, aware the whole time that they were being watched with a mixture of disgust and regard—*good God, it's them again, sugar daddy and his pretty boyfriend*.

"That's a horrendous notion," Damien said, patting Bing's hand. "Ms. Bunny isn't dead. She's getting ready."

"Suppose so."

Bing appreciated the pat, the open display of affection, and hoped the others had spotted it.

I won't be alone, he thought. If it's tragedy, then I'll have someone to support me as I leave. Someone to drive me home, to help me inside. I'm not like you sad sacks, not even close.

And perhaps Damien would hold him in the car. Would that be asking too much? Maybe a hug, or a kiss, or even—

Bing knew it was pointless. Once, while parked in front of

Edward's, he'd leaned forward and kissed Damien on the cheek. Then he kissed his neck. And Damien didn't protest, gave no sign that he was bothered by this older man reaching under his shirt. But then he told Bing to stop; he said it was wrong, said they were friends, just friends. And there was Bing's wife to think about.

"She won't know. No one will. Me and you only. Our secret. No one gets hurt."

"Someone always gets hurt."

"But if we're discreet, if we keep it to ourselves—"

"I'm sorry, Bing, but no. I'm sorry."

"Nothing to be sorry about," Bing said. "I understand."

So they'd be friends. Bing didn't care, as long as he could be associated with Damien. As long as those other queens thought otherwise. Every Thursday they'd go to Edward's, and, at the end of the evening, they'd shake hands. It didn't matter that they both shared and hid the same desires, or that they both loved show tunes and exotic drinks. Or that they had met by chance, not at school, not in the basement men's restroom at the library (a rumored hotbed of sexual activity), but at this piano bar. It just didn't matter.

Anyway, Damien lived with his mother. Bing had a wife. There was a quarter century age difference. Bing could be his father; he hated that idea. And there was another difference—Damien was obvious, effeminate, a bit prissy; Bing, as he imagined himself, was masculine, a real man, inclined only toward a slight weakness for other men. He wasn't a faggot like Dr. Richards (Richards who lisped when he lectured, who had a boyfriend named Michael). He had always loved his wife, always—and sometimes he strayed. Sometimes he wanted to be held. That's all.

How long had it been?

I don't want to think about it, you see. What was I supposed to do? There was my wife, and then there was Marc. But that was so long ago, and it's painful, you know. The world wasn't like it is these days. There weren't dance clubs like now, those places where boys go and dance and sweat to that dreadful music. There were discos, I suppose, but I was already too old for them. You know, I don't think I've ever been young. Never. I was born an old man. And I'm not feeling sorry for myself because my youth was squandered on the heavens. No regrets. Well, at least not many. But, Damien, I wish I could tell you something about myself, because I did love someone like you. And I lost him too. But that's no one's business except my own. But I was young with him, or younger. I mean, I felt younger, I guess. And he was twenty-four. I was thirty-six—three years older than you are. His name was Marc. He was a poet, my afternoon distraction from work. I loved him for three months and then he was gone. Do you know what he drank? Pink ladies. We drank pink ladies together. But it wasn't Ms. Bunny then—it was Sister Judy. And it wasn't Texas, it was New York. But there are some things that should be kept with one's self. So I won't tell you how long it's been since I've slept with another man. Or how badly I miss him. Or that sometimes I dream about him and I can't even remember what he looked like. You see, it's better not dwelling too much on the past. It's better to talk about the weather instead.

"My god, it's raining men! Hail Mary, hallelujah!"

Ms. Bunny appeared, working the bar as she always did, wandering from man to man, touching chins, brushing cheeks. Soon she'd be at the piano, singing in that throaty voice of hers. But jokes came first, then sad songs.

"It's a Viagra convention in here, seriously. Just kidding, darlings. I'm bad, I know. God bless Viagra, that's all I got to say. Really, that drug is like Disneyland, honestly. You wait two hours for a three-minute ride."

Laughter.

"That's funny," Bing said as he lifted his drink.

Ms. Bunny sauntered between tables, blowing kisses and rolling her eyes.

"She's alive," Damien said.

"What?"

Bing leaned in, putting his shoulder against Damien's shoulder.

"I didn't catch what you said."

But Damien looked away, smiling at Ms. Bunny as she moved toward them.

"Nothing," Damien said. "It's nothing."

Nothing, Bing thought. Of course, nothing at all.

5.

The air smelled of sewage, of waste stirred by the rain. Bing sloshed across the damp lawn, heading for the porch, staggering in the light drizzle. And this was how he brought himself inside—waving to Damien when his VW pulled away from the curb. Then wiping his shoes on the doormat (mustn't make a mess). Then fumbling with the keys (don't forget them in the lock). Then through the front door (don't slam it shut). Then up the stairs—go slow, don't trip, be careful, easy on that squeaky top step—and then there he was, short of breath, tipsy, relieved to be standing in his world.

Home. Why did he hate leaving it? Dread returning to it? He didn't know. And when did the guest room become his bedroom? When was it agreed that the upstairs—with its own bathroom, its wet bar—would be his? The downstairs hers? She got the backyard, the garden. He got the french windows that opened to the balcony. At what point were these decisions made?

A flick of a switch illuminated the study. His bookcases. His couch. The coffee table. Beyond, in an alcove, was his office, his desk, his Frank Lloyd Wright table lamp, more bookcases, the stereo.

"Yes, home is where you hang yourself," he told Pussy, his gray tabby who was curled on the couch. He went to her and stroked her coat. "Isn't that right?" he said, cooing like she was a baby. "Pussy is a pretty girl."

She raised her head just a bit, one eye closed, letting him scratch her chin.

"Pussy loves daddy."

And below his shoes, beneath the rug and floor, down there in his wife Susan's world, the house was dark but not quiet. She was asleep with the TV on—he could hear it droning in her bedroom, a late night religious program filtering into her brain, protecting her from those nightmares where she was drowning under a frozen lake. In the morning they'd talk. She'd make breakfast, serving him toast and orange juice and scrambled eggs with green chili. Then she'd ask for money (a check if he had less than ten dollars on him), something for Brother Van Horn in Atlanta, or The Faith Ministries in Baton Rouge, or Helpful Blessings in Orlando. And he'd give her whatever was in his wallet. And she'd accept his offering without a thank you; her black eyes revealing naught—no promise of salvation, no hope for prayers to be answered—even as her fingers closed around the bills.

But now she slept. And her book was on his coffee table, that slim volume of poetry, published the same year they both started teaching (astrophysics for him, English literature for her), before her brain played its tricks and ended her career. Even then there were little clues, foretelling stanzas, lost on him until later.

To be only what I am, floating,
Carried somewhere else, transported
From one end to the other;
All my days are really the same
With varying degrees of cold and cold.

How could he have known?
And how strange it was when Marc (that afternoon distraction of so many years ago—that lover of poets, of Bing) once quoted her as they lay together after sex. She had already changed, had stopped writing and teaching, but the distraction spoke her words, making them sound somehow new and significant: "Our needful embrace, a reminder that we are alone within ourselves."
"That's my wife," Bing said, matter-of-factly. "You know that, right?"
Marc began speaking the words again, slyly, whispering them.
But Bing cut him off.
"Please don't. She's ill and it seems cruel."

the **Advocate**

The national gay & lesbian newsmagazine. Since 1967

www.advocate.com

NO POSTAGE
NECESSARY
IF MAILED
IN THE
UNITED STATES

BUSINESS REPLY MAIL
FIRST-CLASS MAIL   PERMIT NO. 145   MOUNT MORRIS IL

POSTAGE WILL BE PAID BY ADDRESSEE

the **Advocate**

PO BOX 541
MOUNT MORRIS IL 61054-7847

Marc turned on his back, breathing heavy through his nose for effect.

"You love her more than me?"

"I can't say. It's different. It's not the same thing."

"Isn't it?"

Marc folded his arms over his chest; his right leg scooted off the edge of the bed, his foot dropped to the floor. Then how uncomfortable that bed was, how suddenly useless. Yet, the following afternoon, it would become wanted—the single mattress with baby-blue sheets, belonging to an English student, existing in a low-rent apartment (Marc had given Bing a key, a coffee cup, a hanger for his jacket and slacks).

He touched Marc's neck with his fingertips.

"You don't understand what it's like. It's rather complicated. She's my wife."

Marc looked at Bing as if some terrible lie had been uttered.

"You love her. That's why you're here with me."

"Daddy is parched."

Bing wandered to the wet bar, and Pussy followed, rubbing and weaving between his ankles. He fixed a gin and Sprite, pouring the drink into a dirty glass that was stained with bourbon. Then he crossed to his office, clicked the stereo on, listening as static crackled from the speakers. His favorite classical station had signed off for the night. Still, he let the racket continue, preferring the bothersome hiss over the muffled rumble of his wife's TV. "It's the universe's song," he often told his students, when explaining electrostatic disturbances. And, while unlatching the french windows, that's what he told himself.

"Cosmic radiation in E," he said, enjoying the sound of his voice.

Pussy meowed at his feet. She joined him on the balcony, where they both sniffed the foul air. At last the rain had quit. And glancing skyward, Bing saw the reflection of the city lights, the clouds above glowing with a pinkish hue. The constellations were up there somewhere, he knew, but even on clear nights it was impossible to stargaze in Houston; the city ate darkness within a thirty-mile radius—and Bing longed for the country, a farmhouse atop a hill, a year's supply of gin, a telescope, a landmark discovery bearing his name.

"Daddy hates Tong."

He nudged Pussy with his shoe. Then, shaking his head, sipping his drink, he imagined what moved beyond those clouds—Cassiopeia, the Winter Triangle, Tong's dying star.

"No, no, I don't. I don't hate him. I love Tong, Pussy. He's my friend."

I'm plastered, Bing thought. I'm wrecked.

To begrudge Tong was unjust. To despise the Trinity of Rot was noble. They were getting the better of him, and now he felt miserable. Sometimes he convinced himself that it didn't matter—the petty politics, the nasty gossip—that by ignoring the slights he could even the score. Other times he wanted to scream, to leave Houston and never return. But that's what they wanted him to do.

"Fuckers!"

His voice frightened Pussy, who poofed her tail and crouched. He lunged forward, pressing his waist against the railing, and threw his glass down into the backyard.

"Someone cares," he said. "Someone cares."

He stepped away from the railing, taking a deep breath. Then he knelt—calming Pussy with his fingers, caressing her ears—and a strange notion slowly filled him, a notion that had taken time to surface. He started whistling, sensing the lessening of his mood, the righteousness of having been wronged, the desire for equity, the unexpected realization that moments ago seemed distant.

Someone cares.

What was his name? Like Marc. No, Mick. No, Nick. Nick. With a fondness for Whitman. Not a poet though, or an astronomer. But he'd read Bing's paper, was curious about vacuum decay. And Bing would show the Trinity that they could only do so much; they couldn't prevent a teacher from engaging a student, or the creation of an independent study (if Nick was interested). And how easy it would be, how simple. The Origins of the Universe would become secondary. Vacuum Decay and Cosmic Locality would be the important class—just him and one student. It was perfect.

He lifted Pussy, cradling her. The same instant, he felt rain on his brow and nose. A thick mist began spraying the balcony. The cat, startled by the moisture on her coat, attempted to jump from Bing's arms, but he gripped her tightly, clutching her at his chest.

"There, there," he said, as her claws fastened into his jacket.

A thunderclap erupted—the static surged from the speakers—and Pussy struggled, emitting a tragic growl.

"There, there."

Bing shut his eyes for a moment, and made a wish. The same wish he made most nights: Remember everything tomorrow. Don't forget.

"Don't let me forget."

Then he released his hold, allowing Pussy to escape. But he remained for a while outside, swaying in the whirl of mist, as water cascaded down his face, licking his lips like a thirsty fool. At the piddliest hour of the night, he was the only man in the city praying for a flood.

Pasta Night

Jameson Currier

I don't remember when I began cooking so much. Nathan was always the one of us who cooked, but now I found myself helpless with so much restless time on my hands, unable to stop silently worrying about the prospects for Nathan's health and unable, really, to concentrate on anything else. Unwilling to return to work and with Mrs. Solloway usurping the cleaning chores, I began roaming the aisles of the grocery store, bringing home heavy brown bags of cans and jars of gourmet sauces, protein-enriched breads, plastic-wrapped vegetables and vitamins and herbs. I knew nothing about cooking; nothing more than how to fry a hamburger or a grilled cheese sandwich or, perhaps, how to heat a frozen entree or reheat a slice of pizza. The kitchen had always been Nathan's domain; I had never cultivated the patience for cooking.

At first I began by cooking large pots of pasta, then progressed to throwing fruits, milk, ice cream, and protein powder into a blender to create shakes, then, more boldly, experimented with pureeing broccoli, asparagus, and potatoes into soups. Food was what would save Nathan, I had decided; we had, by then, lost too many friends already from the inadequacy of medicine. Nathan was amused when I would walk into the bedroom and say, "Try this sauce, I just made it," and that delight is what sustained me when I returned to the kitchen to cook something else. Food had become a new weapon in our war; hope could be created out of weight and mass.

Nathan had been sent home from the hospital with a stash of

prescriptions: Compazin for his stomach, Nizoral for the thrush in his mouth, Cyclovir for the herpes sore on his chin. Dr. Nyquist had also given him prescriptions for Halcion and Xanax, for help with sleeping and anxiety, and had also started Nathan on a four-hour cycle of a new drug that was just completing clinical trials—Retrovir, soon to be more commonly known as AZT. Whether it was these medications that made him better, my cooking, or my prayers, I am not sure, but he did grow stronger daily. Nathan's mother went back to Hartford, friends calmed down, I went back to work, and Nathan was faced with being a man who was living with an HIV infection and diagnosed with AIDS.

I tried, at first, to find a regimen for us to maintain: a trip to the gym or working out in the morning at home, vitamins, medicine, work, monitoring his temperature and breathing and lymph nodes—all a way to keep disorder from breaking through our lives again. I thought if I kept a list of things I had to do during the day, to remind Nathan, for instance, that he should look into other therapies, such as vitamin C injections, or consult an herbalist whom a friend of a friend had gone to in Chinatown, things would seem rational, logical and ordered, that I had a handle on things, when, of course, there is nothing rational about a life-threatening illness. Frailty shines through life like light through a crystal, only the colors are distorted and frightening when seen in this way. Nathan and I tried to work it out in his mind that he was not living with an illness but coexisting with a virus, but everything seemed to funnel into one fatalistic question: How much time did he have left?

And then a phone call came that Sam was back in the hospital, the KS had spread to his right lung and time was running out. Nathan had taken the call, Sam's mother had phoned that morning, and when I got home that afternoon Nathan was shaking with fright. "I can't go," he said, over and over, knowing he should go but couldn't—it would mean him facing his own mortality as well, something he did with himself every day but did not want to have to do in front of someone else or be forced to do again in the corridor of a hospital.

"I'll go after dinner," I said, mentioning I would stop by the pharmacy first. I knew that in Nathan's mind I had resolved the matter, as if my going back to the hospital was proof there was nothing out of the ordinary to the call, that I would return with good news, that Sam had been given drugs and treatments, that he would be back home in a few days.

When I got to the hospital it was close to 8 o'clock and I took the elevator to the room number Nathan had scribbled down on a slip of paper. When I got to the room Sam was not there, and his name was not listed on the wall beside the door either; two other men occupied the room. I walked to the nurses' station at the center of the floor to check the room number and asked the nurse on duty, a striking young Hispanic woman, what room Sam Karan was in. She seemed disturbed by my question, bowed her head, and said quietly, "Mr. Karan passed away early this afternoon," then backed away slightly from the counter.

Shocked, I found myself graciously bowing to her in reply, as if she had treated me with the utmost hospitality. I felt a scream growing inside me—a combination of fear and hate, and I backed myself away from the nurse, holding my breath till I reached the elevator. It opened almost immediately, and I stepped inside, my body at once relaxing as if I had reached a protective cocoon, and I followed a man out when the doors reopened a few seconds later when I thought we had reached the ground floor. Instead, I was on an unfamiliar floor, and I realized my mistake almost instantly and stood by the elevator bank insistently pressing the call button for the elevator's return.

"I see you back," I heard a familiar-sounding voice speak behind me, and I turned and saw it was the Jamaican nurse I had met several times before.

She must have noticed the looks of horror and grief that were blended into my expression. "He went peacefully," she said. "His brother was here with him." She took my hand and patted it, and

I remember being struck by the heavy-looking silver rings she wore on each of her fingers. "Come," she said, and it was here that she motioned to me, as if she had been awaiting my arrival all day.

I followed her down the hall, around the corner, and through a set of swinging doors. She led me into a large room with beds framed with steel criblike structures, white sheets tucked tightly into tiny mattresses. She handed me a small gauze mask that I slipped over my mouth. "This is Tina," she whispered through the mask she had slipped over her own face, motioning a finger to where her lips were, to indicate that I should stay quiet. In the bed a small, caramel-colored baby lay sleeping, an IV needle stuck into the heel of its foot. I looked abruptly around the room, struck by the quiet I had stepped into. There were babies in each of the cribs, one child was attached to a respirator; along the wall was a row of glass-encased incubators, one of which held a child the size of my palm. "This is Darren," she said, leading me to a bed where an eight-month-old baby lay awake, looking skyward with dark choco-late eyes. She lifted him into her arms, rocking him into a smile. "All they want is to be held," she said, stretching her arms out for me to hold the baby. I hesitated, frightened by the baby, but his eyes looked up into mine and I instinctively took him into my arms. "His name is really Darryl, but I call him Darren, because I like that TV show so much." I nodded to her, rocking Darren in my arms. He opened and closed his fist and then relaxed his head against my chest.

"He's a miracle baby," she said. "The last month he's been test-ing negative."

Again I looked around the room, suddenly aware of where the nurse had led me. These babies had all been born HIV-positive. "They are not all so lucky as Darren," she said. "Tomorrow they're transferring him to Grove House."

"*Grove House?*" I asked.

"Martha Grove. In Harlem," she nodded as if I would immedi-ately recognize the name. "She keeps a house with babies."

She lifted Darren out of my arms. "Come with me," she said. "Mother Grove always need help. And bring your friend with you. I know he like the babies too."

□   □   □

"It's a surprise," I said to Nathan, which was the only way I could guarantee his coming with me.

"Nothing surprises me anymore," he said flatly, following me up the gray concrete steps of a brownstone on the upper west side. It had been a difficult day for both of us; Nathan had been in a particularly stressful conference with a client, and when it was over he realized he had missed taking his AZT. Last night the news of Sam's death had shaken him and he was unable to fall asleep, sitting on the couch till 4 in the morning, trying to distract himself by reading. Now I had pulled him away from work early, after a day where I had taken a simple assignment—installing ceiling fans in a loft in Soho— and turned it into a fiasco by accidentally popping open an old sealed gas line.

I rang the buzzer and a stern, overweight black woman opened the door. "We're here to see Mrs. Grove," I said.

"I'm Mrs. Grove," she said suspiciously. "Who you?" she added harshly, as though to frighten us away.

Just then Dora, the nurse, appeared at her shoulder, and said, "These are the boys I talk about." Dora took the door from Mrs. Grove's hand and opened it wider. "Come," Dora waved. "Come in, come in."

Mrs. Grove's haughty expression followed us inside. She smelled of cinnamon and baby powder, and was crisply dressed in a pressed cotton dress covered by a white apron stained with what appeared to be red paw prints but under closer inspection was the tomato-smudged handprints of a child, the fabrics noisily rubbing together as the fleshy rolls of her waist shifted as she walked. Nathan, at this point, was certainly surprised by the two women, but not, really, very much amused. We were led into a large room filled with small chairs

and children's toys, and stood awkwardly in front of Mrs. Grove
while Dora disappeared. None of us said anything to one another:
Mrs. Grove glaring at us, Nathan confused, myself trying to find
something, anything, to say. Then Dora reentered and placed Darren
in my arms. "A familiar face," Dora said, though I was uncertain
whether it was directed at me or to the child. Nathan and Mrs. Grove
eyed each other suspiciously and then turned and looked at me rocking Darren. Mrs. Grove seemed to relax a bit, shrugging herself into
a resolve. "Well, you boys can help," she said. "It's pasta night."

"*Pasta night?*" Nathan and I answered, incredulously, at the
same time.

She gave us another disapproving glance, as if we should have
known what we had walked into. "Come on," she said and led us
into another room filled with small tables and children's high chairs.
"Dora, find them some rags," she said, and disappeared through a
swinging door. Around the room there were children, small infants
ranging from three months to three years old in high chairs or in
cribs, a roll of toilet tissue unraveling on the floor, a bright orange
beach towel draped over the arm of a chair. There were three other
women in the room, two black and one Hispanic, all much younger
and more slender than our heavyweight host, stooping before babies
with forks and spoons and large bowls of pinkish spaghetti and pasta,
but each of these ladies looked up at us and smiled or nodded when
we entered the room. Nathan slipped his coat off, walked around a
Cabbage Patch doll and a foam football on the floor, and took
Darren out of my arms and placed him into a chair. Dora handed me
a warm washcloth, and Nathan took a bowl of spaghetti Mrs. Grove
had reappeared with, and he crouched in front of Darren trying to
get him to grasp a fork. Darren was more interested in sticking his
fingers into the spaghetti than putting it into his mouth or even
wanting to acknowledge the fork, so Nathan and I sat on the floor,
cross-legged, observing politely but still trying to feel involved, till
one of the other ladies asked Nathan to watch another child while
she went into the kitchen and got more juice.

"Wait," Nathan said, a little too sharply as the woman rose to leave the room. It was loud enough for all of us to hear, sending, at once, a shock through the room. At first I thought Nathan was scared of being alone with the child.

"What's her name?" Nathan asked the woman, softer, aware of the disturbance he had caused.

"Georgia," she answered.

"Georgia," Nathan repeated and sat down in front of the baby, taking his wash rag and wiping the baby's face into a smile.

☐   ☐   ☐

When Nathan and I first began living with each other, we defined our relationship with certain boundaries. Monogamy would not be an issue between us, we decided, but discretion would be. If one of us tricked with someone, we would not discuss it with the other. We were also adamant about keeping our identities separate, making sure to define ourselves as individuals, not entirely as a couple. To help us achieve this, we agreed we would give each other a night off every week from the relationship. Tuesday nights fell into being our nights to do as we planned, whether going out separately with a friend or out to a bar or just spending time alone. Nathan set the pattern very early on in that he would be the one who would be out of the apartment on Tuesday nights, which I readily accepted; I always considered Nathan as the more adventurous one of us. The first Tuesday night without Nathan I remember I sat and listened to an album on the stereo, smoked a joint, looked at myself nude in the mirror, then fell asleep in front of the television; such was the extent of entertaining myself. The next week I was more prepared—Denise and I went to dinner, then I went home and did laundry. Gradually over the years, Tuesdays came and went and our regimen of individuality fell away or reasserted itself whenever necessary. So it was not a surprise when Nathan mentioned a few days after going to Grove House for the first time—just before he was turning off the lamp beside the bed—that he was going out Tuesday night. My only concern was how taxing it would be to him; the weather was still chilly, and he was trying to maintain a full work schedule, but I refused to voice my concern, not letting myself seem to nag him or worry him in that manner. I didn't ask what he was doing, that was not the scenario between us; Tuesday nights were always reserved for their privacy as well. "I'm going back to pasta night," he said, which did surprise me. I lifted my eyes to him and gave him a grin, wounded a bit, though, that he had not asked me along, pleased, however, that he had found something to do that could give him some sort of psychological support in regard to his own health.

"Do you think she would let me bring Georgia home?" he asked as I slipped my body around his, ready to fall asleep.

"*Bring Georgia home?*" I replied. Now he had stunned me.

"Just for a weekend, maybe," he said, testing me, to gage my reaction.

"Nathan," I said, a bitterness rising and catching in my throat as I reached across him for the lamp switch. "Don't set yourself up for disappointments."

☐   ☐   ☐

There is an energy to working with wood, especially older wood, that makes the work become therapeutic. There is the sanding, the staining, the wiping and polishing, the way the wood feels to the touch, the texture one minute silky with dust, another slick with sand, a corner, perhaps, stubbly and rough against the fingertips. Not all of the energy, of course, emanates from the wood or the work, but from the repetition, the constant touch of the wood, the stroking, the rubbing, the action that brings to it a quality akin to meditation. I can think about a lot of things while working with wood, or nothing at all, transcending a problem, for instance, with a repeated rhythmic motion that soothes, something like what I have seen in people who practice tai chi.

A few weeks before Nathan and I went to Grove House for the first time, I found a pair of high-back dining room chairs on the street, the seats kicked out, a support spoke missing from one chair, another broken off midway on the back of the other. I carried the chairs back to the apartment and set them at the end of the hallway, thinking I would be able to repair and refinish them, possibly even give them to Alex to resell. I needed a new project to absorb my attention while at home; my experiments with cooking had waned as Nathan became stronger and began spending more time at the office. And I knew the chairs were more than a hundred years old; there is a feeling to aged wood that is different from wood that has been cut today. I think it has something to do with the wisdom the wood achieves with age, the way the fibers soak in time and history, or at least that's what I would like to believe. The Tuesday night that Nathan went back for a second visit to Grove House I decided to strip the paint off the chairs—someone had painted them a lemon-yellow color that had faded over the years into an industrial discolored beige. That Tuesday night I set newspapers on the floor, found some old rags, and began to wipe away the old paint, sanding the wood in a few hard-to-remove places. I only made it through one chair that night, opening the window and airing out the fumes before Nathan returned. I fell asleep before he came home but felt him when he crawled into the bed beside me.

The next day he mentioned nothing about the chair in the middle of the floor, the sight of which would usually irritate him; he mentioned very little about his visit to Grove House except that he was glad he had gone and Mrs. Grove had let him read a story to the children before bedtime. He didn't mention whether Dora had been there, nothing was said, either, about the prospects of Georgia's visit; I assumed Nathan had not yet approached Mrs. Grove about it. I knew, in time, she would either shoot it down or let it happen; such, it seemed, was her nature. But I was surprised when later in the week Nathan mentioned he would like to go Grove House on Sunday, and did I want to come along with him? Sunday, it seemed, was "song night."

□   □   □

I took the corner of the sheet and tucked it under the mattress, then watched Dora lean over the bed and flatten out the wrinkles.

The room with six cribs was lit only by a small, clown-shaped lamp; the dark blue light of evening filtered through a sheer curtain covering the window. Below us, the rumble of a bass guitar thumped through the plaster seams of the wall. Song night was led by Mrs. Grove's seventeen-year-old nephew, Gabriel; in fact, I discovered Grove House was staffed almost entirely by Mrs. Grove's relatives; Dora, I learned, was Martha's second cousin. I had followed Dora upstairs when the mood became too surreal for me, watching Gabriel pound out a sing-along to Robert Palmer's "Addicted to Love" and Nathan join in, playing a tabletop like a drum with two pencils. I would never have guessed Mrs. Grove's requests would be tunes by Cyndi Lauper and Tina Turner; at one point, during a particularly spirited rendition of "Karma Chameleon," she nodded at me and yelled, "The babies love Boy George the best."

Now I felt a weariness shift into my chest as I stood in the deep light of the window and looked down at the street, taxis and cars floating beneath me as if I were on a bridge. I felt, then, an urge to smoke a cigarette, something I had not done since Nathan and I began living together. It had bothered me to watch Nathan doting on Georgia. It wasn't really that I was jealous; I was worried he was becoming attached to someone and something unattainable for him—that what he wanted from Georgia, that unconditional love one expects, for instance, from a pet, was not possible from this child. Georgia looked deceptively healthy; earlier this evening, Nathan had held her up by the arms, helping her walk on tiptoe like a precocious ballet dancer on point. Dora had told me Georgia's mother was a crack addict, which in turn had bequeathed Georgia neurological problems, which were further complicated by too many months in a hospital crib with her feet straight out. If Nathan were to have let go of Georgia's hands, she would have collapsed to the floor like a rag doll. Nathan had mentioned to me last week that Mrs. Grove had shown him how to massage Georgia's legs to help relieve the cramping. And then Dora had made a stray comment as we were changing the bed linens that Darren was likely to be adopted in the next few weeks. Even though I had only seen Darren a few times, had not even bonded with him, I felt so oddly unbalanced by the news, crushed, really, by the weight of my own disappointment, as if I half expected someone to suddenly reveal a plot device and announce the boy as my son.

In the room that night, watching Dora change pillowcases, she said to me, "When I was a girl in Jamaica, I had all the boys chasing me. I know it looks silly—but true. And in the evenings we would go down to the beach and play the music and drink and smoke and dance till we were too tired. Then one day I met a man and I fell in love with him and stayed with him and didn't go to the beach no more, no more swishing the skirt. But he was killed in an accident offshore—he was a fisherman. I was a wailin' and a moanin' girl then, but years made the screaming softer, and one day my sister said, 'Dora, why don't we go down to the beach and go dancing, like old times. When we got there, there were signs posted KEEP OUT, NO TRESPASSING; the beach was contaminated by an oil spill. You change, life changes you, and then the world changes without you. You will live a long life, Robbie, but things will change many times for you in many ways."

She wrestled the clean pillowcase onto the pillow, and I felt, then, that this woman knew how my life would turn out. "How is it you know so much about me?" I asked her.

"Easy," she answered. "You a child of God."

☐　　　　☐　　　　☐

I have often wondered why God spared me instead of others; wondered too, really, if there even is a God. Is it God who is so judgmental or his Christian followers? Is suffering the punishment of sin or is sin the punishment? Was Georgia being punished because her mother was a crack addict? Was Nathan suffering because he was in love with another man? Was evil the root of the hatred that could sometimes crack my poise as swiftly as a thunderbolt? Religion falters, I believe, when it teaches that gay men should be failures, pariahs, unloved and unlovable outcasts. Society suffers as well by treating these same men as exiles; families disintegrate when their sons become expatriates. But if, to me, AIDS is not a retribution, is there some sort of meaning in the challenge it provides? Is there meaning in suffering or merely meaning from experience? And how, in that experience, do I find the manifestation of God?

What saved me from death or harm, for instance, the day when I was four years old and fell off a swing set? What saved me, years later, as I narrowly missed stepping in front of a Manhattan bus? Why did my mother die at an early age while my father survived to haunt me as an adult? Is there some grand scheme to the way my life unfolds before me, why one day I cook pots of pasta in hopes of saving Nathan, another day I scrape paint off a chair to calm my soul?

Nathan would have said, of course, that I was looking for too much meaning in things. Why, for instance, couldn't I just live in the moment? Nathan was always the one of us who could find meaning in action, not in forethought, which is why he began going to Grove House every evening now after he got off work. He didn't need to explain this to me, however; I knew he received as much from the children as they did from his help, knew that by placing himself in the company of terminally ill children, he was also accepting his own mortality.

Time passed, then, without Tuesday nights being officially separated from our lives. I worked each evening on the chairs when I got home, fielded phone calls from friends checking in, sat with Nathan when he arrived home, exhausted, still able to eat, however, a piece of pie or high-calorie milkshake I would urge upon him. Those were the days I felt for hope in everything—within the stillness in the apartment, within the steam heat rising through the pipes, within the sounds of the streets filtering through the closed windows. But there was nothing I could do to keep the hope suspended before me—it was so fleeting—nothing I could do, either, about the chill seeping through the room, for instance, worrying that if I was so cold here in the apartment, how was Nathan feeling on the sidewalk, rushing from work to Grove House?

Mrs. Grove was adamant about not letting Georgia out of the

house overnight. The weather was a problem—winter was stretching out its icy hand to the bitter end. And then there was the equipment that was at Grove House in case of emergency—the respirator, the IV, the lotions, thermometer, and disinfectants—all things Nathan and I did not possess in our apartment or that we could not arrange to Mrs. Grove's satisfaction. She did agree, however, to allow Nathan to give Georgia a ten-month-old birthday party at our apartment.

The party was more a spontaneous event than a planned celebration; Nathan had only found out Thursday evening that Mrs. Grove would let Georgia visit for a few hours with us on Saturday, and only on the condition that Georgia was not coughing when she woke up that morning and that the weather was not brutally unmanageable. Nathan's parents were coming down for a visit from Hartford that day, and instead of meeting them for lunch we decided to cook a meal for the party.

The party was, I believe, more festive for the adults than for Georgia; how much awareness does a child of ten months possess, beyond what, perhaps, is immediately thrust before her eyes? Nathan brought crepe paper streamers from the party store on the corner. Mrs. Solloway arrived carrying Mylar balloons, Mr. Solloway reluctantly helping her tie them to the table. I cooked a large pot of pasta, several types of sauces, and made a large bowl of salad. Jerry brought a small chocolate cake, and Martin brought taco chips and dips. We asked our neighbors, Debbie and Andrew—a young couple who lived next door—to stop by; and Abby, Nathan's secretary, stopped in for a few minutes on the way home from seeing a movie. Neither Brian nor Alex showed up; both had made other arrangements earlier in the week. Dora and Mrs. Grove were also conspicuously absent—both had been invited—but Gabriel showed up with a small electric piano that Nathan plugged into our stereo system. Mr. Solloway frowned throughout the party till Jerry convinced Gabriel to stick to old Motown tunes; suddenly, Nathan, Jerry and, Martin started entertaining the party as if they were the Supremes, Mr. Solloway snapping their photos with his camera as if he were a photographer for *Vogue*.

There is something about looking into the face of a child that is more absorbing than any movie or television show. There is something that infects the spirit upon hearing a laugh spill around the room and work its way into your bones. I was surprised to find I had so many moments alone with Georgia that afternoon; surprised too by the need for all of us to feel so festive. Had things been so gloomy for us for such a long period? Alex called during a spirited rendition of "Ain't No Mountain High Enough" to again offer his apologies for not being at the party, and while trying to explain the scenario to him, I noticed the two unfinished chairs in the corner, face-to-face, holding between them the small suitcase Nathan had brought back when he had picked up Georgia from Grove House. It was then it occurred to me I could make the chairs into a crib, cutting a large panel that would cover and weld both of the seats together, using some newel posts from an old stairway Alex had stored in his studio to make the sidings. Nathan said if all went well today, Mrs. Grove would allow Georgia a visit once or twice a month; there was even the possibility of her allowing more children to visit. If there is a God, I believe he was with us at that party; if there is a God, at that moment he gave me a plan.

In the cab back to Grove House that afternoon, Nathan held Georgia wrapped between the folds of a pale blue blanket.

"You think this is all so silly, don't you?" he asked me when the cab came to a stoplight near Tenth Avenue. A burst of warm spring-like weather had infused the end of our day with even more optimism.

"Of course not," I answered, my eyes searching out the end of a overhead walkway between two buildings. The sidewalks were empty in this portion of town; the buildings dark and squatty and industrial-looking.

"I wish I could give you a child," Nathan said.

"What?"

"You remember," he said as the cab lurched forward. "All those years ago. I used to go to the sperm bank?"

I nodded, smiled a bit too wistfully. "Why did you stop that?"

"I didn't have to do it anymore," he answered. "I didn't have to prove myself, prove I was an adult, or a young man, or a hot property. I just settled into me."

"I wish *I* could give you a kid," I answered, feeling, all at once, the impossibilities our lives presented us with.

"Maybe someday they'll create a way for two men to have a biological baby. That would be wild, wouldn't it?"

I leaned into him and Georgia as the cab turned up 17th Street and started heading east. "I'm sure you'd be the first one to sign up," I said lightly, placing my hand against his thigh for balance.

"The guinea pig," he laughed. "I'd be the guinea pig for that."

I was wearing a sweatshirt underneath a denim jacket that day, and he used his free hand to lift up my sweatshirt. He moved Georgia over closer to me and pressed her fingers against my stomach.

"This is why," he said, brushing her fingers up through the hair of my chest. "Why it's so important. To touch another life. To have another life touch you." He lifted her away from me, and in that instant I felt abandoned, Godless, fearful of sinking into loneliness without Nathan.

The cab stopped in front of Grove House and I said, "Nathan, you'd make a good father." But he hadn't heard me; he and Georgia were already out the door.

☐   ☐   ☐

Time is what you fight with AIDS. It robs you of plans and a future. It's a disease of inches, difficult to chart, at times, on a day-to-day basis. Those were the days I realized I knew so little about HIV, the way the virus replicates itself within the body, realized too how little hope the doctors could provide, what a gamble, a crap-shoot, medicine was, after all. Why does one antibiotic work for one man and not another? Why does one man develop KS while another struggles with pneumonia? Now, at night, I would awaken after a few hours of sleep, my body tensing because my mind was rested, ready to resume thinking. It was then, deep at night, that I could no longer fight off my hatred. I would get out of bed, move to the couch or a chair, try to read, but instead, I would be focused, resolutely so, on why this was happening to us. I searched and searched through my memory for someone to blame—Hank? Will? Pat? The Prince? My exercise was futile, of course; between Nathan and myself there must have been more than two hundred men, and so I would just sit there hating myself, hating my situation, trying with all my conviction not to blame Nathan, not to hate him for bringing this into our lives— this, this unexpected virus. And so I would find myself rigid with thought even away from the bedroom, and I would roll my neck to unwind the stress, stand and stretch and return to the bed, unable to sleep, though, instead watching Nathan sleep beside me, his face squashed against the pillow or sometimes at my chest, listening to his breathing, the body repairing itself with small strokes of air. Sleep, now, was no longer an escape for me; such was the way anxiety inhabited my world.

AIDS creates fear in surges; for every calming stroke I applied while working on the chairs, another, more distressful one would surface. Every gay man facing AIDS reviews, at some point, the sexual contacts he has had in his lifetime. It's not really to try to pinpoint the source of infection—there is seldom a way of knowing what encounter was the source—and between Nathan and myself we had slept with many, many, many men. I believe this review, this inspection, is to reassure ourselves that the act of sex itself was not the cause of the problem—sex, after all, is what defines and unites gay men, it is their God and their religion, the way they dress and talk and sing and move down the street, the way they meet their friends and lovers, the way too they define their community. What was at fault was a virus, a *retrovirus,* no one could have predicted. A virus that could possibly be transmitted between two men during a sexual act. How had an act that could bring both life and pleasure suddenly become darkened by illness and death? The act of sex, I felt, no, I decided, finally, was not at fault. What had to be accepted, what I had to remind myself over and over, was that sex between two men does not cause them to die. There were ways now to prevent the transmission of the virus; hadn't Nathan and I been practicing safe sex for years?

I finished building the crib in less than two weeks; the newel posts had turned out to be too large for the sides, so I had created a railing from some doweling I found in Alex's studio. I borrowed a drawknife to create the curves and slopes of the headboard and baseboard. By the time I began staining the wood, spring had arrived and I could open the windows as I applied the varnish, a sweet, warm breeze blowing the fumes around the apartment like incense. Nathan brought Georgia back for two more visits to the apartment; the second one she spent in the crib, her fingers clutching for the Mylar balloon we had kept since her first visit and that now floated above her, tied to one of the sides of the crib. With the crib done, Nathan's health maintaining a sort of status quo, I was able to feel more relaxed in the evenings. Alex had sent me to a job at a midtown construction site where I was helping with Sheetrocking, and in the evenings I would arrive home smelly and dusty, but I would go into the kitchen and chop vegetables before showering. The ritual had attained an invigorating rhythm; after showering I would experiment with sautéing the vegetables in a wok.

And then one night Nathan was in the kitchen cooking when I got home. I was surprised to see him home, surprised to find him hunched over a bowl of boiled potatoes that he was mashing with a fork.

"I needed a night off," he said before I had a chance to ask him what was going on. "You want broccoli or beans?"

"Broccoli," I answered, and went into the bedroom, flipped on the stereo, and began to undress. My routine had been disrupted, but before I stepped into the shower I felt something was wrong; Nathan was trying too easily to push me away, without a fight, which meant he wanted me to nag him, force him to tell me what was wrong. I slipped a towel around my waist and went back into the kitchen.

"Did you see the doctor today?" I asked.

"Nothing's wrong," he answered abruptly.

I turned and noticed there were candles placed at the center of the table; Nathan had also bought fresh flowers, irises for the vase on the bookshelf. I knew, then, something was *very* wrong.

I looked at him sternly, unwilling to budge, willingly embarrassing him there with my flesh, my exhaustion, my body screaming for him to open up and tell me what was wrong.

"I think I'm going to leave the firm," he said. "I'll be able to keep my insurance going; that's not a problem. I'll sell some of my prints." He nodded to the animated artwork on the walls of our apartment that he had collected over the years. "The cash will help us float for a while, you know."

"Are you sure?"

He nodded. "I've spoken to Mrs. Grove about it. She's offered me a full-time position at Grove House."

"*Grove House?*" I answered, a bit too surprised. All at once I felt jealous of Mrs. Grove, jealous of Georgia and Dora and Gabriel and all the things pulling Nathan away from me. "I need to do it," he said.

"Do you *want* to do it?"

"Yeah," he answered, turning away from me and opening the freezer door. I left the kitchen and went into the bathroom, trying to relax the stiffening muscles of my shoulders under the warm water.

I felt better after I had dried myself, dressed in clean clothes, and combed my hair, as if I had washed away a forgotten self. When I went back into the kitchen, I was surprised to find Nathan seated with his head resting on the edge of the table, crying.

"Georgia died this morning," he said, briefly looking up at me, then buried his face back into his hands.

☐   ☐   ☐

If there is a God, why does he abandon you when you need him most? If there is a God, why does he take from you the things that give you hope? When a person is diagnosed with AIDS, more than one life is affected; change reverberates through lovers and families and friends, out into society and politics and the fabric of the world. Though I was not ill myself, the anxiety of Nathan's illness produced as much damage to me as the virus was one day planning for him. Though Georgia's death did not touch me the way it touched Nathan, it touched me nonetheless. How does faith survive when it is constantly tested by disappointment? How does hope survive when constantly facing death?

The following day I could not get out of bed to go to work. Nathan had left the apartment, and I could not even find the energy to get up to eat. I fell into a feverish dream, and when I awoke it was late afternoon. From the bed I could see the crib I had made sitting in the darkened corner of the hallway, and then I remembered the day my mother died, how she had lifted herself from her bed and cooked me a hamburger. I was stunned to see her standing that day—she was frail and thin; the chemotherapy had sapped her to nothing. "We survive by doing things," she said, and sat at the table and watched me eat. Then she went back to her bedroom and died. That memory lifted me out of my own bed that afternoon, and I dressed and went out of the apartment, down the steps, and into the streets of Manhattan. It was already rush hour, and even in this part of the Village I could sense the purposeful walk of those whose jobs were over and who were on their way home. There was, then, an agitation to the traffic—taxis blaring their horns, cars cutting pedestrians off at crosswalks, messengers on bikes weaving on and off of the sidewalk. As I headed uptown I found, however, a rhythm in my steps, found myself, oddly, repeating the lyrics of "Addicted to Love," again and again in my mind till I was actually singing while walking.

Later, when Mrs. Grove answered the door, she wasn't startled to see me; she welcomed me graciously as if I were an old friend, so differently, I was aware, from how we had greeted each other at our first meeting. Dora was in the hallway, working her way up the stairs, and she smiled softly down to me and pointed me in the direction of the kitchen, as if she knew all along I had been on my way here. It was Tuesday, and Nathan was in the kitchen pulling down the boxes of food he would be using for pasta night. I could tell right away he was surprised to see me, thinking, I know, something was wildly wrong with me, or that, perhaps, I had arrived, now, with my own set of bad news.

"Hi," I said casually, picking up a box of pasta from the counter, calmly glancing at the directions printed on the side panel. "I'm here." I looked over at him. "Let me help you cook."

Power

Robert Drake

It is ten days since the morning after the waltz party, the morning Emory left.

In the morning, I am awakened most usually by a bugle blowing "Reveille." I leap out of bed to scamper over to the window where I look out and watch three dress marines go through the paces of the ceremony for flag raising at the academy. There is a moment, after they have approached the flagpole, when they must turn, and they do so in perfect unison, executing a series of high steps that remind me of nothing so much as the high prancing of the Royal Lipizzan stallions I used to watch at the circus with my father.

Sometimes, if I wake up before the bugle, I look out the windows of the living room onto the pavement of Gate Three. I watch as the white van filled with the marines in their white pants, their navy blue jackets, their caps, the red trim, arrives and stops to discharge the men. I watch the marines who will raise the flag talk to the marines who are guarding the gate, and I envy them their camaraderie, their easy jocularity. I watch them jostle one another, watch them straighten out jackets and smooth the creases of their pants. I watch as the time comes to raise the flag and the three marines from the van separate from the two others, their lighthearted mood falling away, seriousness and patriotic duty infusing their every step as they approach the sidewalk that marks the starting spot for the ceremony. The one in the center carries the flag, folded neatly to a triangular field of blue with white stars. The bugle starts, a small riff of attention, and the three marines are off, stepping in perfect unison across pale cement, moving toward the then-empty flagpole.

In the ten days that I have watched this movement, I have never once seen a woman among the marines entrusted with this duty, nor at guard upon the Gate.

I clean today, quickly and sloppily, but surfaces are dusted, floors are vacuumed, beds are made and laundry is done. When I am done cleaning I make myself a simple lunch of sliced French bread, some hard butter, a ball of fresh mozzarella, and a sliced tomato, the latter two drizzled with olive oil and sprinkled with basil, ground pepper. The tastes are good in my mouth; the flesh of the tomato firm and wet, the cheese chewy and smooth. I wash the meal down with mugfuls of strong coffee, into which I pour half-and-half and sprinkle sweetener. This meal is breakfast too.

I shower, and dress in a pair of olive drab walking shorts, a black T-shirt Matthew was given when he read at Borders Books in Philadelphia a while ago, as his first novel was being published. Barefoot, my hair wet, I walk downstairs with a book in one hand— Milton's *Paradise Lost;* I have never before read it—a glass of water in the other and settle into a chair on the front porch.

I read for a bit.

When the sun is higher in the sky and the feeling of the day is late afternoon, I toddle back upstairs and place the empty glass in the sink. I set the book on the dining room table as I leave that room, and walk toward the bathroom. I relieve myself, then fall upon the bed in the bedroom, where I nap.

I sleep for a few hours. I don't dream. I've yet to start dreaming well, really; dreaming so I remember the dreams full upon waking. But I've begun to feel them, though, the good dreams. Nestled right below the surface of my thought, I do feel them more than anything else; I feel them struggling to break through this barrier of my mind, I feel them struggle to effect a kind of reunification between consciousness and unconsciousness, between mind and spirit, body and soul.

I wake to a darkening sky and a lowering flag outside my window, the bugle playing "Taps," the marines stiffly in position. The marines at the gate have turned and are saluting the flag as it descends; all traffic, all work, even joggers stop and salute the flag as it is taken in for the night.

I change clothes. I pull on a pair of navy blue shorts, swing into a USNA T-shirt I bought the second day after my arrival, a shirt exactly like the shirts the mids wear when they exercise. After the evening bugle blows, no civilians are allowed onto the Yard without some specific purpose, such as an evening class at the community college that rents out space in the buildings during off hours, or an event such as boxing or, say, a movie. I pull on white athletic socks, lace up New Balance running shoes, and leave the apartment, heading down the stairs again and then out, across the porch, to the sidewalk, and I head south, toward the dead end of the street. Hanover Street is a yellow brick street, its end thick with foliage, low hanging trees, weeds, ivy that has grown over the chain link fence separating the end of the street from the Academy.

I listen for voices, for the sound of runners on the other side of this gray, ten-foot brick wall. I hear nothing, and so I climb, I vault the wall, landing neatly on my feet behind the Academy chapel. I stand, I look about. I see no one. I start off southward on my run. The perimeter of the Academy is five miles in length, and it is a fine, even course. At a good clip, I will run it in less than an hour.

I am in better physical shape now than I have ever been, which is ironic since I haven't shared myself with anyone since Matthew died and before then, while decently maintained, I was always a bit soft. The running, the enthusiasm for physical exercise, the eager, almost hungry response of my body to these rigorous pleasures is something new and vital. The tingling, that tingling I felt throughout my body after the beating that took Matthew from me continues, but it has become a part of me, and most of the time, I am no longer aware of it any more than I am aware that I have a heart sturdily pumping blood from the middle of my chest throughout my body. Its feeling is a subtler form of the feeling I used to feel whenever my leg would "go to sleep": a prickly, tingling sensation. But my arms, my hands, my legs never go to sleep anymore, and better yet, my ankles no longer go out on me. Before the beating, I had trick ankles—weak—

and I would fall now and then to the ground, where I would sit for a bit before dragging myself upright to hobble about until the ankle worked its way toward normal function. The worst part about the falling was that it always had to happen twice; once the ankle went out, it would need to go back in again. These usually happened within a week or two, and then I was fine for several months, if I was careful and watched my step. Those ankles had kept me from enjoying a good run for most of my life; they did not keep me from anything now.

I am passing the visitors' center and have passed the superintendent's house, several homes of Academy faculty, a fighter plane, a small submarine. I turn to head east, along the opening mouth of Annapolis harbor. The water is blue, a graying blue, and rather calm. A few boats—one, a beautiful white sailboat with Canadian registry and blond wood trim—bob in the water where the harbor widens toward the Bay. I'm passing the parked cars of "firsties" now—seniors at the Academy. A young man passes me, his T-shirt damp from his run, his body healthy and trim, his blond hair plastered to his head with sweat. He nods as he passes. I nod back and notice his blue eyes, his freckles, a pug nose. I turn around shortly after he passes me. His back is broad and tapered, his heinie compact and firm. I smile at these observations, then turn to continue with my run. I pass a football practice field; I follow the curve of the road to head north.

It is getting darker. I run a bit faster, my legs pumping, and feel a sweat break across my forehead. I reach to swipe at it with my left forearm and keep going. It is almost dark now; only a glimmer of light remains in the sky to my left, a small patch of twilight amid the onrush of night. I look up: I see stars, the absence of a moon. I feel the steady pounding of my feet upon the asphalt I run over, I listen to the light rasping of the breathing that feeds my body, feel the tingling lurking there, beneath my muscles, beneath my bone, within everything I think, do, and am.

When I fought Michael that last time there was something that happened, some kind of release, that was not sexual in nature but equally as visceral. I remember it as a literally blinding onrush of power, a white wave of pain and anger and noise, the crashing, breaking as internal barriers succumbed to whatever it was that fed through me. I remember it as capability, and I feel the edges of it hinting about me now and again, whispering their presence, and they are there whenever I step up my speed in running, as I did a few moments ago. They push me. They push me to reach toward things I have always thought beyond my grasp; toward things I have never thought possible. I am stronger now than I ever was; I am more agile too. The leaping of the wall earlier, to run here, does not even cause me to break a sweat and takes but seconds; before the beating, this would have required a serious bit of clumsy effort. And there are the voices, my vision.

I'm approaching a wooden bridge that spans the mouth of College Creek. The water that I looked at when I stood shoulder to shoulder with Emory flowed under this bridge moments later. I cross the bridge, enjoying the different thumping sound of my feet upon its planking.

I am running the perimeter of the scrimmage field now, running on a thin strip of dirt and gravel bordered on one side by the low cement sea wall of the Academy and on the other by the grass of the field. I listen; I look. I am the only one running here tonight. I head toward the northernmost end of this part of the Academy, beyond it the rising arc of a fifty-foot-high bridge crossing the Severn River. At the feet of this tall bridge stretch the remnants of the older draw-bridge it replaced, now a walking path for tourists and choked with crabbers when in season. It too is deserted; the only evidence of life other than myself is found in the passing lights of cars high above, upon the surface of the tall bridge. I am almost at the edge of this field; I slow my run.

There is something that has been pulling at me for a while, strongest eleven days ago when I stood overlooking College Creek, slightly drunk on champagne and waltz parties. It pulls me upward, to try the impossible, to dare the dreams of childhood toward reality.

I stop running. I am at the edge of the field. Before me are the bridges, the water of the river. I stand, I collect my thoughts, I breathe in and out, letting my lungs settle from the run. To touch what I believe is possible I need only step forward. I dangle my right foot out, over the water. There is nothing between it and the water but air. I let it hang there and look down at it. There can be no thought. I look up. I step after it.

I fly.

I drift slowly upward, turning in a breeze that buoys me off the river. I move gently at first, letting myself flow with the air, simply being in the moment of this happening. I let what has happened sit with me, until complacency falls away with the onrush of a grin and I remember every image of people flying I have ever seen: Sally Field as *The Flying Nun* and the way as a child I stuffed myself with food until I weighed ninety-eight pounds—what she weighed—then waited for the chance to soar; Superman, and boyhood afternoons spent running around after friends as fast as I could, my arms pointing forward as I "flew," chasing them in their evil villain incarnations; the pictures in the comic books, from *Superman* to my still-beloved *Legion of Super-Heroes* in the old days, when they had their flight rings; and of course, *Superman: The Movie.*

Like the latter two, I pointed my fist heavenward, I drew my body into a tight line and I shot upward, to touch the canopy of this moonless sky. I shot upward until I felt I had gone far enough and then I turned, gracefully, tilting my body to cut into the wind, my arms now out before me and I headed east, toward the lights of the Chesapeake Bay Bridge. As I approached the bridge I lowered myself, arcing out toward the Eastern Shore and zigzagging back through the obstacle course of the bridge's pylons, swooping free of them toward the open water of the bay, my body dipping low toward the water, my arms pulling back along my sides and reaching down, my outstretched fingers, the outstretched blades of my hands touching now the hard black surface of the water, ripping its fabric into a small, even sort of wake. Somehow flying is something I trust and know; I am not afraid. I like the cool touch of the water on my fingertips, the sound of its splashing to my ears. I slow myself, bringing my hands up from the water, centering myself so I stand erect upon the air. I lower myself carefully until I feel the soles of my running shoes against the top of the water, and there I wait. My hands hang loose at my sides. I look up at the bridge before me; I turn around, splashing slightly, and look out at the vast body of water that is this bay. I ball my hands into fists and place them on my hips: a true superhero stance. In the distance, the light of a solitary cargo ship blinks a pale red.

I am alone with the night. Alone with my capability. Alone with whatever the fuck has happened to me.

Again, I allow myself to rise slowly with the wind before turning and taking control of my flight, directing myself back to Annapolis. I return to the edge of the Academy scrimmage field from whence I first stepped into the air. I stand there and savor the feeling of earth beneath my feet. I walk home slowly, past the hospital, past the graveyard, past the houses of more Academy faculty, their windows facing out to the street and revealing families sitting down to supper, a couple dancing to some slow jazz, a lone youth sitting in silence and reading a book.

I love folk music.

This is a surprise to many who know me, as I have always been considered something of a musical disaster to the ears of my friends. They find my appreciation for boys such as Pierce Pettis, Martyn Joseph, and, of course, David Wilcox to mesh perfectly with their appreciation of Mary Chapin Carpenter and other folk songstresses.

I don't know what it is about the music that draws me so. I like the guitars, the rhythms found in folk; somehow they sound natural and close to me. I like the laying of a man's voice above the music of the guitar, the drums, the bass and mandolin. I like the emotional intimacy of folk, perhaps, but then I've always been attracted to music rich in emotional intimacy, what others call sentimentality.

I'm sitting in a café called The Moon, its tables covered with tapestry beneath slices of glass. I'm drinking what they call a Joe: simple, good, American coffee. I'm sitting here with the headphones plugged into the Walkman and blasting Martyn Joseph's "Being There" into my head. My biggest fear is that suddenly, in mid song, I'll look up to find everyone staring my way, only to realize I've been air-guitaring for the past few minutes or, worse yet, singing along and loudly so. I studied voice during my undergrad years and became famous on my dorm floor for belting out show tunes at the top of my lungs until the boys in the room next to me would come pounding on the door, barking out something about "...trying to study!" and this would make me put on the headphones, volume clenched to maximum, and lie back on my bed for a vigorous hum.

I look around the café. The waiter is a tall, young, handsome man, with well-cut hair and a well-managed physique; you could serve coffee on the broad panels of his chest. If you could genetically design coffeehouse waiters with an ambiguously desirable sexuality, you would clone this lad and watch him prosper in artistic neighborhoods worldwide. I wonder if he ever gets hit on but find it almost unimaginable; he is too beautiful. Approaching him, talking to him shatters every myth created in the shadow of his presence and by the force of his suggested promise. He heads toward the back room of the café, where other handsome young men with slicked-back dark hair nurse brown cigarettes and slip whiskey into their coffees when they think no one is looking, while talking poetry technique, lit crit, and art.

I have been thinking about responsibility this evening. After my run, my shower, and the stroll down here, I found myself trying to puzzle out the boundaries of an individual's (my) responsibilities. I remembered an evening conversation with Ophelia in a restaurant blood-red with tablecloths where we talked ideas of community and responsibility among gays and lesbians, people of color, women and men, people. I'm bitter and disillusioned over the fragmentary nature of what has come to be popularly labeled as the gay and lesbian community; Ophelia's disgruntled over what she sees as the black community's penchant for self-betrayal and destruction. She's filled with revulsion at the way young black men prey upon each other and their families in America's inner cities. She draws uncomfortable parallels with this and the self-serving, soul-destroying efforts of the black people who sold other black people into slavery over the course of the Civil War. She wonders if this penchant for self-betrayal is universal or particular to black men; I argue for universality, but she doesn't want to hear it. She lost her younger brother to this kind of infighting three years ago, and the bleeding-heart chatter of pale liberals about the responsibility of the white patriarchy to the darker underclass makes her all but physically ill. She yearns to hear someone speak of self-responsibility, but the only place that tries is the Sunday morning gospel service at the church on the corner, and the women there already heard the message, long, long ago.

I am a white male. What does that mean, politically and socially? Am I empowered? OK, all right, sure I can fly, but I doubt this will mean shit to the government: If all queers could fly, would we suddenly have equal rights? I don't think so, but the image is amusing. Some people view my gender, my race, these things I was born with that are beyond my control as a gift, a blessing that gives me access to wealth and privilege beyond my wildest dreams. This is laughable, richly ironic to a man who had only a small savings account after three decades of life and who lives now on the money left him by his dead lover's insurance policy. Every cup of coffee I drink, every brioche I chew, Matthew died to pay for.

White male privilege, my ass. But, hypothetically, let's assume it's a given.

Let's assume the pundits are right for a moment. Am I responsible for the care and condition of every other human embraced under the citizenry of the planet, or am I responsible solely for the actions of myself, most particularly, myself toward others? I down some more coffee. Is perceived privilege a license to disempower or empower or both, and if you say the latter, is it necessary that the disempowered group always disempower the empowered to realize their own sought-after empowerment, or could there be a simple, equal alignment of power realized among all peoples, and if so, why don't the various self-concerned factions of our society work toward this end?

Perhaps because they are selfish and self-concerned, and I sound like a scary, overcaffeinated dyke. Ophelia only lets me use forms of the word "empowered" five times in any given conversation on this subject, regardless of the discussion's length. And she never, never lets me get away with using "impact" as a verb.

I finish my coffee. I have serious doubts as to whether the movements acknowledged by "isms" are truly movements for equality, as they claim, or movements whose true goal is the obtaining of a kind of favored-person status. The latter, I'm against.

We must extend the same rights to everyone. We must not establish one section of the populace as preferable to another section of the populace. That is what has caused all the trouble from the outset. We must respect boundaries and differences, even as we each see to it that our own boundaries are recognized, respected, and ensured.

I try to see if I'm enough of an optimist to believe what I've said is achievable. It doesn't matter. Gays and lesbians as a whole today seem more concerned with having differences to argue about than celebrating common strengths to build upon. Oppression's like a monster, in a way, and the gay/lesbian/queer/homosexual idealists "we" canonized seem to hold a greater interest in working to feed the monster than they do in working to feed the people. So, while the efforts of the recognized go toward well-stoking the monster's belly, the rest of us who want change and seek an uncompromising assimilation, a happy joining with the human community, waste away from lack of nourishment. The beast grows stronger while the people starve. But if it weren't for the beast, these pundits would have no source of income or "glory," and I'm back at the ruling self-interest again. No dragon, no need for the knight.

I'm beginning to think I've had too much coffee for this late an hour. Still, I've but touched the tip of the iceberg, for all my kvetching.

Responsibility.

How responsible was I to Matthew for letting what happened to him happen, for letting him die, while I lived? There may be those who find this to be a trite line of questioning, but I couldn't care less because when it comes down to what you honestly feel, believe, or question, it is impossible to be trite as long as you are sincere. There are no new ideas, anyway, only the continual refabrication of the old. I do believe this.

Matthew died. I lived. Could I have done anything to change that? Could I have stopped Michael? I did stop Michael, but I stopped him before he could kill me, after he had killed Matthew. Why didn't I stop him earlier? OK, I had the shit kicked out of me at the time, but does that matter or change things? I read today in Emory's copy of Plato's *Symposium* that "[The gods] honored Achilles and sent him to the Islands of the Blest, because when his mother told him that if he killed Hector he would die, but if he did not kill him he would return home and live to be an old man, he dared to choose, by helping his lover Patroclos and avenging him, not only to die for him, but in his end to perish over his body: Hence, therefore the gods, admiring him above measure, honored him particularly, because he set so high the value of his lover."

Did I fail Matthew by not somehow pressing forward to make that ultimate sacrifice? Would I have found meeting death with him preferable to living life without?

People had been killed prior to Michael's attack on Matthew and me; why did it take the personal intrusion of this brutality into my life to push me toward doing something to stop Michael, to stop his violence, to make the city a safer place to be for other faggots? Why didn't I do something earlier? And when I was pushed toward this action, why did I let it take me along the road that I traveled; why this costume? Why the Man? Why me?

Couldn't I have just organized a neighborhood patrol?

I look up again, and around. The handsome waiter must still be in the back. A gang of midshipmen pass by the large glass windows fronting the coffeehouse. I watch them walk past. I shake my hand out from where I've been writing parts of this down in a letter to Ophelia.

Ophelia. Elizabeth's in a rehab program, and Ophelia rattles about their apartment, taking care of the dog, Bruce, doing her work, going to sleep, going to the grocery store to load up food for the two of them, her and Bruce. She's miserable, and I can't blame her, but I eventually fled when confronted with her situation, the situation of living in a place where everything you see or touch reminds you of something good, that good then swallowed whole by something horrible you absolutely do not want to think about.

But Ophelia can't get away. She's responsible. She's got a contract to deliver the news for Channel Seven and a health insurance policy Elizabeth desperately needs right now. There's the care and feeding of Bruce; Ophelia stays because she's responsible. She toughs it out.

Not that fleeing makes the escape of memories any easier. I look down at the place setting on my table, the fork; there are some memories whose triggers follow you everywhere. It's hard for me to look at a fork, for example, still, without remembering I know how it feels to slam silver tines into a man's eye, feeling the flesh of that orb give and break, the silver sinking into thick, greasy fluid.

I shake my head to clear away this thought. I've gotten good at keeping the bad memories at bay while awake. I take the headphones from my ears. I look up and around, and consciously keep myself from trying to eavesdrop on surrounding conversations. I say "consciously" because I could, if I wanted to. Not because the people sit so close to me, their conversations so near, but because I find that I can hear and see things these days. I've been awakened nights from a sound sleep by voices. Not the loud yelling of the unconscious through dreams, but the coming cries of a couple—the sound somehow tells me—a few blocks away; I can hear her sighs pour about his ears, her fingernails raking the flesh of his back enough to scrape him, lightly, but not to draw blood, and his rough sob as he collapses into her. I can hear the marines at the gate across the street from Emory's apartment: their talk, their footfalls, the sound of their urine splashing against the porcelain of the john when they relieve themselves.

I can see too. Should I choose, I can see anything within my field of vision as closely as if I were examining it from a few inches away. Detail is rich in my eyes now, from a flower growing between cracks in the sidewalk at my feet to the steadfast bolting of the Bay Bridge a few miles away, across the water.

I can see. I can hear. I can fly.

How does this affect my boundaries of responsibility?

I push my chair back from the table and stand. I put the head-phones back in my ears and head back toward the bathroom, the Walkman still at my side, Martyn Joseph singing away again in my headset. The handsome waiter sits in the back; he is the first thing I see when I walk into that well-lit, green-painted room. He is sitting at a table of smokers, but he is not smoking, and he laughs full, opening his mouth, smiling, the muscles of his throat moving with the sound.

I look away, marching myself into the bathroom. I go. I wash. I dry. I come out of the bathroom and refuse to look over at him as I pass by, returning to my table.

Responsibility.

I don't sit again at the table, stopping only long enough to pull a few dollar bills from my wallet for the coffee and to gather my things. I leave quickly, and the warmth of the night assaults me after the deep coolness of the air-conditioned café. I stand on the corner and look both ways for cars; I see none that pose an immediate threat to my journey. I cross the street against the glow of a red light.

The walk home is swift and uneventful. Inside the apartment, I shed the Walkman and the other stuff I had brought to the café—my book, my pen, the unfinished letter to Ophelia with its ready enve-lope—onto the smooth emptiness of the dining room table. I stand in darkness. I move through the shadows of the apartment to stand at a living room window and peer down upon marines talking at the gate; a midshipman passes by and chats with them briefly before heading on, the white of his uniform swallowed by the darkness of the Yard. I return to the dining room. In the dim light falling through its one window, I pick up the pen and bend to sign my name to the unfinished letter. I fold the letter and stuff it into the envelope whose flap I moisten and seal. I tuck the envelope deep within the front right pocket of my pants.

I turn about and twist a key that unlocks the closet door of the dining room, and I gently pull this door open. I reach inside, past jackets and heavier winter coats, for a Banana Republic shirt box I know is there: a box I remember placing there shortly after Emory left, moments after I had pulled the box from my suitcase. I find the box, hold it, and pull it free from behind the clothing, turning to carry it to the dining room table. I open the box, taking hold of its top and shaking it lightly until the weightier bottom falls free, falls to the surface of the table. I set the lid of the box aside. My hands reach out to run across its contents, the feel of the cloth beneath my fingers, the leather of the pink triangle patch upon the left breast of the garment: the mask.

I close the box. I place it back in the closet. I take out a thin gray windbreaker and put it on, pulling up the zipper to cover my stomach. I check its pockets and find a handkerchief that I let be.

I leave the apartment again, testing the door lock behind me. I move quickly down the stairs and into the warm night, my head bowed, my hands stuffed into the pockets of my pants. I mail the letter to Ophelia. I don't look at the marines as I pass, but I can hear them talking and notice the slight change of inflection in their voices as I pass and they wonder whether they will be called upon to acknowledge me.

I look ahead; I look up. The sky is empty of stars. I move along quickly down this paved section of Hanover Street, stepping gingerly though pools of lamplight. I reach the end of the street, walled off by another section of the academy, and pause to look around. I am alone.

I leap upward as a car turns down Hanover Street toward me, but by the time the light from its headlamps reaches the wall where I stood, I am gone, sailing upward, beyond the reach of human sight.

The cobblestones of the alley are cool and damp in the night air. I squat to touch them, gently, my fingertips brushing about their surface. I stand and look about me. There are trash cans, the red brick of buildings to either side and blackened by night. Behind me—if turn about, before me—there is the passing of cars, the pools of light from streetlamps not far beyond the lip of this darkness.

I am back.

I turn from the light of Washington Street and walk into the deepening darkness of the alleyway. I stuff my hands into the pockets of my windbreaker, its shell still zippered over my belly. The rational part of my mind tells me I have nothing to fear: Michael is in prison, his followers dispersed; Jimmy is dead and there is the matter of my ever-burgeoning capabilities. There is Police Chief Yates' hunt for The Man, but he is looking for a costumed vigilante, not a former English teacher in shorts and a gray windbreaker. This knowledge does nothing to prevent a shiver from playing about my spine, or a cold grip of fear from tightening quickly about my heart at every sound I do not immediately recognize, every movement I think I see from the corner of my eye.

I look up and see the gray shadow that is the opening to this alley. I see the darkness we moved toward in search of safe hiding from three boys who chased after us with baseball bats and scratching cries of "Faggot!" I look down and see the slick cobblestones we ran on to reach the end of the alley, and I turn to look that way as well, to see the place where I knelt and Matthew stood, before the lead pipe cracked his skull and Michael wrought his handiwork upon us. I shut my eyes, but it's too late; I have already seen the body of Matthew as it was thrown clattering atop the silver metal of these trash cans.

I look up, at the end of the brick walls to either side of us, at the opening of the night beyond, at the pinpoints of starlight suspended in the dark blue water of the heavens. My flight here was wonderfully free and without thought. I know how to fly as I know how to walk, and though I understand you have to learn and, in some cases, relearn how to walk (I did just this, after a broken arm in the fourth grade pinned me flat on my back for six weeks of traction), it would appear that I have been flying for most if not all of my life. I mean this in the sense that flying seems wholly familiar to me; it isn't new at all.

"Hi."

I look down sharply, and he stands there as he stood when I last walked with him down these city streets. He is at the far end of the alley, and he walks toward me now as I blink, as I see him, as my heart or something inside me shudders and shatters and he moves to stand before me as the moon slips free of clouds and her light pours down upon us. I reach to smooth the collar of his blazer where it has turned under. "Adam," he says.

"Matthew," I say, and I'm crying. He takes me in his arms and holds me.

I sob like that for a good while, both of us crouching upon the slick surface of the cobblestones, and I lean into him and let myself be held. I remember this body so well: the smallness it had compared to mine yet the strength it held, this strength I felt whenever it held me, whenever he held me, as he does now.

"Adam," he says, when my crying is through, and he has held a handkerchief for me to blow my nose into. After, we kiss, and my hand reaches to move behind his head and feel the soft thickness of his hair beneath my palm, between my fingers. He tastes as I remember him. "Adam," he says, "take me flying."

We stand.

"Take you what?"

"Take me flying," he says, and he smiles that boyish smile at me, the smile that always let me know that through propriety or charm he would manage to get his way.

I shake my head. I step back from him. I feel in the pockets of my windbreaker and find my handkerchief, my own handkerchief that I had held to my face and blown my nose into after crying myself blind in this alley just moments ago. I stuff it back into my jacket. I look up.

He still stands there. "You're dead," I say.

He doesn't say anything.

"You're dead," and the words fall dryly from my mouth to rustle about the cobblestones before blowing out, onto the street.

He shrugs. He folds his arms across his chest. Then he looks at me. "Teach any great minds today?"

I shake my head slowly. "Not lately," I say, then, recognizing the ritual, "You?"

He unfolds his arms to gesture expansively. "I've written more great books than you would believe," he says, "and the critics, the great thing about the critics here is that they all love you in ways that are intellectual, not smarmy, provocative instead of provoked, and they all get what it is you're trying to do with your work."

"Sounds like heaven."

He shrugs, smiles, and asks again, "Adam, please, take me flying?"

"Matthew, you're dead," I say again. "And flying, flying, I don't know flying. You being here, you make me question if I've ever flown before, if I've ever flown at all," I look up, exasperated "—flying! What the fuck makes you think I can fly?"

"You flew here."

I ignore him. I've started pacing. I'm unwinding like a giant broken spring. "People, people don't fly. Birds fly and bugs fly and airplanes, with the right amount of fuel and speed and lift, they fly, but people alone don't fly, Matthew, people alone don't fly."

"You're not alone if I fly with you."

I stopped pacing long enough to flash him a look of warning. "Please," I said, "please promise me you are not about to start singing 'Wind Beneath My Wings' because you know I always hated that damn Bette Midler version that came along and replaced the great, previous Gary Morris version in virtually everyone's mind but mine." I pause in my rant and scratch at my head. "This is so like you," I say, then look to him, "Where was I?"

He is gentle. "'People alone don't fly.'"

"Oh, yeah. Right." I look at him. I move my arms out to my side in a gesture of helplessness. "What do I do?"

He is nothing if not persistent. "Take me flying?"

I give up. He wins. I extend my arms to him. He takes my hands. I draw him close, wrapping my right arm about his waist and remembering how well he fit against me like this. I lift my arm up to the sky, I nibble lightly at his ear; he looks back and smiles at me, patting my right hand where it sits atop his tummy. I look up and we rise gently, our feet pulling slightly as they leave the cobblestone and then we slip past the edge of the buildings and I turn to head southeast, across old town, across the water of the harbor and away from the lights of the city.

Matthew stays with me, his hands clasped atop mine. We fly. He is smiling, a happy smile, and his eyes gleam with a thrill, a reveling in what it is we are doing. I do not ask any questions of it for now; if this power, this capability has been given to me so that I may be with Matthew like this and make him happy, then it is enough for me.

We soar above Annapolis; I point to the rooftop of Emory's apartment building. We fly beyond, and in the darkness it is easy for us to land on the beach of Sandy Point State Park. Matthew stamps his feet a few times, readjusting to the solid ground beneath us, and he turns to look at the lights of cars upon the nearby Chesapeake Bay Bridge, their gleaming brightness in the night. The moon sits full in the sky now, and everything is silver.

"Wow," Matthew says, then turns to me. "Adam, that was great."

I shrug.

He turns and walks toward the waters of the bay lapping upon this beach, stopping halfway to take off his shoes and socks, which he leaves there upon the first darkened patches of damp sand. As he walks the rest of the way toward the water, I look down for his footprints and see them. Somehow this reassures me. I pull off my sneakers, my socks, and leave them next to his before walking out to join him where the tide will wash over the tops of our feet before pulling away. Matthew bends down and picks up a rock; he pitches it out toward the water and I watch it skip twice before sinking.

He turns to me: "Didja see that?"

"Yep."

He turns back to the water. "I know." He points at the cars traveling across the bridge. "Bet you could hear what they're talking about too, if you wanted to."

I don't want to, but I do, for a moment, before I turn it off. It was a bit of Rush Limbaugh on someone's radio, and I shudder quickly, happy I've some squelch control over this newly developing power of mine.

I don't want to be alone anymore. I step up to him and take him in my arms, holding him next to me, feeling the warmth of him, feeling the steady rhythm of his breathing and the pressing weight of his body as he leans back into me. All of these things I remember well.

"Flying, seeing, hearing," I murmur into his ear, "all these things I couldn't care less about, having you back with me again."

"Adam, I am dead." He begins to feel lighter within my grasp. "I am dead, but I am here, and this, the hows and whys, what is memory what is imagination, what is real is unimportant compared to knowing you're loved," he turns to face me now, still wrapped in the cradle of my arms, "and you are loved, Adam. I will always love you."

I smiled; I was remembering an overblown 1993 pop song we used to make fun of. He knew what I was thinking, and he slapped me for it, lightly, on my upper arm; he also grinned as he reached his arms about me and hugged me hard and quick, his face turning upward, toward the pantheon of stars visible from the darkness of the beach.

"Stop it," he said, "you know what I mean." He moved, leaning into me again, looking out at the black wasteland the night claims at the broad base of the horizon.

Arguable statements about the quality of sentiments mined from cheap pop songs set aside, yes, I knew what he meant.

I stood with him on the edge of this great body of water, happy at feeling the stuff of him against me, memory made life from scraps of how it used to feel when I had held more often the luxury of taking him for granted, which I did, I admit; we all do after a while, even if we work against it.

"Penny for your thoughts." I felt the rise and fall of his stomach beneath my arms as he breathed.

"These powers, Matthew, these things." I lowered my chin to rest atop his shoulder. "What's happening to me?"

"Why'd you put on a mask to roam about seeking Michael and trying to stop him?"

"I don't know."

"You could've just let the police handle it."

I was silent then. "I could've."

"But you didn't."

"I didn't." I paused before saying, "I didn't think the cops would care as much, or do as good a job, had as much at stake as I did."

Matthew continued, ignoring my rationale, "You put on a costume—"

"Yes."

"—and you played superhero and worked to catch the bad guys."

"Yes." Pause; more rationale: "It was necessary."

"And did you?"

I frowned, momentarily lost. "Did I what?"

"Did you catch the bad guys?"

I didn't follow. "All the bad guys? In the whole world?" The thought staggered me. "No, Matthew. I caught Michael. I stopped—"

Matthew turned in my arms again to kiss me. "Take care of things, Adam," he said, and I felt him lighten, felt him separate himself from me, slipping through my arms. "You're responsible." I stood and watched as he started to walk off along the beach, toward the structure of the bridge.

"Take care?" I muttered to myself. "What am I supposed to take care of?" I called after him, then hollered, "Hey! Matthew! What am I supposed to take care of?"

The words echoed into silence, and I watched Matthew's shape as it was swallowed up in the night while I stood, trying to figure things out. I admit I have always found what I did to be a bit loony tunes: putting together, then putting on, a costume and skulking about backstreets and alleyways in an effort to keep people from getting killed, but no one else seemed to be doing anything effective; community patrols simply didn't go as deeply as I would go, and besides, this had worked in the comic books. Dressed up in the outfit, shadows didn't frighten me. I felt powerful.

But the powers changed everything. I had folded up my costume the night Michael was arrested, and I hadn't worn it since. Was I to take it out again? Was I to wear it again? Did I have some kind of fresh obligation now? Did I owe somebody something, by virtue of myself or my new and—I have to add this part—unasked-for capa-bilities or powers? Did the fact that I had been yahoo enough to put on the outfit in the first place and also act for what I understood to be the greater good while wearing it mean I was now responsible for carrying the ideology further? I rubbed my arms to chase away the chill that threatened to run through me. I was a man then. What am I now? And what did Matthew mean; who am I responsible to?

The thought propelled me upward quickly, with a jolt that left me scrambling to get into the rhythm of flying. I was sent upward, high-er and higher through the sky, hurtling through clouds until I had reached such a height where I could see the curve of the Earth before me and stretching out from the curve and toward me, beneath me, behind me a twinkling of lights representing cars, homes, people. Despite the altitude, I did not feel cold; even the promise of a chill from moments ago was gone. I let myself fall back toward Earth, slowing myself for a light touchdown upon the shores of Sandy Point State Park. My shoes sat there, lightly wet from an attempted claiming by the tide. Matthew was nowhere to be seen, and when I looked for his footprints where he had walked or stood, I found they had been washed away by the surf.

The Rose City

David Ebershoff

Roland Dott—who for years had been thinking about changing his name to Roland Montague or Rolando du Brul—drove to the Pasadena Athletic Club on an October morning. He had first joined the club before it moved into its new building on Walnut, when he still went by the name of Rol, sounds like a roll of mints. There was a boy, Charlie Emily, in his class at John Muir High who used to call him that. Watcha doing after the game, Rol? Emily would ask, tugging on his ear. Oh, you know, Charlie, Roland would answer. This and that. He was always too embarrassed to call Charlie Emily "Emily" even though that's what the whole school, even the football coach, called him. Emily. With his oily dark blond hair and his sneakers squeaking against the linoleum tiles in Western Civ and his habit of picking at the tunnel of his ear. Emily, whom every girl at John Muir wanted to date, or, to be more precise, screw; whom many girls—as Roland overheard through the aluminum air vent that connected the boys' room to the girls'—already had.

At the club, in the men's locker room, Roland took off his clothes and stood in front of the mirror. He kept his locker down a side aisle, where traffic was light; this allowed him to stand in front of the mirror for a long time. Once he was plucking the hairs from his nose when two men, sweaty from the squash courts, came upon him, his left nostril turned inside out. "Dig deep," one man said. The other laughed. And inside Roland, who by then had given up on the name Rol, smoldered a vicious little anger. But instead of saying anything, he fled to the steam room, hiding his face in the puff of wet heat.

But today was a Friday, mid morning, meaning the type of men

who sweat abundantly on the squash court were at the office, mois-
tening beneath their stay-stiff collars and inside their khakis. Roland
stood in front of his mirror, plucking the silver-white lining of his
nostril. There was also the patch of hairs, like curbgrass, between his
brow. And the strays that sprouted outside the neat little tuft that
grew prettily between his breasts. Pluck, pluck, pluck. Already he
looked better, Roland knew. He smiled, then thought about Graham
because today was Friday and they'd fallen into the habit of having
lunch on Fridays. "Roland, is it you?" Graham had said when Roland
literally bumped into Graham nine months ago in the cologne aisle
at Bullock's. They went for a cinnamon coffee across the street in a
narrow shop that used to be Huggin's Shoes. They chatted about
nothing important, although Roland admitted he had checked into
a fat farm outside Cathedral City a few years back, when things
weren't good for him. This had caused Graham to stop, his lower lip
pushing out, and it was then that Graham proposed, "We should get
together every now and then. For lunch." And Roland replied, the
cinnamon coffee souring his breath, "And for a laugh."

He lived above a garage on Bellevue Terrace on the estate of an
entertainment lawyer and his family of six. The garage apartment had
sloped ceilings and windows that rattled nervously when the Santa
Anas blew. It wasn't far from the club on Walnut, or from Pasadena's
downtown, which was called Old Town, now that a group of concerned ladies had revitalized it and the stores specializing in casual
clothes had moved in. Behind the Pasadena Civic Center was the
Holiday Inn, which was there years before Old Town, and which still
served a nice salad bar in its Rose City Lounge during the week.
True, the booths could stand reupholstering, but the salad bar had a
diet Thousand Island dressing that Roland—he told Graham every
Friday—could just die for. Sometimes, during the week of the
Emmys, television people from New York stayed at the Holiday Inn
and came to the Rose City for a bite. Of course, only technical people or junior costars would stay at the Holiday Inn, but Roland liked
to sit in his booth, the one located behind the hostess stand, and
watch the men with longish hair and horse-bit loafers come in and

ask for tables for ten. A comedian who went on to win that year Roland once saw at the salad bar; he liked to think he'd seen George Clooney at the Rose City the year before he became famous, and if George Clooney had ever been fat, it was most definitely him.

Graham is on the Santa Monica Freeway right now, Roland was thinking as he toweled himself down after his aerobics class. He would have time for a quick steam, the only thing that could clean out his pores. As he sat on the wet tile bench, the steam vent coughing like a phlegmy old man, Roland thought about Graham in his little silver Honda. Roland preferred his cars European, anything from the continent with two doors, although he drove an old green Malibu. But Graham was crossing town on this Friday afternoon, as he did nearly every Friday afternoon, to have lunch with Roland, in his little silver Honda which was so reliable that were Graham ever to phone and say he couldn't make it because of car trouble, Roland would know Graham was lying. Not that Graham would cancel on Roland. Why, he wouldn't dare!

"Oh, Graham, you take everything so seriously!" he'd said years ago, and really Graham hadn't changed. Like the Friday afternoon lunches; such an inconvenient time for most people, but Graham shuttled himself across town to stick to their date, even when things were tight at the doll company where he worked, even the day the doll company's president had gone into labor in her office. During Vietnam, when nobody did such a thing, Roland and Graham had lived together for nearly two years. Roland had invented a hyphenation: Roland Gee-Dott. Not much of a tongue-roller, so you can understand why he dropped the Gee when it was over.

Roland left the steam room, getting out of the way of a college kid who wanted to sprawl out. Roland would never forget the look on Graham's mother's face when she came to visit them in their apartment and asked where Roland slept. How could she be so stupid, Roland had thought. Later, after Mrs. Gee left, he said the same thing to Graham: so stupid? "Hey, that's my mother you're talking about," Graham replied, hurt by the whole afternoon.

Roland was an usher at the Pasadena Playhouse when they had

first met. He had led Graham and his mother and his sister Wendy
to their seats. The maroon velvet usher suit fit Roland well, with its
jacket cropped snugly at the waist. Roland had made a point of dropping their programs in the aisle and bending to pick them up. It was
a little cheap, this move, but it brought Graham back to the
Playhouse the very next night, this time alone. "You remind me of a
little bird," Graham said when they went for their first drink at the
Miyako Inn—Roland's suggestion.

Over the years he'd learned that the Miyako's kimono ladies
didn't care whom Roland drank sake with or how much he stroked
the hand of his date; they would just pour and cluck and present the
bill in a little blue bowl and a dish of quartered oranges. It might all
sound quaint now, but listen, boys, not so long ago the world was
like this and the Miyako Inn was the only place in Pasadena for you
and me.

When they met again nine months ago, Graham had said nearly
the same thing: a sweet little bird. He seemed to notice Roland's narrow waist, Graham's hand falling to the small of Roland's back when
they entered the shop for a cinnamon coffee. And the way Graham
stared into Roland's eyes, he knew Graham still saw the sapphires in
them. Roland had taken to frosting the tips of his bangs, a trick for
washing out the gray. When Graham reached out and playfully
rubbed Roland's hair, in a way that Emily used to back at old John
Muir, Roland knew the frosted tips worked; up until that moment he
hadn't been so sure.

"You're too thin," Graham had said a few weeks ago, just as he
used to. He never understood that even two pounds could balloon
Roland up, hanging like sandbags from the handles above his hips.

In many ways Graham was still the same. His thick blond hair,
Mrs. Gee's greatest gift to her son, had a little silver in it, but that
suited good old Graham. His face was still handsome, if creased
around the eyes, and he still had the tall, lean body of a high school
basketball star. He'd stayed current with fashions, coming to the
lunches in ironed khakis and Casual Friday shirts and a big silver
tank watch. He was an engineer, designing dolls for a company in

El Segundo; he'd told Roland his latest doll appeared in those television commercials with the doll touring the White House. Graham
had gone on to live with someone else, but after nearly twenty years
with him, the someone else upped and died on Graham. And it was-
n't the nasty old A, if that's what you're thinking.

"Busy week?" Graham asked at the Rose City. He had been a little late, which was a good thing since Roland himself got waylaid at
the Club when the college kid in the steam room had seemed to send
a little signal that he wanted Roland to stay. Something in the way
he sprawled out, scratching his belly and yawning with exaggeration.
So Roland had gone right back into the steam and sat around for fifteen minutes, keeping his back straight as the tile wall. But nothing
had come of it, and when he'd rushed into the Rose City and saw no
Graham, he held his panting chest with relief.

"Not too busy," Roland said. There had been an audition for a television commercial, which had not gone well, and a scare at the doctor's over a strange purple blotch, which turned out to be nothing
more than an age spot—not that an age spot is an easy thing to swallow. "Not too busy," he repeated.

"Join me in some penne alla Norma?" Graham suggested. "You
hungry?"

"Just the salad bar for me. They have a diet Thousand Island I
could just…" He didn't finish his sentence. He didn't know why.
Roland lived on his veteran's disability; not a week in Saigon and he
was stabbed in a park, beneath a coconut palm that was green in the
trunk. Shouldn't have been in the park in the middle of the night,
but he was. His disability plus the little he skimmed from his mother's checking account. His mother, living the way she did in the
home down in Carlsbad-by-the-Sea, had more than enough.

"I saw your commercial again," Roland said. "It was on just after
my favorite soap."

"Which one was it?"

But this caught Roland in a little white lie because he hadn't seen
it, he'd said so only to make conversation, only to make Graham feel

good. Roland turned to flag the waiter, suddenly thirsty for his lunchtime Manhattan. He would ignore the question. Yes, that would be best.

"You're looking well," Graham said. "Been in the sun?"

This brought Roland's attention back to the table, and he turned in the booth. "Every morning for an hour," he said. "The lawyer lets me use the pool when the family's gone." Roland's doctor, the one who identified the age spot, had warned him against sunbathing. Maybe he'd give it up next month, Roland was thinking. Once the weather cooled down and no one expected you to be tan.

Roland didn't know why he had been unfaithful to Graham when they were together. There were a few times down at Venice Beach, which Graham never knew about because Roland would return to their apartment smelling too much of sea salt and coconut oil and beer for the odor of another man, possibly two, to come through. No, that wasn't how Graham guessed it. It was when they went to a Christmas party in the Hollywood Hills at William and David's, and Roland left with an actor named Blaylock. How could Graham not figure it out, what with Roland sneaking back into their little bedroom on Christmas Eve, the bedroom blue from the twinkle lights wrapped around a neighbor's balcony rail. He'd said it would never happen again, crying in Graham's arms, but it did. Again and again, until Graham threw Roland out, on a Friday afternoon in the middle of his favorite soap.

"Remember how your mother used to leave our apartment thinking we were going straight to hell," Roland said. "Remember that little look she'd give us, with her pointy little chin. The world's changed, hasn't it, Graham? Changed right before our eyes." Mrs. Gee had died a little more than a year ago. Poor Graham, his live-in and then his mother both in twelve months. But we've all got to move on, Roland thought, chewing his cherry. Last week there'd been a woman at the bar who could tie a cherry stem into a knot with her tongue. The woman said she and Norman Mailer's wife shared that particular talent. Not the wife he stabbed, but his current wife, whoever she was.

"My mom changed too," Graham said. "She came to love Peter like a son." Peter had been the live-in. Roland never met him. Saw pictures, though. Handsome enough. Owned six gas stations, if you can imagine.

"Do you remember that time you came home from the office and found me with all those clothes I bought at Bullock's? The whole living room covered with Bullock's bags and you told me to take everything right back, every last thing. But I told you no. Told you you'd have to take them back yourself, I wasn't going to. And you said, 'Fine,' but you never did. Remember that time?"

"No," Graham said.

"Wasn't that you?" But then Roland realized it wasn't.

The waiter brought Graham's penne alla Norma and an empty plate for Roland's trip to the salad bar. The waiter was tall, with dark hair cut close and sideburns. He wore a gold hoop in his left ear, and, as far as Roland could tell, waxed his chest. He'd been working at the Rose City for about eight weeks. His name was Johnny, and he wore his jeans high, tucking his order pad into them at the small of his back.

"Not too busy today, Johnny?" Roland said, taking the empty plate and holding it to his chest. "I just love your salad bar, Johnny." Johnny asked if there was anything else he could bring them, and Roland said, "Will you throw in an extra cherry in my next Manhattan, Johnny?"

From the salad bar, Roland watched Graham waiting politely at the table, pulling on a dinner roll. At the bar, Johnny was waiting for the bartender to fix the drinks. That was the way Roland liked it: his men waiting, Graham over there in the half-circle booth, Johnny at the bar, his jeans riding high. Roland filled his plate with iceberg lettuce; a cherry tomato popped out of the tongs and onto the carpet. Back when he lived with Graham, a man not unlike Johnny worked at Huggin's Shoes; every few weeks Roland would go into the shop and try on a pair of penny loafers, arching his foot just so, but the man never paid him any attention; he never seemed to notice Roland buying the same pair of shoes each week and returning them the next.

Roland settled into the booth again. What was keeping old Johnny at the bar? Roland thought about the woman who could tie a cherry stem with her tongue; how far could a talent like that take you? But look at Norman Mailer's wife, whoever she was. Probably the only reason he married her.

"What?" Roland asked. He hadn't heard what Graham had asked. The lunches, going on for nearly nine months, had become dull. He would look forward to them until the moment when he arrived at the Rose City and scanned the room. Then the boredom would creep into Roland as he stood at the hostess stand. And there, always, was good old Graham, waiting patiently in the booth and playing with his silverware.

"You still thinking of moving out of the lawyer's garage?"

"Maybe next year," Roland said. "It depends on this part I'm up for. It could be big."

"Rol, that's great," Graham said. "Tell me about it."

"Don't want to jinx it," Roland said, sealing his lips. In fact, there was no part on the horizon, hadn't been for a while. But Roland kept up his hopes, thinking one day would be his day. One day they'd come a-knocking, and he'd be ready. That's why he aerobicized at the club in the mornings and pluck, pluck, plucked away any long strays and kept his body as brown as a ham. But he was also waiting for someone else, for the heavy-knuckled knock of someone who could turn everything around. One day his Hubby-Hub would come to the garage-apartment door and bang away until Roland let him in. You had to believe in your H.H.—which is how Roland thought of him because if you start saying it too often, the actual words, then the H.H. might skip right by your door.

"Thanks for the extra cherry," Roland said, sitting forward in the booth. Johnny wiped his hands on his jeans, and old Graham said, "Looks good." Leave it to Roland to drool over a Rose City waiter with a big waxed chest. It's what the faggy-fags were doing these days, waxing their chests and who knows what else. Not that Roland couldn't stand in a bar and hold his own; not that a good old-fashioned plucking didn't do the trick for him. Not so long ago, at the club, a young man with a face like a TV star had asked Roland to join him in the steam. But the young man definitely wasn't his H.H.

"I'm just interested is all," Graham was saying. But Johnny seemed to know what was going on, what Roland's intentions were. He'd set the Manhattan down close to Roland's hand. I've still got it, Roland thought. That sparkling little tilt of the neck that Emily used to talk about. "You just tilt your neck in such a funny, soft way. It's funny but nice," Emily would say, tousling Roland's hair and kicking the rye grass of the John Muir field.

"The newest things are mixed-race dolls," Graham was saying. "It isn't so easy to get the skin color right. I had to hire an agency to find people to model." Graham picked through his penne alla Norma. "There's potential, though. At least that's what Sales says."

From another table came a burst of laughter. They were two men and a woman, salad plates for all. Faggy-fags, Roland thought, eyeing the two men's haircuts. A couple, you could tell. But from the way the blond kept himself up, with his pressed shirt and mud-mask complexion, Roland knew what was going on. Why, just now the blond's eye was following Johnny's butt across the Rose City! The couple would last another two months, Roland thought. There'd be a hurled dinner plate and screaming in the parking lot of a bar.

"Black-Chinese, Hispanic-Irish, Norwegian-Eskimo," Graham was saying. "You got to get the colors right. The last thing a doll company can afford is a controversy."

Johnny began to clear the table of three, then there was a second burst of laughter, this time louder and deeper because Johnny was laughing too. The blond was turning red in the throat from the humor; then his eyes roamed right up Johnny's thigh. Make that six weeks.

Peter, the live-in, had come from Bakersfield. The son of an oil-field worker, heir of nothing. "He made himself," Graham had once said, at one of the first lunches. "That's what I liked about him." They bought a bungalow over on El Molino, smallest house on the block, but they fixed it up and grew a wall of bamboo around the backyard. After a few years, they dug a pool. Their neighbors were all in the Junior League, but no one seemed to mind the two of them, Graham reported. "No trouble in twenty years. They were always as nice as can be," he said. No trouble—that's what Graham thinks! Poor old Graham. Not a Junior Leaguer in the world who could deliver a banana bread to the faggy-fags who just moved in next door without thinking at least once of attaching a card that read: PLEASE LEAVE.

"Johnny," Roland called out. "Could you bring me a fresh plate? Think I'll make a second trip to the salad bar. Your diet Thousand Island. I could just—" But Johnny was still clearing the table of three and he held up a single finger, asking Roland to wait.

"I'm repapering the guest room," Graham said. "Well, not me. I've got a good paperhanger." Graham tried to smile, he tried to catch Roland's sapphire eyes. "Plaid," he said. "A nice plaid paper."

"Oh, yes," Roland said. "Plaid. Sounds like you." Johnny had disappeared into the kitchen. The table of three was discussing a movie, and Roland tried to hear which one. It had the word *love* in the title, that's all he could make out. But Roland couldn't think of a movie he'd seen recently with *love* in its title.

"Paper's a tough thing to pick out," Graham continued. "Maybe plaid isn't right. Maybe you could give me a hand, Roland. You've always had a good eye."

That's what Mrs. Gee had said about him too. Roland and she once went shopping for lamps, and when he found one with a glass-jar base, she'd said, "Such a good eye." It was the only nice thing she'd said about him in the two years. Roland used to wonder if she'd known he cheated on her son, but that was impossible. People like Mrs. Gee, who was as Junior League as they come, didn't think like that. She didn't have it in her. Perhaps it was Roland's greatest mistake when he assumed the same about dear old Graham.

"It's a nice house, Roland," Graham said. "Bigger than it looks from the outside. A sun room too. And now with the bamboo, the back is real private. You can sunbathe in the nude."

"Sunbathe in the nude?" Roland asked. He could hardly believe Graham had said that. Graham? With his shoulders that sizzled even on a cloudy day and his baggy swim trunks that hung shyly to his knees? Roland had taken his mother to Hawaii once, to Maui. Right before he checked her into the home in Carlsbad-by-the-Sea. A package deal to the Maui Prince Hotel, with its lobby aviary and sunset hula shows; around the bend was a nude beach where Roland met an avocado farmer. Got such a bad sunburn that Roland had to spread a whole jar of Noxzema across his ass in one night. "You ever been to Hawaii?"

Roland asked Graham.

"Sure," he said. "Peter and I used to love Hana. You know, the road to Hana."

"We can get married over there," Roland said.

Graham pushed his hands across the table, closer to Roland's. "What do you mean?"

"Gays. We can go over there and get married. It's incredible."

"Well, not exactly," Graham said. "It isn't exactly like that. Not exactly married. There's still…"

Roland wanted to go back to Maui, to the nude beach around the bend. If he could ever get the money together, he'd fly over for a week. What with these new laws, there's bound to be an H.H. or two on that beach. Just last month he asked his mother for the money, but she said she simply couldn't spare it, her face whitening in the sun that baked the home's patio. "Fixed income and all," she explained, as if she had to tell Roland. "Wish I could."

Then Johnny appeared with the fresh plate. "They just refilled the lettuce," he said.

"You've tried the diet Thousand Island, Johnny?" Roland said. "It's to die for, Johnny. You don't know what you're missing."

Graham sat back in the booth, pushing away his penne. Johnny cleared the plate, and a drop of cream sauce plop-plopped onto Roland's hand. But Johnny didn't notice.

Neither did Graham.

"You thinking of going back?" Roland asked. "To Hana?"

"Hadn't thought about it." And then, "No one to go with." Graham's eyes lifted. Same blue eyes as the day he threw Roland out. Graham had been real quiet about it. Only said, "I'll be gone for an hour. When I come back I want you out." Not even a door slam. Left Roland alone to scream at the walls.

The table of three got up to leave, and the blond put his hand on the other man's shoulder; the blond leaned in and whispered. Six weeks, Roland thought again. Give them six weeks. When the three were gone, they were replaced by a pair of businessmen, rep ties hanging above their belts. Married, Roland thought. You could tell. The stomachs pushing against the rep ties, the fingers growing fat around the ten-karat bands. They could let themselves go, had nothing to keep themselves up for. The businessmen leered across the Rose City for the waitress, a girl named Harriet, who was, unfortunately for them, working another section. They'd have to do with Johnny. Speaking of which, where did Johnny Boy get to now?

"Rol?" Graham was saying. "What do you think?"

Graham hadn't called him Rol in years, and it made Roland nervous, reminding him of something, but he wasn't sure what. "Think about what?" Roland said.

"Hawaii," Graham said. "Hana?"

"What about it?"

"Didn't you hear me? Maybe we could go some day." Johnny reappeared, took the businessmen's cocktail order. "Rol?" And then again, "Rol?"

"God, sorry," Roland said. "Go to Hana? To hunt for an H.H.?"

"A what?"

There'd been others, of course, since Graham. A gemologist in San Diego, who first told Roland about the home in Carlsbad-by-the-Sea. A lab technician in Chicago, but one winter shivering and mugged in Hyde Park ended that. Hundreds of others, to tell the truth, but only those two he actually lived with. Each lasted a few months, or less. Each ended with a fib, an infidelity, a secretly borrowed MasterCard. If only he could marry, Roland often thought. It was because he couldn't marry that he'd blown so many chances. Marriage would force him to change his ways. Would give him more of a stake in the world. Would let him say to the man winking at the door to the steam, "I can't. My husband—"

His H.H.

"You've got plans after lunch?" Graham asked. "Going to the club?"

"Not sure."

"You finished here?" Johnny asked. His shirt had split open another button, revealing more waxed chest. Pluck, pluck, pluck. Maybe Roland should try a wax. What did he have to lose? That's what he was thinking, and: How could old Graham not even take a peek at Johnny Boy? Was Graham even alive? His white bloodless cheeks made you wonder.

"You been to Hawaii, Johnny?" Roland asked. "Been to Hana?"

"Just Waikiki. Pretty." He spread his feet a bit farther apart. "Climbed into Diamond Head. Saw a snake. A green one."

"A snake!" Roland squealed. "Did you kill it?" He scooted to the edge of the booth. "I bet you ripped it in two with your bare hands." Already, Roland knew he must look a bit silly to old Graham. But Roland couldn't help it; something would flutter up in his chest and carry him, or so it seemed, to every available man in the world. And even a few who weren't so available. Just yesterday there was the garbage man picking up the dumpster from behind the lawyer's garage. A garbage man fetching dumpsters! Even Roland had to admit there was no chance of him being his H.H. The worst thing is, the garbage man clapped his industrial mitts together and said, "You're pathetic, man."

"I didn't think there were snakes in Hawaii." Was that old Graham picking on Johnny Boy, calling him a liar? No snakes in Hawaii? Poor old Graham. He'd never change. Still insisting on the truth even when it didn't matter. It made Roland shudder. Graham and that shaggy shower cap of blond hair. And then Roland remembered that when Graham was little his nickname was Crackers. What a name, Roland thought. And you know what, he couldn't help think that maybe Graham had gone a little crackers during his time with Peter the Live-In. Why else would he cross town for a Friday lunch with sweet Roland, whose eyes lifted effortlessly from Graham's tight face to the swell in Johnny Boy's jeans and back. What was the point, Roland sometimes thought. Old Graham was no more his H.H. than the garbage man with the stained gray mitts. "We can get married there," Roland heard himself saying. "In Hawaii."

"Excuse me?" Johnny said.

"Those of us who are interested in settling down can fly over there for a quickie wedding. People tell me it's turning into our Vegas."

"Oh, that," Johnny said. "But it doesn't really count, does it? If no one else recognizes the marriage. I mean, what's the point of that?"

"Well, there's always Denmark," Roland said. "Never been there, though. Not interested either. I don't like blonds. I like them dark, Johnny. Wouldn't touch a blond with a ten-foot pole. Of course what really matters is inside, don't you agree, Johnny Boy? The first thing I look at is inside. And then I look to make sure they're not a blond."

Graham shifted in the booth and touched his head. "Maybe we should go," he said. "Maybe we should get the check and go."

Johnny left their table, crossing the Rose City, hostility hunched in his shoulders. The businessmen tried to flag him, but he passed them without even looking. But Roland hadn't offended Johnny. If anyone should be upset, it should be old Graham. What with that comment about blonds. Roland shouldn't have said it, even if it was true.

Roland and Graham sat in the booth, quiet. A busboy cleared the last of the plates, leaving the table empty except for an oily glob of diet Thousand Island. It sat there between them, a salmon-colored dollop, as unpleasant and embarrassing as a zit on the end of the nose.

Johnny brought the check and two pink-and-white mints. Roland quickly popped one in his mouth and said, "Johnny Boy, when are you going to start working nights? When am I going to see you at the Rose City at night?"

"From what I hear, you can't see anybody by the time you leave here at night," Johnny said. "Besides, I've got acting class at night. If things go well with this part I'm up for, you won't be seeing me at the Rose City at all." Then Johnny left with an efficient turn.

Roland's throat suddenly felt sore. He felt as if he was still talking even though he wasn't. He sat back in the booth and watched Graham pay the check. He thought to himself, Something had better change.

"You're giving Johnny too much tip," Roland said to Graham. "He wasn't all that good. He doesn't deserve that much. You got to send them a signal that the service wasn't all that good."

But softy Old Graham ignored Roland and left the tip.

"Let's go," he said, his chin sinking into this throat, his fingers dejectedly patting his blond hair. Of course, technically Emily had been a blond. His hair was darker than Graham's, but if you read his driver's license—which Rol did every night in high school after he swiped it from Emily's wallet—it said blond. There was a night in their senior year, at a party over on San Raphael, when Roland and Emily found themselves waiting for a bathroom to free up and then found themselves in there together, the door bolted, Rol on his knees. It happened only once, and Emily never spoke to Roland again, never again on the football field, never again in Western Civ.

Outside the Rose City, the sun was blank and bright. Roland put on his sunglasses. They were a new pair, Vuarnet, but Graham didn't even notice. Said nothing at all. Not that you could expect Graham to know Vuarnet. If anyone didn't understand things French, it was old Graham.

"You've been coming to the Rose City at night?" Graham asked.

"Sometimes. For a drink or two. When I can't sleep. Or on my way home from the Miyako. You never know who you'll meet." You never know on what door your H.H. will knock.

"I see," Graham said. They began walking toward Roland's car. The sun beat down on their necks, and the sky was brown with smog. There were mountains out there, the purple San Gabriels, but you wouldn't know it what with the smog hanging like a fire curtain.

"What were you saying about the wallpaper?" Roland asked. This was the point in their lunch date when Graham usually asked if they'd be getting together next Friday.

Roland would always say, Oh, I don't know, but then they always did. "You were thinking of a stripe? I'm not so sure about a stripe. It depends on the size of the..."

"Thanks," Graham said. "I'll keep that in mind. But it's picked out already. It'll be fine." And then, "It's a nice plaid."

"Plaid?" Roland said. "Someone else was telling me about wallpapering in plaid." But Roland couldn't imagine who.

Then they were at Roland's Malibu, its green vinyl baking in the sun. "If you ever need anything," Graham said. "Please give me a call."

"Of course." But what would Roland need between now and next Friday? Old Graham, always worrying about little Roland. Old Graham would never change, thank God for that.

They kissed good-bye, right there in the parking lot.

Actually, it was Graham who kissed Roland on the cheek. Roland would never kiss another man in public, the way the faggy-fags did on Santa Monica Boulevard. Save it for the bedroom, Roland would think. "But why shouldn't we?" Graham had once said. "If straight people can..."

But Roland didn't think like that. Instead, what he thought was: Never had a man who I wanted to kiss good-bye on the street. And sometimes, when the Rose City threw him out at 2 in the morning: Never would.

That evening, Roland returned to the Rose City Lounge. It was different at night, after dinner was served. They pushed aside the salad bar, clearing the way for a small dance floor. There were lights in the ceiling with colored plastic gels that rotated, giving the room a disco feel.

On each table burned a candle in a glass bulb covered in white netting. And the staff changed. Of course, as you know, Johnny Boy wasn't there, and neither was Harriet. The bartender was a guy with a chest so hairy you could catch a fly in it. Jesse. And there were two or three cocktail waitresses who wore short skirts that poofed out from the tutus of tulle beneath. The waitresses all had faces of smoker's lines and sun damage, and they knew Roland even better than Johnny did. "Maybe even better than I know myself," Roland would sometimes joke to whatever stranger he ended up talking to.

You see, if Roland knew anything at all, he knew his H.H. wouldn't turn up in the Rage or any of the other faggy-fag bars along Santa Monica Boulevard. And certainly not in that local Pasadena trap, the Incognito, with its Charlie's Angels pinball machine and its nick in the wall from when Roland had thrown a bottle of beer. He knew because he had tried. If only he could count the number of potential H.H.s he'd met in a gay bar after midnight who proved themselves the furthest thing from being an H.H. by 6 A.M. But there were too many to count, too many to even remember.

After 10, the Rose City was the home to wandering-eyed business men. Men in Pasadena for a 9 A.M. sales call. The two businessmen with the rep ties were there tonight, in Roland and Graham's booth and flirting with the short waitress, Elaine. Roland would have made his way over to the booth if it were just one businessman. It was easy enough. Even if they were married. Especially if they were married. Liquor them up. Talk about cunt. Go up to their room to watch a late-night game on cable. Gratefully drop to your knees. That's all there was to it. And yet even Roland knew that he had a particular talent because not just anyone could pull it off.

But that would be later. It was still early, and Roland was on his first Manhattan. Jesse was out of cherries. So apologetic was he that he made Roland's first a double. "Nothing for your tongue to play with tonight," Jesse joked, because Roland had repeated the Norman Mailer tidbit to everyone in the bar at least three times.

Graham and Peter the Live-In had had one of those commitment ceremonies. A hundred people in the bamboo yard. A gazebo laced with roses. Matching tuxedos. The whole bit. Once Graham brought the photo album to lunch, and it had made Roland just about burn alive with jealousy. It had made him think: What was Roland doing wrong?

Not that there wasn't tonight for Roland. You always had to remember tonight. Friday night in the Rose City. It was a bit quieter than during the week; the sales reps had made their last leg home.

But there were potential H.H.s dotted about the room. The silver-haired man talking to Jesse at the bar. The Chinese guy in the corner, talking on his phone. The fellow in the polo shirt with letters on the breast that read: '94 Spring Sales Conference, Carlsbad-by-the-Sea. Roland couldn't rule out any of them.

And then there was always the door. You always had to keep one eye on the door. Because just as you were about to give up and settle on a guy who wasn't your H.H. but instead your F.E.—your future ex—just then at the door, filling its frame with his shoulders, drawing the eyes of the three cocktail waitresses and all your other lonelyheart competition slouching over their drinks in the Rose City, there he was: your Hubby-Hub, scanning the lounge, rubbing his hands together, licking his lips, hunting for you.

Whose Song?

Thomas Glave

Yes, now they're waiting to rape her, but how can they know? The girl with strum-vales, entire forests, behind her eyes. Who has already known the touch of moondewed kisses, nightwing sighs, on her teenage skin. Cassandra. Lightskinned, lean. Lovelier to them for the light. How can they know? The darkskinned ones aren't even hardly what they want. They have been taught, have learned well and well. Them black bitches, that's some skank shit, they sing. Give you VD on the woody, make your shit fall off. How can they know? Have been taught. Cassandra, fifteen, in the light. On her way to the forests. In the light. Hasn't known a man yet. Hasn't wanted to. How can they know? She prefers Tanya's lips, the skin-touch of silk. Tanya, girlfriend, sixteen and fine, dark glider, schoolmate-lover, large-nippled, -thighed. Tanya. Who makes her come and come again when the mamas are away, when houses settle back into silent time and wrens swoopflutter their wings down into the nightbird's song. Tanya and Cassandra. Kissing. Holding. Climbing and gliding. What the grown girls do, they think, belly-kissing but shy. Holding. She makes me feel my skin, burrowing in. Which one of them thinks that? Which one flies? Who can tell? Climbing and gliding. Coming. Wet. Coming. Laughing. Smelling. Girlsex, she-love, and the nightbird's song. Thrilling and trilling. Smooth bellies, giving face, brushing on and on. Cassandra. Tanya swooping down, brown girls, dusky flesh, and the nightbird's song. How can they know? The boys have been watching them, have begun to know things about them that watchers know or guess. The boys, touching themselves in nightly rage, watching them. Wanting more of Cassandra because she doesn't want them. Wanting to set the forests on fire, cockbrush those glens. How can they know? They are there and they are there and they are watching. Now.

Sing this tale, then, of a Sound Hill rape. Sing it, low and mournful, soft, beneath the kneeling trees on either side of the rusty bridge out by Eastchester Creek; where the sun hangs low over the Sound and water meets the sky; where the departed walk along Shore Road and the joggers run; where morning rabbits leap away from the pounding joggers' step. Sing it far and wide, this sorrow song woven into the cresting nightbird's blue. Sing it, in that far-off place, far up away from it all, where the black people live and think they've at last found peace; where there are homes, small homes and large, with modest yards, fruit hedges, taxus, juniper trees; where the silver hoses, coiled, sag and lean; where the withered arms hanging out of second-story windows are the arms of that lingering ghost or aging lonely busybody everybody knows. In that northerly corner of the city where no elevated IRT train yet comes; where the infrequent buses to Orchard Beach and Pelham Bay sigh out spent lives and empty nights when they run; where the Sound pulls watersmell through troubled dreams and midnight pains, the sleeping loneliness and silence of a distant place. Sound Hill, beneath your leaning trees and waterwash, who do you grieve for now? Sound Hill girl of the trees and the girlflesh, where are you now? Will those waters of the Sound flow beside you now? Caress you with light-kisses and bless you now? The City Island currents and the birds rush by you now? O sing it. Sing it for that yellow girl, dark girl, brown girl homely or fine, everygirl displaced, neither free nor named. Sing it for that girl swinging her ax through the relentless days, suckling a child or selling her ass in the cheap hotels down by the highway truckers' stop for chump change. Sing it for this girl, swishing her skirt and T-shirt, an almost-free thing, instinctual, throwing her head back to the breeze. Her face lifted to the sky. Now, Jesus. Walk here, Lamb. In thy presence there shall be light and light. Grace. Cadence. A witness or a cry. Come, now. All together. And.

How could we know? Three boys in a car, we heard, but couldn't be neighbors of ours. Had to be from some other part of the world, we thought; the projects or the Valley. Not from here. In this place every face knows every eye, we thought, what's up here in the heart always is clear. But they were not kind nor good, neither kin nor known. If they were anything at all besides unseen, they were maimed. Three boys, three boys. In a car. Long legs, lean hands. In a car. Bitter mouths, tight asses, and the fear of fear. Boys or men and hard. In their car. Who did not like it. Did not like the way those forest eyes gazed out at those darker desert ones, at the eyes of that other who had known what it was to be dark and loathed. Yo, dark-skinned bitch. So it had been said. Yo, skillet ass. Don't be cutting your eyes at me, bitch, I'll fuck your black ass up. It had been said. Ugly black bitch. You need some dick. Them eyes gone get you killed, rolling them at me like that. It had been said. Had to be, had to be from over by Edenwald, we thought. Rowdy, raunchy, no kind of class. Nasty homies on the prowl, not from this hood. How could we know? Three boys, fretful, frightened, angry. In a row. The burning rope had come to them long ago in willed and willful dreams, scored mean circles and scars into their once-gorgeous throats. The eyes that had once looked up in wonder from their mother's arms had been beaten, hammered into rings, dark pain-pools that belied their depth. Deeper. Where they lived, named and unnamed. How could they know? Know that those butterflies and orchids of the other world, that ice-green velvet of the other world, the precious stones that got up and wept before the unfeeling sky and the bears that slept away entire centuries with memories of that once-warm sweet milk on their lips, were not for them? So beaten, so denied, as they were and as they believed, their own hands had grown to claws over the years; savaged their own skin. Needles? Maybe, we thought. In the reviling at large, who could tell? Pipes, bottles? Vials? So we thought. Of course. Who could know, and who who knew would tell? Who who knew would sing through the veil the words of that song, about the someone-or-thing that had torn out their insides and left them there, far from the velvet and the butterflies and the orchid-time? The knower's voice, if voice it was, only whispered down bitter rains when they howled, and left us only the curve of their skulls beneath the scarred flesh on those nights, bony white, when the moon smiled.

And she, so she: alone that day. Fresh and wet still from Tanya's arms, pajama invitations and TV nights, after-dark giggles and touches, kisses, while belowstairs the mama slept through world news, terrorist bombings, cleansings ethnic and unclean. Alone that day, the day after, yellow girl, walking out by the golden grayswishing Sound, higher up along the Shore Road way and higher, higher up where no one ever walks alone, higher still by where the dead bodies every year turn up (four Puerto Rican girl-things cut up, garbage-bagged, found there last year: bloated hands, swollen knees, and the broken parts); O higher still, Cassandra, where the fat joggers run, higher still past the horse stables and the smell of hay, higher yet getting on to where the whitefolks live and the sundowns die. Higher. Seeking watersmell and sheen for those forests in her eyes; seeking that summer sundown heat on her skin; seeking something away from hood catcalls and yo, bitch, let me in. Would you think she doesn't already know what peacefulness means, contains? She's already learned of the dangers of the too-high skirt, the things some of them say they'd like to put between her knees. The blouse that reveals, the pants that show too much hip. Ropes hers and theirs. Now seeking only a place where she can walk away, across the water if need be, away from the beer cans hurled from cars, the What's up, bitch yells and the burning circle-scars. Cassandra, Cassandra. Are you a bitch out here? The sun wexing goldsplash across her now says no. The water stretching out to Long Island summerheat on the other side says no, and the birds wheeling overhead, OK, OK, they cry, call down the skytone, concurring: the word is no. Peace and freedom, seasmell and free. A dark girl's scent riding on her thighs. Cassandra. Tanya. Sing it.

But they watching. The three. Singing. Listen: a bitch ain't nothing but a ho, sing those three. Have been taught. (But by whom?)

Taught and taut. Taught low and harsh, that rhythm. Fierce melody. Melodylessness in mixture, lovelessness in joy. Drunk on flame, and who the fuck that bitch think she is anyway? they say—for they had seen her before, spoken to her and her kind; courted her favor, her attentions, in that car. Can't talk to nobody, bitch, you think you all a that? Can't speak to nobody, bitch, you think your pussy talks and shit? How could they know then?—of her forests, smoldering? Know and feel?—how in that growing silent heat those inner trees had uprooted, hurled stark branches at the outer sky? The firestorm and after-rain remained unseen. Only the lashes fluttered, and the inner earth grew hard. With those ropes choking so many of them in dreams, aware of the circles burnt into their skins, how could they know? How could they not know?

Robbie. Dee. Bernard. Three and three. Young and old. Too old for those jeans sliding down their asses. Too young for the rope and the circle's clutch. Too old to love so much their own wet dreams splashed out onto she they summoned out of that uncentered roiling world. She, summoned, to walk forth before their fire as the bitch or cunt. So they thought, would think and sing: still too young for the nursing of that keening need, the unconscious conscious wish to obliterate through vicious dreams who they were and are, have been, and are not. Blackmenbrothers, lovers, sons of strugglers. Sharecroppers, cocksuckers, black bucks and whores. Have been and are, might still be, and are not. A song. To do away with what they have and have not; what they can be, they think, are told by that outer chorus they can be—black boys, pretty boys, big dicks, tight asses, pretty boys, black scum, or funky homie trash—and cannot. Their hearts replaced by gnashing teeth, dirt; the underscraping grinch, an always-howl. Robbie Dee Bernard. Who have names and eyelids, fears, homie-homes. Watching now. Looking out for a replacement for those shredded skins. 'Cause that bitch think she all a that, they sing. Word, got that lightskin, good hair, think she fly. Got them titties that need some dick up in between. The flavor. Not like them darkskinned bitches, they sing. (But do the words have joy?) Got to cut this bitch down to size, the chorus goes. A tune. Phat pussy. Word, G! Said hey-ho! Said a-hey-ho! Word, my brother. My nigger. Sing it.

So driving. Looking. Watching. Seeing. Their words a blue song, the undercolor of the nightbird's wing. Is it a song you have heard before? Heard it sung sweet and clear to someone you hate before? Listen:—Oh shit, yo, there she go. Right up there. Straight on. Swinging her ass like a high-yellow ho. Said hey-ho! Turn up the volume on my man J Live J. Drive up, yo. Spook the bitch. Gonna get some serious pussy outta this shit.—Driving, slowing, slowing down. Feeling the circles, feeling their own necks. Burning skins, cockheads fullstretched and hard. Will she have a chance, dreaming of girlkisses, against that hard? In the sun. Here. And.

Pulling up.—So, Miss Lightskin, they sing, what you doing out here? Walking by yourself, you ain't scared? Ain't scared somebody gonna try to get some of your skin? Them titties looking kinda fly, girl. Come on, now. Get in.

Was it then that she felt the smoldering in those glens about to break? The sun gleaming down silver whiteheat on her back? And O how she had only longed to walk the walk. To continue on and on and on and through to those copses where, at the feet of that very old and most wise woman-tree of all, she might gaze into those stiller waters of minnow-fishes, minnow-girls, and there yes! quell quell quell quell quell the flames. As one of them then broke through her glens, to shout that she wasn't nothing anyway but a yellow bitch with a whole lotta attitude and a skanky cunt. As (oh, yes, it was true, rivers and fire, snake daggers and black bitches, she had had enough) she flung back words on what exactly he should do with his mother's cunt, 'cause your mother, nigger, is the only motherfucking bitch out here. And then? Who could say or know? The 5-0 were nowhere in sight; all passing cars had passed; only the wheeling birds and that drifting sun above were witnesses to what they could not prevent. Cassandra, Cassandra.—Get in the car, bitch.—Fuck no, I won't. Leave me alone. Leave me—trying to say Fuck off, y'all leave me the fuck alone, but whose hand was that, then, grabbing for her breast? Whose hand is that, on her ass, pressing now, right now, up into her flesh?—Stop it, y'all. Get the fuck off before—screaming and crying. Cursing, running. Sneakered feet on asphalt, pursuit, and the laughing loud. An easy catch.—We got you now, bitch.— Who can hear? The sun can only stare, and the sky is gone.

Driving, driving, driving on. Where can they take her? Where will they? They all want some, want to be fair. Fair is fair: three dicks, one cunt. That is their song. Driving on. Pelham Bay Park? they think. But naw, too many people, niggers and Ricans with a whole buncha kids and shit. (The sun going down. Driving on). How about under the bridge, by Eastchester Creek? That's it, G! Holding her, holding, but can't somebody slap the bitch to make her shut up? Quit crying, bitch. Goddamn. A crying-ass bitch in a little funky-ass car. Now weeping more. Driving on.—Gonna call the police, she says, crying more; choking in that way they like, for then (oh, yes, they know) in that way from smooth head to hairy base will she choke on them. They laugh.—What fucking 5-0 you gonna call, bitch? You lucky we ain't take your yellow ass over to the projects. Fuck your shit in the elevator, throw your ass off the roof. These bitches, they laugh. Just shut up and sit back. Sit back, sit back. Driving on.

Now the one they call Robbie is talking to her.—Open it, he says. Robbie, O Robbie. Eager and edgy, large-eyed and fine. Robbie, who has a name, unspoken hopes; private dreams. How can they know? Will he be dead within a year like so many others? A mirrored image in a mirror that shows them nothing? A wicked knife's slide from a brother's hand to his hidden chewed-up heart? Shattered glass, regret. Feeling now only the circle around his neck that keeps all in thrall. For now he must be a man for them. Must show the steel. Robbie don't be fronting, he prays they think, Robbie be hard. Will they like you better, Robbie, then, if you be hard? Will the big

boys finally love you, take you in, Robbie, if you be hard? But it's
deep sometimes, isn't it, Robbie, with all that hard? Deep and
low....—he knows. Knows the clear tint of that pain. Alone and lonely...unknown, trying to be hard. Not like it was back then when then
when he said you was pretty. Remember? All up in his arms...one of
your boys, Darrell J. In his arms. Where nobody couldn't see. Didn't
have to be hard. Rubbing up, rubbing. Kissing up on you. Licking.
Talking shit about lovelove and all a that But naw man he said the
first time (Darrell J., summertime, 10 P.M., off the court, hotwet,
crew gone home, had an extra 40, sweaty chest neck face, big hands,
shoulders, smile, was fine), just chilling whyn't you come on hang
out?—so said Darrell J. with the hands and the yo yo yo yo going on
and on with them eyes and mouth tongue up in his skin my man—:
kissing up on Robbie the second time, pretty Robbie, the third time
and the fourth and the we did and he kissing licking holding y'all
two and O Robbie Robbie Robbie. A homie's song. Feeling then.
Underneath him, pretty. In his arms. Where nobody couldn't see
didn't have to be hard kissing up on him shy shy and himinyou
youinhim Robbie, Robbie. Where has the memory gone? Back then,
straddling hips, homiekisses and the nightbird's song. But can't go
back there, can you? To feel and feel. Gots to be hard. Can't ever
touch him again, undress him, kiss his thing...feel it pressing against
the teeth and the slow-hipped song. Black skin on skin and—but he
was holding onto me and sliding, sliding way up inside sucking coming inside me in me in hot naw didn't need no jimmy aw shit now
hold on holding him and I was I was Robbie Robbie Robbie Darrell
J. together we was and I we I we came we hotwet on his belly my
side sliding over him under him holding and we came we but naw,
man, can't even be doing that motherfucking punk shit out here.
You crazy? You bugging? Niggers be getting smoked dusty for that
shit. Y'all ain't never seen me do that. Gots to be hard.—So open it,
bitch, he says. Lemme get my fingers on up in there. Awright,
awright. Damn, man, he says, nobody don't got a jimmy? This bitch
stinks, man, he says, know I'ma probably get some VD shit on my
hands and shit. They laugh.—He a man, all right. Robbie! Ain't no

faggot, yo. Not like we heard. They laugh.—Just put a sock on it, the one they call Dee says. Chillchill, yo. Everybody gonna get their chance.

And the sun. Going down, going down. Light ending now, fire and ice, blue time watersheen and the darkened plunge. Sink, golden sun. Rest your bronze head in the Sound and the sea beyond. The birds, going down, going down. Movement of trees, light swathed in leaves. Going down, going down. And.

Hard to see now, but that's OK, they say. This bitch got enough for everybody here under the bridge. No one's around now, only rusty cars and rats. Who cares if they shove that filthy rag into her mouth and tie it there? It's full of turpentine and shit, but the night doesn't care. The same night that once covered them in swamps from fiery light. Will someone come in white robes to save a light-skinned bitch this time?

Hot. Dark. On the backseat. Burning bright. Burning. On the backseat. Fire and rage.—Naw, man, Robbie, not so hard, man. You gone wear the shit out 'fore I get my chance. Who said that? Which one in the dark? O but can't tell, for all are hidden now, and all are hard. The motherfucking rigorous shit, one of them says. Shut up, bitch. Was that you, Bernard? Did you miss your daddy when he went off with the one your mama called a dirty nigger whore, Bernard? Was that where you first learned everything there was to learn, and nothing?—there, Bernard? When he punched you in the face and left you behind, little boy Bernard? You cried. Without. A song unheard. A song like the shadowrain—wasn't it? The shadowrain that's always there so deep, deep down inside your eyes, Bernard. Cold rain inside. Tears and tears. Then fists and kicks on a black shitboy's head. Little punk-looking nigger dumped in a foster home, age ten, named Bernard. Fuckhead faggot ass, the boys there said. The ones who stuck it up in you. Again and again. The second and the third...—don't hurt me, don't!—screamed that one they

called the faggot ass pussy bitch. You, Bernard. How could they
know? Know that the little bitch punk scrunched up under the bed
had seen the whole night and afterward and after alone? Bernard?
Hurts, mama. Daddy—. Rain. Little faggot ass punk. Break his fucking face, yo. Kick his faggot ass down the stairs. Then he gone suck
my dick. Suck it, bitch, 'fore we put this motherfucking hammer up
your ass. The one you trusted most of all in that place, in all those
places...everywhere? Bernard? The one who said he'd have your back
no matter what. Little man, my man, he said. Smiling down. His
teeth so white and wide. Smiling down. Smiling when he got you by
the throat, sat on your chest and made you swallow it. Swallow it,
bitch, he sang. Smiling down. Choking, choked. Deep inside the
throat. Where has the memory gone? Something broken, then a
hand. A reaching-out howl within the rain. A nightbird's rage. A
punk, used up. Leave the nigger there, yo, they said. Til the next
time. And the next. On the floor. Under the bed. Under. Bleeding
under. You, Bernard.

The words to every song on Earth are buried deep somewhere.
Songs that must be sung, that must never be sung. That must be
released from deep within the chest yet pulled back and held.
Plaintive and low, they rail; buried forever beneath the passing flesh,
alone and cold, they scream. The singer must clutch them to the
heart, where they are sanctified, nurtured, healed. Songs that finally
must be released yet recalled, in that place where no one except the
singer ever comes, in one hand caressing the keys of life wounded,
ravaged, in the other those of the precious skin and life revealed. The
three of them and Cassandra know the words. Lying beneath them
now and blind, she knows the words. Tasting turpentine and fire, she
knows the words.—Hell no, yo, that bitch ain't dead.—A voice.—
Fucked up, yo. The rag's in her mouth, how we gon' get some
mouth action now?—Aw, man, fuck that shit.—Who says that?—My
turn. My turn.—They know the words.
　　Now comes Dee. Can't even really see her, has to navigate.
Wiggles his ass a little, farts softly to let off stress.—Damn, Dee,

nasty motherfucker! they laugh. But he is busy, on to something. Sniffs and sniffs. At the bitch's asshole. At her cunt.—'Cause yeah, yo, he says, y'all know what's up with this shit. They be saying this bitch done got into some bulldagger shit. Likes to suck pussy, bulldagger shit.—Word?—The phattest bitch around, yo, he says. Bulldagger shit.

Dee. DeeDee. Someone's boy. Has a place that's home. Eastchester, or Mount V. Has a heart that hates his skin and a mind half gone. Is ugly now, got cut up, but smoked the nigger who did it. Can't sleep at night, wanders seas; really wants to die. The lonely bottle might do it if the whiffs up don't. The empty hand might do it if the desire can't. What has been loved and not loved, what seeks still a place. The same hand, pushed by the once-winsome heart, that before painted angels, animals, miraculous creatures. Blank walls leaped into life, lightspeed, and light. When (so it seemed) the whole world was light. But was discouraged, led into tunnels, and then of course was cut. The eyes went dim. Miraculous creatures. Where have the visions gone? Look, now, at that circle around his neck. Will he live? Two young ones and a dark girl waiting back there for him, frightened—will he live? Crushed angels drowned in St. Ides—will he live? When he sells the (yes, that) next week to the undercover 5-0 and is set up, will he live? When they shoot him in the back and laugh at the stain that comforts them, will he live?

But now he's happy, has found it!—the hole. The soft little hole, so tight, down there, as he reaches up to squeeze her breasts. Her eyes are closed, but she knows the words. That bitch ain't dead. How can they know? When there is time there's time, and the time is now. Time to bang the bulldagger out of her, he sings. Listen to his song:—I'ma give you a baby, bitch. (She knows the words.) Got that lightskin, think you all that, right, bitch? Word, I want me some lightskin on my dick, yo. When I get done, this heifer ain't gone be half a ho. You know know? Gonna get mines, til you know who you dis and who you don't. Til you know we the ones in con-trol, sing it! Got the flavor.—Dim-eyed, banging out his rage. Now, a man.

Banging out his fear like the others, ain't even hardly no faggot ass.
Def jam and slam, bang bang shebam. On and on as he shoots high,
shoots far...laughter, but then a sense of falling, careening...sudden
fear. It doesn't matter. The song goes on.

Night. Hell, no, broods the dim, that bitch ain't dead. Hasn't
uttered half a sound since they began; hasn't opened her eyes to let
the night look in again; hasn't breathed to the soft beating of the
nightbird's wing. The turpentine rag in place. Cassandra, Cassandra.
The rag, in place. Cassandra. Is she feeling something now?
Cassandra. Will they do anything more to her now? Cassandra, will
they leave you there? Focusing on flies, not meeting each other's
eyes, will they leave you there? Running back from the burning
forests behind their own eyes, the crackling and the shame? Will they
leave you there?—Push that bitch out on the ground, the one they
call Dee says.—Over there, by them cars and shit.—Rusty cars, a
dumping ground. So, Cassandra. Yes. They'll leave you there.
  Were they afraid? Happy? Who can tell? Three dark boys, three
men, driving away in a battered car. Three boy-men, unseen, flesh,
minds, heart. Flame. In their car. O my God, three rapists, the pretty lady in her Volvo thinks, locking her doors at the traffic light. In
their car. Blood on the backseat, cum stains, even hair. Who can tell?
It's time to get open now. Time to numb the fear.—Get out the
whiff, yo.—40s and a blunt.—That bitch got what she deserved.—
Those words, whiffs up, retreat, she deserved it, deserved it—and
they are gone. Mirrored images in shattered glass, desire and long-
ing, chill throbbing, and they are gone. The circles cleaving their
necks. Flesh, blood and flame. A whiff and a 40.—We fucked that
bitch good, G.—Night. Nightnight. Hush dark silence. Fade. They
are gone.

  Cassandra. What nightbirds are searching and diving for you now?
What plundered forests are waiting for you now? The girl-trees are
waiting for you, and so is she. Tanya. The girl-trees. Mama. How can
they know? Their eyes are waiting, searching, and will soon be gray.

The rats are waiting. They are gray. Cassandra, Cassandra. When the red lights come flashing on you, will they know? Fifteen, ripped open. Will they know? Lightskinned bitch nigger ho, went that song. Will they know? Girl-trees in a burning forest…they will know. And the night…

Where is she, they're wondering, why hasn't she come home?

They can't know what the rats and the car-carcasses know.

Cassandra? they are calling. Why don't you answer when night-voices call you home?

Night…

Listen now to the many night voices calling, calling soft, Cassandra. Come. Carrying. Up. Cassandra. Come. Out and up. What remains is what remains. Out and up. They will carry her. A feeling of hands and light. Then the red lights will come. Up and up. But will she see? Will she hear? Will she know?

The girl-trees are screaming. That is their song.

It will not appear on tomorrow's morning news.

But then—come now, ask yourself—whose song, finally, shall this be? Of four dark girls, or four hundred, on their way to lasting fire in Sunday school? Of a broken-backed woman, legs bent? Her tune? Of a pair of hands, stitching for—(but they'll never grow). Of four brothers rapping, chugging?—a slapbeat in the chorus? Doing time? Something they should know?

A song of grieving ships, bodies, torch-lit roads?

(—But then now O yes remember, remember well that time, face, place or thing: how those ten thousand million billion other ashes eyelids arms uncountable dark ceaseless burnt and even faces once fluttered, fluttered forever, in someone's dream unending, dream of no escape, beneath a blackblueblack sea: fluttered, flutter still and descend, now faces ashes eyelids dark reflection and skin forever flame: descend, descend over laughing crowds.)

A song of red earth roads. Women crying and men. Red hands, gray mouths, and the circle's clutch. A song, a song. Of sorrowing suns. Of destruction, self-destruction, when eyes lay low. A song—

But whose song is it? Is it yours? Or mine?

Hers?

Or theirs...—?

—But a song. A heedless, feckless tune. Here, where the night-time knows. And, well—

Yes, well—

—So, Cassandra. Now, Cassandra.

Sing it.

Deep Green, Pale Purple

Scott Heim

Had God stretched his gentle giant's fingers across the dustpaths of our road, across our nighttime porch, to open in one twist of the wrist the entire south front face of our house—walls, windows and doors out-turned together like a casket or tiny portalled dollhouse—and had God peered into our exposed rooms for inventory, for study of secrets, he would have seen this: the red reclining chair, empty, with the seat, my father's seat, unsprung and threadbare; the television, still warm but now silent and dark; sun-starched curtains sleeving windows tinted a paranoid's shade of gray to allow no spies, little light; my father sleeping alone in his room; my mother sleeping, alone and fumy with booze, in hers; money, hidden money, worry and skimp, the rolls of coins and rubber-banded bills stashed in decades-old cigar boxes, in tobacco tins scrubbed shiny long ago by my grandfather, now soiled blackly green with the soil of money; invoices and bills, filed, from the orchard store; Bible on the bookshelf, for two generations unstudied; the cracked cement square beneath the potbelly woodstove where my brother once constructed and Krazy-Glued a wee warped cabin of Popsicle sticks, then set it ablaze—the ash-black scar remained still, and I doubted he'd forgotten my father's elm-switch punishment; blue bowl of apples on the table, red skins freckled with hazel, one bitten by my mother during a dead-of-night drunk, her white bite time-tainted to dark umber; unsmiling wall portraits of my father's parents; hard water from the faucets with an acid, eggy smell and never running long enough for altogether hot; damp socks, most snagged or darned with snarls of thread, filed on the couch and chairs to dry; and lastly, back there, our bedroom door, shutting Paul in, me in, now closed and quiet and black.

But tonight, if the meddling, gigantic God had opened that door, had overturned and shaken the room to search and search, he could not have found us. Secretly we had escaped. Riled by the heat, my brother and I outwitted sleep to slip from the house in the calmest hour of night, armed with our pillows, deserters for the forbidden cool of the backyard. It was after 2; 2:30, perhaps. We lay side by side on grass laced lethal with sandburs and chiggers. Somewhere up there hovered stars, mysterious glittering planets, a jet plane sailing much too swift with its high winking fairy-tale light, but we saw none of it, lulled only by an occluded dark, a threatening storm, a sky flimsy and thrilling as a promise.

Beside me, Paul lay storklike in his sleeper flannels. A scatter of blond hair furled free from the edges of the ragged red stocking cap; I placed my hand there. "It's getting long," I said.

"But I want it longer. In a little bit I'll be able to put the bangs behind my ears. Miriam says only four inches more until enough for a ponytail." Miriam Crowhurst was our neighbor, a stout-set black girl Paul's age, conspicuously outcast in our small-town school but still his best friend. I knew she had taken to styling his hair, tucking it into his cap to prevent our father from noticing. Paul had told me their fears of some future midnight when the broad-shouldered shadow might slip inside our room: the mouth crooked victorious, the bend toward the bed, the scissors' staccato glint.

We told ourselves we loved him; a son should be mired in love, devoted. Sometimes, though, the love felt proximate to hate, and sometimes further the hate overtook, leaving Paul, me, airless and trembling. Under him like a curse: steering the tractor, rotary motion, through the orchard; plucking his apples from trees to snuggle them into whichever basket he designated; sidearming the bruised or wormholed to the sky. The coming shutdown of autumn meant enduring his orders and rules. It meant his imminent birthday, so important, his fiftieth. Now older than our mother by a decade and a half—shouldn't this day be important, she'd asked, shouldn't we surprise him real special? Octobers previous, Paul and

I had searched racks at corner drugstores, our mother standing patient with the dollar bill. Cards with photographs of racehorses and stock cars; cartoon drawings of burly policemen, all-star wrestlers, lifeguards. But the greetings inside proved misdirected and false. "Daddy," some began, but we'd never called him Daddy. Others muted us with "love": disqualified. In the end, our mother chose for us. No sentiment, no singsong poem, best suited this man we flanked at the dinner table, in the apple truck; whose questions bloomed lumps in our throats; whose daily fieldwork changed his eyes deep-set and black, his finger pads hard as thimbles.

The wind surged and stilled and surged again, smelling of rain, rustling the bowed heads of roland grass and shivering shadows from the trees. I crept one leg closer to Paul; aimed my voice for his ear. "Pretty soon it'll be lots colder," I said. "We can take down the big brown blanket again."

"Nope. The stuffing kept coming out. If Dad was smart he'd throw it away."

The blanket was my favorite, and its smell had set permanent in my brain, easily conjured, that fragrant peppery warmth of its fleece, early winter mornings, oozy in-and-out of slumber with my brother beside me, chrysalised, lapsed within a dream, both of us snuffly and dulled with first colds. Its borders wore patches from one of my mother's faded gingham skirts. I couldn't imagine spending January, February nights without it, and to sway Paul's opinion I grasped for something untrue. "Mom fixed it," I said, "last spring. She sewed it up so we can't get rid of it."

He huddled closer to his pillow. "I'd rather freeze my feet all night than wake up with that fluff all over us."

At that I sat up, leaning even with his knees. "I wouldn't let them get cold." In two quick tugs I shucked the socks from his feet. This was ritual: Sometimes, late nights before sleep soothed blackly in, I would gather Paul's feet to my chest and massage them. His body swiveling sideways, head and arms dangling over the bed, Adam's apple pulsing as he swooned. I adored it, slaving for him, so again, in tonight's backyard chill and darkness, I brought his feet to my lap.

My fingertips bridging the toes, my palms aligned with arches soft-skinned and curved delicate as a girl's. Kneading and pressing the callused heels. Sometimes Paul made little moans, but tonight, as I began my intricate aggression, he knew to stay silent, careful of waking our parents.

For a medley of minutes the clouds broke, and between them, nobly, the moon appeared: full, as the kitchen calendar predicted, a knob of bone dragging its white weight across the sky. It shone on the parallel wires of backyard clothesline. On the sheets and pillowcases that quivered there like souls of the orchard's ghosts. On the pair of rusted trash barrels, anchored in the sand, away from the grass, filled with the ashes from past tandem days. And on Paul and me. I resumed rubbing, rubbing. Then the clouds again dressed the light and, far behind our field, came the bark of Dusty, the Crowhursts' pepper-haired German shepherd, faintly lonesome.

"I'm scared," I told Paul. "The other day I was in the orchard and something came after me. Back by the last rows. A ghost. I could hear it breathing."

"Matt," said my brother, using my real name now instead of Maggot, the nickname given by my father. "There's nothing back there. No ghosts." And, softly: "I'll protect you."

Looking down I noticed the nails on Paul's toes were clipped perfectly and colored ten colors which, under the moon-blazed clouds, seemed ten separate hues of purple. I didn't have to ask. Miriam had done this before, had streaked Paul's hair with wash-off dye, had painted his lips and nails in stripes and glitters and swirls. When our father traveled, Miriam sometimes visited, and after she left I would find remnants of dress-up clothes she'd brought, a trash can of tissues smudged with mascara. I knew if our father discovered these secrets he would brand Paul a sissy, Miriam a filthy nigger. But Paul kept his games confidential, and I, Maggot, didn't mind: My knowledge was a thirteen-year-old's knowledge, without upshot or bias, and I was nowhere near our father, not even close, caring less what my brother created and daydreamed behind bolted doors with his silly chubby dark-skinned girl.

"That's enough," Paul said, moving his feet away, retrieving his socks. "Much obliged, sir." As I eased back beside him, a wet flicker brushed my face. The first hint of rain. Wind hit the tree limbs to launch their pinnate leaves, scattering, swooping upon our makeshift bed like bats. Soon the rain would fall fully upon us. But we would never surrender: we would brave the hot or cold, the dry or insufferably wet. We had no mother or father; we were nomads, drifters from town to purgatorial town, sleuthlike, rash, needing no one.

Paul put one arm between his pillow and the grass and turned to face the house. The hair shook from his shoulder and revealed, at the height of his spine, a pimple, beaded exquisitely white. Soon silence reigned, but I longed to stay awake, wanted Paul to keep speaking, to unravel one of his hundreds of late-night stories. No, he wasn't sleeping. I sensed an unease, a concern, in the curved tension of his body. As I whispered "Paul" I slid closer, toeing the back of his knee with the softness of a moth.

"It might not matter soon," Paul said, returning to the discussion of the blanket, our parents. "I might not always be there in that stupid crowded bed with you anyway."

His words frightened me a little; slow words, apprehensive, and I almost heard, inside them, his shivery heartbeat. At last I asked, "Why not?"

"Can't you tell things are changing? Mom's with Crowhurst all the time. Can't say I blame her either because he pays ten times the attention Dad ever has. And how do you think she gets her booze?" In the pause I pictured Mr. Crowhurst, his dark liquid eyes and pressed white shirts, father to Miriam and husband to the freakish shut-in wife I'd never seen. So out of place on his land; his race, his easy nature, his ignorance of farming. I thought of his embarrassed smiles when our father, in the orchard with Paul and me, caught him tending to his boxes of bees, his hobby, in his back stretch of pasture. I'd heard Paul's stories of the affair but couldn't believe it, not quite; couldn't vision my mother together, with him, in some top-secret motel.

Paul continued. "Don't be mad at her, though. It's rough for her with Dad. At least now she's found someone who pays attention."

"I'm not mad," I said. "But what's that got to do with you? How's that mean you won't always be here?"

He turned now to face me: a mark from his charcoal pencils on the side of his chin. "Dad's going to find out about Mom," Paul said. "If he doesn't know already. Because he knows a lot of things. He knows about me too. You know what I'm saying? He's taking me along Saturday so it can be us, just us two, alone. He wants to talk to me."

For the weekend Paul would join our father in the fruit truck, another journey delivering apples across the state. Suddenly I understood Paul's meaning, the weight and danger, and I protested. "No. Don't tell him. Wait."

"Until when? Some day you might have to get by without me. On your own." He hesitated, and my terror swelled, palpable in the drizzly air. Finally he smiled. "But not for good. I'd never leave you for good." Still, his smile made a weak bandage. Already I felt our father's fury; already, my brother slipping. Above, leaves trembled like pennants, spraying us. "It's them," Paul said. "They're the reason I'd go, not you."

And in this darkest part of night the drizzle stopped its tease and began dropping, heavy, from above. Half-speed, it seemed, this rain we'd needed for weeks, swirling down—yet we would not go inside, we refused to think of our father's ire, the money it would waste to launder our flannels, our muddied pillowcases. I couldn't form other questions for Paul; panicked still at his imminent standoff with our father, I merely waited out the night and watched the rain, blinking only when it sprinkled my eyes.

Minutes and hours. I hovered a hand above Paul's face to prove his sleep; indeed he was gone, long gone, and again I touched the hair around the stocking cap. Wet, his curls went silky in my hands, oily too, like the sweet filaments of yellow inside a pod of corn. By now the rain was so thick we could have punctured it. It had to penetrate the trees to get to us, the overhanging drapery of leaves, and by the time the water hit our bodies it had turned a bubbly green. Our clothes and skins were smeared with it, leaf-bled rainshade, and

although anticipating my father's wrath, I cared nothing nonetheless
and let the stains deepen. In retrospect this green, this specific night,
seems so fleeting, it may never have existed at all. I wish I could have
savored it, wish I could have held my brother closer, turned a deeper, a durable and darkly indelible, shade of green.

But I fell asleep. Paul fell asleep. On waking, the rain had tapered,
and bunches of those wet leaves lay along our bodies. Even in pre-
dawn I saw their heraldry, mostly greens, but also coppers, also tea-
shade tans; in my fingers they tingled, waxy and firm. Touching them
was like touching money. I heard a noise behind us, far behind, in
the orchard perhaps, and mindful of the ghosts I pulled tight to my
brother. Fear fluttered through me; I placed my head against his rail-
boned chest. I couldn't imagine him leaving, ever. The solace, the
security. Paul had tumbled deep-sleep so my burden, against him,
mattered nil, lodged now in his commencing dream. I listened for
his heart, tuning out the shudder and hiss of drizzle, the surrounding night. At last, its velvet thrum. My eyes closed for what seemed
seconds and when I opened them again the rain, the deep green rain,
had whirled conclusively away, a far-off bird was trying first notes,
and the sky had gone pale as paper, meaning morning.

Work, postdinner, loading the truck for tomorrow: All around us
the late-fall apples, a shallow sea of yellow, of reds both deep-dark
and pinkish, overflowing and bumping from baskets. We moved gently, cautiously, about them. If the sky outside had set afire, had fall-
en in shards to the earth, we wouldn't have noticed, stuck as we were
inside the fruit trailer, dark rectangular box behind our father's
truck, with nothing to see or smell but apples. Pectin and pulp in our
hair, our ears. Sweat dripping beads from our temples, spreading bibs
at our shirtfronts. Our footheels and backbones would ache at
school—first semester only three days away—but we couldn't stop.
By the time I followed Paul inside the house, a dark-of-night drape
had lowered and we were tired, too tired for anything but sleep.

The house was dangerously quiet. In the kitchen, we discovered
he had joined her in drink: fifth of gin on the table, orbited by her

stolen dwarfish bottles; twin glistening hoops of sweat from glasses they had carried to his room. Although we couldn't hear them, we knew. She only went to his bed when he too drank, forced there by some threat behind his eyes. Having learned about Owen Crowhurst, I realized my mother's imperative; perhaps now, as I stood with Paul at the sink, she was tricking my father, further erasing suspicion, closing her eyes and forcing soft fraudulent sighs. I could smell my father's cheap cologne, dabbed to his neck for her, for this. I imagined his hands on her, cold as guns. And her hands too, the raw scratched skin, the knuckles pearling white as she clutched at the mattress, endure, endure, surrender.

Paul worked his palms over the pink cake of soap. Tomorrow he would leave with our father, off to the smaller towns, Halstead, Medicine Lodge, and the larger, Derby, Wellington, Coffeyville. Overnight, returning on Sunday for school the next morning. Along the way they would supply fruit stands, the merchants of each city, our antonyms: whites whole levels above our Trash; blacks nothing like the crazy Crowhursts; dads and sons who would steal snickers and winks as my father and brother drove away. I had traveled cross-state with my father before. Sometimes I rode with Paul, and sometimes, before Halloween, I cramped in the truck with both Paul and my mother, the trailer stocked with pumpkins, with cobwebbed fall-colored husks of Indian corn. On these special October trips, she costumed us, romanced our faces with rouges, paints, to surprise the town-by-town sellers. Past years, Paul and I transformed to long-haired apemen, Cracker Jack clowns, dime-store vampires or ghouls. But now, September, Halloween waited weeks away. I couldn't guess what it held. Between now and then: what secrets Paul could reveal, what risks my mother could let slip.

We stayed at the kitchen table until they emerged. My father fixed two new drinks; neither looked into our faces, yet both seemed acutely aware, the way they'd treat two dying boys. She had tissued the lipstick from her mouth. Its red smudged neither my father's cheeks nor chin, but a stain showed on the inner crease of his fingers as he poured his bourbon and her gin. His hand had kept her quiet.

"Pop for you two," he told us, stepping into the adjoining room. "Keeping it cold in the freezer." He shut the light and clicked the television's silver knob; the glass went between his knees as he eased into his chair.

So we would drink with them. Mine was regular cola but he had remembered Paul's favorite, grape, the dull-labeled generic brand, but still grape. We sat at the table, our backs to him, the television's nimbus teetering about the rooms. "Thank you," I said, because I knew I should. Quickly Paul gave thanks as well. My mother smiled and sat with us. Her sweatshirt, gray with dimmed penny-orange tiger, seemed too warm for the weather; when she exhaled, the kitchen air went flammable from her evening of drink.

Our flannels lay rain-stained and green in the pile of dirty laundry, waiting for my mother's patient scrubbing. As I thumbed the top of the can I sensed my father's anger still, his silence throwing its dense blanket across us. We should give more thank-yous, I thought; should show extra satisfaction for his mercy, these little unexpected gifts. Try harder, yes, I would. I tipped the can to my lips and swallowed, and then, equally quiet, Paul opened his. But the grape must have jostled, must have overturned or shaken in the freezer, and with the release of pressure came a firecracker hiss. Paul outthrust the can, far from his clothes, trying to shield its top with his hand: the pop came gushing free regardless, a fuss of violet fizz, sparkling the table, dripping foam to the kitchen floor.

Paul's eyes widened to our mother. When she drank, we could always easily gauge her; her face would flush, and we knew she felt strangely secure, lodged within some shifted city we wouldn't discover for several years, a place where the sounds slurred and the ceilings and walls went calm, wobbling and loosely drifting. A few drinks and my mother would relax, often pull us toward her, and her hugs felt good, warm, a warm like dipping gently into limitless summer water. Yet my father was opposite. His drunks, infrequent as they were, bore no resemblance to hers: Sullen, squinting at us, he stammered orders and stomped through rooms, a knifeblade, shimmery with violence. And so we felt this father rising for us. Felt the blade opening. The grape made pools at Paul's feet, and suddenly my father stood there, over the mess with him, triggered by my brother's clumsiness. "Just like a girl," he said. Only in his rage did the stuttering vanish, and he continued, flawlessly taunting. "Stupid. I buy you something, you spill it. Can't steer the tractor right, can't get the fence fixed, can't even open a goddamn can."

My mother straightened in her chair. "Now, Robert," she whispered.

"Keep shut," he told her. He reached for the can, not taking it, just waiting until Paul moved his arm to lift it fatherward. The sides were trickled with purple but my father squeezed it in his left grip, took Paul's arm with his right. "Little faggot," he said. "That's what we got here. A maggot and a faggot." From my place at the table I sensed the pride rising in my father's chest, the laughter at his own joke, his rhyme. "Maggot and Faggot, Faggot and Maggot."

"Stop," my mother said, threading the word between her clenched teeth. As the sound hit the air, his hand curled tighter around Paul's arm, and he looked at her, furious. She nodded. "Cease fire, right now."

He laughed then, not really a laugh but more a growl, the can held out before him like a beacon, its purple dribbling to the table. Within the achy motionless silence I couldn't guess what he would do. Maybe he had planned it all, had shaken the can before lodging it skewed in the freezer. Maybe he would leave now, walk outside as he'd done before, to stay away for hours. The quiet continued. He stared her down. Finally my mother opened her mouth, nodding again at his hand on Paul's skin. "I said stop it."

In a single white-blurred instant he flung his arm forward, the arm with the can, and turning to my mother I saw what he'd done: her face now damp with it, the pale bubbled grape, bubbling and dropping and lining parallel streams down her shirtfront. He pistoned his arm again, a second aim to douse her face with the rest, but even on its splash she made no sound. My father dropped the can. It knocked the table with a soft click and rolled, emptied, one weak arc toward my chair. As he left the room he mumbled, his gaze at his feet. "Teach you yet." He paused at the door; before it slammed, the rest of his words. "Like a goddamn corpse in bed and still takes their side."

Gone, gone; only his cologne left, the hum of him, only the print of a fingernail on Paul's arm, a slit I could have fit a dime through, now seeping a crescent of blood. Without warning the kitchen had become a cell; we were a trio of prisoners, trapped and taunted by the warden. I could hear the echoey racket of his billy club against the bars. Could feel the air shattering apart, the shatter of a window as the victim's body crashes through. There were shotguns in the house, there were pocketknives and pills and snake-coiled rope. And three of us, waiting to be ripped, turned inside out.

We began to clean the kitchen. No one spoke, not her, not him or me. And as we cleaned, I remembered a story I'd heard from Paul: When he was younger, just a little boy with me only a baby, there had been an accident in the orchard. Strong winds, fallen ladder, fire-power lightning bolt: Whatever the source, Paul didn't know, but an outsized peach-tree branch had broken and fallen on him. The branch was sturdy and thick and knobbed like knucklebone, and Paul lay pinned beneath it, helpless, his leg nearly fractured. He recalled the scratch of leaves against his face, the sand in his mouth as he writhed against the earth. He could not remember the pain or the blood. But he did know the smell of the rescuing father, the man's sudden miracle of arm as it hugged the branch, lifted, and bandied it to his side. He pressed his son close to his chest and patted his head, gently touched the wound and whispered OK, you're OK.

Paul had told this story many times, often late night when we stretched pre-slumber in our beds and murmured to each other, cautiously, face to flashlit face. Yet I couldn't imagine that man, saint and superhero who had saved my brother, the identical man as this. Maggot and Faggot. Surely some change had happened, some diminution or sorcery. The man in Paul's memory had carried the boy back, all dense orchard lanes and pasture scrub, to the house; the man had laid him warm in blankets, had taken the blue bandanna from his overall pocket and after a gentle rib-tickling tied it bandit-style around Paul's head. Had patted his forehead and soothed his voice into his ear. Sweetheart, the voice said. Not Stupid. Not

Faggot. Much, much later, after Paul had left home and I was older, I would think of this accident—the slender leg curved crooked in the sand, the wreck of peaches and leaves—and, missing Paul and wanting to know more, would request details from my mother. But she would only stare, her eyes deadwater-blank, the story unknown and missing from her mind. "I'm sorry, Matthew…nothing like that ever happened." Maybe Paul had resurrected the wrong man. Maybe he had stretched the truth. But it was how he wanted to picture our father, the rescuer, the intrepid, the strongman saying *sweetheart*. For years I went along with this hero, Paul's hero. For years I remembered him that way too.

The Term Paper Artist

David Leavitt

I.

I was in trouble. An English poet (now dead) had sued me over a novel I had written because it was based in part on an episode from his life. Worse, my publishers in the United States and England had capitulated to this poet, pulling the novel out of bookstores and pulping several thousand copies.

Why should I have been surprised? My publishers were once Salman Rushdie's publishers too.

I didn't live in Los Angeles then. Instead I was on an extended visit to my father. After his retirement a few years ago, he moved down from the Bay Area to Glendale because his wife, Jean, teaches at a university not far from there. They own a newish house, rambling and ceremonial, rather like a lecture hall. This house, which originally belonged to a movie producer, includes a "media room," the electronic controls of which are so complex that even after five years, neither one has figured them out; a lighting system more various and subtle than that of most Broadway theaters; a burglar alarm they can never quite explain to Guadalupe, the cleaning lady, who seems always to be tripping it accidentally. The trouble may be that the house was built in the mid '80s, when technology was already amazing but not yet simple. And because technology, like money, is measured by our needs—had she lived in our age, George Eliot might have said that most of this gadgetry, by the turn of the decade, was obsolete. These days machines, like clothes, seem to lose their value merely with the passing of seasons.

In any event, it was to my father, and his complicated house, that
I had come that fall. I had come because I couldn't write in my own
house and also because I was dating an actor: an actor who, as it happened, had gotten a part in a movie almost as soon as I'd arrived,
then flown off to spend six weeks in the Andes. And as I was inclined
neither to visit him in the Andes nor to return to New York, where
I had fallen into bad habits, I settled down into the life of my father's
guest room, which is a pleasant, lethargic one except in one detail:
Because New York wakes up three hours earlier than California,
when I got out of bed in the mornings, it was invariably to find faxes
of a not very pleasant nature lying outside the door to my room. And
this particular morning—the morning of the day I would meet
Eric—the fax that lay outside the door to my room was particularly
unpleasant. My American publisher, it told me, had decided to sus-
pend publication of the paperback edition of my novel; in spite of the
revisions I had made over the summer, in spite of the book already
having been announced in the catalog, "counsel" had decreed it still
too dangerous to print.

There was a bad smell in the room, mossy and rotten, as if the fax
itself gave off noxious vapors.

I mentioned nothing to my father except the smell. As a rule, I
was trying to learn to take blows better, or at least to take them
without letting them distort the natural progress of my days. So, as
usual I had my morning coffee at the local Starbucks. Then I drove
around for a while, listening to Dr. Delia, the radio shrink. Then I
tried out the computerized massage chair on display at the Sharper
Image in the Beverly Center, and then I stopped in at Book Soup on
Sunset to thumb through the latest issues of *The New Yorker, The
New York Review of Books,* and *The New York Times Book Review* as
well as whatever books happened to have landed that morning on
the "new arrivals" table. You see, it was terribly important to me in
those days to stay abreast of what my confrères in the writing trade
were up to. Competitiveness, not to mention a terror of losing the
stature I had gained in my early youth, played a much more singular
role in my life than I have heretofore admitted. Indeed, I suspect it

plays a more singular role in most writers' lives than they are willing to admit. And the level of success makes no difference. The young poet cringing to learn that his enemy has been awarded the Guggenheim for which he has been turned down is merely a miniature version of the hugely famous novelist cringing to learn that her university colleague has won the Nobel Prize for which she has shamelessly campaigned: We are speaking, here, of the emotions of vacancy, which scale neither enhances nor mitigates; for panic and emptiness (the words are Forster's) always feel like panic and emptiness, no matter the degree.

After Book Soup, I ate lunch alone at the Mandarette Café on Beverly, then drove over to the UCLA library to research the new novel I was working on, which concerned the aftermath of the Cleveland Street Affair. This was a scandal that took place in London in the years immediately preceding the Oscar Wilde trials. Essentially, in 1889 Her Majesty's police had stumbled upon a homosexual brothel at 19 Cleveland Street, the clients of which included Lord Arthur Somerset, a major in the Royal Horse Guards and equerry to the prince of Wales, whose stables he supervised. Telegraph boys—one of whom had the astounding name of Charles E. Thickbroom—provided the "entertainment" at this brothel as well as most of the evidence against Lord Somerset.

My idea was to merge his story with that of his brother, Lord *Henry* Somerset, who had fled England for Florence ten years earlier after his wife had caught him in flagrante delicto with a boy called Henry Smith. (Lady Somerset would later become a famous temperance advocate.) History has tended to confuse, even to fuse, the brothers, and I was following history's lead.

So there I sat, in a carrel in the stacks of the UCLA library, with an open legal pad and a pile of books in front of me, doing, if truth be told, very little. Partially this was because by nature I am not a researcher. I grow impatient with facts. And yet I cannot deny the more pressing reason for my indolence: It was fear. An aureole of worried expectancy seemed to surround the prospect of this next novel. I thought I could hear it in the voice of my agent, my editor, even my father. Would I ever be allowed to forget what had happened with *While England Sleeps?* I wondered. Or would the scandal that had attached itself to the novel's publication—to quote a helpful journalist—"taint my aura" forever? I couldn't yet say.

Thus my UCLA afternoon, like all my UCLA afternoons, proceeded. Instead of studying the "blackmailer's charter," which in England criminalized "acts of gross indecency between adult men in public or private," I got a Diet Coke from a vending machine. Instead of reading up on the Italian Penal Code of 1889, by virtue of which Italy became such a mecca for homosexual émigrés, I martyred myself to *Publishers Weekly*.

Instead of investigating Florence's amazingly casual attitude toward sodomy, I investigated whether anyone sexy was loitering in the photocopy area. Finally around 3, having devoted at best a paltry hour to the skimming of history books and the jotting down of notes, I left. Impending traffic on the 210 was my excuse. And yet somehow I managed, as always, to find time for a visit to the Circus of Books on Santa Monica Boulevard, where I wasted just enough minutes browsing at the porn magazines to ensure getting stuck in the same rush hour traffic I'd departed the library early to avoid. It was 6:30 by the time I pulled into my father's driveway.

Feeling rather cross, I got out of the car and went inside. Three people I didn't know were drinking iced tea in the living room. They looked at me. I looked at them. "Hello," we all said, and then Jean and my father—one bearing a platter of raw vegetables, the other a bowl of mushroom pâté—emerged through the swinging door from the kitchen. "Oh, hi, David!" Jean called cheerily, and introduced me.

The three people, all of whom stood, turned out to be Cynthia Steinberg, a sociology professor at Rutgers and a colleague from Jean's graduate school days; her husband, Jack; and their son Eric. Eric, I quickly learned, was an economics major at UCLA who hoped to attend Stanford Business School; and as my father has taught for several decades at that august institution, this little drinks party had been arranged so that Eric could ask questions, get advice, and perhaps (this is my conjecture; it was never stated) ingratiate my father into writing him a letter of recommendation.

Now, it has actually become quite a common occurrence for old friends of my father's and Jean's to bring their children over for academic advice. And probably because I was so used to the well-heeled, eager-eyed boys and girls I tended to encounter, all of them hell-bent on making an executive impression, Eric surprised me. For one thing, he had large, placid blue eyes with which, as I accepted Jean's proffered glass of tea, he stared at me: a stare that had no caution in it. Eric wasn't exactly handsome; his nose obtruded, and he had thick, stupid lips—the best for kissing. Still, imperfect features can fit together with a mysterious harmony that is altogether more alluring than beauty. And it was this somewhat cobbled-together aspect of his appearance that attracted me: his long legs in khaki pants, which he could not keep still; his brown loafers, above the scuffed edges of which, when he slung one leg over the other, a tanned and hairy ankle was exposed; his too-short tie and brown jacket; and the hair that fell into his eyes: Yes, I am back at his eyes; I always end up back at his eyes. For what took me off-guard, as I sat across from him (Jean was talking about GMATs), was their frankness. They were like the eyes of children who are too young to have learned that it is not nice to peer. And Eric did peer; at me, at my father, at the garden through the plate-glass windows. His mother asked all his questions for him. He only nodded occasionally, or muttered a monosyllable.

It took me ten minutes before I realized how stoned he was.

Eventually, talk of business schools dried up. "So are you living in L.A. now, David?" Eric's father asked.

"Just visiting," I said.

"David lives in New York," my father said brightly. "He's out here working on his new book."

"Oh, you're a writer?" This was Eric speaking—the first question he'd asked since I'd arrived.

"When I'm able to work," I said, "I call myself a writer."

"David's done very well for himself," Mrs. Steinberg informed Eric. "You know I wasn't going to say anything—I figure you must hear it all the time—but I really loved *Family Dancing*."

"Thanks. Actually, I don't hear it all the time."

"What do you write?" Eric asked.

"Novels, short stories," I said, and braced myself for the question that would inevitably follow: *What kind of novels? What kind of short stories?* But Eric only smiled. His teeth were very large.

"And you make a living at it?"

"Usually."

"What did you major in?"

"English."

"Great. Where'd you go to school?"

"Yale."

"Cool. My teacher—I'm taking this English lit class? My teacher went to Yale. Her name's Mary Yearwood. She's probably about your age."

"I don't know her."

"She's an expert on Henry James. Did you go to grad school?"

"No. I pretty much started publishing out of college."

"I'd really like to read some of your books. Maybe you could tell me the titles."

"Well, we'd better be going," Mrs. Steinberg said, rising very suddenly from the sofa. "We've kept you folks long enough."

"No, no." My father did not sound very convincing, however, and soon the Steinbergs were moving toward the door, where farewells were exchanged. Meanwhile I hurried into the kitchen and wrote the titles of my books on a memo pad advertising Librax.

"Thanks," Eric said, as I handed him the list. "I'll definitely pick one up." And he held out his hand.

We shook. His handshake was—everything about Eric was—long, loose, generous.

They left.

"A nice kid," my father said.

"Very nice," Jean agreed. "Still, Cynthia's worried. Apparently he's a whiz with computers—but not exactly verbal."

"C's in English won't get him into Stanford," my father said. (We had all strolled into the kitchen.)

"What does English matter if you want to go to business school?"
I asked.

"It didn't use to. But then there were always too many techni-
cians, and so what we're looking for now are all-around students
with a good background in the humanities. You, for instance, my
boy"—he put a hand on my shoulder—"would probably have had an
easier time getting into Stanford than Eric Steinberg will."

"But I didn't want to."

"I still wish you'd applied. You could have been the first student
in the school's history to get a simultaneous MFA and MBA—"

"Yes, I know, Dad."

Jean went up to her study while my father took some yellow beets
from the freezer and put them in a microwavable dish.

"By the way, do you still have that stink in your room?" he asked.

"Yes," I said. "It's the strangest thing. I started noticing it after
the tremor."

"Tremor! What tremor?" He walked over to the intercom. "Jean,
did you feel a tremor?" he shouted.

"No, I didn't!" she shouted back. For some reason they always
yelled at each other through the intercom, as if they didn't quite
trust it to carry their voices.

After that I changed my routine. Instead of wasting my mornings
on the road, I went directly from Starbucks to the library, and stayed
there until lunch.

I wish I could say I got a little more work done over the course of
those days than I might have otherwise, but I didn't. Instead I spent
most of my time looking up various literary acquaintances in the
periodicals index to see how much more work they had published in
the previous year than I had; or chasing down those bad reviews of
While England Sleeps that my publisher had had the good sense not
to forward to me (the worst of these, in *Partisan Review,* was by one
Pearl K. Bell, whose son had been my classmate); or reading and
rereading the terrible press I'd gotten during the lawsuit. Also, I
looked every day to see if anyone (Eric?) might have checked out any

of my books. (No one had; I took the occasion to autograph them.) After which I'd lunch, drive around, and end up more often than not (no, I am lying: every day) at the Circus of Books.

Coming home one evening, I walked through my father's door only to hear Jean shouting through the intercom that I had a phone call.

"It's Eric," Eric said when I picked up. Not "Eric Steinberg," just "Eric"—as if he took it for granted that I'd remember him.

"Eric, how're you doing?"

"All right, yourself?"

"Great."

"Cool.

There was a silence. Naturally I presumed that since Eric had called me, he would also shoulder the responsibility for keeping the conversation going. He didn't.

It soon became apparent that if I didn't say something, no one would.

"So what are you up to?"

"Oh, you know, the usual. Studying. Partying." Another silence. "So I bought one of your books."

"Really. Which one?"

"*The Secret Language of the Cranes.*"

"Oh, right."

"Yeah."

Long pause.

"And did you like it?"

"Yeah, I thought it was pretty cool. I mean, to write all that! It takes me an hour to write a sentence."

"It's just a matter of practice," I said. "Like sports. Are you an athlete?"

"Not really."

"I was just asking because you looked to be in pretty good shape."

"I swim three times a week."

"At UCLA?"

"Uh-huh."

"Is there a good pool?"

"Pretty good. Olympic size." More silence.

"Well, I appreciate your calling, Eric," I said. "And buying the book. Most people who say they're going to never bother."

"That's OK. I don't read much generally, but I thought your book was pretty interesting. I mean, it showed me a lot of things I didn't know, not being gay myself."

"I'm glad to hear you say that," I said in one breath, "because sometimes I think gay writers only write for a gay audience, which is a mistake. The point is, human experience is universal, and there's no reason why straight people can't get as much out of a gay novel as gay people get out of a straight novel, don't you think?" (I grimaced: I sounded as if I were giving an interview.)

"Yeah" was Eric's reply.

A fifth, nearly unbearable silence.

"Well, it's been great talking to you, Eric."

"My pleasure."

"OK, so long."

"Later."

And he hung up with amazing swiftness.

The next morning I was at the library when it opened.

I stayed all day. Did you know that Lord Henry Somerset's father, the Duke of Beaufort, invented the game of badminton, which was named for his estate? Well, he did. Also, Osbert Sitwell once wrote a poem about Lord Henry, in which he lampooned the notorious expatriate as "Lord Richard Vermont," whom "some nebulous but familiar scandal I Had lightly blown... over the Channel, I Which he never crossed again."

Thus at the age of twenty-seven
A promising career was over,
And the thirty or forty years that had elapsed
Had been spent in killing time
—or so Lord Richard thought,
Though in reality, *killing time*

Is only the name for another of the multifarious ways
By which Time kills us.

When I got home that evening, there was a message in my room that Eric had called.

"Hey," I said, calling him back, calmer now, as well as more curious.

"Hey," Eric said.

Apparently it was not his conversational style to phone for any particular reason.

"So what's up?"

"Not much, man. Just kicking back"

"Sounds good. You live in a dorm?"

"No, I'm off campus."

"Oh, cool." (Lying down, I shoved a pillow behind my head, as I imagined Eric had.) "And do you live alone?"

"I share a house with two other guys, but I've got my own room." He yawned.

"And are your roommates home?"

"Nope. They're at the library."

"Studying?"

"You got it."

"And don't you have studying to do?"

"Yeah, but I bagged it around 7. Actually, I was feeling kind of bored, so I started reading another one of your books."

"Oh, really? Which one?" (How I longed to ask what he was wearing!)

"*Family Dancing*. And you know what's weird? It really reminds me of my family—especially the one called 'Danny in Transit.' I'm from New Jersey," he added.

"Wow," I said. *Family Dancing* was the last thing I wanted to talk about it. "So what do you do with your spare time, Eric? Besides swim three days a week."

"You've got a good memory, Dave."

"Thanks. It goes with the territory."

"Like that story of yours! So let's see, what do I do with my spare time." (I heard him thinking.) "You mean besides jack off?"

"Well—"

Eric laughed. "Let's see. Well, I like to party sometimes—"

"I'm sorry to interrupt, but I have to ask—when you say party, do you mean literally party, or get high?"

"Can be both, can be both."

"You were stoned at my father's house the other day, weren't you?"

"Shit! How'd you know?"

"I could just tell."

"Do you get high?"

"Sometimes."

"Man, I am so into pot! Ever since I was thirteen. Listen, do you want to come over and get stoned?"

I sat up. "Sure," I said.

"Cool."

Long pause.

"Wait—you mean tonight?"

"Yeah, why not?"

"No problem, tonight's fine. I just don't want to keep you from your studying."

"I told you, I bagged it."

"OK. Where do you live?"

"Santa Monica. Have you got a pencil?"

I wrote down the directions.

Through the intercom, I told Jean I was going out to a movie with my friend Gary, after which I got into the car and headed for the freeway. The rush hour traffic had eased, which meant it took me only half an hour to arrive at the address Eric had given me, a dilapidated clapboard house. In the dark I couldn't make out the color.

From the salty flavor of the air, I could tell that the sea wasn't far off.

Dogs barked as I got out of my father's car and opened the peeling picket gate, over which unpruned hydrangea bushes crowded. The planks of the verandah creaked as I stepped across them. In the windows, a pale orange light quavered.

I knocked. Somewhere in the distance Tracy Chapman was singing "Fast Car."

"Hey, sexy," Eric said, pulling open the screen door.

I blinked. He was wearing sweatpants and a Rutgers crew T-shirt.

"Glad you could make it." He held the door open.

"My pleasure," I said.

I stepped inside. The living room, with its orange carpet and beaten-up, homely furniture, reminded me of my own student days, when I'd shopped at the Salvation Army or dragged armchairs in from the street.

"Nice place," I said.

"It's home," Eric said. "I mean, it's not like your dad's house. Now *that's* what I call a house. Say, you want a beer?"

"Sure." I wasn't about to tell him I hated beer.

He brought two Coronas from the kitchen, one of which he handed me.

"*L'chaim,*" he toasted.

"Cheers," I said.

Then Eric leapt up the staircase, and since he gave no indication whether or not I was supposed to follow him, I followed him. He took the stairs three at a time.

At the top, four doors opened off a narrow corridor. Only one was ajar.

"Step into my office," he said, passing through. "And close the door behind you."

I did. The room was shadowy. An architect's lamp with a long, folding arm illuminated a double mattress on the floor, the blue sheets clumped at the bottom. Against the far wall, under a window, stood a desk piled with textbooks. Clean white socks were heaped on a chair, beneath which lounged a pair of crumpled Jockey shorts.

In the space where a side table might have been, a copy of *Family Dancing* lay splayed over the Vintage edition of *A Room With a View.*

"Have a seat," Eric said. Then he threw himself onto the mattress, where, cross-legged, he busied himself with a plastic bag of pot and some rolling papers.

"You can move all that," he added, indicating the chair.

Gingerly I put the socks onto the desk, nudged the shorts with my left foot, and sat down.

Unspeaking, with fastidious concentration, Eric rolled the joint. Much about his room, from the guitar to the recharging laptop to the blue-lit CD player (the source of Tracy Chapman's voice), seemed to me typical UCLA. And yet there were incongruous touches. For one thing, the posters did not depict acid rock musicians or figures from the world of sports. Instead Eric had thumb-tacked the Sistine Chapel ceiling onto his ceiling. Over his bed hung the *Last Judgment*. Caspar David Friedrich's *Wanderer in a Sea of Mist* stared into the back of the door.

"Have you spent much time in Europe?" I hazarded.

"Yeah, last summer. I went to Italy, France, Amsterdam."

"You must have liked Amsterdam."

"I basically don't remember Amsterdam."

I laughed. "And Italy?"

"Man! Rome was amazing! Rome really blew me away!" Licking the joint, he sealed it, then picked up a lighter from the floor.

"The last time I went to Florence I tried to find the hotel where Forster stayed," I said. "I only mention it because I see you're reading *A Room With a View*."

Eric lit the joint. "Come on down here," he said, slapping the other side of the bed like someone's behind.

"I'd better take off my shoes."

"Yeah, Dave, I'd have to agree that would be a good idea."

He was mocking me, but agreeably, and, flushing, I did what I was told. Down among the sheets the world smelled both fruity and smoky.

Eric toked, passed me the joint. Lying back, he stretched his arms over his head.

"Two weeks in a Virginia jail," Tracy Chapman sang, "*for my lover, for my lover.*" And on the next line, Eric joined in: "*Twenty-thousand-dollar bail, for my lover, for my lover…*"

"You've got a nice voice," I said when he'd finished the song.

"Thanks."

"Me, I'm tone-deaf. I get it from my dad."

"Your dad seems like a decent guy."

"He is. I liked your parents too. Have they left yet, by the way?"

"Finally." He breathed out bitter fumes. "I mean, my parents, they're nice and all, but after a few days—you know what I mean?"

"Sure."

Propping myself on one elbow, I looked at him. His eyes were getting red. In silence, I watched the way his swollen lips seemed to narrow around the joint, like some strange species of fish; the way his stomach distended and relaxed, distended and relaxed; the meshing of his lashes, when he closed his eyes.

"This is good pot," I said after a while.

Eric had his feet crossed at the ankles. From beneath his T-shirt's hem, the drawstring of his sweatpants peeked out like a little noose.

I forget what we talked about next. Maybe Michelangelo. Conversation blurred and became inchoate, and only sharpened again when Eric looked at me and said, "So do you want to give me a blow job?"

I opened my eyes as wide as my stoned state permitted. "A blow job?"

"Yeah. Like in your book. You know, when Eliot's sitting at his desk and Philip sucks him off."

"Oh, you remember that scene."

"Yeah."

"And what makes you think I'd want to give you a blow job?"

"Well, the way I see it, you're gay and I'm sexy. So why not?"

"But you have to want it too. Do you?"

"Sure."

"How much? A lot?"

"Enough."

"Are you hard now?"

"Yeah, I guess."

"You guess?"

I reached over and grabbed his crotch. "Yeah, I guess so too."

"Well, go ahead." Eric crossed his arms behind his head.

Untying the little noose of the drawstring, I pulled back his sweat-pants and underwear. Like his handshake, his cock was long and silky. It rested upon a pile of lustrous black pubic hair rather like a sausage on top of a plate of black beans: I apologize for this odd culinary metaphor, but it was what entered my mind at the time. And Eric was laughing.

"What's so funny?"

"Nothing, it's just that... you're really gay, aren't you?"

"Is that a surprise?"

"No, no. I'm just...I mean, you're really into my dick, aren't you? This is so wild!"

"What's wild about it?"

"Because it's like, here you are, really into my dick, whereas probably if you saw, you know, a vagina or something, you'd be sort of disgusted, or not interested. But if you showed me your dick, I'd be like, I could care less."

"You want me to show you my dick?"

"Not really."

"You want me to give you a really great blow job, Eric?"

"Actually, I had something else in mind."

All at once he leapt off the mattress. I sat up. Putting his cock away, he started rummaging through the mess on his desk.

"Here it is," he said after a minute, and threw a copy of *Daisy Miller* at me.

"*Daisy Miller*?"

"Have you read it?"

"Of course.

"I have to do this paper on it. It's due next Tuesday." He read aloud from a photocopy on the desk: "Compare and contrast Lucy's and Daisy's responses to Italy in Forster's *A Room With a View* and James's *Daisy Miller*. This is for Professor Yearwood," he added.

"Uh-huh."

"And I've really got to ace this paper because I got a C on the midterm. It wasn't that I didn't do the reading. I'm not one of those guys who just reads the *Cliffs Notes* or anything. The problem was the essay questions. What can I tell you, Dave? I've got great ideas, but I can't write to save my ass."

He lay down on the mattress again and started flipping through *Daisy Miller.* "So last year my friend bought a paper from this company, Intellectual Properties Inc. They sell papers for $79.95, and they've got, like, thousands on file. And my friend bought one and got caught. He ended up being expelled." Eric rubbed his nose; "I can't risk that. Still, I need to ace the paper. That's where you come in."

"Where I come in?"

"Exactly. You can write my paper for me. And if I get a good grade, you can give me a blow job." He winked.

"Wait a minute," I said.

Eric reached for, and switched on, his laptop. "Actually I've already started taking notes. Maybe you can use them."

"Hold on! Stop."

He stopped.

"You don't honestly think I'm going to write your paper for you, do you?"

"Why not?"

"Well, I mean, Eric, I'm a famous writer. I have a novel under contract with Viking Penguin. You know, Viking Penguin, that gigantic publisher, the same one that published *Daisy Miller*? And they're paying me a lot of money—a *lot* of money—to write this novel. On top of which, what you're proposing, it's unethical. It goes against everything I believe in."

"Yeah, if I were asking you to make up the ideas! But I'm not. You can use my ideas. I'm just asking you to put the sentences together." He stubbed out the joint. "Shit, you're a really great writer, Dave. I'll bet you never got less than an A on a paper in your life, did you? Did you?"

"No."

"Exactly." He brushed an eyelash off my cheek. "So the way I see it is this. I've got something you want. You've got something I need. We make a deal. I mean, your dad teaches at Stanford Business

School. Hasn't he taught you anything? Now here are my notes."

He thrust the laptop at me. Words congealed on the gray screen. I read.

"Well?" Eric said after a few minutes.

"First of all, you're wrong about Daisy. She's not nearly so knowing as you make out."

"How so?"

"It's the whole point. She's actually very innocent, maybe the most innocent character in the story."

"Yeah, according to Winterbourne. I don't buy it. I've known girls like that, they only act innocent when the shit hits the fan. Otherwise—"

"But that's a very narrow definition of innocence. Innocence can also mean unawareness that what other people think matters."

"I see your point."

"Oh, and I like what you say about George being part of the Italian landscape. That's very astute."

"Really? See, I was thinking about that scene with the violets— how he's, like, one with the violets."

"Which book did you enjoy more?"

"*A Room With a View*, definitely."

"Me too. I don't—what I should say is, I'll always admire James. But I'll never love him. He's too—I don't know. Fussy. Also, he never gets under Italy's skin, which is odd, because Forster does, and he spent so much less time there."

"The paper's supposed to be ten to fifteen pages," Eric said. "I need it Tuesday A.M."

"I haven't said yes."

"Are you saying no?"

"I'm saying I have to think about it."

"Well, think fast, because Professor Yearwood deducts half a grade for every day a paper's overdue. She's a ballbreaker."

"And what'll you do if I do say no?"

"You won't say no, Dave. I know you won't because I'm your friend, and you're not the kind of guy who lets down a friend in need."

It seemed natural, at this point, to get up off the bed and head downstairs, where Eric put a paternal arm around my shoulder. "Dave," he said. "Dave, Dave, Dave. Dave, Dave, Dave, Dave, Dave."

"By the way," I said, "you do realize that both Forster and James were gay?"

"No shit. Still, it makes sense. The way they seem to understand the girls' point of view and all." He opened the creaking screen door. "So when do I hear from you?"

"Tomorrow." I stepped out onto the verandah.

"It'll have to be tomorrow," Eric said, "because if you don't write this paper for me, I've got to figure out some alternative plan. And if you do—" Pulling down his sweatpants, he flashed his cock, which was hard again—if it had ever gotten soft.

"How old are you, by the way?"

"Twenty last month. Why?"

"Just wondering."

He reached out a hand, but instead I shook his cock. "Whoa, no way!" Eric said, laughing as he backed off. "For that you have to wait till Tuesday."

"Only kidding," I said.

"Later," Eric said, closing the door, after which I headed back out into the salty night.

"Society garlic," Jean said the next morning.

"What?"

"That smell in your bedroom. It was the flowers. They're called society garlic because they're pretty but they stink. And Guadalupe picked them and put them in your bedroom. You remember she took that ikebana course?" Jean sighed loudly. "Anyway, we're airing the room out now."

"Guadalupe didn't realize it at the time," my father said. "She just thought they were normal flowers."

Jean poured some cold tea into a mug and put it in the microwave. In the wake of last night's adventures, I'd completely forgotten about the odor in my bedroom, which had apparently troubled my father to a considerable degree. "Yesterday while you were at the library I must have spent an hour and a half going through your room," he said. "Top to bottom, and I still couldn't figure out where the smell was coming from. Toward the end I was worried something had crawled into the wall and died."

"What movie did you see last night?" Jean asked.

"Oh, we didn't end up going to a movie. We just had coffee."

"Gary's a nice fellow."

"I forgot to tell you," my father said. "That other friend of yours phoned last night. Andy, is that his name? And he says he's in the Andes." He laughed.

"I know. He's making a movie."

"He left a number. I'm not sure what the time difference is, but I can check."

"Don't worry. I can't call him back now anyway. I've got to get to the library."

"You certainly seem to be working hard these days," Jean said. Then she took her cup of tea up to her study. My father started the *Times* crossword puzzle. "Younger son of a Spanish monarch," he read aloud. "Seven letters."

"Infante," I said. Needless to say, it worried me to imagine him searching my room top to bottom: Had he discovered the stash of pornography in the dresser drawer?

After that I left for the library. You will notice that in my account of these weeks I have not made a single reference to the act of writing, even though it is the ostensible source of my income and reputation. Well, the sad truth was, for close to a year, my entire literary output had consisted of one book review and two pages of a short story (abandoned). Research was my excuse, yet I wasn't really interested in my research either, and so when I got to the library that morning I bypassed the 1890s altogether, opting instead for a battered copy of Furbank's biography of Forster. According to Furbank, Forster met James only once, when he was in his late twenties. The master, "rather fat but fine, and effectively bald," confused him with G.E. Moore, while "the beautiful Mrs. von Glehn" served tea. Yet even as Forster felt "all that the ordinary healthy man feels in the presence of a lord," James moved him less than the young laborer he encountered on the way home from Lamb House, smoking and leaning against a wall. Of this laborer, he wrote in a poem,

No youthful flesh weighs down your youth.
You are eternal, infinite,
You are the unknown, and the truth.

And he also wrote,

For those within the room, high talk,
Subtle experience—for me
That spark, that darkness, on the walk.

Poor Forster! I thought. He'd never had an easy time of it; had passed his most virile years staring at handsome youths from a needful distance while his mother dragged him in the opposite direction. Rooms "where culture unto culture knelt" beckoned him, but something else beckoned him as well, and the call of that something— "that spark, that darkness, on the walk"—he hadn't been able to answer until late in his life. No, I decided, he wouldn't have warmed much to James, that conscientious objector in the wars of sexuality, exempted from battle by virtue of his "obscure hurt." (How coy, how typically Jamesian, that phrase!) Whereas Forster, dear Forster, was in his own way the frankest of men. Midway through his life, in a New Year's assessment, he wrote, "The anus is clotted with hairs, and there is a great loss of sexual power—it was very violent 1920–22." He gathered signatures in support of Radclyffe Hall when *The Well of Loneliness* was banned, while James distanced himself from Oscar Wilde during his trials, fearful lest the association should taint. And this seems natural: Fear, in the Jamesian Universe, seems natural. Whereas Forster would have betrayed his country before he betrayed his friend.

I closed the Furbank. I was trying to remember the last time a boy had inspired me to write a poem. Ages, I realized; a decade. And now, out of the blue, here was Eric, neither beautiful nor wise, physically indifferent to me, yet capable of a crude, affectionate sincerity that cut straight through reason to strum the very fibers of my poetry-making aeolian heart. *Oh, Eric!* I wanted to sing. *Last night I was happy. I'd forgotten what it was like to be happy. Because for years, it has just been anxiety and antidotes to anxiety, numbing consolations that look like happiness but exist only to bandage, to assuage; whereas happiness is never merely a bandage; happiness is newborn every time, impulsive and fledgling every time. Happiness, yes! As if a shoot, newly uncurled, were moving in growth toward the light of your pale eyes!*

I got up from where I was sitting. I walked to the nearest pay phone and called him.

"Hello?" he said groggily.

"Did I wake you?"

"No problem." A loud yawn. "What time is it anyway? Shit, 11." A sound of nose-blowing. "So what's the word, Dave?"

"I've decided to do it."

"Great."

"You need the paper Tuesday, right? Well, what say I come by your place Monday night?"

"Not here. My roommate's sister's visiting."

"OK. Then how about we meet somewhere else?"

"As long as it's off campus."

I suggested the Ivy, a gay coffee bar in West Hollywood that Eric had never heard of, and he agreed.

"Till Monday, then."

"Later."

He hung up.

I went back to my carrel. I gathered up all the 1890s research books I'd kept on hold and dumped them in the return bin. (They fell to the bottom with a gratifying thunk.) Then I went into the literature stacks and pulled out some appealingly threadbare editions of *A Room With a View* and *Daisy Miller,* which I spent the afternoon rereading. Believe me or not as you choose: Only four times did I get up: once for a candy bar, once for lunch, twice to go to the bathroom. And what a surprise! These books, which I hadn't looked at for years, steadied and deepened the happiness Eric had flamed in me. It had been too long, I realized, since I'd read a novel that wasn't by one of my contemporaries, a novel that smelled old. Now, sitting in that library near a window through which the fall sun occasionally winked, a naive pleasure in reading reawoke in me. I smiled when Miss Bartlett was unequal to the bath. I smiled when the Reverend Beebe threw off his clothes and dived into the sacred lake. And when Randolph Miller said, "You bet," and the knowing Winterbourne "reflected on that depth of Italian subtlety, so strangely opposed to Anglo-Saxon simplicity, which enables people to show a smoother surface in proportion as they're more acutely displeased." That was good. That was James at his best. *Oh, literature, literature!—I was singing again—it was toward your pantheon that fifteen years ago, for the first time, I inclined my reading eyes: Not the world of lawsuits and paperback floors, the buzz and the boom and the bomb; no, it was this joy I craved, potent as the fruity perfume of a twenty-year-old boy's unwashed sheets.*

That afternoon—again, you can believe me or not, as you choose—I read until dinnertime.

"Dad, are you using your computer?" I asked when I got home.

"Not tonight."

"Mind if I do?"

From his crossword puzzle he looked up at me, a bit surprised if truth be told, for it had been many weeks since I'd made such a request.

"Help yourself," he said. "There should be paper in the printer."

"Thanks." And going into his study, I switched on the machine, so that within a few seconds that all too familiar simulacrum of the blank page was confronting me.

Very swiftly—blankness can be frightening—I typed:

"That Spark, That Darkness on the Walk":
Responses to Italy in *Daisy Miller* and *A Room With a View*
by Eric Steinberg

After which I leaned back and looked admiringly at my title.
Good, I thought, now to begin writing. And did.

I dressed up for my meeting with Eric at the Ivy that Monday.
First I got a haircut; then I bathed and shaved; then I put on a new
beige vest I'd bought at Banana Republic, a white Calvin Klein shirt,
and fresh jeans. And at the risk of sounding immodest, I must say
that the effect worked: I looked good, waiting for him in that little
oasis of homosexual civility with my cappuccino and my copy of
Where Angels Fear to Tread. Except that it hardly mattered. Eric
arrived late and only stayed five minutes. His eyes were glazed, his
hair unwashed, his green down vest gave off a muddy smell, as if it
had been left out in the rain.

"Man, I feel like shit" was his greeting as he sat down.

"What's the matter?"

"I haven't slept in three nights. I've got this huge econ project
due Wednesday. Airline deregulation."

"You want some coffee?"

"I have had so much coffee in the last twenty-four hours!" He
rubbed his eyes.

We were silent for a few seconds. Waiting, I'd been curious to
know what he'd make of the Ivy, the clientele of which consisted
pretty exclusively of West Hollywood homos. Now I saw that he
wasn't awake enough to notice.

"So do you have it?" he asked presently.

"Yeah, I have it." Reaching into my briefcase, I handed him the
paper. "Seventeen pages, footnoted and typed in perfect accordance
with MLA style rules."

Eric thumbed through the sheets. "Great," he said, scanning.
"Yeah, this is just the sort of shit Professor Yearwood'll eat up."

Stuffing the paper into his backpack, he stood.

"Well, thanks, Dave. Gotta run."

"Already?"

"Like I said, I've got this econ project due."

"But I thought…"

My voice trailed off into silence.

"Oh, that," Eric said, smiling. "*After* I get my grade. I mean, what if she gives me a D?" He winked. "Oh, and *after* I'm done with fucking airline deregulation. Well, later."

He was gone.

Rather despondently, I finished my cappuccino.

Well, you've learned your lesson, a voice inside me said. Ripped off again. And not only that, you can never tell anyone. It would be too embarrassing.

I know, I know.

Alas, it was not the first time this voice had given me such a lecture.

I drove home. My father and Jean were out. Locking myself in the guest room, I took off my Banana Republic vest, my Calvin Klein shirt, my no longer fresh jeans. Then I got into bed and called the phone sex line, a particularly desperate form of consolation, to which I had not resorted for several weeks. And as is usual in that eyeless world (Andy calls it "Gaza"), various men were putting each other through panting, frenetic paces on which I couldn't concentrate; no, I couldn't concentrate on "the bunkhouse" by which one caller was obsessed, or the massage scenario another seemed intent on reenacting. Finally, feeling heartbroken and a little peevish, I hung up on Jim from Silver Lake in the middle of his orgasm, after which I lay in bed with the lights on, staring at the vase from which the society garlic had been emptied; the phone, smug on its perch, coy as a cat, not ringing; of course it wasn't ringing. For Eric had his paper, and so there was no reason he would call me tonight or tomorrow night or ever. Nor would I chase him down. Like Mary Haines in *The Women*, I had my pride. He'd get his A. And probably it was better that way, since after all, the terms of the arrangement were that he would let me suck him off once, and if I sucked him off once, I'd probably want to suck him off twice; and then I'd want him to do it to me, which he wouldn't. Falling in love with straight boys—it's the tiredest of homosexual clichés; in addition to which Los Angeles circa 1994 was a far cry from Florence circa 1894, from that quaint Italian world to which Lord Henry Somerset had decamped after his divorce, that world in which almost any boy that caught your eye could be had, joyously, for a few *lire*, and without fear of blackmail or arrest. And though they would eventually marry and father children, those boys, at least they had that quaint old Italian openness to pleasure. I'd thought Eric had it too. But now I saw that more likely, he viewed his body as something to be transacted. He knew what a paper was worth—and he knew what he was worth; what his freshness and frankness were worth, when compared with some limp piece of faggot cock from the Circus of Books; some tired-out, overworked piece of dick; the bitter flavor of latex. (Do I cause offense? I won't apologize; it was what I felt.)

And in the morning, I did not go to the library at all. Made not even the slightest pretense of behaving like a writer. Instead I spent the whole day wandering the city. (The low business in which I got myself involved need not be catalogued here.)

Likewise the next day. And the next.

Then Eric called me.

At first, glancing at the Librax pad, I didn't quite believe it.

I thought perhaps it was another Eric—except that I recognized his number.

"Dave, my man!" he said when I phoned him back "You have got the Midas touch!"

"What?"

"An A, man! A fucking A! And an A- on my econ project!" I heard him inhale.

"That's great, Eric. Congratulations."

"Thanks. So now that you've done your part, I'm ready to do mine."

"Oh?"

"What, you're surprised?"

"Well—"

"Dave, I'm disappointed in you! I mean, do you really think I'm the kind of guy who'd let you write his paper and then just, you know, blow you off?"

"No, of course not—"

"On the contrary. You're the one who's going to do the blowing. You just tell me when, man."

I blushed. "Well, tonight would be OK."

"Both roommates away for the weekend. Plus I've got some great pot...I bought it to celebrate."

"Fantastic. So—I'll come over."

"Cool. See you in a few." He hung up.

Feeling a little shaky, I took a shower and changed my clothes. By now the beige vest from Banana Republic had gotten stretched out, and the Calvin Klein shirt had a ketchup stain on it. Still, I put them on.

"Hey, Dave," he said at his door half an hour later. And patted me on the shoulder. Eric was drinking a Corona; had put *Sgt. Pepper's Lonely Hearts Club Band* on the stereo.

"Hey, Eric. You're certainly looking good." By which I meant he looked awake. He'd washed his hair, put on fresh clothes. On top of which he smelled soapy and young in that way that no cologne can replicate.

"I feel good," Eric said. "Last night I slept fourteen hours. Before that, I hadn't slept in a week" He motioned me upstairs. "And you? What have you been up to? Hard at work on another best-seller?"

"Oh, in a manner of speaking."

We went into his room, where he shuffled through the pile of papers on his desk. "Here it is," he said after a few seconds. "I thought you'd want to see this." And he handed me my paper.

On the back, in a very refined script, Mary Yearwood had written the following:

Eric: I must confess that as I finish reading your paper, I find myself at something of a loss for words. It is really first-rate writing. Your analysis of both texts is graceful and subtle, in addition to which—and this is probably what impresses me most—you incorporate biographical and historical evidence into your argument in a manner that enriches the reader's understanding of the novels (in my view, *Daisy Miller* must be looked upon as a novel) without ever seeming to intrude on their integrity as works of art. Also, your handling of the (homo)sexual underpinnings in both the James and Forster *oeuvres* is extremely deft, never polemical. And that extraordinary early poem of Forster's! Wherever did you find it? I applaud your research skills as well as your sensitivity to literary nuance.

Looking back at your midterm, I have trouble believing the same student wrote this paper. Never in my career have I seen such a growth spurt. Clearly the tension of the exam room strangles your creativity (as it did mine). Therefore I have decided to exempt you from the final. The paper, thought out quietly in privacy, is the form for you, and so I shall assess your future performance purely on that basis.

Last but not least, if you're not averse, I'd like to nominate this paper for several departmental prizes. And if you have a chance, why don't you stop by my office hours next week? Have you thought of graduate school? I'd like to discuss the possibility with you.

Grade: A

I put the paper down.

"So?" Eric said.

"I guess she liked it," I said.

"Liked it! She went ape shit." Kicking off his shoes, he sat down on the bed and started working on a joint. "You know, when I first read that part about the midterm, I choked. I thought, Shit, she'll say it's too good, someone else must have done it. But she didn't. She bought it!"

"I tried hard to make it sound, you know, like something a very smart college junior might write. I mean, as opposed to something Elizabeth Hardwick or Susan Sontag might write."

"And now I don't even have to take the final!" He laughed almost brutally. "Stanford Biz School, here I come! You really slung it, Dave."

"Well," I said.

My pulse quickened.

Very casually he put down the joint, unbuttoned and took off his shirt. Then his T-shirt.

He lay back. What a friend of mine called a "crab ladder" of hairs crawled from his belt up over his navel to disappear between small, brown nipples.

He lit the joint, took a puff.

"Dave Leavitt, come on down," he said. "You're the next contestant on the new *Price Is Right*."

He started taking off his socks.

"Let me do that for you," I said.

And did. I licked his feet.

Above me, I heard him exhale. Reaching up, I felt his warm stomach rise and fall.

"Eric," I said.

"What?"

"I want to ask you something. I know it wasn't part of the bargain. Even so—"

"You can't fuck me," he said.

"No, not that. What I'd like to do—I'd like to kiss you."

"Kiss me!" He laughed. "OK, sure. As your bonus for getting me out of the final."

I pulled myself up to shadow his face with my own; licked the acrid flavor of the pot from his tongue; sucked his soft, thick lips.

"You're a good kisser," I said after a few minutes.

"So they tell me."

"Who, girls?"

"Yeah."

"And how do I kiss, compared to girls?"

"Not bad, I guess."

"Afterward, you'll have to tell me if I do something else better than girls do."

"To tell the truth, I'm kind of curious to find out myself," Eric said.

Then for about half an hour, though he made other noises, he didn't speak a word.

II.

Things started looking up. My editor moved from Viking Penguin to Houghton Mifflin, which decided to bring out the paperback of *While England Sleeps* as well as my new novel. "So it's a done deal," my agent said on the phone. "Oh, and by the way, I'm putting down a March of '96 delivery. Is that feasible?"

"Sure," I said. "Why not? I'm working harder than I have in years." Which was true. The quarter was drawing to a close, and I had two term papers to finish: "Mirror Imagery in Virginia Woolf" for Mary Yearwood, plus "Changing Attitudes toward Sex and Sexuality in 1890s England" for European History. Also, the day before, I'd come home from the library only to get a message that someone named Hunter had called. Needless to say, I'm not of the generation that knows many people named Hunter. Still, I called back. Hunter told me he was a sophomore, a buddy of one of Eric's roommates. Could I meet him for lunch at the Fatburger on Santa Monica? he wanted to know. He had a business proposition to discuss.

Of course I went. Hunter turned out to be one of those muscular blond California boys who drive Jeeps and really do call every male person they know except maybe their fathers "dude."

"I'm a friend of Eric's," he began.

"Oh?"

He nodded. "And we were partying the other night, and I was telling him I was up shit creek with my World War II history paper, so he goes, 'Why don't you call up this dude I know, Dave Leavitt?' "

"He did."

"That's right. He said, well, that you could help me out. I mean, how am I supposed to finish this history paper, *and* my comp sci project *and* my poli sci project, in addition to which I've got this huge econ final? Huge." Hunter took an enormous bite out of his Fatburger. "You understand my problem, dude?"

"Sure," I said. "As long as you understand my arrangement with Eric."

"I'm listening."

"I mean, did he explain to you how he, well, pays me?"

"Yeah."

"And are you willing to pay the same way?"

He crossed his arms. "Why not? I'm open-minded."

Mimicking his gesture, I sat back and looked him over. He didn't seem to mind. He had dark skin, longish blond hair brushed back over his ears, abundant blond chest hair, tufts of which poked upward from the collar of his shirt. An unintelligent handsomeness, unlike Eric's. Nor did he provoke in me anything like the ample sense of affection Eric had sparked from the first moment we'd met. Still, there is something to be said for the gutter lusts, and so far as these were concerned, Hunter possessed the necessary attributes— muscles, vulgarity, big hands—in abundance.

"So what's the assignment?" I asked.

"That's the trouble. I've got to find my own topic."

"History of the Second World War, right?" I thought. "Well, something that's always interested me is the story of the troops of black American soldiers who built Bailey bridges in Florence after the armistice."

"Bailey what?"

"Temporary bridges to replace the ones that were bombed."

"Cool. Professor Graham's black. He'll like that."

"Almost nothing's been written about those soldiers. Still, I could do some research—"

"It's supposed to be a research paper," Hunter added helpfully.

"When's it due?"

"That's the bitch. The twenty-first."

"The twenty-first!"

"I know, but what can I do? I only found out about you yesterday."

"I'm not sure I can manage a research paper by the twenty-first."

"Dude, please!"

He smiled, his mouth some orthodontist's pride. I don't know what came over me, then: a lustful malevolence, you might call it, that made me want to see just how far I could go with this stupid, sexy, immoral boy.

"All right," I said. "There's just one condition. With this time constraint, the terms are going to have to be—how shall I put it?—more exacting than usual."

Hunter put his elbows on the table. "What did you have in mind?" he asked.

"OK, how does this sound? Just to be fair, if you get a C or lower on the paper, you don't have to do anything. If you get a B, it's the same as with Eric: I give you a blow job. But if you get an A—"

"You can't fuck me," Hunter said.

Why did these boys all assume I wanted to fuck them?

"That wasn't what I was going to propose," I said. "What I was going to propose was...the opposite."

"That I fuck you?"

I nodded.

"Sure," Hunter said swiftly. "No problem."

"Have you ever fucked another guy?"

"No, but I have, you know, fucked a girl...back there."

"You have."

"Uh-huh."

"And did you like it?"

"Well..." He grinned. "I mean, it felt good and all, but afterward—it *is* kind of gross to think about. You know what I'm saying?"

I coughed. "Well, I guess it's a done deal, Hunter."

"Great."

We shook.

"Oh, and Hunter," I added (what possessed me?), "just one more thing. There is the matter of a security deposit."

"Security deposit?"

"Didn't Eric tell you?"

"Well, naturally I require a security deposit. On my work. I'm sure you understand that."

"Sure, but what... kind of security deposit?"

I gestured for him to lean closer.

"Do you wear boxers or briefs?" I whispered.

"Depends. Today briefs."

"Good. All right, here's what I want you to do. I want you to go into the bathroom, into the toilet stall, and take off your pants and underwear. Then I want you to jack off into your underwear. You know, use them to wipe up. Then I want you to put them in your coat pocket. You can give them to me when we get outside."

"But—"

"You don't have to worry, there are locks on the stalls."

"But Eric didn't—"

"Or we could just forget the whole thing..."

He grimaced. Suddenly an expression of genuine disgust clouded his handsome face, so forcefully that for a moment I feared he might knock over the table, scream obscenities, hit or kill me.

Then the expression changed. He stood up.

"Back in a flash," he said, and strode into the bathroom.

Exactly five minutes later—I checked my watch—the bathroom door swung open.

"Ready?"

"Ready."

We headed out into the parking lot.

"Here you go, dude." Surreptitiously Hunter handed me a wad of white cotton.

My fingers brushed sliminess as I stuffed it into my pocket.

"And are you always that quick?"

"Only when I need to be."

He climbed into his Jeep and switched the radio on loud. "So I'll have the paper for you the afternoon of the twentieth," I shouted over the noise.

"Sounds like a winner."

"Oh, and incidentally, Hunter, if you don't mind, maybe you could do it in the back of your Jeep."

"Do what?"

"If you get an A."

"Oh, man!" Hunter laughed. "Shit, you have really got a filthy mind. I like it." Then he nearly slammed the door on my fingers.

Simple as that, I became an industry.

Days passed more quickly. I got up early in the mornings, sometimes as early as my father, who was usually weeding in the garden by 6. Then I went to the library. Did you know that at the end of World War II, after the Germans bombed the bridge of Santa Trinità in Florence, all four Statues of the seasons which graced its corners were recovered from the river? Everything except spring's head. Posters went up, in which a photograph of the head appeared under the words, HAVE YOU SEEN THIS WOMAN? $3000 REWARD. Rumor had it that a black American soldier had kidnapped the head. Only no one ever turned up to claim the ransom.

Not until 1961—the year I was born—was the head finally found, buried in mud at the bottom of the Arno.

Actually, I'd known this anecdote well before I started researching Hunter's paper. I'd even seen a reproduction of the poster itself when I'd gone to Florence a year earlier with Andy: Heading into the Palazzo Medici-Riccardi one morning to look at Benozzo Gozzoli's frescoes of the *Procession of the Magi*, we'd stumbled on a photo exhibit commemorating the bombings that had nearly destroyed the city's medieval center. And there, amid the rubble-strewn piazzas and the women cheering the American liberators and the children in bread lines, the poster had hung, boldly American in its idioms, like the WANTED posters I used to study anxiously while my mother waited in line at the post office. Around it, in photographs, young black enlisted men—one of whom had been suspected of the theft—built Bailey bridges. If they felt the sting of injustice that must have been their daily lot in the military, their faces didn't show it. Instead, expressionless as ants, they heaved steel beams, and gradually restitched the severed city.

As I recall, Andy didn't take much notice of the soldiers. Good homosexual that he is, he was in a hurry to get over to the Accademia and see the David. And I should have been more interested in the David too; after all, he is my favorite sculpture, as well as the erotic ideal in pursuit of which Henry Somerset and his brethren had poured into Italy all those decades ago. And yet it was those soldiers—not the David—whose faces bloomed in my mind as we trudged up Via Ricasoli; to which I should add that I was in the middle of being sued then; in Italy, as it were, in flight from trouble; invention was almost painful to me. So why, at that particular moment, should a novel have started telling itself in my head? A novel I knew I could never write (and all the better)? A novel in which a young black soldier comes to Florence; from a distance, as he hammers planks, an Italian boy watches him, every morning, every afternoon...

The thing I need to emphasize is this: I never wanted to write that novel. I wanted just to muse on it as a possibility; listen to the story unfurling; drift with it, the way as a boy I used to keep up a running soap opera in my head. Every day I'd walk in circles around the pool outside our house in Stanford, bouncing a red rubber ball and spinning out in my mind elaborate and unending variations: pure plot. Sometimes I'd look up and see my mother watching me from the kitchen window. And when my ball got a hole in it, my father was always ready with his little packet of patches to seal it up.

A curious thing about my father: When, many years later, he moved down south, he gave away without compunction most of the sentimental objects of my childhood. Stuffed animals, Corgi cars, books. Yet he kept that ball. He still talks about it. "David's ball," he says, which I must have bounced a thousand miles in circles around that pool, in those days when invention was the simplest sort of pleasure or folly.

I think that was what I was trying to recapture: all the gratitude of authorship, with none of the responsibility implicit in signing one's name.

And how hard I worked! Mornings in the library, afternoons at my father's computer. For Eric's history project, I was able to cannibalize a good deal of the research I'd already done for the Somerset novel—that novel which, like the Bailey bridge novel, I was now certain I would never write. An essay I'd done in college on *Between the Acts* formed the basis for "Mirror Imagery in Virginia Woolf." And Hunter: well, thanks to that unwritten, even unwhispered bit of story, he ended up getting the best paper of all three.

And why was that? This is the thing of which, I suspect, I'm going to have the hardest time convincing you. After all, a bond of genuine affection united Eric and me: It made sense that I should want to do well by him. Toward Hunter, my feelings could best be described as an admixture of contempt and lust. Nor did he like me any better than I liked him. Contempt and lust: How is it possible that from such a devalued marriage as this, art could have been conceived? Yet it was. Indeed, as I look back, I recognize that there was something startlingly clear, even serene, about my partnership with Hunter, which no yearnings for domesticity defiled. Eric, on the other hand, I was always calling up and asking if he wanted to have lunch. He'd meet me when he had time, which was rarely, since lately he'd gotten busy with his juggling lessons.

Yes, juggling lessons.

Sometimes I'd go over to his house and lie on his bed, stoned, while above his head he hurled three red pins, or three sticks, or three white balls. Only the occasional "shit" or "fuck" interrupted his quiet, huffing focus. A ball bounced toward the window, or the pins clattered. Then he picked up the pins and started fresh, as the dense odor of his sweat claimed the room.

He said he was hoping to get good enough to juggle on weekends for extra cash. He said he was working up to fire.

And need I mention that those evenings never evolved into the erotic? Of course one hoped. Yet Eric was scrupulous, and—more to the point—not that interested. Sex with me, to his view, was a reward for a job well done.

With Hunter, by contrast, sex was payment for services rendered. I hope I've made the distinction clearly.

And of course he got his A. I learned only from Eric, who'd gotten A's too and called me up before Christmas break to whoop about it. "Hasn't Hunter told you?" he asked when I inquired, and when I said no, went silent. Then I tried to phone Hunter, but he was never at home. This didn't surprise me, betrayal being the usual result when one starts making gentleman's agreements with people who are not gentlemen.

Anyway, what more should I have expected from a boy who buys a term paper, then tries to pass it off as his own?

In the end I had to track him down at the UCLA pool. Dripping chlorine, the golden hair on his chest made my mouth water. I wanted to drink him.

"Hey, I've been meaning to call you," he said as he toweled himself.

"I've been trying to call you too. You're never home."

"Sorry about that, dude. I've been busy. By the way, my professor really loved that paper! I appreciate it."

"No problem."

He dried under his arms.

"So anyway, the reason I'm here, Hunter, is that I'd like to know when you intend to fulfill your half of the bargain."

"Softer, your voice carries!"

"What, you don't want any of your friends to know I wrote your paper for you?"

"Softer!" He pushed me into a corner. "Look," he said, his whisper agitated, "it'll have to be after I'm back from break. Right now I'm too busy."

"No, it'll have to be before you leave for break. Didn't your mother teach you it's never a good idea to put things off?" I patted him on the arm. "Tell you what, why don't you come over to my dad's place tomorrow around noon? He's away for the weekend. We can put the Jeep in the garage."

"The Jeep."

"You did get an A, Hunter."

"But I—"

"What, you thought I was just going to write that paper for nothing? Uh-uh. You be there at noon."

I gave him my address, after which he limped off toward the showers.

He was not a bad kid, really. It was just part of his affably corrupt nature to try to get away with things. Of such stuff as this are captains of industry made.

Probably the aspect of this story that puzzles me most, as I look back, is how word of my "availability" circulated so quickly through the halls and dormitories of UCLA those next months. I don't mean that it became common knowledge among the student body that David Leavitt, novelist, was available to write term papers for good-looking male undergraduates; no articles appeared in the *Daily Bruin*, or graffiti (so far as I am aware) on bathroom walls. Still, in a controlled way, news got out, and as the spring quarter opened, no less than five boys called me up with papers to be written. And how had they gotten my number in the first place? I tried to imagine the conversations that had taken place: "Shit, Eric, I don't know how I'm supposed to finish this paper on 'Ode to a Grecian Urn' by Friday." "Why don't you call up Dave Leavitt? He'll do it for you if you let him give you a blow job." "A blow job, huh? Sounds great. What's his number?"

Or perhaps the suggestion was never so direct. Perhaps it was made in a more discreet language, or a more vulgar one. The latter, I suspect. In fact I'm sure that at some point all the boys, even Eric, made rude, humiliating remarks about me, called me "faggot" or "cocksucker," then qualified those (to them) insults by adding that I was "still a basically decent guy." Or some such proviso.

Business got so good, I started turning down offers, either because I was overworked, or because the boy in question, when I met him, simply didn't appeal to me physically, in which case I would apologize and say I couldn't spare the time. (I hated this part of the job, but what could I do? Profit was my motive, not charity. I never gave anything for which I didn't get something back. You'd think I had gone to business school.)

All told, I wrote papers for seven boys—seven boys toward most of whom I felt something partway between the affection that enno-bled my friendship with Eric and the contempt that characterized my dealings with Hunter. The topics ranged from "The Image of the Wanderer in English Romantic Poetry" to "The Fall of the Paris Commune" to "Child Abandonment in Medieval Italy" to "Flight in Toni Morrison's *Song of Solomon*" to "Bronzino and the Traditions of Italian Renaissance Portraiture."

Of these boys, and papers, the only other one I need to tell you about is Ben.

Ben got in touch with me around midterm of the spring quarter. "Mr. Leavitt?" he said on the phone. "My name's Ben Hollingsworth. I got your number from Tony Younger."

"Oh?"

"Yes. He told me to call you. He said you might...that we could—"

"Relax. There's no need to be nervous."

"Thanks. I'm really...I don't know where to start."

"Why don't we meet?" I offered, my voice as honeyed and pro-fessional as any prostitute's. "It's always easier to talk in person."

"Where?"

I suggested the Ivy, only Ben didn't want to meet at the Ivy—or any other public place, for that matter. Instead he asked if he could pick me up on the third floor of the Beverly Center parking lot, near the elevators. Then we could discuss things in his car.

I said that was fine by me.

We rendezvoused at 10:30 the next morning. It was unusually chilly out. Ben drove a metallic blue Honda, the passenger door to which was dented. "Mr. Leavitt?" he asked as he threw it open.

"In the flesh."

I climbed in. Altogether, with his carefully combed black hair and short-sleeve button-down shirt (pen in breast pocket), he reminded me of those Mormon missionary boys you sometimes run into in the

European capitals, with badges on their lapels that say "Elder Anderson" or "Elder Carpenter." And as it turned out, the association was prophetic. Ben was a Mormon, as I soon learned, albeit from Fremont, Calif., not Utah. No doubt in earlier years he'd done the very same European "service," handing out pamphlets to confused homosexual tourists who'd thought he might be cruising them.

"I really appreciate your taking the time to see me, Mr. Leavitt," he began as I put on my seat belt.

"Call me David."

"I'd feel more comfortable calling you Mr. Leavitt."

"OK, whatever. And what should I call you?"

"Ben."

"Ben. Fine. Anyway, it's no problem."

We headed out of the parking lot. "I just want to make one thing clear," he said. "I want you to know that I've never cheated on anything in my life. Not a test, not a paper. And I've never stolen anything either. I don't drink, I've never used drugs. I'm a clean liver, Mr. Leavitt. I've had the same girlfriend since I was fifteen. And now here I am driving with you, and we're about to enter into an unholy alliance—at least I hope we are, because if we don't, my GPA will go below 3.5 and I need higher than that to get into a good law school. I'm so desperate that I'm willing to do things I'll be ashamed of for the rest of my life. You, I don't know if you're ashamed. It's none of my business."

We turned left onto San Vicente. "Probably not," I said.

"No. And it must sound terrible to you, what I'm suggesting. Still, the way I see it, there's no alternative because one day I'm going to have a family to support, and I've got to be ready. Most of these other guys, they've got rich parents to fall back on. I don't. And since I'm also not black or in a wheelchair or anything, it's that much more difficult. Do you hear what I'm saying? I don't really have any choice in the matter."

"You always have a choice, Ben."

Opening the window, he puffed out a visible sigh. Something in his square, scrubbed, slightly acned face, I must admit, excited me.

His cock, I imagined, would taste like Dial soap. And yet even as Ben's aura of clean living excited me, his shame shamed me. After all, none of the other boys for whom I'd written papers had ever expressed the slightest scruple about passing off my work as their own; if anything, it was the sex part, the prostitutional part, that made them flinch. Which, when you came to think about it, was astounding: as if the brutal exigencies of the marketplace had ingested whole, in each of them, all shopworn, kindergarten notions of right and wrong.

In Ben, on the other hand, those same kindergarten notions seemed to exert just enough pressure to make him worry, though not quite enough to make him change his mind.

"So what's the class?" I asked.

"Victorian History."

"And the assignment?"

"Are you saying you'll do it?"

"You'll have to tell me what the assignment is first."

"Jack the Ripper," Ben said.

"Really? How funny. I was just reading about him."

"You were?"

"Yes. Apparently a lot of people thought he was Prince Eddy, Queen Victoria's grandson and the heir to the throne. Since then that's pretty much been disproven, though."

"Wow," Ben said. "That might be an interesting angle to take…if you're interested. Are you interested? I hope you are, because if you're not I'll have to figure out something else, and buying a term paper with cash is something I just can't afford right now."

"Ben, slow down for a second. I have to say, this whole situation worries me. Are you sure you know what you're getting yourself into?"

"Do you mean do I understand what I'll have to do in exchange? Of course, Tony told me, I'll have to let you—you know—perform oral sex on me. And no, I can't pretend I'm comfortable with it. But I'm willing. Like I said, I have this girlfriend, Jessica. I've never cheated on her either."

We stopped at a red light, where Ben opened his wallet. From between fragile sheets of plastic, a freckled girl with red hair smiled out at us.

"Very pretty," I said.

"She will be the mother of my children," Ben said reverently.

Then he put the picture away, as if continued exposure to my gaze might blight it.

The light changed.

"Of course, if you say no because I'm not so good-looking as Tony, well, there's nothing I can do about that. Still, I do have rather a large penis. I understand homosexuals like large penises. Is that true?"

"Sometimes." Laughing, I patted his knee. "Look, you know what I think? I think you should write your paper. And I'll read it over for you, how does that sound? Free of charge, as it were. And if you do get a C in history, well, so what? It won't matter in the long run. And meanwhile you won't have cheated on Jessica, or compromised your ethics."

"But I'm fully prepared to compromise my ethics." Ben's voice grew panicked. "Also the security deposit. Tony told me about that too, and I've already taken care of it. Look."

Reaching across my lap, he opened the glove compartment. A bleachy odor of semen wafted from the opening.

Pulling out a pair of rumpled boxer shorts, Ben tossed them into my lap.

"When did you do this?" I asked, caressing slick cotton.

"Just now. Just before I picked you up." He grinned. "So what do you say, Mr. Leavitt? Will you do it?"

"All right." My mouth was dry.

"That's great. That's terrific."

He turned onto Saturn Street.

I wiped my fingertips on my jeans.

As I'd told Ben, I already knew a little about Jack the Ripper. This was because Prince Eddy, whose candidature for the post

"Ripperologists" were forever bandying about, stood also at the center of the Cleveland Street scandal. Indeed, several historians believed Lord Arthur Somerset had fled England primarily to take the heat off Eddy (also a regular client at the brothel) as a favor to his old friend and protector the prince of Wales.

It would have been interesting, I thought, to write a paper linking Prince Eddy's homosexuality with the hatred of the female body that seemed to have been such a motivating element in the Ripper crimes. Unfortunately, fairly hard proof existed that Eddy had been off shooting in Scotland on the date of two of the murders, and since Ben's assignment was to make a strong case for one suspect or another, I decided I'd better look elsewhere. M.J. Druitt, a doctor whose body was found floating in the Thames about seven weeks after the last murder, was certainly the candidate toward whom most of the evidence pointed. Yet for this reason, it seemed likely that many of Ben's classmates would argue for Druitt.

Who else then? Among the names that came up most frequently were those of Frank Miles, with whom Oscar Wilde had once shared a house; Virginia Woolf's cousin James Stephen, who had been Eddy's tutor; the painter Walter Sickert; and Queen Victoria's private physician, Sir William Gull. Indeed, a large percentage of the suspects seemed to have been physicians, which is no surprise: to disembowel a woman's body as precisely as the Ripper did that of Mary Kelly, you would have to possess a detailed knowledge of human anatomy. And if Donald Rumbelow is correct in proposing that the Ripper's weapon was a postmortem knife "with a thumb-grip on the blade which is specifically designed for 'ripping' upwards," the evidence that he was a medical man appears even stronger.

So: the Ripper as doctor, or antidoctor. As far as this "angle" went, the argument that intrigued me the most came from someone called Leonard Matters, who in 1929 had published a book claiming that the Ripper was in fact a "Dr. Stanley." His brilliant young son having died of a venereal infection after traveling to Paris with a prostitute named Mary Kelly, this good doctor (according to Matters' theory) had gone mad and started scouring the alleys of Whitechapel,

bent on revenging himself not only against Mary Kelly, but prostitutes in general.

A second possibility was to talk about class. This struck me as an
interesting if somewhat experimental approach because regardless of
who actually committed the crimes, the Victorian imagination—of
which gossip is the strongest echo—associated Jack almost obses-
sively with Buckingham Palace. If he was not a member of the royal
family, then he was someone close to the royal family, some mad fail-
ure of stately blood who would periodically troll the streets of East
London in search of whores to murder and eviscerate. And couldn't
that be looked upon as an allegory for the exploitation of the working classes by the upper classes through history? A Marxist argument
proposed itself. After all, as victims Jack chose exclusively prostitutes
of an extremely degraded type: older women, alcoholic, with too
many children and no qualms about lifting their petticoats in a
squalid alley to pay for a drink. To write about the Ripper as a per-
sonification of the bourgeoisie's contempt for the workers would
certainly provide a provocative twist on the assignment. Or perhaps
such a twist would be *too* provocative, especially coming from a boy
like Ben.

A third possibility was to talk about xenophobia: for if the Ripper
suspects could be categorized, then the last rough category (after
doctors and aristocrats) was immigrants.

And as I mulled over each of these angles, the one thing I could
not get out of my mind was a police photograph I'd seen of the
corpse of Mary Kelly, the last of Jack's victims and the only one to
be killed in her room. Her body had been found on the bed, quite
literally split down the middle. The nose had been cut off, the liver
sliced out and placed between the feet. The kidneys, breasts, and the
flesh from the thighs had been dumped on the bedside table, and the
hand inserted into the stomach.

Even in my own epoch of serial killers and snuff films, of Charles
Manson and Jeffrey Dahmer, I'd never seen anything quite like that.

Three days passed in research. Each morning I'd wake vowing to
conclude the afternoon with a decision, and each afternoon I'd go

home having failed. Then only a week remained before Ben's paper was due, and I hadn't even started writing. It felt as if something had seized up in me, the way the screen of a computer will sometimes freeze into immobility. Nor did it help when Ben stopped by my carrel one afternoon to give me a book I'd already read and returned. "It's called *The Identity of Jack the Ripper*," he said. "And according to this guy, at first they thought the Ripper was a Polish barber who went by the name of George Chapman, but then they found out that he had a double, a *Russian* barber, and that this double—"

"Also sometimes used the name Chapman. I know."

"Oh, you've already read it? Well, never mind, then. I just thought in case you hadn't—"

"Thanks."

"Say, you want a 7Up or something?"

I said why not.

We repaired to the vending machines, then, taking our drinks outside, sat on a bench in the library courtyard. It was a warm spring day, better than most only in that the air was unusually clear. A breeze even seemed to carry the scent of mountains.

For a time the only noise in that courtyard, aside from the buzz of yellow jackets, was the pop of our drink cans opening. Then Ben said, "Strange, all this."

"What?"

"Just...our sitting together."

"Why?"

"I'm not sure quite how to explain. You see, in the church—did I tell you I'm a Mormon?"

"No."

"Well, in the church we have this very clear-cut conception of sin. And so I always assumed that if I ever committed a really big sin, like we're doing now...I don't know, that there'd be a clap of thunder and God would strike me dead or something. Instead of which we're sitting here in this courtyard and the sun's shining. The grass is green."

"But what's the sin?"

"You know. Cheating."

"Is cheating really a sin?"

"Of course. It's part of lying."

"Well," I said, "then maybe the fact that the sun's shining and the grass is green means God doesn't really care that much. Or maybe God doesn't exist."

Ben's face convulsed in horror.

"Just a possibility," I added.

Ben leaned back in disillusion. "So you're an atheist," he said. "I suppose I should have expected it. I suppose I should have guessed most homosexuals would be atheists."

"Oh, some homosexuals are very religious. It wouldn't surprise me to find out one or two were Mormons."

"Ex-Mormons."

"A lot more than two of those. But to get back to what you were saying, I wouldn't call myself an atheist. Instead I'd say I'm a skeptical lapsed Jew, distrustful of dogma."

"Tony's Jewish too. Last night he was telling me about his circumcision."

"His *bris*."

"—and how in Israel they use the foreskins to make fertility drugs." He shook his head in wonder.

"Are you circumcised, Ben?"

"No, actually." Blushing, he checked his watch.

We got up and walked toward the library. "Well, back to the salt mines," Ben said at the main doors. "By the way, I hope you realize I'm working my butt off too. I really bit off more than I could chew this quarter."

"Oh, I'll bet you can chew more than you think."

"Probably. Still, I wanted to make sure you knew. I mean, I wouldn't want you thinking that the whole time you were sweating out this paper, I was playing pinball or something." He wiped his nose. "By the way, have you decided who did it yet?"

"Not yet. The problem is, everyone has a different theory about the Ripper, and every theory has a hole in it." Which was true.

Indeed, looked at collectively, the theories ramified so far afield that the actual murders began to seem beside the point. For if you believed them all, then the Ripper was Prince Eddy *and* Walter Sickert. The Ripper was Frank Miles *and* M.J. Druitt *and* Sir William Gull. The Ripper was an agent provocateur sent by the Russian secret police to undermine the reputation of their London brethren. The Ripper was a Jewish *shochet*, or ritual slaughterer, suffering from a religious mania. The Ripper was a high-level conspiracy to squelch a secret marriage between Prince Eddy and a poor Catholic girl. The Ripper was Jill the Ripper, an abortionist betrayed by a guilt-ridden client and sent to prison, and therefore bent on avenging herself on her own sex.

Not to mention the black magician and the clique of Freemasons and (how could I forget him?) Virginia Woolf's cousin (and possibly Prince Eddy's lover), the handsome, demented James Stephen.

But which one? Or all of them?

Saying good-bye to Ben, I returned to my carrel. As it happened I'd left the photograph of Mary Kelly's corpse lying open on the desk. And how curious! As I sat down, that "butcher's shambles" no longer made me nauseated. Perhaps one really can get used to anything.

And upon this degraded body of the late nineteenth century, I thought, some real demon swooped, ransacking its cavities like a thief in search of hidden jewels, and finding instead only a panic, an emptiness, a vacancy.

But what demon? Who?

I looked up.

Modernism and espionage, Diaspora and homosexuality, religious mania and anti-Semitism and most vividly—to me most vividly—desire and disease, gruesomely coupled.

"Fantastic," I said. For all at once—sometimes inspiration really is all at once—I saw who Ben's Ripper had to be.

The Ripper was the spirit of the twentieth century itself.

I worked fast those next days, faster than I'd ever worked on anything else. Looking back, I see that the pleasure I experienced as I wrote that paper lay in its contemplation as a completed object, like the Bailey bridge novel I was sure I would never begin. Or a Bailey bridge, for that matter. Bank to bank I built, and as I did a destination, a connection, neared. It was the same end I'd hoped to reach in my Somerset book: a sort of poeticization of that moment when the soul of my own century, the soul of vacancy itself, devoured the last faithful remnants of an age that had believed, almost without question, in presences.

After that, from the unholy loins of Jack the Ripper, whole traditions of alienation had been spilled, of which I was merely one exemplary homunculus. Eric was another: Eric with his cheerful, well-intentioned immorality. And Hunter. Even Ben. We were the nightmare Mary Kelly had dreamed the night she was murdered.

I finished, to my own surprise, three days early. That same afternoon my agent called. "Congratulate me," I said. "I've just done the best work of my life."

"Congratulations," Andrew said. "Now when do I get to see pages?" To which request I responded, rather unconvincingly, "Soon."

How could I have explained to him that the only thing that made it possible for me to write those pages was the knowledge that they would never bear my name?

I called Ben. He sounded happy and surprised at my news, and as before we arranged to meet on the third floor of the Beverly Center parking lot.

He was waiting in his car when I pulled up. "Nice to see you, Mr. Leavitt," he said.

"Nice to see you too, Ben." I climbed in. "Beautiful day, isn't it?"

"Mm." He was staring expectantly at my briefcase.

"Oh, the paper," I said, taking it out and handing it to him.

"Great," Ben said. "Let's go up to the roof and I'll read it."

"Read it?"

"What, you think I'm going to turn in a paper I haven't read?" He shook his head in wonderment, then inserting the key in the ignition, drove us up into sunlight. To be honest, I was a little surprised: After all, none of the other boys for whom I'd written had ever felt the need to verify the quality of my work. (Then again, none of the other boys had been remotely scrupulous in the second sense of the word, either.) Still, I couldn't deny Ben the right to look over something that was going to be turned in under his name; in addition to which the prospect of seeing his astounded face as he reached the end of my last paragraph did rather thrill me; even in such a situation as this, I still had my writer's vanity. So I sat there, my Ripper's eyes fixed on the contoured immensity in his polyester slacks, and only balked when he took a pen from his shirt pocket and crossed out a line.

"What are you doing?"

"I just think this sentence about Druitt is a bit redundant. Look."

I looked. It was redundant.

"But you can't turn in a paper all marked up like that!"

"What, you thought I was going to turn in this copy? Are you kidding? No way! I'll type it over tonight on my own computer."

He returned to his reading. Periodically he jotted a note in the margin, or drew a line through a word or phrase. All of which made me so nervous, he might have been Michiko Kakutani sitting in the next seat, reviewing one of my novels while I watched.

Finally Ben put the paper down.

"Well?" I said.

"Well…" He scratched his head with his pen. "It's very interesting, Mr. Leavitt. Very…imaginative. The only thing is, I'm not sure it answers the assignment."

"How so?"

"The assignment was to make a case for someone or other being Jack the Ripper. And basically, what you're saying is that it doesn't matter. That any of them, or all of them, could have been Jack the Ripper.

"Exactly."

"But that's not what Professor Robinson asked for."

I spread my hands patiently on my lap. "I understand what's worrying you, Ben. Still, try to think about it this way. You have a murder mystery, right? A whodunit. Only there's no clear evidence that any one person did it. So the B student thinks, I'll just make a case for the most likely suspect and be done with it. But the A student thinks, More is going on here than meets the eye. The A student thinks, I've got to use this as an opportunity to investigate a larger issue."

"I can see all that. Still, this stuff about twentieth-century modernism—I have to be honest with you, Mr. Leavitt, to me it sounds a little pretentious."

"Pretentious!"

"I mean, very intelligent and all. Only the spirit of twentieth-century modernism—that can't hold a knife. That can't strangle someone. And so I'm afraid Professor Robinson will think it's—I don't know—off-the-wall."

Clearly Ben had the limited vision of the B student.

"Well, I'm sorry you're disappointed," I said.

"Oh, I'm not disappointed exactly. It just wasn't what I expected."

"Fine. Then I'll go home this afternoon and rewrite it. You just have to tell me who you think actually did do it—"

"Mr. Leavitt—"

"Was it M.J. Druitt, or James Stephen, or Dr. Pedechenko? Or how about Jill? It could have been Jill."

Ben was silent.

Then: "Mr. Leavitt, you can't blame me for being worried. A lot rests on this paper for me. You, you've got nothing to lose."

Was that true?

"And *you* don't risk expulsion if you get caught."

"Well, naturally, and that's exactly why I'm offering to rewrite it." (My anger had dissipated.) "After all, Ben, you're the customer, and the customer's—"

"Do you have to make it sound so...commercial?"

"Isn't it?"

"I'm not sure," Ben said. "I never have been."

Once again he took out his pen. From the bottom of his breast pocket, I noticed, a tear-shaped blue ink stain seeped downward. "You must have put your pen away without the cap," I said.

"Did I? I guess. I do it all the time."

"Me too."

With my forefinger, I stroked the stain. Ben's breathing quickened.

"Look," he said, "about the paper. You don't have to rewrite it. I mean, if I didn't appreciate it, it probably says more about me than about you, right?"

"Not necessarily—"

"And anyway, I didn't come to you to get a B paper, I came to you to get an A paper. And if I don't recognize an A paper when I see one, all that points up are my limitations."

"Maybe." I moved my finger downward, to brush the cleft of his chest. "Or maybe it only points up the fact that I have a wider experience of these things. Remember, I've never gotten anything less than an A on a paper in my life—for myself or anyone else."

"Mr. Leavitt, please don't touch me like that. Someone might see us."

"I'm sorry." I took my hand away.

"Thank you," Ben said, clearing his throat. "And now I guess I owe you something, don't I?"

"Oh, don't worry about that. For that let's just wait until you get your grade. Then we can—"

"No, I'd rather get it over with, if you don't mind. Not have it hanging over my head." He played with his collar. "Obviously we can't do it here. Where can we do it?"

"My dad's place," I said swiftly. "He and his wife are in Singapore."

Without a word, Ben switched on the ignition and drove me back to my car. "Follow me," I said, and he did, down Santa Monica to Cahuenga and Barham, then onto the 134, the flat, trafficked maze of the Inland Empire.

Around 1:30 we pulled into my father's garage. "Come on in," I said, switching off the burglar alarm. "Make yourself at home. You want to take a swim in the pool first?"

"I didn't bring a suit."

"You don't need one. No one will see you but me."

"Actually," Ben said, "I'd rather just—you know—get down to business, if that's all right with you."

"Fine," I said. "It's this way." And we headed together down the long corridor into my bedroom.

"This is nice.

"Thanks. It's not really mine. Just the guest room. But I try to put in some personal touches when I'm here. That little painting, for instance. My friend Arnold Mesches did it."

"What is it, a turkey?"

"A portrait of a turkey."

"That's funny."

I took off my shoes. "By the way, would you rather I leave the lights on or off?"

"Off."

"All cats are gray in the dark, right? All right, then, why don't you just...take your clothes off and lie down on the bed. And I'll be back in a minute."

"OK."

Like a discreet masseur, I stepped into the bathroom, where I brushed my teeth and got out some condoms. Then I walked back in. Ben was sitting naked on the edge of the bed, shivering a little.

"Are you cold?" I asked. He shook his head.

"Wow," I said, sitting down next to him. "Lucky I've got extra-large condoms."

He wrapped his arms around his chest. "Mr. Leavitt, you embarrass me when you say things like that."

"Look, Ben," I said, trying to sound paternal, "I've been thinking about it, and if you don't want to—"

"No, it's OK."

"But it's also OK if you don't want to. I mean, you can still have the paper. Don't tell Tony, though." I winked.

"What's his like?" Ben's voice was surprisingly urgent.

"Tony's? Oh. Fine. Smaller than yours, of course."

"Straight or curved?"

"Straight."

"The other night he was telling me that in his fraternity, they take the pledges and shave their balls."

"Yeah?"

"If they pass out from too much drinking."

Something occurred to me. "You're not in a fraternity, are you, Ben?"

"No."

I brushed my fingers against his scrotum.

"Your balls are pretty hairy. I could shave them for you, if you wanted." I hesitated. "You know, we could pretend you were the pledge."

Ben started shaking.

"Or that I was Tony—"

"Shut up."

And pulling my face toward his, he thrust his tongue down my throat.

Don't think he wanted me. He didn't. Yes, he stayed that night, allowed me to initiate him into even the most specialized modes of intimacy—and initiated me into one or two as well. Yet as we sat down across from each other at breakfast the next morning, I could tell from his eyes that it wasn't me he was thinking about. Maybe Jessica, or God. Probably Tony. Not me.

He left shortly thereafter, having first extracted from me a promise never to tell anyone what had happened between us—a promise I naturally kept. And as I watched his car disappear onto California Boulevard, I couldn't guess whether he'd ever do it again, or do it only once again, or change his life and do it a thousand times. I knew only that during our night together, the marrow of identity had been touched. Whether it had been altered, however, I couldn't say.

A lull ensued. Spring break took most UCLA boys to a beach. With my father and Jean still in the Orient, I resorted to old habits: an hour each morning at the library, followed by Book Soup and lunch at the Mandarette Café. Then Andy was back in town for a few days between shoots; and my friend Matt Wolf from London. I got busy.

Something like my old life claimed me.

Naturally I was curious to find out, when spring break ended, what grade Ben had gotten on his paper; also, whether he'd bother to call and tell me what grade he'd gotten on his paper.

When finally I heard news of the matter, however (this was early April), it wasn't from Ben but from Eric.

Eric and I hadn't been in touch much lately. My suspicion was that he had a new girlfriend, the sort of thing he would never have discussed with me. So I was surprised and happy when he called me up one Sunday morning at 7 and ordered me to meet him for breakfast at Ships on La Cienega.

He was waiting in a corner booth when I got there. A placid, sleepy smile on his face, he held the menu with fingers marked by little burns. "Juggling fire?" I asked.

"I got fifty bucks on Venice Beach last Sunday," Eric said.

"Congratulations." And I sat down. His skin was porphyry-colored from the sun.

"I must say, I never expected to hear from you at 7 in the morning," I said. "You're not usually such an early riser."

"Depends on the season. Anyway, I had some news to tell you."

"Tell me."

"I just thought you should know, apparently some guy you wrote for—Ben something—got caught last week."

"Caught?"

"Tony Younger called me. Banana waffles for two," he added to the waitress, "and another cup of coffee. Anyway, yes. Apparently what happened was that when this guy Ben got back from spring break he found a message waiting from his history professor, the gist of which was to get over to her office hours pronto. So he went, and she basically told him that after reading his paper, and comparing it with his other papers, she'd come to the conclusion that it wasn't his own work. Too sophisticated or something. Then she gave him a choice. Either he could admit he hadn't written the paper, which case he'd get a C and the incident would be dropped, or he could protest, in which case he'd get an F and the whole thing brought before the honor board."

"Damn. What did he choose?"

"That's the clincher. Apparently this Ben, this idiot, not only confessed he hadn't written the paper, he practically got down on his knees and started begging the professor's forgiveness. Tony's roommate was outside the office, he heard the whole thing." Eric shook his head in disgust. "After that he went straight to his room, packed up his things, and left. And since then—this was three days ago—no one, not even Tony, who's one of his best friends, has heard a word from him."

"Eric," I said, "I have to ask. Did he mention me?"

"Always thinking about others, aren't you, Dave? But no, he didn't."

"As if it matters. As if it makes it any less my fault."

"Hey, take it easy." The waffles arrived. 'You're too quick to blame yourself," Eric went on, pouring syrup. "I mean, it's not as if this Ben guy didn't know the risks. He came to *you*. Don't forget that. And he could have fought it. Me, I would have said"—his voice went high— " 'Miss Yearwood, Miss Yearwood, how can you think I'd *do* something like that!' And cried or something. Whereas he just gave in. You can't break down like that! The way I see it, they're testing you twenty-four hours a day. They want to see if you can sweat it out. If Ben couldn't take the pressure, it's not your problem. Still, I'd say it's probably better if you kept a low profile around campus for a while." He patted my hand. "Me, I'm lucky. I've finished my humanities requirements. And if I win a prize for that paper, it'll go a long way toward Stanford Biz School, provided I get a high enough score on my GMATs. Did I tell you I have GMATs coming up?"

He hadn't—a lapse he now corrected in lavish detail—after which we said good-bye in the parking lot, Eric cheerful as he drove off into his happy future, me wretched as I contemplated the ruin of Ben's academic career, a ruin for which, no matter what Eric might say to assuage my guilt, I understood myself to be at least in part responsible. For suddenly it didn't matter that I hadn't gotten caught; it didn't matter that no one knew what I had done except the boys themselves, none of whom would ever squeal on me. Because I had written my paper, and not Ben's, he had suffered.

Blame could not be averted. The best I could do was try to bear it with valor.

I got into my father's car. For some reason I was remembering a moment years before, in elementary school, when a girl called Michele Fox had put before me an ethical dilemma familiar to most American schoolchildren at that time: If a museum were burning down, she'd said, and you could save either the old lady or the priceless art treasure, which would you choose? Well, I'd answered, it depends. Who is the old lady? What is the art treasure? To which she responded—wisely, I'm sure—"You're missing the point, David Leavitt." No doubt I was missing the point—her point—since Michele had few doubts in life. (She grew up to be a 911 operator.) As for me, I tortured that little conundrum for years, substituting for the generic old lady first my aunt Ida, then Eudora Welty; for the priceless treasure first the *Mona Lisa,* then Picasso's *Guernica.* Each time my answer was different. Sometimes I opted for life, sometimes for art. And how surprising! From this capriciousness a philosophy formed itself in me, according to which only particularities—not generalities—counted. For principles are rarely human things, and when museums burn—when any buildings burn—the truth is, most people save themselves.

What I'm trying to say here is, I made no effort to get in touch with, or help, Ben. Instead, that afternoon I booked a flight to New York, where by the end of the week I was once again installed in that real life from which the episode of the term papers now turns out to have been merely a long and peculiar divagation.

III.

I ran into Ben about a year later. This was in the Uffizi Gallery, in Florence, where I'd gone to research (I am actually now writing it) my Bailey bridge novel. I was looking at Bronzino's portrait of Eleonora di Toledo, and Ben was looking at Bronzino's portrait of the baby Giovanni, fat-cheeked and clutching his little sparrow, and then quite suddenly, we were looking at each other.

"Ben?" I said, not sure at first that it was he.

"Mr. Leavitt!" To my relief, he smiled.

We walked upstairs, where in the little coffee bar on the roof, I bought him a cappuccino. Ben looked better than he had when we'd first known each other. For one thing, his hair was both longer and messier, which suited him; also, he'd foregone his old Mormon uniform in favor of denim, down, hiking boots: ordinary clothes, boy clothes, in which his body, somehow ampler-seeming, rested with visible ease. Nor did he appear in the least surprised to be sitting with me there. "Actually," he said, "since I've been in Florence I've bumped into six people I knew from school. It might as well be Westwood Village." He took a sip from his cappuccino. "I never knew coffee could be so good before I came to Italy."

"How long have you been here?"

"In Florence, three days. In Italy, two weeks. I'm with my friend. No—I guess I should say my lover." He leaned closer. "Keith and I talk about this all the time. Lover's stupid, and friend's too euphemistic, and partner sounds like a business arrangement. So Keith says, just say you're with Keith.' But then people say, 'Who's Keith?' And I'm back to square one."

"Well, you don't have to worry with me," I said, smiling. "Anyway, how did you meet Keith?"

"It was after I quit school, while I was living with my parents in Fremont. The thing was, I just kept having this yen to go into San Francisco. The usual story. So one night I was driving up and down Castro Street, and finally I worked up the courage to stop in at a bar. The next thing I knew someone was buying me a beer."

"And that was Keith?"

"Oh, no. Keith came later." Ben's cheeks reddened. "He likes to tell people we met at a party, but the truth is we met on the street. He cruised me, we went back to his apartment and fucked. The rest is history." Ben drained his coffee cup. "And what about you, Mr. Leavitt? What have you been up to this year? Still living with your father?"

"No, I'm back in New York."

"Oh, great. And who are you writing term papers for there? NYU boys? Columbia boys?"

"Actually, I'm working on a novel."

"Better, I guess." His tone was somehow reproachful and affectionate all at once.

We were quiet for a moment. Then I said, "Ben, about that paper—"

"So you heard what happened."

"Yes. And I'm sorry. Probably you were right, probably it was pretentious. Or at least, not the right thing for you. I always tried to make my papers sound like they came from the people they were supposed to be coming from. I guess in your case, though, I got carried away. Infatuated, almost. The thing was, I fell in love with an idea."

"You're a writer. Writers are supposed to fall in love with ideas."

"Exactly. And that's why I should have been more careful. After all, if I'd done the paper the way you'd asked me to—"

"If you'd done the paper the way I asked you to, I'd be graduating from UCLA and on my way to law school and engaged to Jessica. Or graduating from UCLA and on my way to law school and a queer with a whatever you want to call him. Instead of which I'm drinking coffee with you on the roof of the Uffizi." He leaned back. "I'm not saying you didn't screw things up for me. I'm just saying the jury's still out on whether it was all for the best or not. And of course I'd be a hypocrite if I pretended it was only for the paper. It was never only for the paper."

"So what are your plans?"

"Well, for now I'm studying social work at San Francisco State. My goal is to go for my master's, then work with PWAs."

"That's great."

"Oh, and also—this may surprise you—I've been trying my hand at fiction writing."

"Really."

"Well, I figured, why not? See, since I moved in with Keith, I've been reading every gay novel I can get my hands on. I even read two of yours. I liked *The Lost Language of Cranes* all right. I didn't much like *Equal Affections*."

"I probably should have written it as a memoir. I still might."

"Interesting. As for me, I was thinking our little adventure might make a terrific story."

"That's a good idea," I said. "Writers often disguise their lives as fiction. The thing they almost never do is disguise fiction as their lives."

There wasn't really any way to answer this remark, and so for a few more moments we were both silent. Then Ben said, "And how about you, Mr. Leavitt? Do you feel comfortable with what you did?"

I spooned up the last remnants of my cappuccino foam. "Well, I'll never look at it as the proudest moment of my life, if that's what you're asking. Still, I'm not ashamed. I mean, is it wrong for the ghostwriter to say yes to the First Lady because she can't write? Was it wrong for Marni Nixon to dub Natalie Wood's voice in *West Side Story* because she couldn't sing?"

"You tell me. Was it?"

But I couldn't answer.

We got up shortly after that. It was nearing 1, when Ben and Keith had a date to meet outside Café Rivoire. From the spot where Savonarola had burned the vanities, I watched them kiss each other on the cheek, two handsome, nicely dressed young men. Then, arms linked, they strolled together down Via Calzaiuoli.

And how did I feel? Ashamed, yes. Also happy. For the one thing I hadn't explained to Ben—the one thing I could never explain to Ben—was that those papers, taken together, constituted the best work I'd done in my life. And perhaps this was precisely *because* they were written to exchange for pleasure, as opposed to those tokens with which one can merely purchase pleasure. Thus the earliest troubadours sang, so that damsels might throw down ropes from virginal balconies.

Still, I couldn't have said any of this to Ben, because if I'd said any of this to Ben—if I'd told him it was the best work I'd done in my life—he would have thought it a tragedy, not a victory, and that I couldn't have borne.

From Savonarola's circle, I turned toward the Uffizi corridor, opening out like a pair of forceps. Pigeons, masses of them, circled in the sky, sometimes alighting on the heads of the Statues: the imitation David, Neptune, Hercules, and Cacus, with their long fingers and outsize genitals. *And toward this nexus, great waves of men once moved*, I thought, *drawn by the David himself by the dream of freedom itself.* It would have made a wonderful paper... Meanwhile bells rang. Ben and his companion had disappeared. "Time for lunch!" called an old man with bread, and the pigeons flocked and swooped to the earth.

Virgins and Buddhas

Russell Leong

for Ronald Lewis, a virgin in spirit and a Buddha in action

I don't get up early in the morning. Before Ma goes to the grocery store she wakes Ba and me up. She puts his walking cane right near their bed. I can hear the soft thud of his feet and the click of the cane on the tile floor when he makes his way to the bathroom. She knocks on my door and calls me *lan doi* or lazy kid. I never see her smile, only her puffy eyes.

Sometimes she mutters in Spanish. No one can understand her except, perhaps, the wooden statue of the Virgin Mary next to the Buddha altar in the hallway. The statue was one of the two things she brought with her from Lima, Peru, where she was born, raised, and stolen away by my father. The other thing was her torn brown leather photograph album.

One time she showed my brother and me a photograph of her and her mother, posed in front of a broad European-style avenue with trees framing white colonial buildings. She was smiling and holding onto her mother's Chinese-style dress. "Lima," in a careful child's handwriting, was penciled in under the sepia-toned image. Her grandfather, who had been sent to Peru as a coolie to work on sugar plantations, had harvested sugarcane, tapped wild rubber trees in the Amazon, and dug for gold. Saving his money, he imported a woman from China to be his wife. They had worked hard and left the Amazonian backwaters of Iquitos, where they had settled originally, to open a general supply store in the capital.

Before we finish our rice soup, Brother has revved up the green pickup parked outside our apartment. He's the only normal one around here. But as soon as he finishes junior college he's planning to join the Navy. Out of here for good.

Some of us go to the clinic in the morning, the rest in the afternoon. If we don't check in, the social workers call our parents or guardians, or our aunts or uncles who sign the state SSI—state disability forms.

I go around noon when the clinic gets leftover doughnuts free from the Hop Luck Pastry Shoppe around the corner. The Pacific Mental Health Center is on the southeastern corner of Stockton Street, beneath the Ping Yuen Housing projects, right through this wooden and glass door.

Through this door is another world. It's as murky as water reflected on the scaly skin of a fish, any of the gray-white ones piled high on the aluminum pans on Grant Avenue. Daylight barely reaches the inside of the clinic; here we are just soft bones, stagnant blood, and slow fins serving out our time.

But they can't lock us up. For sure we would die in the state wards. I remember visiting my ex-girlfriend at Agnew's Asylum in Napa. It took me two hours to get there by bus. Before I even walked into the large corridor waiting room I could hear the screaming and moaning. It was how I imagined cattle or ducks or pigs sounded when they were being slaughtered for market. She was pale-looking, and we had nothing to say to each other because her eyes were washed out. Emptied. They didn't see me anymore. From the screaming noises, I expected to see blood on her white smock. But it was clean. I left her staring at me because I couldn't stand to look at her. As none of us have yet committed serious crimes—kidnapped or gunned down anyone important—prison's really not the place for us either. You must understand that for them to keep their jobs they keep on prescribing pills and make sure we go to the outpatient care clinic. No one looks up at me when I arrive, just the social workers who, after all, are paid to pay attention.

The main room is lined with brown metal folding chairs, with big tables in the middle. Seven-Up bottles with one or two cutout paper flowers decorate the tables. The back wall has a long counter. Behind that is where a secretary and a couple of social workers and staff have their desks.

I almost bump into Diana. She's hunched over as usual, her head staring down at the table, at a doughnut crust and a Styrofoam cup of coffee.

"Diana!" I yell in her face, otherwise she would not hear me, or pretend not to. Her gentle face peeps up from the yellow knit sweater with the Chinese symbols for longevity embroidered on it. She will live a long time, her mother hopes, and I cross my fingers hoping she will.

"Do you know what this red thing here is?" I ask her, pointing to my heart. Every time I come here I ask her the same thing, to make sure she and I still mean the same to each other.

"It's me," she says, smiling and pointing to my chest. "It's me, and you, one on the left and one on the right. I finished my dough-nut. *Nei yiu* doughnut *ma?*"

"Mmm, Di. I don't see any left."

Someone taps my shoulders. "Welcome back, Lee. Good to see you. You haven't been to the clinic in a week. We were worried."

"Yeah? Miss Woo, guess if I don't come around you don't meet your quota."

Miss Woo drops her smile and walks away. Quickly, out of the cor-ner of my good eye, I see her scribbling furiously on a yellow legal pad, and putting the note in Dr. Lau's mail slot. Dr. Lau was my doc-tor. He was the one who prescribed the orange pills. He was the one who saw me every Friday. Just another Chinaman, from Hong Kong. This place was full of 'em; half the people who came here and most of the docs and shrinks and workers were from there.

I find a seat next to Diana. John winks at me from across the table. He's the one you always see walking around Chinatown, wearing a checkered sports jacket, his head in the air, not looking to the right or to the left. One time I followed him for a dozen blocks, and he only stopped twice: once to look at a Chinese movie billboard and the other to look at a window display of plastic toy ducks dipping their beaks into a bucket full of water. He looked at the ducks for a long time.

John always looked like he had somewhere to go, but he just walked in circles everyday. People around here were used to seeing him, unchanged over the past five years. Every morning rain or shine you could see him leaving the Victory Hotel on Clay Street at exactly 7:30 A.M.

Some said he escaped from a Vietnamese fishing boat in 1973; others said he was the son of a rich Chinese-Vietnamese banker from Cholon who had sent enough money to the clinic to take care of John for nine more lives. He never talked. The social workers treated him nice. A man like that didn't bother folks. I nodded to him. I had a gut feeling he knew more than he could ever say. I wanted to be there just in case he opened his mouth one day.

This Wednesday was quiet, except for Rowena's radio: Smoky Robinson and the Miracles. Rowena Gee: 5 foot 5 in thigh-high boots with five-inch stiletto heels walked in with her six-foot tall boyfriend, Herbie. Baby-faced. She must have been over thirty but no lines, no wrinkles at all.

"Hiya, and you, and you, and Di, and Johnny baby," she coos. Today her makeup is thicker. Green eye shadow and orange lips.

"Herbie," Miss Woo says, "please turn your radio down. This is not a public park."

Herbie worked in a North Beach Radio Shack about a mile or so from here. He and Rowena had been tight for almost as long as I could remember. As the social workers had said, speaking softly among themselves in Chinese, not only was he Black, but five years younger than Rowena. "But at least he has a job."

I keep track of people, where they go and what they do, especially the doctors. Got to make sure they're doing an honest job. Because no one else here does.

About Rowena and Diana and John: I have to point out that most everyone in here has two things in common: They are baby-faced and they never wore no hats, including me. The face business—there are all kinds of reasons but I have my explanation: we don't let the world bother us too much.

As for hats—none of us have been or ever will be accepted into the U.S. military. None of us are businessmen—with the black fedoras; none of us are old China women—with the tight knitted skullcaps. None of us work in poultry and fish shops and wear those white paper hats. No felt hats, knit or paper hats, or greasy hats. Unlike the rest of you, we bare our heads to the air and sky. How many times we have uncovered our heads to Chinatown social workers and doctors who don't know what to do with us?

Hatless, we're part of Chinatown. Yet we're not. Not working. The state pays us general disability, and we're supposed to get taken care of by these grease-ball social workers. The truth of the matter is: I'm the caretaker for all of us who wear no hats. The hatless family. They're my best friends. That's why I'm writing this in my own long-winded way, before they change the medications on us or ship some of us to the funny farm like they sent my ex-girl.

I don't know exactly what changes each capsule causes in me. I take them, though—it's been two years now. Otherwise I get edgy and nervous. Don't know much about the different ones they give me, but they're supposed to calm me down. Don't get me wrong. I am a lot calmer now. That's why I'm still coming here, until I get perfectly calm.

Maybe Doc is right. Sometimes I need those pills. Especially with Ma yelling at me at the grocery store. I hear her yelling all the time, even though no one else can hear her.

Brother says I'm crazy. "Ma's not yelling at you, all she said is will you go downstairs and turn the fire down beneath the pot of abalone on the stove." I thought she was yelling at me.

Ba gives me a drowsy look. I wish he would fall flat on his eighty-two-year-old face. That's not nice for a son to say, I know. But he might as well fall. He sits there, dreaming of when he was a middle-aged man. When he went to Hong Kong to marry my Ma. They sent my beautiful Ma, she was only twenty-one then—from Lima to

Hong Kong to marry a fifty-year-old man she never even saw before. She was one of five daughters, and there weren't enough eligible Chinese men in Peru, at the time, to marry all five off.

Through family connections, what she saw was a photograph of a much younger man, not the old one who finally met her at the Kowloon wharf in 1958. On the ship, she told me, she had made friends with a young Chinese man, from Caracas, who was coming to Hong Kong to meet the village girl arranged for him. An arrangement in reverse. Talking about her trip was the only time I saw her eyes soften, but she quickly brushed her eyes with the corner of her apron and told me to get back to work.

I think she remembered that man because of the Chinese customer from Venezuela who had come into the store one morning to buy tins of Canadian beef jerky and packages of dried Hawaiian pineapple for a trip he was planning to make to Latin America. From the back of the store where I was unloading crates of preserved duck eggs, I didn't see the customer clearly, just the shadow of his straw fedora and pencil mustache. About an hour later, she began telling me about the voyage she had made over twenty-five years ago, but it was as if she was talking to herself. I didn't say a word.

She got a raw deal. Ba outlived his other two wives and I can see why. I think Ma cries alone in Spanish at home, after Ba, Brother, and I go to sleep.

She's yelling at me again. I duck behind the stack of boxes that read HANDLE WITH CARE, SOYA SAUCE and stick my hands on top of my ears until the yelling stops. Then I walk down the damp wooden stairs to the basement kitchen.

The leathery odor fills the store. Dried abalone has been boiling for hours. I turn up the fire, then wipe the grease from my fingers on my pants. I go over to the sink and start washing the lunch dishes. The sink has no drainpipe, so I dunk the cups, chopsticks, and bowls carefully into the plastic pan with cold suds, and then slosh them through with hot water. After stacking the bowls and cups I carry the dirty water to the toilet and dump it all down. The water gets on my pants and sneakers. But I don't let it bother me. We live like fishes here. Fishes swimming in clogged watery basements. Carp, eel, rock cod, salmon, flatfish, bass, floating clean or slimy, dead or alive through the streets.

I don't wear hats, like the old folks. They're always protecting their heads, afraid maybe something is going to happen to them, that heaven is going to fall down on them. That somebody from a family association third floor balcony will spit a wad or drop a cup of red Hawaiian Punch on their heads. I can't worry about such futuristic things. I'm swimming through my life, in the here and now. Fish don't wear hats, never seen any with them.

I scramble up the stairs. Ba is still slumped on the wooden chair, the cold cigar on the ashtray next to him. He snores, right in front of the customers' faces. Longevity, what good is it? I hope Diana dies young, happy in her yellow sweater. She don't deserve to end up like Ma, in a fixed marriage, serving some guy old enough to be her father. He sits on that rattan chair snoring through the afternoon, then wakes up for dinner. After Brother drives them home in the pickup, he sleeps again until his breakfast porridge. Sleep and eat. Day in and day out.

At least Diana still smiles when I yell her name. Ma just gives me a pained look when I call her name, and takes a five-dollar bill out of the cash register and hands it to me. "No gamble," she warns.

"Ma, I got to go to the clinic now."

"*Gei dim fan oak?*" she asks me.

"I'll be home around 4," I answer.

Suddenly her eyes light up, with fire or something else. "Be sure you go. The doctors are good for you. Don't run away. *Chinos cimarrones.* If you don't go they stop the checks."

"Ma, I know they'd stop them—what did you say?"

"They used to call coolies that—runaway Chinese—when they ran away from the fields. Grandfather told me he ran away from the plantation once. Whipped because he still hadn't paid up his fare from China."

I turn out the door. I don't tell her sometimes I felt like tearing them up and dangling the torn checks in her face. Maybe she likes me to stay sick, as sick as she is for staying here with Ba. On the other hand, where would she go? She couldn't swim back to Peru because there was no one there for her anymore: Her parents were dead and her four sisters were scattered throughout the world, from Canada to Hong Kong. So we hang together here, sinking in the basement water.

If I got well, clerks downtown would nod at each other and say to themselves, "Lester Kwok-Lee is finally well. Scratch him off the list. We only pay for sickos."

I sprint the three blocks up the hill to the clinic. Thursday is dance day. The big room is empty. The mural on one wall shows Chinese laborers working on the railroads and digging for gold. Everyone's face was tinted yellow in the picture. Maybe they were eating the gold whole or had yellow fever or hepatitis. The corner of the scratched and dusty mural was signed, "James Leong, 1952." I wasn't even born yet. Strains of "The Hawaiian Wedding Song" drift into the clinic from the yard. I walk out the open back door.

Diana and John are hand in hand, marching under an arch of arms formed by Miss Woo and another social worker. They look like they are getting married, right here in the project yard, stepping delicately over gobs of weathered dark bubble gum pressed into the asphalt. Rowena is off to the side, by herself, fondling her Hawaiian lei made of pink toilet tissue paper during craft day yesterday. I cup my hands like I was blowing into a shell and let out a big fartlike sound with my lips.

I yell: "Hooray for John and Diane, hooray for the bridesmaids, happy Hawaii, happy Chinatown."

Rowena blows me a kiss and completes the ceremony by taking a dollar bill out of each of her black boots and giving it to the bride and groom. A half dozen people on the wooden benches look away, past the scrawny bushes below the project walls.

"Lee," Miss Woo interrupts. "Dr. Lau wants to see you. You go into the office in about five minutes."

She was afraid of me. She knew I was running this place, making sure all of them did their jobs, filled the forms, checked the right names, picked up the pink box of stale doughnuts every afternoon. Behind her pointy Hong Kong face, under her polyester blouse and blue skirts she wore everyday, she knew that I knew. That's why I didn't bother her much. As long as I came to the clinic two out of five days, they wouldn't stop the SSI checks coming. She wouldn't dare.

Dr. Lau is waiting in his office, smiling. He strokes his receding chin with his left hand. He has one of those pickled smiles that looked as if he had a sour Chinese plum stuck to both sides of his upper gums.

"Lee, have a seat. Haven't seen you for a while. Just thought I'd check up on you. We cut the Demerol, you know. You're getting much better."

"Doc, I get used to the pills. The color. Now that you've switched it to blue I feel lost. I liked those orange ones best."

"Lee, you know how you used to pick on Miss Woo, pick on Diana, and all the others in here. Since we've given you the new medication, Thorazine, you seem much more relaxed. Do you feel relaxed?"

"I don't trust you. Or Miss Woo. What did she write you in that note the other day?"

"You mean Wednesday? She just told me you had showed up after a week's absence, and she thought it was time for you to see me again. That's all."

"I don't care. Still don't trust her. Any of you from China."

"Lee, it is true that most of us were born in China. I myself am Chinese, but I was born in Burma. We can communicate better with Chinese—from everywhere. For instance, John is from Vietnam. He speaks *chiu chou,* another Cantonese dialect. But I'm able to speak with him."

"I don't think he talks to anybody. Does he say anything to you?

"Not much, not much. But we want to find out about you."

"Doc, I want to tell you not to worry. The clinic is running fine. I've checked everything out. You don't have to worry about me, or

Diana, or Rowena, or my mother or father or brother. They're just fine. But I don't want to talk to you anymore today."

"All of us feel antisocial at times. But that's perfectly normal. Just understand that I'm—we're here when you need us."

"That's it?

"See you next week. I'm glad everything is working out. No more yelling in your ears?"

Doc's sneaky, like the oriental painting of two birds on a branch behind his desk. The birds probably just finished eating a hundred worms. But they just sit there looking all pretty and innocent. Doc's done his duty for the week, another mark on my chart. Seen Diana, seen John, seen me, and all the rest. He can go home and relax. He gets paid good. I should be the one paid. I take care of them.

Once you pass through the scales of the fish you never come out. Scales and bones and fins and gills get stuck in your throat. You don't see light in the same way again. No one understands what I'm trying to say. Maybe Diana, if she had five percent more brain cells. I'm not putting her down. It wasn't her fault how she was born or whatever happened to her, to Ma, or to me.

One Friday last year, we took a trip outside Chinatown on the number 30 bus early in the morning. It was gray, not sunny, and I had my warm parka on. We had bag lunches. There were ten of us. We transferred to the 5 McAllister bus to Golden Gate Park. We were going to the Aquarium and the Japanese Tea Garden.

I'll never forget that day. My orangeade dripped through the paper bag. It was a defective carton. That meant my roast pork bun tasted like orange drink later on. Then, as we were getting off the bus, Rowena almost got killed. She was standing on the street, on the pavement, adjusting her black nylon stockings. A motorcycle almost ran her down. That didn't seem to bother her. She blew a kiss to the motorcyclist, who was already half a block away. Miss Woo was panicky—I saw it in her eyes. I laughed, and she threw me a dirty look.

In order to get to the aquarium section, we had to pass through the reptile section first. The glass cages were full of colored snakes that looked edible. That's what I heard—Chinese in China eat everything that can be skinned, fried, boiled, or steamed. That's logical; anything tastes good if it's prepared right.

I passed out copper pennies to everyone, and we started to pelt the sleepy alligators in the algae-green pond below the steel railing. I could tell Miss Woo didn't like what we were doing, but she didn't say anything. I imagined we could, all ten of us, lift her up and toss her in.

The huge room was lined wall-to-wall with glass windows. Tiny fish as big as your little finger zipped this way and that. Some were like neon, with fluorescent coloring. These were live fish, arranged against backdrops of rock and ocean weeds. I would like to have one of those tanks one day. Diana stood tall and straight, her head at attention like a soldier, entranced by the little fish that were like electric blue sparks.

The fish room opened up suddenly to the dolphin chamber, with a wider and taller picture window glass. Rowena pressed the red button on the wall. We could hear dolphins yelping in their own language, which none of us could understand. But we listened. The dolphin pool was bare, no ferns, weeds, or rocks. They swam around and around in the blue water. They were like birds in the sky. But then my hands brushed the cool glass walls of the transparent tank.

We were watching them. Kids poked their greasy fingers, leaned their noses, and made funny faces at the dolphins. I stood with John and watched the dolphins and the people. I looked at John, and he was smiling, not saying a word. A plaque by the tank said dolphins were one of the most intelligent animals on Earth, and that scientists were studying and testing them for the good of mankind.

I turned away, without telling anyone where I was going. I ran out of the dolphin room and past the fish tanks. Making a left, I went through the dark hall of reptilian cages, circled around the alligator pond, and cut out of the entrance.

The gray sky had turned to a light drizzle. My feet picked up speed, and I found myself between the green benches of the music concourse. I dodged an old woman with a white cane and ran through the wooden gate into the Japanese Tea Garden. We were supposed to visit here later, so my friends would eventually find me.

Rounded hills and bushes. Each tree was shaped by gardeners. I saw a Filipino man raking fallen leaves into piles of red, brown and yellow. My eyes were wet, but not because of the rain.

Dolphins were beautiful smooth-skinned creatures. But their watery tanks that I had thought were so big a while ago grew smaller and smaller until they shrank to a droplet inside my head.

I walked on the stone paths through the garden. No pathway was straight. Sometimes I found myself walking in small circles, back to where I started. Under a pine tree facing me, a greenish statue of Buddha sat peacefully with his hands folded on his lap. His expression looked like my kung fu teacher's when he was doing his White Crane breathing exercises.

I wish I had a camera. I would stand behind Buddha and ask a friend to take a picture of me hidden behind. Nobody would be able to see me in the photograph. Only Buddha and I would know where I stood. Ma had her Virgin Mary, silent and wooden, which reflected the light of the votive candle Ma used sometimes on special holidays. But she bowed to Ba's ancestral shrine and lit incense up at the same time. When I was a child, I waited to see which would go out first: the wick of the candle or the orange point of the lit punk stick. Who would win: virgins or Buddhas.

I continued walking, past the wooden teahouse crammed with tourists, drinking tea and eating fortune cookies. Glass wind chimes tinkled from the gift shop next door. I crossed a stream. Water was flowing freely. Over the pond a strange humped Japanese wooden bridge looked steep. There were no steps, just rungs. A few people were clambering up, taking photos. I watched until everyone had deserted the bridge. Then I started on the first wooden rung. Each rung was a piece of split bamboo that nicely caught your heel. Nineteen steps to the top, half of my life. Reaching the top rung, I stopped and looked at the green garden spread out below me.

It looked different from above. The people looked smaller. I could see some circular pathways I had missed. About ten yards away, I saw my bare-headed friends straggling in, some eating from their lunch bags. Miss Woo, wearing a scarf to protect her permed hair from the drizzle, was leading them, holding on to Diana's hand.

Diana had the same kind of expression that my Ma had in the Peruvian photograph, holding on to her mother. Trust. I spit into the water. They sold you down the river, Ma. Now we are gone, and we can never swim back.

I decided to stay on top of the bridge until they saw me. If they missed me, I knew how to get back to Chinatown by bus. I would tell them they had gotten lost, not me.

Into a Mirror
Excerpt from The Same Embrace

Michael Lowenthal

(*The Same Embrace* is the story of Jacob and Jonathan Rosenbaum, identical twins who, though close as boys, choose radically different lives as adults: Jacob as a gay activist in Boston and Jonathan as an Orthodox Jew in Israel. Present-action chapters alternate with Jacob's childhood memories such as this one, which takes place at the summer home of their Holocaust-refugee grandparents.)

Jacob had noticed the glow the previous summer, on cloudy nights when light hugged the ground. Blue and orange like a flaring gas flame, it made the marsh shimmer with shadows, birthing wispy figures between tall stalks of grass, then just as quickly stealing them away. He had surmised it was the drive-in movie theater, more than a mile by road but maybe closer as the crow flies. He had figured as much, but he lacked conclusive proof.

Now, lying next to Jonathan on their second night at Nana Jenny and Papa Isaac's cottage, he had a brainstorm.

"You asleep?" he asked the dark shape of his brother.

Seconds of silence. A throaty scraping of phlegm. Then Jonathan's croaking reply: "Not anymore."

"Good. Want to see a movie?"

"A movie? I don't know. I guess maybe if it rains tomorrow."

Jacob sat up and pulled on his shorts. "No, stupid. Now. We're going on the roof."

They visited Cape Cod every year for the three weeks before Labor Day, renting the same small house just a block from the place

Papa Isaac bought when he retired as a rabbi. The Cape was a flexed arm extending out of the torso of Massachusetts, from the armpit at Falmouth all the way to the curled fist of Provincetown. When Jacob told anyone his family summered there, they inevitably asked which part; he had learned to hold up his left arm, mimicking the map, and point. They were in the triceps. Not very glamorous, but functional.

But that August, with the twins a month shy of thirteen, their father was attending a geneticists' conference in Switzerland, the dates of which overlapped with their standard vacation. He had taken their mother with him. And so Jacob and Jonathan were staying a full week with their grandparents.

Nana Jenny and Papa Isaac's cottage was a gray-shingled box at the cul-de-sac of a silent lane. The ocean loomed past the backyard, just beyond a narrow swath of reeds and mud. On days when the wind blew in, the house filled with the smells of wet shellfish, rotting seaweed, all kinds of salty decay. The rich scent livened Jacob, sped his metabolism, as if the composted marsh air were fertilizer for his own growth. He could feel his muscles bulking, his body stretching into new, powerful shapes.

The goal was to get onto the garage. The roof of the main house was out of range, so high that even Papa Isaac, when he strained, could barely graze the gutter with his fingertips. But the garage roof was lower, connected to the main house by a short breezeway. If they could make it up here, the rest would be a cinch.

They built a ladder from the old picnic table and its two long benches. Dried by summers of exposure, the table had the disconcerting lightness of a balsa model, its wood parts warped in unruly twists. Balancing the benches on top of one another was as hard as stacking eggs. An inadvertent touch or a wrong look might disrupt the entire contraption.

Jacob hoisted one knee onto the top rung, but just as the second knee was about to make it up, his instincts made him lower the first again. He flailed that way awhile, like his mother riding her Exercycle, pedaling hard but not getting anywhere.

Finally he managed to get both knees on the top bench. He rested a split second, then flexed to stand, but was swiftly flung off as if someone had pressed Eject.

When he had gathered himself and stood upright again, he whispered, "Makes you respect them, doesn't it?"

"Who?" Jonathan asked.

"Olga Korbut. Nadia Comaneci. The balance beam is like, less than *half* as wide as these benches."

Jonathan groaned. "I can't believe you watch that gymnastics crap." He pushed Jacob out of his way and stepped onto the table. "Here," he demanded. "Hold it steady."

Jacob watched his brother climb up, place his palms on the edge of the roof, and propel himself into the air, all in one graceful motion. A sprinkle of gravel settled into Jacob's hair like dandruff.

Jonathan squatted on the roof's edge. "Come on," he called. "It's great up here."

"How'd you do it?" Jacob asked, breathless with awe.

"Cake," Jonathan said. "Just don't think about it."

"I can't not think about it."

"Sure you can. Pretend it's easy, and it will be."

Jacob stepped onto the first bench and was surprised how much steadier it seemed. Then he positioned his knee on the top bench. He was trying not to think about it, the way Jonathan had instructed. He was trying to think instead of eagles and kites, things that soared in the air, trying to forget his body's mass.

The picnic bench tottered, crashed. Jacob's balls sucked into his stomach, and his stomach into his throat—the same plunging nausea as hitting turbulence in an airplane.

"I can't do it," he said. He heard his voice break. His legs quaked as if trapped on a sewing machine's seesawing pedal.

"Here," Jonathan said, extending a thin arm that shone strangely in the starlight. "Make it to the top again and then I'll pull you."

Jacob peeled a rust-colored chip of paint from the bottom bench. "I can't."

"I thought you wanted to check out the glow," Jonathan said.

"I do."

"Well, then get up here."

Jacob tested the top bench. Wobbly as ever. But he knew it was possible. Jonathan had done it.

He stepped to the first level and, without stopping to catch his balance, kept going to the second. The roof's edge was only inches above his head. He reached—higher, higher, *there*. But just as his fingertips brushed the coarse shingles, the world collapsed under him. For a moment he weighed nothing, a marionette suspended in midair. Then he was nothing *but* weight; he fell backward and down.

Something clamped his wrists. A flash of burn and everything stopped. He dangled there, connected to the world only by Jonathan's clenched fingers.

"Don't let go," he whispered, unable to summon his full voice.

Jonathan didn't say anything, but rocked back on his heels, and Jacob was lifted, his stomach scraping the asphalt edge of shingles until at last he hugged the cool roof.

The ivy-covered chimney provided ample handholds. They clambered from the breezeway to the main roof and then stepped—arms spanned like tightrope walkers', one foot on each side of the peak—to the TV antenna's rusty skeleton. They moved on tiptoes, in careful unison. Papa Isaac and Nana Jenny were an unsettling presence below, in the ponderous darkness of the house.

This visit was the first time Jacob had witnessed his grandparents in their daily existence, rather than for just a holiday dinner or special event. They were different people this way, people he didn't like as much. More than anything, it was the silence.

Jacob had known hints of it before: Sometimes in the middle of a Shabbos dinner in Brookline, the phone would ring. Nobody would say anything, but the grown-ups all seemed to know the call was for Nana Jenny. When she returned to the table, she and Papa Isaac would not speak to each other for minutes.

But here the silence was as permanent as the film of soot crusted blackly on the barbecue. Papa Isaac would sit for hours in his armchair, thick-rimmed reading glasses perched on his nose, making no sound besides the snap of prayer-book pages. Nana Jenny didn't talk either, except to herself. Sometimes, as she sat needlepointing a pillow cover, her lips would begin to move. She would tilt her head with a question, pause, then nod firmly with her own response.

Jacob was afraid to cough or chew food too loudly around his grandparents. They acted as though the house were an airtight box made of fragile glass. A disturbing noise might shatter the walls, and the air would escape, leaving everybody gasping.

But he wasn't in the house now. He was on top of it, on the roof, a different world.

The salt breeze swirled seductively, tickling its way into his nostrils. Reflected off the gray shingles, the starlight bestowed milky halos on everything, making objects glow like the ghosts of bones in an X-ray. Jacob imagined he had special powers of vision, superhero eyes.

When he turned to face the marsh, he saw that his hunch had been correct. The drive-in screen was huge, even at this distance, a miracle of dancing light in the sky. The entire shimmering rectangle was visible except for a trio of fuzzy blotches at the bottom, probably trees at the marsh's far edge.

"It's like at the movies," Jonathan said, "only bigger."

"Shh," Jacob whispered. "Can you hear?"

They held their breath in deference to the distant luminescence. There was only the rush of wind, the swish of marsh grass, the quiet roar of a seashell pressed against an ear.

"You can follow it anyway," Jonathan said. "She just told him not to go through that door, but he's not going to listen."

It was some horror thing from the year before, maybe one of the *Halloween* movies. Just as Jonathan had predicted, the male actor opened a door and entered a shadowy room.

"Now she'll follow him," Jacob said, excited by the game. "And the door will slam behind them and they'll be trapped!"

"Unh-unh. Too predictable. She'll wait for him outside, thinking it's safer, but when he comes out the bad guy will have gotten her."

They watched and waited. Jacob wanted to warn the woman, to tell her to follow her friend into the other room, but from this distance she was tragically unreachable. The director had inserted delay shots, panning around the room, close-ups of cobwebbed furniture. The quiet of the marsh was thunderous. Jacob invented music in his head to make the scene more familiar, more like what he expected at the movies. He conjured the menacing wail of violins, creepy black-key piano chords.

Suddenly the man on screen whipped around. Had he heard something? Had there been a scream? He ran out of the room and straight into the blood-soaked body of his female companion, a kitchen knife lodged in her back. Jacob recoiled and grabbed into the night. It was seconds before he realized what he had clutched was not the antenna, not the roof, but his brother's hand. He was embarrassed until he felt the sweaty reciprocating squeeze.

They let go without looking at each other.

"Pretty real," Jonathan said.

Jacob shook imaginary blood from his hands. "*Too* real."

Jonathan concluded, "They should have stuck together."

After the gory murder scene came a long lull of exposition. It made no sense without the dialogue. Jacob grew bored. He found himself looking away from the screen for minutes at a time.

He and Jonathan sat at the very top of the roof, their elbows hooked over the peak. Jacob loved just lying there, soaking in the starry night. He blinked his eyes rapidly, creating strobe effects with the constellations. He imagined he was inside a giant whirling disco ball.

A small-engined plane buzzed overhead, lights flickering like a battalion of colored fireflies. Jacob knew the plane was on its way to the Hyannis airport, the one John F. Kennedy had used when he was president. Their father never failed to point this out, every time they circled the rotary in front of the airport's entrance. "You know JFK flew in here on weekends?" he would say. "They had to extend the runway so it could handle Air Force 1."

"Yes," Jacob and Jonathan always answered dutifully, and then as their father recited his favorite part of the inaugural address, they would mouth the words in unison: "Let the word go forth from this time and place, to friend and foe alike, that the torch has been passed to a new generation…"

Jacob felt for the Kennedys. He knew it was a cliché—*everyone* felt for the Kennedys—but he was sure his connection with the family was special. He thought often of the brothers—Joe, Jack, Bobby, and Teddy—picturing them as portraits on a mahogany-paneled wall. One by one, the portraits shook and fell, the frames cracking on the floor, until only Teddy remained.

Jacob had always sympathized most with Teddy. Teddy, who should have been the pampered youngest, but ended up carrying the entire family's burden. Teddy, who had to watch his brothers, one after another, disappear into their dark, dusty graves. Jacob wondered sometimes what it would be like to lose Jonathan, to have to dress for his own brother's funeral. What would it be like to be a portrait hanging alone?

A surge of warm air washed up the roof's incline. Just as quickly, a cooler wave pushed in, repelling the warmth, the way pockets of different-temperature water torpedoed below the surf at Seagull Beach. Jacob shuddered, inched closer to Jonathan.

"Cold?" Jonathan asked. Without waiting for answer, he scooted over, closing the gap still further. The short hairs on Jacob's calves stood at attention, dozens of tiny arms reaching out, stretching for Jonathan.

His brother lay quietly next to him. His head was tipped back against the sharp peak of the roof, his eyes closed. His nostrils flared wide with every breath as if he were trying to steal all the air for himself. Maybe it was the starlight, or the shifting glow from the drive-in screen, but Jacob was amazed by Jonathan's softness. It was the only way he could describe it—a softness like lamb's wool that compelled him toward it, made him want to bury his face in its plush caress.

Why couldn't things always be this way between them? It occurred to him that it was other people who messed up everything:

their parents, Papa Isaac. If only they could be alone like this.

He had the urge to say something to Jonathan, something big. He thought of Teddy Kennedy, who could never, ever speak to his brothers again. Jacob should not take for granted what he still had. But the only sentences that came to mind were meaningless in their self-evidence: "It's just us" or "You're my brother." He felt the need to apologize for something, to touch Jonathan's arm and whisper, "I'm so sorry." But Jonathan might ask, "Sorry for what?" and he wouldn't know what to say.

Another plane flew overhead, this time heading away from Hyannis. Jacob pictured it swooping out past Seagull Beach and over the Atlantic, then continuing on and on to—where? Greenland? France? Some distant and exotic place. The buzzing of the plane's small engines tickled his neck, the same metallic shock of arousal as when Nick the barber clippered behind his ears. Jacob always squirmed at the electric razor's touch, twisting in the vinyl chair, and Nick threatened haircut disaster if he moved another inch. The clippers' vibrations, combined with the challenge of self-restraint, swelled Jacob's dick to a lump beneath the plastic apron.

It was like that now, hard and itchy in the cotton of his underwear. His heart was a jittering alarm clock. Bullets of hot blood shot through his neck. He shifted to hide the bulge in his shorts, but something inexplicable seized him; he shifted back, leaving it visible.

"You all tingly?" he asked Jonathan. He rubbed his palms briskly on his calves, creating a prickle of friction.

"My legs?" Jonathan asked.

Jacob nodded.

"Kind of," Jonathan said. "But you've got more hairs than I do." He pressed his right leg against Jacob's left.

Jacob thought he saw his brother's eyes glance at his crotch. He couldn't be sure. He trailed his fingers down the valley where their legs were joined. Jonathan's hand met his. Their fingers danced on each other's goose-bumped skin.

And then Jacob was talking, forcing speech through the pounding gully of his throat: "Some of the guys were joking. At camp? About being identical twins." It wasn't true, but Jacob couldn't admit that the thoughts he was about to confess were his own. "They wanted to know did we have identical everything. Like identical dicks."

He tried to say the last word softly, like a secret, but it crackled in the night air. He wished he could pull it back, swallow it, try again. There was a fluttering on his leg. He was too scared to look.

"What'd you tell them?" Jonathan asked.

"That how should I know. That we didn't sit around with our pants off all the time." Jacob was hoping to come off as blasé, the way other guys sounded when they talked about sex, but everything was coming out wrong.

"Have you?" Jonathan asked.

"What?"

"Wondered," Jonathan said. "You know. If they're the same?"

Jacob made a sound that he might be able to claim later had been a cough, not an affirmation.

"I don't care," Jonathan blurted. "I'd do it."

"You serious?" Jacob asked.

Jonathan's eyes flickered with the drive-in light, full of possibility. "Sure," he said. "Yeah. You want to?"

The wind had picked up, making the TV antenna hum like a distant harmonica. A briny smell lifted from the marsh; lingered; passed. They leaned into each other, creating a sheltered canyon. Jacob imagined they were more than twins, that they were the same person, the same brain, coexisting in two separate bodies.

They unbuttoned their shorts. Jacob's Sears briefs were grayer, more worn in spots than Jonathan's. He gripped the elastic band with his right hand so his brother wouldn't see how badly he was shaking.

Jonathan cupped his hand over his crotch, as if protecting a baby bird. "It's all hard," he said. He lifted his fingers an inch and pretended to peek.

"Me too," Jacob said.

"On three?"

"One...two...three."

Together, they lifted their hips and shimmied down the underwear. Jonathan's dick looked pretty much the same as his—four inches long, as big around as the Magic Markers their social studies teacher, Miss Pinter, used on the butcher-papered bulletin board. But Jonathan's had a freckle, a tiny beauty mark a pinkie's width from the hole. Jacob wondered why he didn't have one too.

Jonathan's crotch was hairless, just a smattering of brown wisps in the smooth exposed V. Jacob knew each of the two dozen hairs in his own crotch by heart. But looking down now at his body, he could see none of them. The strange light obscured everything. Maybe Jonathan too had hair that didn't show.

They leaned closer until their shoulders bumped, balancing their bodies in a sturdy teepee. Every movement Jacob made was matched by Jonathan, as if they were connected by a pivot point. He thought of those dumb slapstick routines when one character encounters another and thinks at first that he's looking into a mirror. He moves left, and the other guy moves left. He raises his hand; the other hand is raised. But then the other character thumbs his nose and the illusion is shattered.

Jacob pushed his dick down so it poked straight at Jonathan. Jonathan did the same. Their dicks were parallel, an equal sign of flesh.

"They're the same length," Jacob said.

"Yeah, but yours is curved." Jonathan pointed with his chin.

Jacob had worried Jonathan would notice this. The deformity got worse every time he checked. "It's not that much," he said.

Jonathan giggled. "I bet it's from playing with yourself too much."

Jacob saw an opening to continue his fabrication. "The guys?" he began, swallowing hard. "They said we probably jerked each other off, because we'd know exactly what felt good."

Jonathan giggled again, harder this time, and the convulsions were contagious. They collapsed together laughing. Jacob's left arm was trapped between them, but he didn't mind. The tightness felt good, a hot security.

"Pretty dumb," Jonathan said. He wiggled closer.

"I know," Jacob said. "Really dumb."

Something brushed against his dick. It was an accident of motion. Neither of them pulled away.

"But they could be right," Jonathan said.

"They could," Jacob agreed.

He touched Jonathan first. His brother's dick was as hard as his, but warmer, the skin gummed with the tackiness of cheese that's been melted, then cooled again. Jacob tried to use the same amount of pressure he used on himself, the same rapid motion with his wrist. But it was different because he couldn't feel the results. He didn't know what adjustments to make, or when.

When Jonathan curled a loose fist around him, Jacob flinched. His brother's fingers had the effect of a hypodermic prick, stinging the flesh and itching and throbbing numbly all at once. But the touch reached other places too, deep below the skin. The sizzled lining of his stomach. His badly aching throat.

They continued silently. Jacob tugged on Jonathan; Jonathan tugged on him. Their arms were like jumper cables connecting car batteries, the current flowing from one body to the other, then back, the circuit complete.

Jacob had had his first ejaculation four months earlier. He'd been lying on the bathroom floor, his legs propped against the tiled wall, rubbing himself against his stomach. It wasn't until he was finished that he noticed the creamy fluid pooled in his belly button. By now he was used to the feeling, the Morse code of muscles in his groin that signaled impending eruption.

Jonathan pulled two, three, four more times and the liquid pulsed deep inside Jacob's body. He was thinking of his brother's name, chanting it to himself. *Jon. Jon. Jon.* The softness of the *O,* an open mouth.

Jonathan jerked away. "Eew," he shrieked, dropping Jacob's dick. "You got stuff on my T-shirt."

"Mmm?" Jacob was still in the trance of his orgasm. He looked down: two wet globs. "Oh," he said. "Sorry."

"It's disgusting! Get it off!"

"Shhh." Jacob pointed at the roof. "Their bedroom's right there."

Jonathan held the T-shirt away from his stomach as if it were soaked in acid.

"What's the big deal?" Jacob said. "It's what happens when you come."

Jonathan's jaw trembled. He looked like he was about to cry or throw up.

"Didn't you come yet?" Jacob asked.

Jonathan kicked him. "Just get it off!"

A shiver ripped through Jacob's body. He felt suddenly exposed, lying there without his pants. Someone could see them. Anyone. Passengers in the planes to and from Hyannis could report them to the police.

He stood and tugged his underwear and shorts together over his hips. Jonathan was still splayed below him, still trying to keep the T-shirt from touching his skin.

"Get up," Jacob said. "We'll get caught."

Jonathan didn't move.

"Come on, get up!"

When there was still no response, Jacob turned away. "Fine," he said. "Stay. I don't care."

He strode across the roof, moving carelessly as if on flat ground. He hopped down onto the breezeway and made his way over to the garage. Loose gravel had lodged in his briefs. The grit scraped the tender skin of his crack, but he ignored it.

He caught himself at the edge of the garage roof, the height twisting his stomach. He'd forgotten that their picnic table ladder had toppled.

Crouched along the roofline, the toes of his sneakers poking just over the edge, Jacob could feel the ground's magnet pull. The grass glistened, starlight glancing off just-formed dew. Somewhere over the ocean, a plane's engine faintly sputtered. He drew a breath and leapfrogged into the emptiness. The world crashed toward him in fast forward, then jammed to a halt. He had landed on his feet.

As he turned to walk to the main house, he heard a scratching from above. Jonathan stood at the roof's edge, kicking his sneakers at the shingles. He had stripped his T-shirt and wadded it into a ball, which he held at arm's length like a dead animal.

"How'm I supposed to get down?" he asked.

"You seemed to get up just fine," Jacob said.

Jonathan looked small from this perspective. Jacob could hold a fist in front of his face and block out his brother's entire figure.

"There were the benches before," Jonathan said. "I can't."

Jacob was going to say mean things, to hiss back Jonathan's own advice—"Just don't think about it"—but decided it wasn't worth the effort. He turned the garage corner and headed for the house, the wet grass spitting on his ankles.

Say Goodbye to Middletown

by William J. Mann

His hands, as I remember them, were like the twisted apples left on the trees after the apple-pickers were through.

Not like the hands of the boys I'm watching now: soft hands, smooth, cupping each other's hard pink butt. They don't know I'm watching them. They think they're hidden, but they're wrong. I'm sitting in my car, pretending to be asleep. They think the bushes around the cold asphalt lot protect them from being seen. But they're wrong.

It's their hands that fascinate me: hands so unlike the ones I have come here to find, hands that remain forever twisted in my mind. They are the hands of the man who first loved me, who I rewarded for a such a gift with a stretch in jail, simply for teaching me the secret of the apples left behind on the trees. I can see the orchards now, finally, after driving the last three hours, leaving the city before the sun was up, eager to get here while it was still morning. Now, here at the rest stop on Eagle Hill just outside town, my contemplation of the orchards and the town they embrace has been disturbed by the sight of two boys fucking each other, with all the vitality I once had in this place, except my passion had been met not by a boy my own age, but by a man, many times older than I.

I reach into my jeans with some difficulty. The steering wheel is cumbersome to get around, but I manage. I touch myself just as the older boy drops to his knees and takes the younger one into his mouth. They are beautiful. The older one, on his knees, is dark and thin. The younger one, with his head thrown back and his eyes now closed against the cold sky, is fair and stocky. There is nothing about them that reminds me of the boys of New York: no goatees or sleeve-less flannel shirts, no clunky Doc Martens boots, no black leather jackets with crack-and-peel slogans accusing the government of hav-ing blood on its hands. No, these are the boys of Middletown, sim-ple boys, the milk under the cream, not the ones who will be siphoned off, stolen by the lure of the city. These are the sons of the boys I once knew, the sons of their experience if not of their flesh, boys who remained in the place where I was born long after I had left it—and them—behind.

We are the only ones here, these boys and I. They lurk behind a cluster of wild rosebushes, stubborn orange leaves shielding them from the lot. But not from me. The younger boy now grabs his part-ner's hair, fucking his face. I stroke myself, watching the scene, like a porno film with the volume turned down, the way I usually have it. But this is even better: This is an unexpected welcome home.

"Yes," I whisper, watching them. "That's the way."

I hear the younger boy moan, even at this distance. I moan too.

The younger boy comes, and I notice with a queer mix of unease and envy that he does not pull out, that the older boy eagerly drinks what has been offered. There is no hesitation, no negotiation. The boy merely comes, the other swallows, and then they stumble out from the bushes, pulling on their jeans and their sweatshirts, mount-ing their respective bicycles and pedaling away with as much energy as they have just fucked, in opposite directions, of course.

I come into my hand, a sorry excuse for a climax, frothy semen bubbling over my fingers.

I take time to breathe. The air is sharp in my nostrils, sharp and cold, sharp and clear, sharp and blue, very blue, the hard blue of a cloudless sky. I look out over the orchards, barren of fruit. It's past time, and the leaves on the trees are red-tinged gold. The ground is becoming hard. I take a deep breath and exhale slowly, thinking about the trees. The apples have been packed into crates and shipped into stores, baked into pies, and dropped into lunch bags. All gone, except for the few twisted ones left rejected on the branches, tiny deformed apples that cling desperately to the cold limbs, ugly little children who have aged too quickly, abandoned by their too-beautiful brethren, picked over and left to rot.

But that is not the whole story of the twisted apples. Below me is Middletown, and I look down at it like a map memorized: I know these streets that crosshatch through the meadow, ending by the river. I know who walks them, who comes out by day and who by night. When I lived here, back in another time, I knew everything there was to know about this town. I would listen to my mother standing at the clothesline, sharing the gossip with the lady who lived next door. I stayed after school to hear the secretaries in the office trade stories about the nuns and the priests. I listened to the clerks at Britta's Grocery, to the waitresses behind the counter at Henry's Diner, to the old men who sat out on the steps of the post office. I listened, and watched. Watched old Mr. Smoke steal a pack of cigarettes at South End News. Watched Ann Marie Adorno make out with Phillip Stueckel in the choir loft. Watched Eddie Piatrowski's father beat off in his basement to a greasy pile of *Penthouse* magazines. Watched Miss Aletha take off her wig when she thought she was alone. Watched, without ever being seen, without ever being heard.

In the town where I grew up, the factories still stand: big old husks of brick and steel and journeymen's ghosts. I stand now at the edge of Eagle Hill, where I doubt an eagle has roosted for more than a hundred years, and gaze out over the valley at the ruined castles below. They have decayed ignobly for decades, many of them since before I was born. I once played among those ruins: a King—more often a Queen—a knight, a mad monk, the hunchback of Notre Dame. "Stay out of those places," my mother scolded, but what child ever paid his mother any mind when the iron claws of a rusting factory awaited his imagination?

My father, many years before, had worked in one of my castles: as a young man, as a young husband, before he finally moved on to better things, like selling shoes—before the factories themselves moved on, leaving the town behind. "Middletown was once a thriving place," the old-timers in front of the post office would say, "til the factories shut down." As a boy I'd listen to them, not comprehending their melancholy.

For as a boy, what was there to be sorrowful for? For grand adventures in ruined palaces? For long and twisting walks along daisy-covered railroad tracks, for discovering forgotten tunnels and the occasional overturned caboose? For the tall, ivy-covered spires of the university, where I would climb and peer out of the green stained glass windows, imagining myself to be Rapunzel, trying to follow the river all the way past the great bend? Then the watchman would arrive, shouting after me to get out, barking at me that townies weren't allowed up here. I'd run out as fast as I could, back to my own castles, where no one dared to chase me away.

They've boarded up the factories now, I can see, even from way up here on Eagle Hill: posted signs to keep out. Those who dare to enter are no longer boys or imagined queens, but rather hard-eyed addicts with maps of the world etched upon their faces—men who, like my father, may have once worked in these ruined places in days gone by. Today, the children of Middletown do not venture into the crumbling fortresses of my youth; the moat has gone dry and the drawbridge has rotted into pulp. The sadness is now—even to children, I suspect—palpable.

It was in such a place that I first had sex with Alexander Reefy.

He is the man I have come back to see, the man who first touched my trembling skin, the man whose life I ruined and sent to jail. He is the man whose hands live on so strongly in my memory, hands that first touched the pink buds of my nipples, hands that stroked my hair and spanked my innocent butt.

It is the morning of Halloween, his favorite holiday. I remember when he dressed as Marilyn and it shocked me. It was the first time I'd seen a man in drag. Now, twenty years later, I remember that night, the party and the costumes, the Richard Nixon masks and the man who came dressed as H.R. Pufnstuf, and how after everyone had gone home, Alexander Reefy took me up into the night-blackened orchard and taught me the secret of the twisted apples left behind on the trees.

Gnarled apples like his hands. Knuckles like tumors. On my skin. Big hands. Rough hands. Soft, baby skin. His hands, and then his breath, hot and smoky, against my face.

He fucked me in the factory behind St. John the Baptist's, on the edge of Dog Town, where he lived in a two-floor brick house with a wooden front porch. "Don't go down there," my mother had warned me. "That's the bad part of town." And it was, indeed: beyond the crumbling factories the old tenant housing remained, housing built by rich WASP factory owners for their immigrant workers at the turn of the last century. Houses built over swamps, where the river swelled its banks twice every spring, where skunk cabbage grew plentiful and tall, where velvety cat-o-nine-tails enticed children to wade across the muddy, stinking water that licked the edges of the tenements. "Don't go down there," my mother had pleaded, but although I listened intently to every conversation dropped in line at Grant's department store, I had long since stopped listening to her.

When I was a boy, the immigrants had moved on from Dog Town: the Irish and the Poles and the Italians lived in Middletown proper, as proper Middletonians. When I was a boy, Dog Town consisted of the blacks and the perverts, those strange, leftover hippies in VW vans and patchwork-covered bell-bottom jeans. "Don't go down there," my mother warned, time and again. But I turned a brazen shoulder to her pleas, hopping upon my bicycle—the very cool 1974 banana bike with the long shiny purple seat, the newfangled handle-bars and the tall silver bar behind my back—and pedaled with every ounce of strength I had all the way from our quiet little subdivision into the swamps of Dog Town.

"Todd," she says now, her arms outstretched, welcoming me home.

Not my mother. My mother still lives in her quiet little subdivision, in the same house where I grew up all too quickly—that is, until the summer I turned fifteen, when I left my mother's house forever and came here, to Elsa.

"Todd," she says again, encircling me.

How old she has gotten. How unlike my memories. But it is her, just the same: Elsa, the woman who took me in, who set me right, whose roses every year win first place in the Middletown Flower Show. Or at least, used to. I do not know if she still competes. We exchange cards maybe once, twice a year. After I first went away, she would come and visit. She came to my college dorm room once. We had a party. We got her high. But I haven't seen her in seven years. She knows little about my life today. As little as I know of hers.

"Elsa." I look down into her soft blue eyes. How strange it feels to be taller than she is.

A tea kettle whistles. "Join me?" she asks.

I nod. Her kitchen, unlike her, is exactly as I remember: cluttered and odoriferous, with a tanginess underneath, as if something in the refrigerator has gone bad. But it's not an unpleasant smell: the candied scent of overripe fruit or the tempting promise of old wine.

She pours me some tea, and we sit at the table overlooking her yard. A few roses, a deep red-purple, cling to the vines along the trellis. I point this out to her.

"Yes," she says, smiling. "Some of them last this long. But tonight there will be a frost." She sips her tea.

"Will you bring them inside?" I ask.

"I can't save them all," she says.

One of her cats rubs against my ankles. I reach down to stroke it.

"Your letter came as quite a surprise," she says to me.

"I'm sure it did."

"You don't even know if he will want to see you."

"No," I admit. "I don't."

"I was sorry to hear that your lover died," she said.

I look back out the window, at the purple rose on the vine trembling against the cold wind.

"Had you been together long?" Elsa asks.

"Just a year," I tell her. A year of many dreams. I turn my eyes to her. "Do you know I turned thirty-three this year?"

She smiles. "A babe."

I smile back. "Thirty-three. Christ's age. When he was crucified."

She shakes her head. "Since when did you become religious?"

"I'm not. It's just a strange age, that's all. I remember the nuns talking about it, at St. John the Baptist. As if it were magical or something. The double threes. The Holy Trinity." I smile. "There are a lot of threes in Christianity."

She shrugs. "I don't believe in symbolism."

"And I asked myself: What has my life been like in thirty-three years? What have I done, compared to Christ?"

Elsa gives me a stern look. Even with her pure white hair and thousands of wrinkles, it is still the same look she gave me all those years ago—a look much more serious than any my own mother ever gave me, a look that said: "You are being foolish, but I love you anyway." I receive that look for what it is, and I smile.

Elsa lives on Oak Avenue, in a great old Victorian house that was her grandmother's. It's in an old part of town just up from Main Street, and some of the houses are not as well cared for as Elsa's. Many of them are now subdivided into two, three, or even four apartments. University kids mostly and a scattering of black families, taking their first halting steps out of Dog Town. Elsa's been here as long as most folks can remember, and for just as long, everyone has known that she's a lesbian. She's been harassed—not often, but sometimes cruelly: it comes and goes in waves. Right now it's quiet. She thinks maybe she's getting too old for people to care anymore.

"You think thirty-three is an age to be reckoned with," she says to me now. "I'll be seventy next year."

Elsa at seventy. It boggles. Seventy used to seem so old to me. So did thirty-three. But being with Elsa, despite the wrinkles and white hair, is the same as it ever was, sitting here across from her, just as I did years ago, telling her my dreams. "Elsa," I say, "it feels good to be here."

She smiles. "I'm glad."

"I didn't know how I'd feel," I admit. "Coming back here..."

"...is difficult," she says, finishing my sentence. "But you'll write about it?"

I shrug. Perhaps she assumes that is why I've come back. To be sure, it would make a great piece. *Boy returns to face the man he accused of rape.* But I'm a news reporter. I don't do features. I deal with facts. And there are no facts to explain why I have returned.

"Do you still work with the kids?" I ask.

"Sometimes. There's a center now. The Community Health Collective. There's a regular Friday night gathering."

I'm surprised. "For queer kids?"

"That's what you call them now," she says. It's a statement. Nothing else. "There are about six or seven every Friday night."

"That's so hard to imagine. *Here.* If only—"

"Yes," she says, understanding. "If only there had been such a thing for you." She laughs. "Or can you imagine for me? You didn't have it easy, but think about me. Forty years before you came along, needing help."

"But how much had really changed between your time and mine?" I ask. "In 1976, as compared to anytime before? How much was really different for me? Who had heard of Stonewall in Middletown?" I've thought about this a great deal, working as a reporter for a New York alternative weekly. I've written about it, in fact: interviewing a dozen New York transplants from places like Mount Pleasant, Mich., and Wilmington, Del. Stonewall came to the provinces much later than it did to the big cities. "Strange how it seems sometimes that mine was the last generation, the last of a long line of invisibles, that I have more in common with you than I do with these kids who gather every Friday night, even though forty years separates you and me and less than fifteen stands between me and those babies."

"You could be right." She pours me some more tea. "But we're still invisible here."

"That's not so. There's a center, there's a room, there are pink triangles on pickup trucks, I saw two as I drove down Main Street—"

Elsa shakes her head. "I'm talking about *us.* Not the children. Hurray for the children, and God save them all. But who will teach them? Who is left? There is me, an old lesbian grandmother, and a handful of sick old queens."

I understand. "So they will leave. The kids. In their time."

"As they all do. As you did."

"But I had to."

"Yes," she says. "I suppose you did." She stands up, shifting on tender joints to find some balance, and opens her old refrigerator. "Do you still like cheese sandwiches?"

"Sure," I tell her.

She makes me lunch. How often I once sat here, especially in the beginning, sat right here at this table, watching her there, at the counter, preparing a meal, not wanting to ever leave this warm, fragrant kitchen.

"So who's died?" I finally ask.

"All of them," she says.

"All?" I ask.

"All of those you'd remember." There's a pause, very slight. "Except him, of course."

Her back is facing me as she makes the sandwiches. "Do you see him often?" I ask.

"No," she says. "Nobody does."

"He doesn't ever come to the center—?"

She turns to face me, as if I had just said something completely absurd. And maybe I have. "No," she says, turning back to the cheese. "He has never come down to the center. Not since he started it."

"He—?"

"Yes," she says. "It was him."

"Even after he'd been in jail? He came back, and still was involved?"

"As much as they'd let him."

I ask her what she means.

"He spent a year in prison, but that's not what was really so bad," she says. She opens the refrigerator, pours me a glass of orange soda. "It was afterward. You know, things started happening here in Middletown after you left. Some of us tried to put together a community center. And we got a political group going. Did you know we got a civil rights bill passed in the state?"

"Yes," I say.

She places the sandwich and the soda in front of me. "We did some good things. But then ten years ago somebody came along, some do-gooder from down from the state capital, and he says that it's not a real good idea to have a convicted child molester playing such a public role. Bad for the image. The *community*, he said. Think of the *community*."

I look up at her.

"Do you want a pickle with that?" she asks.

"No," I say. "Tell me. What did Zandy say? How did he respond?"

"I'll always remember it. He stood up at the meeting, the very first one we had at the community center. 'Child molester?' he said. 'Is that what I am?' And Miss Aletha, God bless her old heart, she stood up and said, 'Well, I guess you don't think drag queens should be part of this community either?' And the do-gooder got all flustered and said, 'Oh, drag queens are OK. You know, Stonewall and all—' "

"Miss Aletha was always ready to stand up and be—"

"But he won, the bastard." Elsa turns away, back to the sink. "They voted to expel him from the board. Only Miss Aletha and I voted in favor of keeping him."

I'm quiet for a long time, watching the day get colder outside her window. I can tell the temperature is dropping: The purple roses shiver on their vine, and big gray clouds now obscure the sharpness of the blue sky. I decide I want to walk to his house, not drive. I want to feel the air, breathe in its coldness.

"He was the first to tell me stories of New York, of Greenwich Village, of Christopher Street, of Fire Island—and now I live there." She knows this. She lets me talk. "San Francisco and Provincetown too, he told me about these places, places where gays could walk in the street, holding hands. They were like fairy tales." I take my first bite of the cheese sandwich. It's as good as I remember. "He taught me about gay liberation, about how we were going to change the world—"

"He was a leftover hippie," Elsa says. It's just a statement. Nothing else.

"I use the stuff he taught me every day. In my work. The way I see myself, the way I see us, as a community—that all came from Zandy. He was never ashamed of who he was or what he did. Never. Not even when—"

I don't continue. "No," Elsa says. "He was never ashamed."

"He taught me so much," I tell her, more softly now. And I think of his hands, on my body.

"You tell him that, " Elsa says, "when you see him."

It was my statement to police that caused Alexander Reefy to be arrested for statutory rape.

I gave it willingly. To say otherwise now would be a lie. My parents did not coerce me. I walked into the police station ahead of them, and even spelled his name for the officer sitting behind the desk. I can remember him still: Officer Joseph Garafolo, a big man with eyes that never looked at me. He had been eating a pear when we came in, and bits of it clung to his bushy black mustache all through our conversation.

And then he sent out a cruiser to arrest Zandy, and never again did Zandy touch me.

I was fifteen years old.

Alexander Reefy first touched me when I was thirteen, back in 1974, the year I got my banana bike. The year I was first allowed to stay up past 9 o'clock and watch *Rhoda*. I was in love with Joe. I'd jerk off into my underwear as I lay in front of the TV set humping the braided rug. There was this terrible urgency in my groin at all times. There was no community center then, no gay characters on *Rhoda*, as there are on TV today. I'd flip through the card catalog at the school library, only to find nothing between *homoeans*, a fourth-century Christian heresy, and *Homs,* a city in Syria. Occasionally there was something on the news—"Gay rights marchers paraded down Fifth Avenue in New York City today"—reports that caused me great distress if my mother happened to be in the room, shaking her head silently as if to ask: "What *is* this world coming to?" All I had, really, were the whispers of my classmates: the whispers about a world none of us knew anything about except somehow that it existed, in the dark, marshy fringes of our own world.

The boys in my eighth-grade class at St. John the Baptist knew the word *homosexual*. Those who lived in the neighborhood closest to the school, the neighborhood that bordered the swamps of Dog Town, told me tales of Alexander Reefy, how he would leave his front porch light on whenever he was free and available, how men would stop by and go inside and the light would be turned off for the duration. "They're *homosexuals,*" Eddie Piatrowski would whisper, and all of our eyes would grow wide. Mine especially.

I was a loner in school. I would watch, I would listen: I knew all their secrets. But none of them knew mine: my private thoughts, my private parts, how my body was changing, how I had learned to do strange and fascinating things with it. No one had prepared me for the changes that were taking place in my body: the hair under my arms and around my dick, the white stuff that would shoot out of my slit if I pulled on myself long and hard enough. No one had told me how good that would feel, or how it would make me think of Joe Gerard, his big hairy chest crushing into Rhoda's face. How it would make me obsessed with that front porch light on a house I had never seen, with a man whose face I had never glimpsed, but whose name conjured images and thoughts that consumed my days and the dreams I endured at night.

It was a cold November morning, and Eddie Piatrowski, the closest I came to having a friend, asked me if I wanted to join him and some other boys who were planning on skipping school. We were in the recess yard, before the first bell. Eddie wanted to head south, down along the river, where we could smoke cigarettes and look at the dirty magazines he'd stolen from his father and carefully hidden in his knapsack. Michael Marino preferred the university, where we could maybe bum some beer from a student. I cared about none of those things: I hated the taste of cigarette smoke, hated more the taste of beer, hated most the big fleshy knockers of the women held captive in Eddie's bag.

"Let's go into Dog Town," I suggested.

"Yeah," Eddie said, gleeful. "We can go find the *fag*."

Only a few abandoned factories stood between us and Dog Town, and these were places well known to me, every nook and broken board, my private after-school club house since the third grade. I led the way. For once, I felt important, as if the other boys looked up to me. It was Eddie Piatrowski and Michael Marino and Craig Warzecha, and they were all following me. We crept past an abandoned car, inexplicably hauled into the ruins of the factory and left there to rot. Craig Warzecha wanted to stop and explore, but I urged him on: much more of interest lay ahead.

"There," Eddie pointed, when we climbed out of the last of the factories and stumbled into the marshy field that led to Dog Town. "His light's on."

And it was. We approached like warriors, but there was no plan beyond getting here. No words were spoken now. Eddie picked up a stone and threw it at the window. We followed suit. The tiny pings of the stones against the glass were the only sounds along the street.

He emerged finally, awakened by the stones: sleepy-eyed and disheveled, not shouting as we had expected. From his lair he crept dizzily, not stealthily, not threateningly. "Hey, what—?" he asked, rubbing his eyes, and I tried desperately to get a glimpse. But Eddie barked: "Run!" So we ran, turning on our heels and plunging through the swampy field, foul-smelling mud soaking into our shoes as we tripped over rusting casements of the old factory and dove back into the darkness.

But this I saw: Alexander Reefy, shirtless, a mat of mysterious black fur on his chest, in checkered pajama bottoms, standing on the steps of his house under the dull golden glow of his front porch light, and he was smiling. "Hey, peace and love, you little hooligans," he said, and then he went back to bed.

I walk up Oak Avenue to Pearl Court, crossing over to Washington, the wide boulevard that connects Main to High and to all the new shopping plazas and condo developments out past the orchards. It's these new places that have sapped Main Street of its life, drained away its business. Once there were dozens of shops along Main Street, lined up between South End News on one end, where I bought every issue of *Action Comics,* to Schafer's Shoes in the north, where Dad once worked. I remember Schafer's Shoes with one of the few good memories I have of my father. He'd sit me up on the chair like a little prince and let me try on all the new pairs of Buster Brown shoes. But even back then, back in the days of bustling shops and a regular Main Street bus line, the old men who sat on the post office steps would lament what had become of Middletown. What might they say now, with South End News paved over and Schafer's Shoes boarded up? With a Subway Sandwich Shop in the place of Henry's Diner? With the benches along the street occupied not by fellas with their girls but by the homeless and the mentally ill?

On the corner of Pearl and Washington, I see from the mailbox that the Piatrowskis still live in their big yellow Victorian. There, in an upper room, they used to keep Eddie's retarded older sister, a big-faced girl with pop eyes named Helen. I wonder if she's still there. Helen was always screaming. There was never any reason for it that was obvious. Sometimes poor Helen seemed genuinely terrified; other times, it just seemed as if that was all she knew how to do. Mrs. Piatrowski spent all her time tending to her. I was the only kid Eddie ever invited to spend the night at his house. I remember all through dinner—a feast of cabbage and sausage—Helen screamed upstairs. Her screams unnerved me for weeks—all my childhood, in fact, and whenever I was at Eddie's house, I'd come home shaken, waking up in my own bed convinced I could hear her still. There were times when Helen Piatrowski's screams seemed to echo all through the town: from the brownstone spires of St. John the Baptist through the abandoned factories right into the streets of Dog Town.

Now, as I turn on to Washington Street, the traffic gets heavier. Zandy doesn't live in Dog Town anymore, Elsa had told me. He lives here, on Washington, just before the street ascends the hill to wind its way past the large white homes on High Street, past the stoic, ivy-covered university, ending finally at the shopping plazas, where, behind a Shop Rite, my mother still resides in her quiet subdivision. My father had been very proud to finally buy his own home after renting for so long, even if it was a modular one-story behind a grocery store. Now my father was dead and my mother a vacant memory. Zandy's apartment was as far down Washington Street as I would venture. Going further was not the reason I came back.

And what is? I ask myself, raising the collar of my coat against the wind.

Where Zandy lives now is unremarkable: an apartment complex I remembered being constructed in my youth, over the remains of a small park where once a rusted jungle gym had enticed children. One of those children—a boy or a girl, I don't remember now—darted into the traffic on Washington Street and was run over by a garbage truck. So they closed the park and built the apartments. Boxy red brick. Stone Estates. This is where Alexander Reefy ends up. A square, small apartment on the side of a busy street, with no front porch light to flick on and off as his libido wills.

The wind bites my cheeks. I imagine children are preparing their outfits for tonight. Mothers are sewing on sequins for their daughters' ballerina costumes. Little straight boys are planning to go out dressed like Power Rangers. Little gay boys are turning up their noses at such absurd masquerades, preferring to apply their own hideous makeup to transform themselves into witches and devils and similar creatures of the night. Or at least I would have, anyway. I feel as if I am in costume now. My costume is that of an adult, of a man who has lived long and hard, who has claimed his part of the world as his own, who has lived with some manner of integrity and decision since leaving this town, who has come back to say goodbye to a part of his past. This is the costume I am wearing. This is not who I am.

When I find his name on the list beside the door, I press his buzzer and wait.

When he first fucked me, I cried. There was pain, such pain as I had never known, before or since. He held me around the waist, my face away from his. I felt his smoky breath at my ear as he lifted me up off my feet, holding me in front of him, pushing his dick up inside me, causing me to squirm, to writhe, to cry like a little baby.

I was fourteen.

And how he comforted me after. We built a fire, in an open section of the old factory, where the roof had caved in. There was a pool of oily black water beside us, where he rinsed off the Vaseline from his hands. I sat in front of the fire, feeling my sphincter still contracting, feeling as if I needed to shit, to piss, to pass out. And he came up behind me, wrapped his big arms around my frail, shaking body, and held me tight, kissing my neck as I'd seen Joe do to Rhoda.

I loved him immediately.

Alexander Reefy was not a handsome man. His nose was too long and his eyes too small. And his hands: But I've already mentioned his hands. I never knew exactly how old he was. Not quite thirty, but close to it. Younger than I am now. The thought staggers. To me he seemed much, much older than I, and in truth, he was: But he also seemed ageless, like a genie or an old elf out of Tolkien. And yet, what did I care how old he was or what he looked like? He was a *man*—a man with a penis and a chest like a bear, a man who recognized the urgency within me and affirmed it.

I had made anonymous phone calls to him in the days after we'd pelted his house with stones. I asked: "How would you like to suck my dick?" and he answered: "I might be interested." *Might be interested*. It blew me away. Here was a man acknowledging he *might be interested* in sucking dick. Even though Eddie Piatrowski had told me Alexander Reefy was a homosexual, to hear it confirmed was almost too much for my senses. I jerked off to that phrase for days: "I might be interested."

One night, coiled up like a Slinky ready to shoot across the room, I called him. "Can I come over?" I breathed. How I found the nerve, the appalling guts, to ask such a thing I still can't fathom. My father was snoring in his chair in front of the TV in the living room. In the kitchen, my mother was packing lunches for my sister and me to take to school the next day. It was a Sunday afternoon. I was in my parents' bedroom, my hand cupped around my mouth as I whispered into the phone.

"How old are you?" he asked.

"Sixteen," I lied.

It was an age pulled from the air. Something told me it held some magic. I did not know it was the age of consent in this state. But Zandy did, and he said, "All right. Come on over."

I don't remember much of the ride through town on my purple banana bike, except that it was the longest ride I'd ever taken. I assume I came straight down Washington Street, dodging the traffic, then headed north on Main, around St. John the Baptist and past the factories along River Road. I do remember that his front porch light was on.

That first day all he did was touch my dick. With those hands. No sucking. No fucking. But that was enough. I came in ten seconds flat. Then I was out of there, pedaling back home as fast as my frightened little feet would take me. But I was back the following Sunday, and that's when he gave me my very first blow job. He took me upstairs to his room and sat me down on the edge of his bed, kneeling in front of me and unzipping my fly. He didn't expect me to reciprocate.

Afterward, I didn't run, but hung around for a while. He gave me some apple juice. He was nice to me, nicer than anyone had ever been to me. We sat in his living room, papered with posters of Karl Marx and Janis Joplin and Barbra Streisand, and I cried. I didn't say anything. Just cried. He sat there, nodding his head. "Yeah, yeah," he said softly. "I know."

The next time, I met his friends, people who would become well known to me over the next year and a half. A tall man everyone called Miss Aletha, who wore a blond wig and purple eye mascara; Bertrand, his (her?) boyfriend, a shy young man in his twenties with tattoos on his arms; and Cisco, a dark-skinned kid not much older than I was who always looked at me strangely, as if he resented me.

It was Cisco who said, finally: "That kid ain't sixteen." And Miss Aletha had gotten up and walked out of the room. Bertrand smiled.

Zandy reached over to me where I sat on the couch, sipping my juice, and tousled my hair. He winked at me. It made me feel better.

Zandy taught me the things my father should have: why I had to shower more frequently now that I was sprouting hair, how to wash my dick to keep it clean, how to get rid of an infestation of crabs he said was inevitable for any teenage boy. He taught me that the feelings I had shouldn't be cause for shame or concern. He said being gay was just the most natural thing: "And don't you ever let anyone tell you otherwise," he said. Of course, there was more. He taught me how to give pleasure and how to receive it: the best way to handle a man's dick, the best way to show your partner what turned you on.

But I never sucked his dick. Not once in all that time. He taught me how to do it only through demonstration, never asking me to practice what I had learned. Later, with others, I was eager to get down on my knees and serve. To Zandy I offered my ass without hesitation, but never my lips. And he never asked. In all of our love-making, which was considerable, I never gave him a blow job.

Zandy told the judge later that he had wanted to stop, wanted to send me away. But there was something in my eyes, he said, something that wouldn't let him. Elsa would say, even later, that that was no excuse, that he shouldn't have put the onus on me. "Maybe there was nothing wrong in what he did," she always asserted, "but it was him doing it to you, not the other way around." But she was wrong, one of the rare occasions when she didn't get it right. It *was* me. There *was* something in my eyes.

"Someday," Zandy promised me, "we won't have to hide. We won't have to pretend." The days had become longer for me, the weeks interminable. I lived for my Sunday afternoons, listening to Miss Aletha sing show tunes from her days as a performer at the Follies Café, long since closed. Bertrand could perform magic tricks, and he did lots of them. I still remember the parakeet coming out of his old black hat and how astounded I was. Cisco was always sullen, sometimes (I learned) slipping outside to sell his body to the men who would drive very slowly with their lights off along River Road. Zandy didn't like to talk to me much about that.

That's how I met Elsa, when she came into Dog Town to counsel Cisco. She was a social worker back then. She worked with street kids and poor families. She met with Zandy, who was putting together an organization he called the Gay Liberation Project of Middletown. He was really into it, making up fliers and brochures. Elsa allowed her number to be listed on the handouts as part of a hot-line service. She was a nice lady, and clean and very respectable. I didn't figure she was like Zandy or Miss Aletha or Bertrand. But she was.

"Yes," she said to me one afternoon, after I'd met her on the sidewalk in front of Zandy's. "I'm gay too."

That really just knocked my socks off. Here was this well-dressed lady saying she was just like me. After that, whenever I'd see Elsa on the street passing out her literature or knocking on the doors of poor families' apartments, I'd always hurry up to greet her. And she always seemed happy to see me.

I dreaded the prospect of high school: my classmates were all clamoring to join the Middletown High football team. No, not me, I'd say, backing off, and already the taunts were beginning. "*Fag*," the boys would whisper, "queer boy." I looked forward to Sunday afternoons more than I possibly could have expressed at the time because that's when I felt the most real: sitting in that living room in Dog Town, listening to Miss Aletha sing, watching Bertrand pull parakeets out of his hat, hearing about Zandy's trips to Greenwich Village or his summertime jaunts up to Provincetown.

"Someday, kid," Zandy told me, "I'll take you to a gay pride parade in New York City. It's fabulous. Lots of balloons and banners and great music to dance to. As soon as you're a little older, we'll go and we'll watch all the hundreds of homosexuals walk down Christopher Street. You'd never believe there were so many. Drag queens like Miss Aletha, and dykes on their big old motorcycles, and big hunky guys with lots of muscles. And we'll stay out all night. I'll take you dancing and we'll go into the back room and boy, will you be popular there..."

On Halloween night, Zandy opened his door dressed like Marilyn Monroe. I was shocked, appalled. But Zandy sat me down and explained all about Stonewall, how drag queens have always been the ones on the front lines. "You like Miss Aletha, don't you?" he asked.

I nodded my head.

"Well, she was leading the fight here in this town long before any of us arrived. We've got her to thank for a lot."

He was always teaching me these things. "From here," he said one afternoon, seated in his overstuffed, frayed armchair, beneath a tattered American flag pinned up to the wall with a large peace sign painted over it, "I can see the very edge of the rainbow."

"The edge?" I asked.

"You've got it made, kid," he said. "You and all the little ones to follow. We're making such progress. You'll see. Even here in Middletown."

I couldn't imagine.

"Look. It's 1975. In San Francisco there's a guy running for supervisor. That's like the city council here. And he's gay. And people don't care. His name is Milk. Strange name for a fag, huh?" Zandy laughed. "And he's gonna make it. Looks like he's really going to make it. How about that, huh?"

I raised my eyebrows.

"You just imagine twenty years from now, kid. Just you imagine."

I tried, but couldn't.

"Don't worry," he said, "take my word for it. It's going to be *grand*." And I remember how he kissed me then, his smoky breath in my mouth, putting his hands in front of my lips afterward, letting me kiss them and lick them and suck each one of those knotty, twisted fingers into my mouth.

That night, or a night shortly thereafter, he took me out to the old abandoned factory, just as spring began to thaw the cold earthen floors, and fucked me for the first of many, many times in my life.

Why not me? I asked myself, when my lover died in New York. *Why not me?* I asked again, when Elsa told me that all of them— Miss Aletha and Bertrand and Cisco too, I imagine—were dead. *Why not me?*

Maybe that's why I've returned. Maybe that's why I press his buzzer now and wait for him to answer.

There's nothing. I wonder if he's gone out. But he's too sick to go out, Elsa told me. That's what she had heard. Maybe he's too sick to open the door.

In the street behind me, a motorist slams on his brakes, causing a terrible screeching sound. An angry horn blares. I think of the child run over by the garbage truck here, long ago. I remember how we prayed for—him? her?—in church, how terrified I was of the thought of being run over in the street.

A young woman is suddenly behind me. She smiles shyly and I step aside, allowing her to unlock the door and go inside. I hold the door for her. She's carrying a bag of groceries. She says, "Thank you." I nod and follow her inside. She does not appear to be uncomfortable with my presence, and I follow her up the first flight of stairs. At the landing, she turns and unlocks the door to the first apartment on the right. When she is inside, I hear a chain lock quickly slide into place.

Zandy's apartment is 311. Third floor. I climb another set of stairs.

It smells of mold and mildew in this place. The gray carpeting is stained in places. At the far end of each corridor on each floor a fingerprint-covered window lets in cold blue light. Cigarette butts litter the stairwells, despite the NO SMOKING signs.

I find 311 on my left, at the end of the corridor. The last apartment on the last floor. I knock. I hear nothing. I decide he's gone, perhaps in the hospital. I fear my whole trip here has been in vain. But then I sense a shudder from inside, as if a hibernating animal was just stirring back to life. There's a sound, a noiseless kind of sound, as if from under something: a pile of blankets, maybe, or a mound of pine needles and soil.

"Zandy?" I call.

There's the sound of air, a strange sound, like the flurry of wind in the eaves. Then it's quiet again.

"Zandy? It's Todd O'Riley."

I swallow hard. Why should he want to see me? Who's to say if he's even read the letters I sent? Who's to say he doesn't hate me with all the passion my parents once hated him? And who would blame him?

Then I hear the scuffing: footsteps approaching the door. And then a voice, softly entreating: "Go ahead. Come in."

It was the day Schafer's Shoes closed its doors. Dad hadn't been forewarned. Old Mr. Schafer just told him it was over. "Go on home," he said to my father, handing him his severance pay. "That's what I'm going to do."

The men on the steps of the post office would have something else to cluck over. The little store just couldn't compete with the new Shoe Town that opened up on North Washington, one of the first of the new stores out there, not far from our house. "There's a big parking lot there," my mother would say, by way of explanation, as if parking lots could explain the entire world. Later, my Dad would blame Jimmy Carter, and the Arabs: I'm not sure why, but it was all due to inflation somehow, and Carter and the Arabs were to my Dad the root causes of most our problems.

But on this day Dad said nothing. He just sat on the couch not moving, just staring into the air. I was fifteen now, and when I got home from yet another harrowing day of high school, fending off the taunts of the upperclassmen and the guys who had once been my classmates back at St. John the Baptist, I found him tight-lipped about the whole thing, unwilling to look me in the eye. "Leave your father alone," my mother commanded. "Go to your room and pray."

For what? For Shoe Town to close? For Jimmy Carter to resign? But my younger sister obeyed. I still remember looking into her room and seeing the sad little Sign of the Cross she made that day sitting on her bed, her feet in their black patent-leather shoes not even reaching the floor. But I simply flopped down on my bed and stared at my ceiling. It was a dark day. At least, I remember it that way. I'm pretty sure it was raining. Or maybe I just think I remember the rain because my life had become a drizzly blur, a damp mist shrouding everything I did. Who can explain teenage angst, particularly queer teenage angst? The very last completely happy time I can remember with Zandy was a night shortly after Halloween, when he took me up into the orchards and we filled a basket with the picked-over apples. "Miss Aletha taught me a secret a long time ago, when I first came to Middletown," he told me, and it struck me that I didn't know he had come from anyplace else. "The secret is in these apples. Everybody leaves them behind. But they're the sweetest of the bunch, and they're *free*."

He was right: They *were* sweet. And we picked as many as we could, stumbling in the dark, shivering and laughing and biting into the hard sweet fruit, oblivious of the threat of worms or the chance of being discovered. We went back to his house and baked Miss Aletha a pie, and I remember how she cried, the mascara running down her cheeks, and that was the last completely happy time I ever had with Zandy and his friends.

Because after that things started changing: The taunts at school got worse, my father began to suspect I was becoming somebody he didn't want me to be. "Why aren't you on any sports?" he griped, now that I was in high school. My mother's face simply went tight, abandoning me to his suspicions. But I no longer found solace in my Sunday afternoons with Zandy. Instead, I wanted to appease my tormentors. I wanted finally to be like them, especially the handsome jocks whose images I would jerk off to at night, after a day spent fending off their taunts and insults. I wanted friends my own age, *normal* friends: I wanted to hang out with Eddie, and Craig Warzecha and Michael Marino, as I had on that day when I led them through the factories, the day I first got mixed up in all of this. I was weary of being alone in the hallways, lugging my books spiritlessly from class to class, occasionally having them knocked from my arms by a band of roving jocks. I no longer desired the refuge I found in the arms of Alexander Reefy—that *man*, that *old* man, how dare he do the things he did to me?

This is how I was thinking, in those last several weeks, sitting in Zandy's living room, listening to his stories now with a feeling of revulsion. My Sunday visits became fewer. Zandy never asked why, which made me even more resentful. I became hostile to him, refusing sex. I even told Miss Aletha that she looked foolish one day: "Everyone knows you're just a guy." I wanted to take the words back instantly, because I saw how it hurt her. But Zandy never asked what was going on with me. If he didn't care, I reasoned, then neither did I.

I had stopped riding my banana bike: too faggy. So I'd ask my father for an occasional ride to the center of town, from which I'd walk the mile into Dog Town. Once he turned to me and asked, not expecting an answer, because I never offered one: "What do you *do* with your time, anyway? You don't go out with girls. You don't play football. I don't understand you at all. You can't be a kid of mine."

Maybe I wasn't. Then whose kid was I? Certainly not Zandy's, because by then I hated his hands on my body as much as I hated my father's words. Maybe that's why I went directly to his house the day my father lost his job. Maybe somehow I figured my father would follow. Maybe I wanted what happened to happen. My father *did* follow, and he must have driven real slowly and deliberately because I walked all the way there and yes, I'm sure now that it was raining, because I remember being cold and damp when I finally got to Zandy's, and Cisco was there, on the front porch, with another kid I didn't know, and I ignored them and walked right on inside without knocking. Zandy came out of the kitchen with a towel in his hand and without his shirt—freshly showered, I think, because the hair on his chest was all alive and shiny and not at all matted. He said, "Hey, kid, what's up?" and that's when I heard my father behind me and he was shouting, "We're going to have you arrested, you pervert!" and he did just that: He got Zandy thrown in jail. No. *I* got Zandy thrown in jail, because I told my parents and the police everything. Every last detail. To shock them, perhaps. To repulse them. To drive them out of my life. Them and Zandy too.

My father smacked me across the face that day in front of Zandy's house. Zandy tried to stop him, but then he hit Zandy too, and I remember Zandy's mouth bleeding and Cisco running off down the street with the other kid, and I think they were laughing, the little shits. My father pulled me outside by my hair and shoved me into the car, and by this time I was crying and denying I'd ever been there before, little coward that I was. That was the last time I ever saw Zandy: bleeding mouth and open eyes, listening to me deny he'd ever meant anything to me. I didn't have to see him in court because I was just fifteen and didn't have to go. There was a big scandal and the local newspaper wrote a story using Zandy's name, although mine was not revealed. Still, everyone knew it was me: It went all through school, and the taunting just got worse. So did the beatings at home.

When my father kept hitting me, I ran away. To Elsa's. Somehow she got my parents to agree that I could live with her, even though there were rumors in town that she was a dyke. But I think my parents just wanted to be rid of their faggot son. Elsa was good to me. She got a dentist to cap the tooth my father had broken, and she even sent me to a shrink. But school became unbearable, and Elsa figured it was better if I went away. She arranged for me to go to a prep school in New York. She chipped in to help pay because my father still didn't have a job. If it weren't for Elsa, I'd probably be dead now. But she gave me a chance to start over, and that starting over began the day she drove me out of Middletown in her big brown station wagon to catch the train in New Haven. When I looked out the car window at Middletown receding behind me, I saw my life there just disappear, as if it had never happened, fading away to just a muddy background on which I could paint the rest of my life.

I remember the train ride to New York as vividly as I remember anything. Watching out the window as the train passed the backs of shopping centers and the backyards of suburban, lower-middle class homes, I felt like a voyeur, seeing parts of people's lives I'd never seen before, parts of their lives I wasn't supposed to see. Yet instead of guilt, I felt privileged to have such a glimpse: the backyard swing set, the garbage cans, the flower pots, and the tool sheds. People didn't often have the opportunity to see someone else's backyard, littered with bikes missing wheels, forgotten toys and broken wheel-barrows.

I remember, even now, especially now, the little girl I spotted, swinging dispiritedly on an old rusty swing set behind a one-story house. She seemed lost in thought, oblivious to her surroundings. She didn't even look up as the train whizzed past her house. It must have become so routine for her: the clatter of the tracks, the blowing of the horn. She didn't raise her eyes in excitement at the approach of the train, as most children would: It was something she heard every day, several times a day, and it brought her no particular joy. I wanted to call to her, to tell her to look up, to hop on the train with me. "It can take you away too," I wanted to tell her, suddenly feeling responsible for her, wanting with all my might to grab onto her and take her with me.

But I couldn't, of course. All I had with me was one small bag, all new clothes that Elsa had bought for me. I went to school and did all right. After graduation, I got accepted at Columbia and took up journalism. I came out. There was a gay and lesbian group on campus. Some of the older guys would go out dancing at the Saint or spend all night at the Mineshaft, but I never went with them. Too scared, maybe, after all the shit I'd gone through. By the time I wanted to go, no one was going out anymore—it was 1983, the year of the Big Scare. So I never went dancing all night in New York as Zandy had prophesied. I didn't have a lot of sex. I never did drugs. The promise of gay life being one long never-ending party failed to materialize for me. I admit to being somewhat disappointed: Zandy had made it all sound so dazzling. But gay life had never been that way for me: Why should I have expected anything else?

I *did* have expectations, though. "It's going to be *grand*," Zandy had said. But the first man I fell in love with died—not from the plague but at the hands of some teenage boys from New Jersey, boys not much different from Craig Warzecha and Michael Marino and Eddie Piatrowski. They thought it was a joke: "Let's beat up a fag." They kicked his brains out, left them in a grisly, watery stream all the way down the pier. It made me write to my mother, finally, after all

those years. I don't know why. I told her Zandy had been no moles-
ter, no aberration. She sent me back a long letter, quoting the Bible.
She'd never been religious before, but now she listened to Jim and
Tammy Faye with all the passion of a convert.

When I graduated, I got my current job. I like it OK. I fell in love
for the second time, and then he died too. This time it *was* the
plague. I haven't had sex since, unless you count watching at the
piers or at the rest stop outside Middletown. Then, a few months
ago I got the letter from Elsa: "I thought you might want to know
that Alexander Reefy is sick. He's not doing well. Just thought you
might want to know."

"Todd O'Riley," he whispers now from the darkness of the shut-
tered room behind the door.

"Zandy," I say.

He steps aside to let me in. The apartment is dark, cast with a
strange blue light. The Venetian blinds are pulled tightly shut on all
the windows. The smell is foul: cigarettes and urine and bad milk. A
mix of staleness, sweetness, and sour. He's dressed in a big floppy
flannel shirt, untucked, way too big for him, though it probably fit
him when he was healthy. His gray sweatpants are stained and torn.
He's barefoot.

"Todd O'Riley," he says again.

His face has the skeletal look I've come to recognize as a last sign
of the plague: deep hollow cheeks, wide eyes, protruding teeth. His
breath is rancid; how well I remember Steven's breath at the end,
how repulsive it was, as if all his organs were decaying inside him
with the stench making its way up through his mouth. In Zandy's
case the odor is made worse by the decades of cigarettes: His teeth
are yellow and chipped, his lips a stained brownish green.

He's unshaven, with big tufts of black hair on his cheeks and his
chin. I remember for a while he had grown a beard, and how I
thought he looked magnificent, back in those days when facial hair
was still socially affirmed among gay men. But now the hair on his
face is patchy and ragged, as if whole clumps had fallen out all at once.

"Zandy, I wanted to see you," I begin.

He smiles. His teeth frighten me. "Well," he says, gesturing, "here I am."

I reach over to touch him, shake his hand, something. He folds his arms across his chest. I brush his wrist as he does so. I feel nothing. It's as if I've just swept through smoke, not flesh.

"I want you to know—" I try again.

He laughs. "How sorry you are? Is that it, kid? Is that why you've come back?"

I don't know what to say. "Yes," I try. "Yes. That's part of it. How sorry I am."

For a flash I see the old Zandy: the face hidden behind the death mask. I'm transported nearly two decades back into time, and I feel a strange stirring in my loins.

"And what should I tell you now?" he asks. "What is it that you've come back to hear me say?"

"I don't know," I admit.

"How about 'I exonerate you'?" he asks suddenly, his eyes lighting up, as if the idea had just occurred to him. "Isn't that why you came back? To receive absolution from a dying man?"

"Zandy—"

"Well, you're too late. I'm already dead."

"Look, Zandy, I don't need you to forgive me. I've had to do that for myself."

He just looks at me, and for a minute it's as if I can see right through him: lungs and heart and rib cage, and then the wallpaper beyond.

"I just wanted to say I was sorry," I tell him. "That I was a fucked-up kid who nonetheless loved you very much. And still does. There was so much, so very much you taught me. I am who I am because of you. Everything I know about being gay, about our history, our traditions—you taught me. You taught me not to be ashamed. I owe you enough to at least come back here and tell you—"

"You don't owe me anything." Zandy puts his hands over his face. They're as knotty as I remember, but thinner, so much thinner. He takes a deep breath, then lets it out. He uncovers his face and looks hard at me. "You've become a mere peddler of words," he says at last.

His words take me by surprise. "How do you know what I've written?" I ask.

"You're a reporter. A reporter writes only what he *sees*. Not what he feels. Not what he *knows*."

I don't understand.

"You *do* understand," he says, reading my mind. "Don't pretend you don't. You know what to do."

"Tell the stories," I say.

"Yes," he tells me. "And not from your eyes. Your eyes are only part of it. Your heart, kid. Your heart and your soul and your head and yes, kid, your dick. You write the book I will never get to write."

But I don't know if I can.

"Sure you can," he says. "You tell 'em for me. It's *still* going to be grand."

Then he laughs. "Hey," he asks, "do you remember the secret Miss Aletha taught me?"

I hesitate for just a second. "About the apples?"

"Yes," he says. "How sweet are the twisted apples that they leave behind." Zandy turns to look at me. We hold each other's gaze, and I can see through his eyes.

I know what he means.

"Don't worry," he says. "You can't get infected by a dead man."

And then I understand. Fully, for the first time. I'm not frightened, standing here with a ghost, the ghost of a man who loved me, who I loved in return, the ghost of a man I could have been and still might be. I approach him, falling to my knees in front of him. I gently pull down his sweatpants, my fingers caressing cold, cold flesh. His dick, shriveled and blue, nests in a stinking mat of pubic hair. I take the icy shaft into my mouth. He moans, and for a second I remember that voice: the soft cooing in my ear, the soft promises of a world yet to be explored. And I give him the best blow job that I know how, a skill I learned from him. And when he shoots, I take his come down my throat, drinking every last drop of that sweet freezing liquid that burns all the way down, purifying me.

"He's dead," I tell Elsa.

She's not surprised. She's clipping the purple roses from the vine. "Some warm water," she says. "That'll keep these for a few more days."

The sun is setting in a watery mix of reds and purples. The ghosts and the goblins will all emerge now, going from house to house, collecting their treats and delivering their tricks.

"I want to head out tonight, get back to New York," I say. Elsa understands. "I had thought the dying was hard there," I tell her. "Here, how do you go on?"

She holds me tight for a few moments, then lets me go. "I love you," I tell her, and she smiles.

Her too, I think as I drive out of town. Her story too. I pull off the road to watch the sunset on Eagle Hill, this time oblivious to the boys in the bushes. I can see her house from here, standing out in the red glow cast by the setting sun among the long purple shadows. I can see the factories, the deserted shops of Main Street, the cold brownstone steeple of St. John the Baptist church. I can see Stone Estates too. I shiver, wanting to get back to New York before it gets much later. Before I forget the job I have to do. Before I forget what I have to say.

Before I hear Helen Piatrowski scream.

The Documentary Artist

Jaime Manrique

I met Sebastian when he enrolled in one of my film directing classes at the university where I teach. Soon after the semester started, he distinguished himself from the other students because he was very vocal about his love of horror movies. Our special intimacy started one afternoon when he burst into my office, took a seat before I invited him to do so, and began telling me in excruciating detail about a movie called *The Evil Mommy,* which he had seen in one of those 42nd Street theaters he frequented. "And at the end of the movie," he said, "as the boy is praying in the chapel to the statue of this bleeding Christ on the cross, Christ turns into the evil mommy, and she jumps off the cross and removes the butcher knife stuck between her breasts and goes for the boy's neck. She chases the screaming boy all over the church, until she gets him." He paused to check my reaction. "After she cuts off his head," he went on, almost with relish, "she places his head on the altar." As he narrated these events, the white of Sebastian's eyes distended frighteningly, his fluttering hands drew arabesques in front of his face, and guttural, gross croaks erupted from the back of his throat.

I was both amused and unsettled by his wild, manic performance. Although I'm no great fan of B horror movies, I was impressed by his love of film. Also, I appreciated that he wasn't colorless or lethargic like so any of my students; I found his drollness and the aura of weirdness he cultivated enchanting. Even so, right that minute I decided I would do my best to keep him at a distance. It wasn't so much that I was attracted to him (which is always dangerous for a teacher) but that I found his energy unnerving.

Sebastian started showing up at least once a week during my office hours. He never made an appointment, and he seldom discussed his work with me. There's a couch across from my chair, but he always sat on the bench that abuts the door, as if he were afraid to come any closer. He'd talk about the new horror movies he'd seen, and sometimes he'd drop a casual invitation to see a movie together. It soon became clear to me that because of his dirty clothes, disheveled hair, and loudness, and his love of the bizarre and gothic, he was a loner.

One day I was having a sandwich in the cafeteria when he came over and joined me.

"You've heard of Foucault?" he asked me.

"Sure. Why?"

"Well, last night I had a dream in which Foucault talked to me and told me to explore my secondary discourse. In the dream there was a door with a sign that said LEATHER AND PAIN. Foucault ordered me to open it. When I did, I heard a voice that told me to come and see you today."

I stopped munching my sandwich and sipped my coffee.

"This morning I had my nipple pierced," Sebastian continued, touching the spot on his T-shirt. "The guy who did it told me about a guy who pierced his dick and then made two dicks out of his penis so he could double the pleasure."

My mouth fell open. I sat there speechless. Sebastian stood up. "See you in class," he said as he left the table.

I lost my appetite. I considered mentioning the conversation to the department chairman. Dealing with students' crushes was not new to me; in my time I too had crushes on some of my teachers. I decided it was all harmless, and that as long as I kept at a distance and didn't encourage him, there was no reason to be alarmed. As I reviewed my own feelings, I told myself I was not attracted to him, so I wasn't in danger of playing into his game.

Then Sebastian turned in his first movie, an absurdist zany farce shot in one room and in which he played all the roles and murdered all the characters in very gruesome ways. The boundless energy of this work excited me.

One afternoon, late that fall, he came to see me, looking upset. His father had had a heart attack, and Sebastian was going home to New Hampshire to see him in the hospital. I had already approved his proposal for his final project that semester, an adaptation of Kafka's "A Hunger Artist." I reassured him that even if he had to be absent for a couple of weeks, it would not affect his final grade.

"Oh, that's nice," he said, lowering his head. "But, you know, I'm upset about going home because I'm gay."

"Have you come out to them?" I asked.

"Are you kidding?" His eyes filled with rage. "My parents would shit cookies if they knew."

"You never know," I said. "Parents can be very forgiving when it comes to their children."

"Not my parents," he snorted. Sebastian then told me his story, "When I was in my teens I took one of those IQ tests and it said I was a mathematical genius or something. That's how I ended up at MIT at fifteen with a full scholarship. You know, I was just kind of a loner. All I wanted was to make my parents happy. So I studied hard and made straight A's, but I hated that shit and those people. My classmates and my teachers were as…" he paused; there was anger and sadness in his voice. "They were as abstract and dry as those numbers and theories they pumped in my head. One day I thought, *If I stay here, I'm going to be a basket case before I graduate.* I had always wanted to make horror films. Movies are the only thing I care about. That's when I announced to my parents my decision to quit MIT and to come to New York to pursue my studies in film directing."

His parents, as Sebastian put it, "freaked." They were blue-collar people who had pinned all their hopes on him and his brother, an engineer. There was a terrible row. Sebastian went to a friend's house, where he got drunk. That night, driving back home, he lost control of his car and crashed it against a tree. For forty-five days he was in a coma. When he came out of it, nothing could shake his decision to study filmmaking. He received a partial scholarship at the school where I teach, and he supported himself by doing catering jobs and working as an extra in movies. He told me about how brutal his father was to the entire family; about the man's bitterness. So going back home to see him in the hospital was hard. Sebastian wasn't sure he should go, but he wanted to be there in case his father died.

When Sebastian didn't return to school in two weeks, I called his number in the city but got a machine. I left messages on a couple of occasions but got no reply. Next I called his parents. His mother informed me that his father was out of danger and that Sebastian had returned to New York. At the end of the semester I gave him an incomplete.

In the summer I started a documentary of street life in New York. I spent a great deal of my time in the streets with my video camera, shooting whatever struck me as odd or representative of street life. In the fall Sebastian did not show up, and I thought about him less and less.

One gray, drizzly afternoon in November I had just finished shooting in the neighborhood of Washington Square Park. In the gathering darkness, the park was bustling with people getting out of work, students going to evening classes, and the new batch of junkies who came out only after sunset.

I had shot footage of so many homeless people in the last few months that I wouldn't have paused to notice this man if it weren't for the fact that it was beginning to sprinkle harder and he was on his knees, with a cardboard sign that said HELP ME, I AM HUNGRY around his neck, his hands in prayer position, and his face—eyes shut—pointed toward the inhospitable sky. He was bearded, with long, ash-blond hair, and as emaciated and broken as one of Gaugin's Christs. I stopped to get my camera ready, and, as I moved closer, I saw that the man looked familiar—it was Sebastian.

I wouldn't call myself a very compassionate guy. I mean, I give money to beggars once in a while, depending on my mood, especially if they do not look like crack heads. But I'm not like some of my friends who work in soup kitchens or, in the winter, take sandwiches and blankets to the people sleeping in dark alleys or train stations.

Yet I couldn't ignore Sebastian, and not because he had been of my students and I was fond of him but because I was so sure of his talent.

I stood there, waiting for Sebastian to open his eyes. I was getting drenched, and it looked like he was lost in his thoughts, so I said, "Sebastian, it's me, Santiago, your film teacher."

He smiled, though now his teeth were brown and cracked. His eyes lit up too—not with recognition but with the nirvana of dementia.

I took his grimy hand in both of mine and pressed it warmly even though I was repelled by his filth. At that moment I became aware of the cold rain, the passersby, the hubbub of the city traffic, the throng of New York City dusk on fall evenings, when New Yorkers rush around in excitement, on their way to places, to bright futures and unreasonable hopes, to their loved ones and home. I locked my hands around his, as if to save him, as if to save myself from the thunderbolt of pain that had lodged in my chest.

"Hi, prof," Sebastian said finally.

"You have to get out of this rain or you'll get sick," I said, yanking at his hand, coaxing him to get off the sidewalk.

"OK, OK," he acquiesced apologetically as he got up.

Sebastian stood with shoulders hunched, his head leaning to one side, looking downward. There was a strange, utterly disconnected smile on his lips—the insane, stifled giggle of a child who's been caught doing something naughty; a boy who feels both sorry about and amused at his antics. The smile of someone who has a sense of humor but doesn't believe he has a right to smile. Sebastian had become passive, broken, and frightened like a battered dog. Fear darted in his eyes.

"Would you like to come to my place for a cup of coffee?" I said.

"Thanks," he said, avoiding my eyes.

Gently, so as not to scare him, I removed the cardboard sign from around his neck. I hailed a cab. On the way home we were silent. I rolled down the window because Sebastian's stench was unbearable. A part of me wished I had given him a few bucks and gone on with my business.

Inside the apartment, I said, "You'd better get out of those wet clothes before you catch pneumonia." I asked him to undress in my bedroom, gave him a bathrobe, and told him to take a shower. He left his dirty clothes on the floor, and while he was showering I went through the pockets of his clothes, looking for a clue to his current condition.

There were a few coins in his pockets, some keys, and a glass pipe, the kind crack heads use to smoke in doorways. The pipe felt more repugnant than a rotting rodent in my hand; it was like an evil entity that threatened to destroy everything living and healthy. I dropped it on the bed and went to the kitchen, where I washed my hands with detergent and scalding water. I was aware that I was behaving irrationally, but I couldn't control myself. I returned to my bedroom, where I piled up his filthy rags, made a bundle, put them in a trash bag, and dumped them in the garbage.

Sebastian and I were almost the same height, although he was so wasted that he'd swim in my clothes. But at least he'd look clean, I thought, as I pulled out of my closet thermal underwear, socks, a pair of jeans, a flannel shirt, and an olive army jacket I hadn't worn in years. I wanted to get rid of his torn, smelly sneakers, but his shoe size was larger than mine. I laid out all these clothes on the bed and went to the kitchen to make coffee and sandwiches. When I finished, I collapsed on the living room couch and turned on the TV.

Sebastian remained in my bedroom for a long time. Beginning to worry, I opened the door. He was sitting on my bed, wearing the clean clothes, and staring at his image in the full-length mirror of the closet. His beard and hair were still wet and unkempt, but he looked presentable.

"Nice shirt," he whispered, patting the flannel at his shoulder.

"It looks good on you," I said. Now that he was clean and dressed in clean clothes, with his blond hair and green eyes, he was a good-looking boy.

We sat around the table. Sebastian grabbed a sandwich and started eating slowly, taking small bites and chewing with difficulty, as if his gums hurt. I wanted to confront him about the crack, but I didn't know how to do it without alienating him. Sebastian ate, holding the sandwich close to his nose, staring at his lap all the time. He ate parsimoniously, and he drank his coffee in little sips, making strange slurping noises, such as I imagined a thirsty animal would make.

When he finished eating, our eyes met. He stood up. "Thanks. I'm going, OK?"

"Where are you going?" I asked, getting frantic. "It's raining. Do your parents know how to reach you?"

"My parents don't care," he said without animosity.

"Sebastian, I'm sure they care. You're their child and they love you." I saw he was becoming upset, so I decided not to press the point. "You can sleep here tonight. The couch is very comfortable."

Staring at his sneakers, he shook his head. "That's cool. Thanks anyway. I'll see you around." He took a couple of steps toward the door.

"Wait," I said and rushed to the bedroom for the jacket. I gave it to him, and an umbrella too.

Sebastian placed the rest of his sandwich in a side pocket and put on the jacket. He grabbed the umbrella at both ends and studied it, as if he had forgotten what it was used for.

I scribbled both my home and office numbers on a piece of paper. "You can call me anytime you need me," I said, also handing him a ten-dollar bill, which I gave him with some apprehension because I was almost sure he'd use it to buy crack. Sebastian took the number but returned the money.

"It's yours," I said. "Please take it."

"It's too much," he said, surprising me. "Just give me enough for coffee."

I fished for a bunch of coins in my pocket and gave them to him.

Hunching his shoulders and giving me his weird smile, Sebastian accepted them. Suddenly I knew what the smile reminded me of: It was Charlie Chaplin's smile as the tramp in *City Lights*. Sebastian opened the door and took the stairs instead of waiting for the elevator.

The following day I went back to the corner where I had found him the day before, but Sebastian wasn't around. I started filming in that neighborhood exclusively. I became obsessed with finding him again. I had dreams in which I'd see him with dozens of other junkies tweaking in the murky alleys of New York. Sometimes I'd spot a young man begging who, from the distance, would look like Sebastian. This, I know, is what happens to people when their loved ones die.

That Christmas I took to the streets again, ostensibly to shoot more footage, but secretly hoping to find Sebastian. It was around that time that the homeless stopped being for me anonymous human roaches of the urban squalor. Now they were people with features, with faces, with stories, with loved ones desperately looking for them, trying to save them. No longer moral lepers to be shunned, the young among them especially fascinated me. I wondered how many of them were intelligent, gifted, even geniuses who, because of crack or other drugs, or rejection, or hurt, or lack of love, had taken to the streets, choosing to drop out in the worst way.

The documentary and my search for Sebastian became one. This search took me to places I had never been. I started to ride the subway late at night, filming the homeless who slept in the cars, seeking warmth, traveling all night long. Most of them were black, and many were young, and a great number of them seemed insane. I became adept at distinguishing the different shades of street people. The ones around 42nd Street looked vicious, murderous, possessed by the virulent devils of the drugs. The ones who slept on the subways—or at Port Authority, Grand Central, and Penn Station—were poorer, did not deal in drugs or prostitution. Many of them were cripples or retarded, and their eyes didn't flash the message KILLKILLKILLKILL. I began to hang out outside the city shelters where they passed the nights. I looked for Sebastian in those places, in the parks, along the waterfronts of Manhattan, under the bridges, anywhere these people congregate. Sebastian's smile—the smile he had given me as he left my apartment—hurt me like an ice pick hammering at my heart.

One Saturday afternoon late in April, I was on my way to see Blake, a guy I had met recently in a soup kitchen where I had started doing volunteer work. Since I was half an hour early and the evening was pleasant, the air warm and inviting, I went into Union Square Park to admire the flowers.

I was sitting on a bench facing east when Sebastian passed by me and sat on the next bench. Although it was too warm for it, he was still wearing the jacket I had given him in the winter. He was carrying a knapsack, and in one hand he held what looked like a can of beer wrapped in a paper bag. He kept his free hand on the knapsack as if to guard it from thieves, and with the other hand he took sips from his beer, all the while staring at his rotting sneakers.

Seeing him wearing that jacket was very strange. It was as though he were wearing a part of me, as if he had borrowed one of my limbs. I debated whether to approach him or just to get up and walk away. For the last couple of months—actually since I had met Blake—the obsession with finding Sebastian had lifted. I got up. My heart began to beat so fast I was sure people could hear it. I breathed in deeply; I looked straight ahead of me at the tender new leaves dressing the trees, the beautifully arranged and colorful beds of flowers, the denuded sky, which wore a coat of enameled topaz streaked with pink, and breathed in the air, which was unusually light, and then I walked up to where Sebastian sat.

Anxiously, I said, "Sebastian, how are you?" Without surprise, he looked up. I was relieved to see the mad grin was gone.

"Hi," he greeted me.

I sat next to him. His jacket was badly soiled, and a pungent, putrid smell emanated from him. His face was bruised, his lips chapped and inflamed, but he didn't seem withdrawn.

"Are you getting enough to eat? Do you have a place to sleep?" I asked.

"How're you doing?" he said evasively.

"I'm OK. I've been worried about you. I looked for you all winter." My voice trailed off; I was beginning to feel agitated.

"Thanks. But believe me, this is all I can handle right now," he said carefully, with frightening lucidity. "I'm not crazy. I know where to go for help if I want it. I want you to understand that I'm homeless because I chose to be homeless; I choose not to integrate," he said with vehemence. Forcefully, with seriousness, he added, "This is where I feel OK for now."

The lights of the buildings had begun to go on, like fireflies on the darkening sky. A chill ran through me. I reached in my pocket for a few bills and pressed them in his swollen, raw hands.

"I'm listed in the book. If you ever need me, call me, OK? I'll always be happy to hear from you."

"Thanks. I appreciate it."

I placed a hand on his shoulder and squeezed hard. I got up, turned around, and loped out of Union Square.

Several months went by. I won't say I forgot about Sebastian completely in the interval, but life intervened. I finished my documentary that summer. In the fall it was shown by some public television stations to generally good reviews but low ratings.

One night a month ago, I decided to go see a movie everybody was talking about. Because it was rather late, the theater was almost empty. A couple of young people on a date sat in the row in front of me, and there were other patrons scattered throughout the big house.

The movie, set in Brooklyn, was gloomy and arty, but the performers and the cinematography held my interest and I didn't feel like going back home yet, so I stayed. Toward the end of the movie there is a scene in which the main character barges into a bar, riding his motorcycle. Except for the bartender and a sailor sitting at the counter, the bar is empty. The camera pans slowly from left to right, and there, wearing a sailor suit, is Sebastian. He slowly turns around and stares into the camera and consequently into the audience. The moment lasts two, maybe three seconds, and I was so surprised, I gasped. Seeing Sebastian unexpectedly rattled me so much I had trouble remaining in my seat until the movie ended.

I called Sebastian's parents early the next morning. This time his mother answered. I introduced myself, and, to my surprise, she remembered me. I told her about what had happened the night before and how it made me realize I hadn't seen or heard from their son in quite some time.

"Actually, I'm very glad you called," she said softly, in a voice that was girlish but vibrant with emotions. "Sebastian passed away six weeks ago. We have one of his movie tapes that I thought of sending you since your encouragement meant so much to him."

Then she told me the details of Sebastian's death: He had been found on a bench in Central Park and had apparently died of pneumonia and acute anemia. Fortunately, he still carried some ID with him, so the police were able to track down his parents. In his knapsack, they had found a movie tape labeled *The Hunger Artist*.

I asked her if she had seen it.

"I tried to, but it was too painful," she sighed.

"I'd be honored to receive it; I assure you I'll always treasure it," I said.

We chatted for a short while, and then, after I gave her my address, we said good-bye. A few days later, on my way to school, I found the tape in my mailbox. I carried it with me all day long and decided to wait until I got home that night to watch it.

After dinner I sat down to watch Sebastian's last film. On a piece of cardboard, scrawled in a childish, gothic calligraphy and in big characters, appeared THE HUNGER ARTIST, BY SEBASTIAN X, INSPIRED BY THE STORY OF MR. FRANZ KAFKA.

The film opened with an extreme close-up of Sebastian. I realized he must have started shooting when he was still in school because he looked healthy, his complexion was good, and his eyes were limpid. Millimetrically, the camera studies his features: the right eye, the left one; pursed lips, followed by a wide-open smile that flashes two rows of teeth in good condition. Next we see Sebastian's ears, and, finally, in a characteristic Sebastian touch, the camera looks into his nostrils. One of the nostrils is full of snot. I stopped the film. I was shaking. I have films and tapes of relatives and friends who are dead, and when I look at them, I experience a deep ocean of bittersweetness. After they've been dead for a while, the feelings we have are stirring but resolved; there's no torment in them. However, seeing

Sebastian's face on the screen staring at me, I experienced the feeling I've always had for old actors I love passionately, even though they died before I was born. It was, for example, like the perfection of the love I'd felt for Leslie Howard in *Pygmalion*, although I didn't see that movie until I was grown up. I could not deny anymore that I had been in love with Sebastian; that I had stifled my passion for him because I knew I could never fulfill it. That's why I had denied the nature of my concern for him. I pressed the play button, and the film continued. Anything was better than what I was feeling.

Now the camera pulls back, and we see him sitting in a lotus position, wearing shorts. On the wall behind him, there is a sign that reads THE ARTIST HAS GONE TWO HOURS WITHOUT EATING. WORLD RECORD! There is a cut to the audience. A woman with long green hair, lots of mascara, and purple eye shadow, her lips painted in a grotesque way, chews gum, blows it like a baseball player, and sips a Diet Coke. She nods approvingly all the time. The camera cuts to Sebastian staring at her impassively. Repeating this pattern, we see a man in a three-piece suit, an executive type, watching the artist and taking notes. He's followed by a buxom blond bedecked with huge costume jewelry; she is pecking at a large box of popcorn dripping with butter, and drinking a beer. She wears white silk gloves. We see at least half a dozen people, each one individually—Sebastian plays them all. This sequence ends with hands clapping. As the spectators exit the room, they leave money in a dirty ashtray. The gloved hand leaves a card that says IF YOU EVER GET REALLY HUNGRY, CALL ME! This part of the film, shot in garish, neon colors, has, however, the feel of an early film; it is silent.

The camera cuts to the face of Peter Jennings, who is doing the evening news. We cannot hear what he says. Cut again to Sebastian in a lotus position. Cut to the headline: ARTIST BREAKS HUNGER RECORD: 24 HOURS WITHOUT EATING.

The next time we see the fasting artist, he's in the streets and the photography is in black and white. For sound track we hear sirens blaring, fire trucks screeching, buses idling, huge trucks braking, cars speeding, honking, and crashing, cranes demolishing gigantic structures.

This part of the film must have been shot when Sebastian was already homeless. He must have carried his camera in his knapsack or he must have rented one, but it's clear that whatever money he collected panhandling, he used to complete the film. In this portion he uses a handheld camera to stress the documentary feeling. I can only imagine that he used street people to operate the camera for him. Sebastian's deterioration speeds up: His clothes become more soiled and tattered; his disguises at this point are less convincing— it must be nearly impossible for a starving person to impersonate someone else. His cheeks are sunken, his pupils shine like the eyes of a feral animal in the dark. The headlines read: 54 DAYS WITHOUT EATING...102 DAYS...111 DAYS. Instead of clapping hands, we see a single hand in motion; it makes a gesture as if it were shooing the artist away.

Sebastian disappears from the film. We have footage of people in soup lines and the homeless scavenging in garbage cans. An interview with a homeless person ends the film. We don't see the face of the person conducting the interview, but the voice is Sebastian's. He reads passages from Kafka's story to a homeless woman and asks her to comment. She replies with a soundless laughter that exposes her diseased gums.

I pressed the rewind button and sat in my chair in a stupor. I felt shattered by the realization that what I don't know about what lies in my own heart is much greater than anything else I do know about it. I was so stunned and drained that I hardly had the energy to get up and walk to the VCR to remove the tape.

Later that night, still upset, I decided to go for a walk. It was one of those cold, blustery nights of late autumn, but its gloominess suited my mood. A glacial wind howled, skittering up and down the deserted streets of Gotham. I trudged around until the tip of my nose was an icicle. As I kept walking in a southerly direction, getting closer and closer to the southernmost point of the island, I was aware of the late hour and of how the "normal" citizens of New York were, for the most part, at home, warmed by their fires, seeking escape in a book or their TV sets, or finding solace in the arms of their loved one or in the caresses of strangers.

   I kept walking on and on, passing along the way the homeless who on a night like this chose to stay outside or couldn't find room in a shelter. As I passed them in the dark streets, I did so without my usual fear or repugnance. I kept pressing forward, into the narrowing alleys, going toward the phantasmagorical lament of the arctic wind sweeping over the Hudson, powerless over the mammoth steel structures of this city.

Mystery Spot

David A. Newman

It never occurred to me that I should tell people I was losing my sight. In a weird way it was like losing weight; I kind of hoped people would notice. I take that back. I didn't want anyone to notice. I preferred to play brave and stoic images of myself to myself until the mere act of waking and turning off a blurry alarm clock felt heroic.

I need to clarify because I've just thought about why I didn't tell anyone and why I pretended things were fine when clearly they weren't. It was because of Ian. And now it sounds sad—a single, divorced woman with sole custody of a six-year-old angel from God. Someone's mommy with so many things, it turns out, wrong with her eyes that the only one anyone's ever heard of or can even pronounce is glaucoma. Except no one's heard of glaucoma in a twenty-three-year-old, which is how old I was when all this shit started six years ago.

Ian loves the car, our private domain. Loves punching radio buttons and flipping ashtray lids to keep time. Every now and then, despite the license suspension and promises to my folks, we sneak out late and head east on the almost-empty 210 at night. Just trucks, unlit billboards, and us moving slowly down the far right lane. We roll the windows down and make wind happen. We hold out our hands and feel warmth flow around our palms. It's the one time I can tell we're moving forward.

You can fool some of the people some of the time. But when the only bill you can accurately identify is the new, Monopoly-looking twenty, you have a problem. When you sit on your best friend Alice's arm because, as she unlocks the passenger door, she drops her sunglasses on your seat and you break the glasses and sprain the arm— it seems like it would be hard to hide. But it wasn't. Initially, I told people I was having problems with my ears. That I was having trouble balancing. It's embarrassing to admit, but I even saw an ear, nose, and throat specialist.

I didn't want Ian to know. He gets so freaked out and is up most nights worrying—general worrying, more now since the divorce— about things, deeper things than I even worry about, like is there enough happy for everyone and will he grow up to be a black basketball player. We're white, so I tell him it doesn't look good. Regarding the happy issue, I don't have the heart to look him in what my mother calls his "new little man eyes" and say, *No, there isn't. Mommy went to San Francisco for what she thought was a lifetime of happiness based on two months of lies, and Mommy came back with you.* And nothing else.

Keys jingle as Ian walks down the hall. He stands next to me, too scared or shy, too boy to bleed himself into me the way he used to, the way my cat Sidney still does. I listen to darkness and crickets and say, "Mommy's tired."

"You're always tired." A tennis shoe kicks at the sofa, a silent kick at a missing father that gets me up. Ian strokes my hand with his index finger before he puts the keys in them. I find his head that grows closer to mine each day and run my fingers through it.

We cut through the night air. This time the radio is on. A girl who sounds like she hasn't had her period yet is singing about an undercover lover. Or an underwater lover. Ian hums along.

"Do you see the bracelets, Mom?" he asks, and I nod. Ian knows that's what highway reflectors look like to me: tiny jewels in a long unfurling bracelet. What he doesn't know is that sometimes, for the briefest of moments, they disappear. A van passes on the left, its taillights blurring into shiny propellers that leave trails of light as it pulls away.

"That car's been to Mystery Spot." Ian slides all the way over to his window. "It says so on their bumper sticker."

"Which looks like?"

"Let's see," he says, excitedly. Ian loves to fill in the details, considers it a challenge, even an honor. "It's yellow and black, kind of like a bumble bee, but in a circular pattern, you know, like the one on the box of Tide."

"Ooh." I wiggle my fingers out the window, trapping air in my nails. "That does sound mysterious."

The air, the nails, the word *mysterious,* the rhythm of the wheels on the road, the sulfur smell of trucks. For a moment I am not a soon-to-be thirty-year-old woman with a degree in sociology, no job, and an ex-husband known to all my friends as Fat Ass. I am in college, driving my first love, a gigantic black '68 Oldsmobile, into the city with Alice and Truit—my best friends, then and now. A warped X tape is stuck in the tape deck. Truit, all raw emotion, bounces beside me in the passenger seat, shrieking along with Exene. Alice, all fishnets and black eye shadow, lies silently in the back with a penlight, studying Proust and the gnarled branches of winter trees.

My eyes are blue and round, wide open. I see us as we were—late-night driving, club dancing, ready to stomp on the world with our big black boots, blissfully ignorant of what the world was readying to stomp on us. For one glorious moment I can see everything: the sun setting purple through the smog, Alice's trance-inducing brown eyes, Truit's bursting-at-the-seams smile. Shadows of trees and faded garbage, the tip of Truit's joint and bright red and white signs for In-N-Out Burger.

"Hey, Mom," Ian slides closer to me, bringing me back to blurred taillights and shimmering bracelets. "Maybe there's aliens at Mystery Spot."

"Maybe."

To Ian, Mystery Spot has become the Promised Land. We planned to go for Alice's birthday last year but spent the day in the hospital instead—planting the seeds of Ian's obsession.

"Maybe there's dinosaurs too," Ian says conspiratorially, even though he knows it can't be true.

"Maybe the UFOs brought the dinosaurs." I smile at him.

"Left, Mom," Ian says. "You're drifting."

"Uncle True!" Ian runs into Truit's arms when we stop by his guest house on foot the next morning.

"Neon Ian!" From the groan I can tell Truit has picked Ian up.

"You look great," Truit says in my direction as he sets Ian down. "Skinny."

I smile. To Truit, skinny is all. It's his metaphor for everything that used to be. Truit used to be skinny but now isn't. He used to smoke pot for fun, not breakfast. He used to make people laugh, not nervous.

"Mom, I'm going to see Tender Ears," Ian says, referring to the multiearringed drag-queen sock monkey Truit keeps in his fantastic garden outside and cross-dresses in elaborate-themed costumes. Last week Tender Ears was Tender Golightly, simply sexy in a black slip dress (showing off his long, lanky sock monkey legs), pearl necklace, and white feather boa. The screen door slams as Ian bounds outside.

"He is so beautiful." Truit blows his nose. "Obviously he doesn't get it from Fat Ass."

I don't even bother to answer. Truit knows my ex is off-limits, which is why he always brings him up. "How's Tender?"

"She's got kind of a Mexican sarong thing going on." He takes the bong—the smooth one we call "Pearl"—and lights it, sucking in. "I call it Tender From Ipanema." I sit on newspapers that cover a chair, more a reflection of Truit's lack of cleanliness than my lack of eyesight.

"Alice doesn't have much longer," I say, bringing up Truit's off-limits topic. Truit hasn't spoken to Alice since she told him point-blank she thought Roger, Truit's double ex (boss and lover), was all the horrible things Roger turned out to be. Greedy. Selfish. Promiscuous. Truit, obsessive and superior in his love, was convinced Alice was jealous. He never imagined he would lose his boyfriend, his job, and his identity on the same Tuesday afternoon, pieces falling from the heart of him that still haven't been found, let alone put back together.

"Here you go." Truit places Pearl in my hand.

"True, can I ask you a favor?"

"That's the last of the pot, I swear." Truit deflects me because he thinks I'm going to ask him to visit Alice, which I'm not.

"I need you to take us somewhere. We took our final drive last night."

"You're not still doing that!" For once, Truit's overly dramatic response is completely appropriate.

"You're right," I nod, inhaling. "We're not."

I leave out the part about Ian helping me pull off the highway because the bracelets disappeared—only this time for a full five minutes. About me crying on the side of the road because I finally agreed with everyone else: It is no longer safe for me to drive.

"I thought your mother took the keys."

"Ian took them back. She'd take the car if they had room in their garage." I finally exhale.

"So where are we going?" He asks, guarded.

"Mystery Spot. He's dying to go, True. Dy-ing. Can you cope?"

For the last two years, ever since Roger, there's been damn little that Truit can cope with. Including leaving the house, forgiving Alice for being right, listening to any CD other than Annie Lennox, and showing up for a little boy's fifth birthday party dressed as a clown, which was his stupid idea in the first place.

"An extraordinary sight to behold?" he asks, reciting the Mystery Spot tagline, plastered on billboards up and down the 152.

"Don't believe everything you read."

"For him...I can cope."

Truit feels sweaty and bigger than I can remember when I hug him. It's then I realize he makes even me nervous. I can't fit the round hole he's become into the square peg of my memory. "We both love you to death." I use my son's feelings to cover my own, even though I know it will always be true. I will always love Truit, no matter how little who we are resembles who we used to be.

"Twice versa," he whispers in my ear.

Now that I'm my mother's sound bite and she practically cuts my food with her brave Nancy Reagan smirk—some images never fade—the question on people's minds is, How blind are you?

It's like this. When we went to the circus with Alice and her brother Leo, I didn't know we were in a tent. I thought it was a warehouse. Thought the clowns looked like bomb-pops and the trapeze artists like unraveling rolls of toilet paper. I fill in blanks with voices and memory. Afterward, when I asked for a full recap, Leo told me about Nancy Kerrigan's legally blind mother who used to sit inches away from a monitor in order to see her daughter skate.

"She was blind?" Alice said, a light dawning. "I wondered why they always showed that old woman with the obstructed view."

Alice is one who levels with me, who says, "It's good you're going blind because you wouldn't like what the last few years have done to your face." Alice is the one who makes me laugh and who insisted on making me over for my first and I promise you my last blind date. Pun not intended.

How do I describe Phil Stein? Dark and mysterious, I guess. That's a joke. *Sesame Street* is dark and mysterious to me these days. As is the toilet. Phil was a therapist. Correction, Phil is a therapist. Not mine, though Lord knows the man tried. He kept saying I was surrounding myself with negative energy. Phil didn't seem to understand that in the last four years incredibly horrifying and life-altering events have occurred to almost everyone in my life. "So it's the other way around, Phil-is-stine," I told him. "Negative energy is slowly and gradually surrounding me."

"Hey, Gramma, what do you call a cow with no legs?" Ian lies in the back of my mother's Continental, holding his Yak Bak, an incredibly annoying toy that records and repeats everything you say. My mother slipped it in his stocking last Christmas, the same year she told him, while I was napping, that I was "visually impaired."

"Not now honey, Grammy's driving." My mother pulls quickly into the hospital parking lot, nearly sideswiping a truck as she parks in a waiting zone. That both Ian and I feel safer with me behind my wheel than with my mother is all you need to know.

"Ground beef!" Ian yells into his Yak Bak, which has two buttons—one for "say" and one for "play." When my mom told him I was visually impaired, Ian told her he already knew. He told her my left eye with the overall blur was the good one. And the right one with no peripheral vision was the bad one. All the same, having it in the open did seem to free him. Christmas Day he kept saying "Are you blind?" and "Why are you blind?" into the Yak Bak and holding it up to my ear. A few days later at the grocery store he whispered "My mom's going blind" and played it for the checker.

"So Alice is worse?" My mom repeats what I told her when I called asking for a ride.

I nod.

"If only she hadn't ignored those lumps." My mom flips down her visor and makes a popping sound—checking her lipstick. "You need to have a mastectomy, by the way. Twenty-eight is not too young."

"Ground beef!" Yak Bak repeats. Ian giggles.

"Twenty-nine, and I hope to God you mean mammogram." I grab my purse. "A mastectomy is when they actually remove your breast."

"Not in front of the boy, Lauren." My mom yanks her head toward Ian who says "mammogram" into the Yak Bak as he climbs from the car.

Last week I caught Ian holding the Yak Bak up to his friend Blake's ear and giggling as the machine repeated his tiny "fuck."

"See you in an hour," my mother says, pulling away.

We wave good-bye.

"Gram-mammogram," Ian tells the Yak Bak, hitting play to immediately repeat the word.

Ian grabs my hand, and we head toward the entrance.

"Shazam-ogram!" Ian yells, pulling me through the revolving door and into the hospital.

It seems oddly fitting to find Alice among the barely living. In college she was obsessed with cemeteries and seances, believed in over-souls and underground clubs. Even then Alice had a sad face and a melancholy way of dancing that made me want to cry. I thought her morbid fascinations had something to do with a bleached-out La Jolla childhood, never imagined her obsession for the dark might become a self-fulfilling prophecy.

"You look amazing!" I say as we walk into the room, a private joke. To me, Alice actually looks a bit like lint—gray and fuzzy.

"Like my hair?" Alice mocks her chickpea head. "I dyed it pink."

"No, she didn't!" Ian runs into the bathroom and hides. He claims to hate our pretend game, but I think, because he can clearly see Alice, these visits are harder on him.

In addition to eliminating both her breasts, Alice says her breast cancer has eliminated her ability to bullshit and her fear of heights. Alice, who wouldn't climb a library ladder in college, took up rock climbing after she was diagnosed, increasing the risk of her climbs in direct response to the progression of her cancer. But this year it's been no contest. The rocks haven't felt her thin and tender hands since November.

"Ready for the latest?" Alice takes the Dr. Pepper I brought and twists it open. "I, Alice Leanora Marcoux, had...an aneurysm!" She says it proudly, like a woman announcing the sex of her newborn. "Remember Truit in college? 'Don't have an aneurysm, Alice!' " She mocks his voice. " 'Chill, Alice. You'll give yourself an aneurysm.' I fucking had an aneurysm, Lauren," she cries, holding her stick arms toward me.

I hug her and we cry and cry and cry.

"Now, now," Alice finally whispers, "Don't have an aneurysm."

We both start laughing. Hard. Alice hands me Kleenex as we finally break apart. "The ass-kicker?" Alice mocks her stepmother's Jersey accent, telling me that, according to her doctor, the aneurysm explains why she, a book-a-week demon, can no longer read. "Apparently my eyes still have the ability, but something in my brain has stopped signaling them to comprehend words. How fucked up is that?"

"Jesus, Al." I rub her thin hand, thinking of rocks, of stones, feeling one in my throat.

"It's the only thing I have left." She cries again and so do I, rubbing her hand so hard I expect a genie to appear, freeing her.

"Shazam-ogram!" I hear the Yak Bak faintly from behind the bathroom door.

"Ian, go play in the children's waiting room!" I yell, and he does, sprinting from the room, thrilled to be released.

"Help me up." Alice reaches for my hand, and I pull her up, feeling in her body what I never do in her words—a very sick, very frail woman, mustering all of her strength to climb from the bed. She slowly spreads her arms out and stretches up on her tiptoes, twirling around slightly. "There's not nearly enough dancing in hospitals," she says, dropping my hand and shuffling into the bathroom.

When she returns I tell her about one of Ian's first word books, *Frederick's Surprise*. "It's about this fish named Frederick who realizes he hates swimming and decides there's no point in being in the water."

"Sounds lame." She sniffs.

"My mother bought it without reading it."

She nods. "So what happens?"

"Well, one day Frederick musters up the courage to leave the ocean and walk up on shore. And at first everything's great, he's all free and filled with possibility." I laugh.

"Don't tell me." Alice pulls her blanket up.

"A page later he dies in the hot sun, discovered too late by a little boy—"

"What a hideous book for a child!" Alice screams.

"I'm not finished! The boy tosses him out to sea anyway, and Frederick comes back to life...and he loves the water in a way he never has, which is really the surprise, the end."

"Fuck Frederick." Alice looks at the television. In my memory her eyes are impossibly light brown and young. She situates herself on the bed. "I think it's worse for you," she says quietly.

"And why is that?" I take her hand.

"Because at least I'm dying. You, on the other hand, have to live like this forever."

299   David A. Newman

Sidney finds me on the couch and curls up on my stomach. His purr warms me. He's a people cat—more so now that Roscoe, the cat-hating German shepherd, moved in next door. I pat Sid's back absently. I'm beginning to feel like one of those weird cat ladies. I haven't had sex in more than a year, have no prospects, and sleep with Sidney every night.

This is what I've become. A woman who lives off monthly alimony checks, who occasionally has sex with her shower massage, whose dapper, doglike cat sleeps with her, pressed close, so tactile and ever-present that it's Sidney's green eyes and not Ian's blue ones that I can still see.

I listen to the aggressive blue jays that rule our backyard and to Roscoe, to repeating chirps and barks, and try not to think of my ex, Arthur. Yes, Fat Ass has a proper name. It's Alice and Truit who refuse to use it.

The first sentence Arthur uttered to Truit contained the word *remuneration,* which sealed his fate. He was talking about sales, talking about a deal he'd closed, talking constantly and always selling. I think everyone has one monumentally bad relationship in their lives. One oil meets water meets a shadow of yourself that no one else will ever know how to bring out, thank God. One least favorite mistake. It's not so much Arthur that I don't like thinking about—it's who I was when I was with him that keeps me awake. Needy. Petty. Wifey. Snobby. As rich as I've ever been. As white as I've ever been. My worst possible me. Terrified of going blind, I spent my last good-eye years looking at all the wrong things.

On our first date I told Arthur what the doctors had told me. In all likelihood my eyes would continue to deteriorate until I was legally blind. He blinked his flat brown eyes and pledged to learn sign language. "I'm going blind, not deaf!" I said, laughing so hard Chardonnay came out my nose. He is the father of my son. He lives in Mill Valley with his new wife, Simi. He plays league tennis and snorts cocaine before big meetings and matches. Alice and Truit despise him. So does Ian, which makes me both very happy and incredibly sad. We see him twice a year. That is all and everything he will ever be to us.

Alice has taken a turn for the worse, Alice's mother tells me Friday afternoon in a wavering voice. *The doctor says it could be as soon as the end of the month.* Alice's mother has only called me once before—when Alice was diagnosed. *I asked him not to tell her, Lauren, and I'm asking you as well.* Alice's mother is a kind and generous woman who sews and bakes and sent Alice to college in Laura Ashley dresses. *I just don't want anyone to discourage her.* Alice's mother has never understood her dark daughter and probably never will.

I hang up. Pour myself a glass of water. Sit down. The wall I've built, the certainty I've always felt that Alice would somehow survive, comes down Berlin Wall–style, swiftly and unexpectedly. What floods through is everything Alice is not going to see. A thirtieth birthday. A gallery opening featuring her twisted paintings and poems. Her long-ago promised Edward Gorey–themed wedding—long, pointy bridesmaids' dresses, everyone in black, ravens released into the air like antidoves. The dark-haired, full-lipped man with an edge she was going to marry as soon as she met him. Ian's first-grade graduation. Her best friend sobbing uncontrollably at the kitchen table.

When he finds out we're going to Mystery Spot in the morning, Ian heads straight to bed. "I want us to get up really early," he says. "I want us to be the first ones there."

I lie on the couch, exhausted from Alice, and my mind travels back, past Alice, past college, and stops, for some reason, on a leadership camp I went to in high school. A week in the woods with a bunch of do-gooders. I went ironically—some guy I liked named Ramon was going, so I followed him. Sometimes I wonder if anyone I met at leadership camp is leading anything, anywhere. The last night, we went on a handicap hike, which at the time seemed noble but now strikes me as perverse. What we, a group of happy, healthy young leaders, did was form groups of five. Then we were handicapped in dramatic ways. Some were made deaf, others put in wheelchairs. I was blind.

Blindfolded, at any rate. What's weird is, I couldn't be blind. Couldn't cope with being instantly cut off. I tried, of course, and no one knew I was peering out the bottom of my blindfold. Back then I had the option. I remember thinking this wasn't something I'd have to master, walking through the woods with freshly showered strangers guiding me by the arm—a sensation I hated even then. Like learning origami or the oboe, preparing to be blind never struck me as a practical skill.

Now I dream about that hike. But in my dreams the blindfold is white and the sun warms my eyelids. Ian runs beside me, keeping up, describing everything. He tells me the trees look like the air freshener ones only not as green and with needles. Then he's gone. A cool breeze passes through my fingers as I reach my hands out before me, locking my wrists, ready to break my fall. I can't peer beneath the blindfold so I stop and kneel. Memories of the happy girls from camp float back as if they're watching from the shadows of the trees, wondering how far I'll make it on my own before they have to step in and lead me to the campfire.

Ian dances around the kitchen chanting and Yak Bak-ing "Mystery Spot!" driving me insane as I make his favorite pancakes. I mix the batter; Ian pours it into the skillet and tells me when it's time to flip.

"Hey, mom!" he says, a smile in his voice. "This pancake's shaped exactly like a heart!"

Before we eat I call Truit to make sure he's up. I get his machine. I simply say "Mystery Spot" and hang up. Five minutes later he calls back.

"I had an outbreak yesterday," he says.

Since college Truit has had sudden, random acne outbreaks that cover his face one or two times a year. We used to call them "Not Pretty in Pink." He used to laugh at them, but over the years I understand they've gotten worse. There's been scarring.

"I can't cope," he says one more time than I can stand.

"Truit, you're going."

"Don't tell me what to do, Lauren," he says indignantly. "I'm not your son."

"We're going, Truit, and you're coming with us."

He hangs up.

I march to the bedroom and feel around my dresser, pulling out a sweatshirt, a skirt, and a wool cap. When I come back out Ian is watching television, moping.

"Ian, get the keys."

"I thought you couldn't drive anymore."

"I'm not!" I reply, not sure what I'm saying. "You are."

"Why don't we just call Gramma?"

"Because I want us to have fun."

Roscoe greets us in the driveway—on top of Sidney, who is wailing and clawing. Ian screams.

"GET AWAY!" I shriek, running forward, kicking at the air, connecting with Roscoe, who lunges at me, then suddenly turns and trots calmly next door. Sidney whimpers on the ground.

"His ear's bleeding, mom."

Without a word, I scoop up a trembling Sidney and gently place him in the backseat.

"There's blood on your dress," Ian says.

"Get in the car."

Ian silently sits on my lap. I start the car and back out. It is harder somehow in the daylight, the sun mutes the shapes I can see, there are no reflectors. It looks like someone has replaced the windshield with a clear, wavy shower glass door. I see trees in triplicate. It is three short blocks to Truit's house. Ian's hands are inside mine on the steering wheel. "We can do this." I say out loud, to myself.

The first block goes well but slowly. "We're going fifteen," Ian says, excited. "Now we're going twenty." There is no one behind us. Sidney, normally frantic in a car, sits silently in the back. The second block ends with a four-way stop. A woman pushes a stroller in front of us, her white T-shirt blurring her face. I wait. And wait. A truck honks behind us. Ian tenses, his ridge-thin back pressed against my stomach. Finally we make a right turn.

When we pull onto Truit's street, Ian spies Truit standing on the curb in front of his house. "Tender Ears is wearing yellow and black," Ian whispers. "He looks like Mystery Spot."

Truit walks over to my window. "Excuse my language, Ian, but your mom is a complete bitch."

Ian giggles.

Truit pulls on the door handle. "You'll have to slide over if you want me to drive."

I shake my head. "My car. I'm driving."

"Oh, this is getting better all the time!" Truit says, walking back around to the passenger side. "Let's all drive off a cliff, shall we!" he says, squeezing into the front seat and tossing Tender Ears in the back. As we pull out, a bloodcurdling cat scream is heard from the backseat. Sidney, it seems, is not a big Tender Ears fan.

"He's killing Tender Ears!" Ian yells, turning back around.

"Oh, let him!" Truit says, laughing, stoned already.

For once, I am thankful Truit is a backseat driver extraordinaire. "Lady with really ugly hair behind you," he says, checking his mirror as we pull onto Bay Road. "Slow it down, Laur. Get in your left lane—it's clear, and OK, there we are." Truit, who hasn't been needed by anyone for anything in far too long, brightens as we travel, relishing his newfound responsibility. But minutes later, as we pull into the hospital parking lot, his mood darkens.

"Now you know why I'm driving," I say, putting the car in park.

"I'm not going in." Truit says.

"Who asked you to? C'mon, Ian."

I fish the skirt, sweater, hat, and a cold Dr. Pepper from the trunk. Ian takes my hand and leads me toward the hospital.

"If I could see how bad you look, I would never do this," I say, dressing Alice in clothes I've outgrown.

"I've been praying for someone dark and brooding to break in and get me out of here," she says through short, shallow breaths. "I was thinking Rufus Sewell."

"He was busy." I bring the cap to her head and she pulls it on.

Alice swims in my tight clothes. We turn on the bathroom sink and leave the door slightly ajar. "Ian, there's a wheelchair in the closet," she says, and he wheels it out. At first it feels like I'm pulling Alice, but after a couple of steps it seems she is pulling me. Ian stands guard, motioning us down the hall when it's free of nurses. I push, barely feeling Alice in the chair. She stifles a laugh as we slide smoothly out of the cancer ward. We turn a corner and head for the elevator. "Faster!" Alice whispers, clapping in delight as her skirt blows up a little.

Truit breaks down when he sees Alice. Just cries and cries, drowning out Sidney, who is still attacking Tender Ears.

"God, I hate you," she says weakly, kissing him on the forehead.

"I hate you more." He helps her into the backseat and collapses the wheelchair, shoving it in the trunk.

Truit opens my door, and I slide over without a word. "We're off to see the wizard!" He sings, starting the car, and we all join in.

Ian sits in my lap, the boy leading the broken.

"Have you ever been to Mystery Spot?" he asks Alice when we hit the familiar freeway.

"Mysteriously enough, I have not," she says. "But I hear it looks a lot like Medjugorje," she mentions her obsession, the town in Bosnia-Herzegovina where a group of children have visions of the Virgin Mary. The town atop a mountain famed for miracles and the masses who journey there hoping for one, climbing the steep, rocky hill where the visions first appeared.

"We're going there when you get out," I say, wrapping Sidney's nicked ear with what's left of Tender Ears' miniskirt.

"Who needs it when you've got Mystery Spot, right?" Alice asks, and we all answer "Right!"

Sidney purrs his megapurr, licking my forearm and dozing off. I wave my nails out the window, loving the rhythm of the wheels on the road. For a moment I am in the Olds, behind the wheel. "Remember when we tried to go to the Petrified Forest?"

Like all truly inspired ideas, it happened when we were stoned. Alice mentioned something about the Petrified Forest, and Truit and I got the giggles. We kept picturing all those terrified trees, just frozen and whimpering with their mouths open. Truit explains all this to Ian, leaving out the stoned part. Ian giggles, one of us, our arrested development merging perfectly with his precociousness.

"The signs all have that Tide box swirl thing except they have question marks in the middle." Ian squeezes my hand as we walk down the gravel path. "You sure Sidney's OK?" he asks.

"He's sleeping, sweetie. He needs rest."

Behind us, Truit tries to push Alice, but the wheelchair sinks, bogged down by the stony path. "Help me up," Alice says Truit does, holding on to her as we start down the path.

"Let's get married," she says.

Truit nods. "I'll design the dress."

"It can't be explained." Ian reads with gusto. "It can't be defined! It can only be experienced! Mystery Spot, thirty feet ahead!" My son pulls me hard to the left, and I feel his excitement, letting it run through me, growing curious myself. I hear other footsteps, a family speaking Spanish, clicking their camera as they pass.

"Let's wait for Truit and Alice to catch up," I say.

Ian pauses, ready to burst with excitement, but being the boy I'm so grateful he is, he waits for Alice and Truit and says, "You're doing great, Aunt Alice," when they finally reach us.

"Medjugorje," I whisper as we help Alice to a drinking fountain and wait as she sits down, catching her breath. We are silent. I keep expecting Truit to make a crack or sing something silly, but he doesn't. Even Ian is strangely calm.

I've heard some things about Mystery Spot. Apparently it is a place where the laws of gravity do not apply—where a compass just spins and spins and brooms stand up all by themselves. After a few minutes, Truit helps Alice up, and together we begin to climb the hill, pausing every five or six steps for Alice to catch her breath. People stream around us in fast-motion, chatting, slurping sodas. We slowly climb to the top of the hill and look down.

"Wow," Ian says softly, squeezing my hand.

"Amazing." Alice whispers, taking my other hand

"It's beautiful." Truit hugs me from behind.

I look where they're looking, seeing nothing but shadows of trees. I tilt my head up. The sun warms my eyes. A cool breeze passes through my fingers, and a tear falls from my right eye, the bad one. I feel light-headed and slightly top-heavy, as if something is trying to force me right off the hill and up into the sky.

I feel I could spread my arms and fly, strong enough for all of us, carrying my friends and my small son on to wherever it is we're supposed to go from here. I feel the strongest, most incredible love pass between the four of us, filling me up from my feet to the top of my head. Instead of wiping away everything that's come between us, it clarifies it, magnifies it, holding it up and covering it in kisses, making it perfect and beautiful. And then, for a moment that I pray will never end, I see faintly, then brightly, the most brilliant white light.

Hair

Andy Quan

1.

First they prepared the eggs. Dai Mo, great-auntie, the one who chose my Chinese name, reached for the carton, her hands turned into a careful claw. She plucked out three oval shapes and placed them in the small pot, filled with water. They added the dye, bought from an herb store in Chinatown, and lit the gas stove. The white shell slowly turned pink, then red; the insides hardened. Dai Mo hit the eggs with the spoon so the shell would crack and the red color would transform the insides as well.

And then they were ready.

I only found this out years later. Mother and I in our basement, she was opening up the big black safe, the kind that belongs on movie sets. I have no idea where my father got it from. She was storing away part of her small collection of jade carvings. Her hand, exiting the safe, paused at one of the shelves, where it reached into a shallow cardboard box and pulled out an envelope. It was marked with my name and the date August 7, 1969. This is a piece of your hair from your first haircut, she explained. We open the envelope gingerly; I don't dare breathe on it. At the bottom of the inside there is a small clump of black down. You had so much hair when you were born!

Dai Mo cracked open the eggs and left the shells on a cloth on the kitchen table. Then she rubbed one of the rubbery hard-boiled eggs all over my small, soft head. Why on Earth did she do that? I asked.

Well, it was to get you used to the feeling of something on your head—scissors, hands—it was for your first haircut, it was so you wouldn't cry.

Well, did I?

I don't remember *that,* said my mother, and I saw her twenty years younger, not so different really: a more youthful face, blacker hair, the same calm pleased look as today, the older relatives all hovering over her, and over me too—grandfather, days before his death, Dai Mo's husband, probably drunk on Scotch like always, some of my father's brothers or sisters. Her youngest son, his first haircut.

2.

I have always had mixed feelings about my name. Things could have been worse: Chinese daughters often get the names of flowers like Peony, Pansy, Jasmine. The sons get names of odd British men, plucked out of history. They are old names like Winston, Byron, Percival. I had a theory about this growing up. However antiquated these names might sound to Anglo-Canadians, Chinese families had no mental associations with them at all. They were simply names, one basically as good as another, though why not have something a little more flashy and important sounding than John, they thought, eyes lit up with ambition.

I suppose that is how I got the name Samson, which I tried to hide under the moniker Sam, but which failed whenever a teacher at school would read out a role call at the start of the year. The biblical reference was not so bad, as most kids didn't know who Samson was anyways, but once it started, it stayed, and from time to time, my classmates in the schoolyard would tease, Samson, oh Samson, where is your long hair? At least it was better than the kids who called me Samsonite, after the luggage company, the name with a faint Japanese ring and sounding like Superman's deadly poison.

However, I always had a certain belief that we are marked at a young age to follow certain paths, as if it were written physically on our bones. Like when you see someone on the street and you can see how they looked like when they were a child or what they will look like when they are very old. There is a child on my street, not more than nine years old—I can see how she will laugh when she is thirty, how she will wear stylish sweaters, how her face will become long and elegant. That is a kind of destiny.

With me it's different. People tell me I look different according to my haircut. If I have it short, I look like a boy; if it is long, I look older. It looks very different if it is in a ponytail than if it is held loose. I always felt that my destiny was linked to my hair due to my name and my biblical namesake. While I surmised that Myrons would always be awkward, that Jeffs would always be friendly, that Louises would tend toward cigarette smoking, I knew that I, Samson, and my strength would always be linked to the long strands of straight Chinese hair springing out of my scalp and downward with gravity.

3.

I went through many phases with my hair.

The first was the barbershop, the Greek barbershop that my father and brothers went to. It smelled of talcum powder and blue after-shave. There were mirrors behind the barber chairs and in front. When I sat down in the worn vinyl, I could see my head multiplied a million times, the smallest one receding off into the distance, some-where so far away that I could not see the end. Someday I figured I would visit that place.

There were four barbers, and I liked Steve the best. Leo would nick my ears; Mike seemed so sloppy. John, Steve's cousin, was OK, but it was Steve I liked, his large hands cupped around my head, the warm buzz of the razor against my neck, the blades of his agile scis-sors hovering around my scalp like the wings of a hummingbird. He would always give me the same haircut, just above the eyebrows, a bit above the ears. He would ask me each time how long I wanted my sideburns. He would shave the nape of my neck up to a precise horizon that curved around just below my ears.

It was when I was a tender fourteen that my outrageous Italian friend, Luis, told me about "model nights" at Hiro's hair salon. Luis was outrageous because he wore stylish Italian clothes that were bought during summer visits to his grandmother's home in Rome, he wore a Speedo bathing suit for swimming instead of baggy athletic shorts like the rest of the boys, and he couldn't care less about the Rolling Stones and Led Zeppelin, the idols of most other kids in the neighborhood. He liked English bands with black dyed spiky hair. Of course, he would know about these special nights at the hair salon. Call them up, he advised. I decided it was time to leave the Greek barbers.

I went in for my first appointment. A young hair stylist named Chachka greeted me and led me to the back of the studio, all angles and black plastic and track lighting. The mirrors here did not reflect each other but instead other parts of the stylish interior. I was placed in a chair, my head placed back in a sink, caressed with sweet-smelling shampoo, massaged by strong lean fingers, my hair rinsed by a glorious spray of hot, hot water.

Chachka spent an hour on my hair, trimming single hairs here and there, consulting with her supervisor, clipping and unclipping metal clips used to divide my hair into sections. Instead of the crude equal lengths of the fluorescent barbershop, here at Hiro's they measured and primped, angled and gelled. She left my hair a bit long on top, incrementally angled upward on the sides from short to longer. She trimmed off all remnants of sideburns and showed me to how to gel my hair, after she'd given me a second glorious shampoo. Blow-dried it all into place, told me to come back in a few weeks. All for five bucks.

I returned many times. It was in those days that I first became conscious of how I appeared to others: I started to spend longer in front of the mirror, squint my eyes to see how I might look differ-ent. I didn't like my face. The eyes were fine, a simple almond shape, like Mom's. I had heard of Chinese who had gotten an operation to have their eyes "fixed' so they would appear more Western. A slit here, a tuck there, voilà! Eyelids. But I didn't mind that mine were hidden. The nose and the jaw were another thing. The former was flat and tended to sprout pimples right in the middle. I would have liked something smaller at the time, a bit more angular and delicate. As for the shape of my face, I couldn't stand its roundness. No one I had ever met who was considered handsome had a round face like mine. They had Superman jaws, angular V's or squared U's. Not my round rice bowl face. Still, there were few alternatives, even though an exercise book that I found in the library said I could tighten up my jaw by twisting it this way and that twenty times a day. If I couldn't change my face, at least I could do something with my hair, which, lucky for me, grew quickly, so I had options.

I went through several variations of the gelled hairstyles that were popular in those years. I received them from a whole series of young, stylish, ambitious men and women who were at various stages in their salon careers. I made idle chitchat, asked how long they had worked there, what they did before the salon, what kind of hair they liked to cut best. One of the stylists, a rough-looking fellow Chinese named Alexander, asked me about high school and studies. Just as he was finishing a final blow-dry, he asked if I had a girlfriend. Or girlfriends? It was not something I had really thought about, although I knew what answer was expected. Still, I was never good at lying. "No," I mumbled and, when pressed, said something about being shy. "Shy?!" he exclaimed. "C'mon, man, you can't be shy about these things." He continued his pep talk as I placed a blue five-dollar bill in his hand and moved toward the door. I didn't return to him.

One of the next stylists, talking with his hands the way many of them did, described a wave in the air and said, "Your hair's getting long enough. You know what I'd do? I'd put a wave in it." I was starting to feel at the time that all Chinese hair was the same, and no matter what I did, I would look like all the other Chinese kids I knew. So I imagined that shape on top of my head, my hair sweeping over to one side, an ocean curve. It seemed daring and original.

Of course, this is not what happened, and I should have stopped it all when the rollers went in. "Samson! What did you do?" Mother asked in mock horror, although I could tell she thought it was quite funny: short at the sides but the rest of my straight Chinese hair bound up into curls on top of my head. Have you seen Chinese people with perms? I hoped people wouldn't think I was trying to hide my cultural roots. How embarrassing! My only consolation was that it was summer holidays and no one from school would see me. Also, it was easy to take care of. Pat it into place each morning; no need even for a comb. It was, however, a long summer, and I decided then that I would grow my hair long.

4.

Long hair! Long black hair! Silky, shiny, thick. The girls flock to it, they feel it, they braid it. "I wish I had hair like this," they exclaim. I reply, "I think you might look a bit odd with Chinese hair." Still, they giggle and flirt. I am different from the other boys. They are attracted to how little I care about the masculine requirement for short hair. However, they cannot seem to guess that I care nothing at all for masculine requirements.

That's not entirely true. The masculine requirement that I truly discard is that I should be interested in these girls who are interested in me. On other fronts I do want to be masculine. Effeminacy frightens me, for effeminate is what I have heard I am supposed to be. I manage to avoid accusations, though, and it takes me some time to understand that as an Asian male, I am viewed as neither masculine nor feminine, or so I believe and so I carry myself. Anyways, it allows me to meet those flirtatious looks with a completely blank stare resembling innocence rather than distaste. Rapunzel, Rapunzel, I wonder. How did you know who you wanted to let your hair down for? Was it really love that climbed up those locks?

I grew my hair long the same time I left for college. While my mother thought the permanent was vaguely amusing, she was horrified by the increasing length of my hair. "Shouldn't you get a haircut?" she asked whenever I would appear home for weekend visits. The repetition would echo in my ears and off the walls, and I knew to expect it two, three, four times a visit. There was no irony or playfulness in her voice when she asked the question. She simply hated that I had long hair.

It was about the same time that I was considering coming out, and somehow I managed to link the two issues firmly together in my mind. If mother couldn't accept my long hair, after my repeated moans and groans to stop asking me to cut it, how would she ever accept it if I told her I was gay? I kept my mouth shut. I kept my hair long.

When the girls would braid my hair, I felt the strands twist around each other, and I felt them twisting around myself, tight lines of constraint that held me in all sorts of manners.

5.

I have forgotten the dates when adolescence arrived. I only remember images. The hair that sprouted above my penis, all twisty like the shrubbery that grows next to the ocean, the curves and bends mystifying the sea wind, rooting itself in place. I think I tried not to look those days; I much preferred to be smooth and hairless. I thought of my dentist's hairy hands reaching into my mouth, the tufts of chest hair rising above his unbuttoned collar. I felt somehow nauseous.

I was lucky, though, since I never grew much hair, hardly any on my arms, a bit on my legs. As for other places, I watched my father cut his nose hairs and hoped I would never have to do the same. Eventually I would, that familiar revelation that we all become our parents one day.

I entered university. I told my parents I was gay, my father was confused and my mother cried, but she stopped complaining about my long hair, and within the year, things were relatively back to normal.

My mother started dyeing her gray hairs black (I hoped that my sexuality and her gray hairs were not linked). On the other hand, I discovered my first gray hair while on a drive in the countryside one sunny fall with a boyfriend, Paul, who was sweet but who would only last three weeks. "I can't believe it. I think I have a gray hair," I exclaimed in panic, holding it up and peering into the side and rearview mirrors.

"Where, where?" asked Paul as he lazily reached over while keeping one hand on the wheel. He found the hair and plucked it out with a sharp quick motion and a smirk. "Not anymore," he said.

Although I was annoyed, it was an easy solution at the time to the problems of aging.

I got crabs from the boyfriend after Paul. While I didn't particularly mind a bit of physical infidelity here and there (mental infidelity was another matter), I was dismayed at the physical consequences it had on me. I was going through a particularly busy time at university and had started swimming again. I convinced myself the itch was due to the chlorine. I almost fainted when I actually saw what was crawling around. Not only at discovering the denial of what my body had been telling me but also the idea of these small horror movie creatures, with their white legs and prehistoric-looking form. I considered shaving off my pubic hair, but realized the simple powder was an easier solution.

After swimming I took up weights. Not only did I get to ogle beautiful men, but it also gave me a good topic of conversation those days, since it seemed every gay man I met was going to the gym as well. Of course, it also appealed to my sense of vanity, and after believing my skinny Asian body could not gain weight, I was quite pleased with the results.

I was amused by another discovery that summer. After admiring innumerable sets of perky, rounded pectoral muscles, some of which would lead down to an incredibly ridged abdomen, some of which would perch on top of a rounded or smooth torso, I started to wonder why they looked all the same, as if put through an assembly line to make parts of cars: hubcaps perhaps, or fenders.

I called my best consultant in the city, Randolph. Although he knew all the latest trends in the gay world, he never got too caught up in them. "Randolph, why do all the men in this city have the same chest? I've been noticing a disturbing trend lately."

"Ah," he put on his academic voice, which became more precise daily as he worked on his doctorate in social anthropology. "Perhaps, my dear Samson, it is because not only are the men body obsessed these days, but they are all shaving their chests to appear even more masculine and true to form."

"But I thought hair was very masculine."

"No, no. Where have you been, my boy, during this crisis? Gay men are dying into a sea of hair and ashes. Now, they all want to appear boyish and hygienic and hairless. The blond boy next door. It seems more healthy that way. Have you been frolicking with the gym Nazis lately?"

Hair. No hair. Shaved hair. Shaved chests. I thought about all of this with some satisfaction and some resentment. Resentment since I could never fit into these gay North American obsessions. I may be a Chinese neighbor, but I would never be a boy next door. At the same time I felt some sort of secret satisfaction. My chest was smooth, I would never have to shave it, I would never have razor cuts over my heart. At least, in a technical sense, according to the whims and styles of the gay community, I was one step ahead without having to do anything at all.

6.

I traveled the country and other continents with my mane of black hair. I reveled in the attention it brought me. Sometimes I would be angry that it was all people could see. Many times I was addressed as "miss" or "madam" and would answer in my deepest, most resonant voice. Watch them adjust their embarrassment and try to hide their surprise. While some white male friends with long hair would tell the same story of people mistakenly approaching them from behind with the wrong call of gender, I don't think they'd ever been met directly in the eye and addressed as a woman.

Where have these people been? I thought. Have they never seen a Chinese face? Can they not tell the difference between my slanted eyes and Suzie Wong's? Is my Adam's apple shrunken like our cocks are supposed to be? Are the breasts of Asian women so flat they look like a thin man's chest? So flat they do not need a bra?

Or do people not look? Do they see only a flash of black hair? A flash of something strange and foreign and unlikable so they turn their heads, so they speak with the first word that arrives to their tongues? So they stand as in Columbus' supposed encounter with the indigenous peoples on this continent, awed by each other's strange tones of skin and manner of movement?

At the same time, I enjoyed hiding behind that hair. I could twist

it when I was bored, I could cover my eyes with it when I did not
want to see. I could hide my ethnicity in mystery. It was the Chinese
who arrived in Canada in great numbers, my grandparents who
owned produce stores and bought property, who raised children
who moved step-by-step further into society. Yet still they did not
understand us, or they believed they understood us too well. The
same questions over and over: What do you eat at home? Do you
speak Chinese? Were you born here?

With long hair I could be almost anything. Few Chinese had long
hair. People would ask me if I was Japanese, Filipino, Thai. They
would ask too if I was Indian, a native Indian; they would not know
what word to use to least offend: Indigenous, First Nations Person,
Indian? I could spin stories like thread, or I could tell them the truth,
which was a long, threadlike story since mother and father came
from different generations of immigrants as well as different coun-
tries, even though all of our ancestors came from villages in the same
province of Canton. If I wanted, I could be the ultimate Chinese. I
was growing my hair, braiding it into a queue, to return to my roots,
to wear my hair as the first Chinese immigrants to Canada did, if they
managed to escape the white man's scissors.

7.

There was another trend in the gay community that took me a
while to notice. Randolph, of course, noticed right away, but knowing some of the background to my long mane of hair and secretly lik-
ing its connection with my name, he kept his mouth shut. Of course,
the trend followed the same reasoning as the shaved chest phenomenon. If a hairless body, at this point in our history, was somehow
more masculine and hygienic, what about hairless heads?

Gay men were shaving their skulls, their pates peeking out into
daylight. Some had blue veins, some had razor cuts, others had odd
bumps and lumps. If they were not shiny bald, then at least, hair was
short. Short, short, like crew cuts. A military allusion. Or impossibly
stylish. Short everywhere except for a cowlick that would rise up
from the brow, like the Belgian comic book character Tintin.

I considered this trend seriously. After all, it had been four years since I had seen my hair short, and I was admittedly tired of the long black hairs that would appear everywhere, thick Asian strands in the carpet, in the sink, in the shower, and on bathroom tiles. I wasn't tired of the attention, but I was tired that it came only from women. There was, I must recount, a roughly drawn poster posted outside Toronto's Glad Day Bookstore that advertised a club for long-haired gay men and men who loved them. But to me, it seemed no differ-ent than the specialty classified ads that appeared in the back of the community biweekly requesting boot-licking slaves or water-sport fanatics. To the mainstream gay man, I was definitely out of fashion.

Still, it was not an easy decision. When I told friends of the idea, most lamented what a shame it would be to lose such hair. Perhaps something clicked when I spoke with Ronnie, an actor friend of a friend. People always told me how intelligent he was, but I could never tell. He seemed to express only mild interest in me, and we only made idle chitchat when we met. Besides, I was envious. I was deeply attracted to his physical form, a blond boy next door with a handsome, rugged face, a football player's physique—a body that somehow avoided looking too planned and precise, unlike those of so many others in the community.

"Don't listen to that crap," he tossed, his eyes elsewhere, sneak-ing a look at who his ex-boyfriend was talking to elsewhere in the bar. "Why would you follow some stupid trend? Why would you need to follow the crowd? Gay people can be so superficial." His attention altered to watch a tall brunet cross the floor. "That's not a comment on you—it's just, why would you need to?"

I adjusted my ponytail, my hair drawn back and held by a thin black elastic. It's a game, I thought to myself. Checkers, Parcheesi, Poker. I want to play, and how can I play if people won't even let me into the game? I got up to leave and felt a flash of anger. I swallowed it. Heat bounced uneasily against my interiors. Ronnie could wear whatever he wanted, the most out-of-style clothes, the most garish colors. He could grow his hair into a river of blond lengths. He could keep his chest unshaved if it wasn't already. He would still be

pursued as he probably had been pursued all of his life, men buck-
ling at the knees at first sight. And he would never know he did not
need to play the game because he was it. He was the game.

When I shaved my head, I felt glorious. It was a nice surprise to
learn my parents had gifted me a strong, round skull. I sent my braid
to a Chinese-Canadian artist friend who thought he could work it
into his next piece, a pseudo–museum display on the cultural artifacts
of a composite Chinese-Canadian family. I showered and felt the hot
spray directly on my head. My hair did not need drying; the number
of hairs in the carpet slowly diminished.

Most important, I walked along sunny Church Street and felt the
weather on the very top of my body, and amazingly, like a miracle
predicted but not believed in, heads swiveled, other eyes caught
mine. If one has never swum in the ocean, there is no way to describe
to those with no experience of it how the salt smell rises into your
head to the heights of your senses, how every inch of what surrounds
you feels alive and in motion, how the salt leaves its traces on your
skin as you leave the water. Ever since I had come out of the closet,
I had had long hair, and I had never known what it was like to be
close-shaven. More accurately, I had never known what it was like to
be recognizably gay and to walk on a gay street on a hot summer day.
With all that mess of hair, the narrow-visioned denizens of my gay
world saw only an exotic creature with foreign roots. They could not
see my desire through the forest of hair, could not name me as one
of them. For with my skin already a different color, they needed
another signal to call me their own. Shaving my head, I had learned
to play the game I wanted to play.

How many of you have ever seen your head bald, seen the lines
and veins and patterns of the skull, to see how nature has formed that
skull without the adornment of hair? That summer I saw it, and it
was a revelation. Its round form showed me the shape of the world
in which I was learning to take part.

8.

When I arrived in Europe to start my first real job, in the office of a human rights organization, my hair was fuzzy, thicker than the skin of a peach but not so thick that the white of my scalp was hidden from view. Still, it was starting to jut out from behind my ears, it was losing its clean and even look. I was far too busy packing my bags before I left to give myself a quick shave; now I realized the shape of the plugs was different here than in Canada, and before I did anything, I would have to find something to convert or adapt my razor.

It took me another handful of days to find an electrical shop, and even then the man handed me a small white plug that to me did not look sturdy enough for anything. When I tried it out, my plug still wouldn't fit into it. "Oh, that's easy," said my French coworker, Paul-Marc, as a pocketknife suddenly appeared in his hands and he deftly enlarged the holes.

That night I was to meet an American friend. He had also just arrived to work for a European branch of an American newspaper. We were ready to explore the gay bars of Brussels for the first time since we'd arrived. He would meet me here at the apartment where I was staying that belonged to a friend, Thomas, who was away for the weekend. I finished work early and decided after eating some pâté on bread that I would shave my head, take a bath, and be ready for action.

I stripped off my clothes, plugged in the razor, and knelt in the bathtub, a mirror in one hand, and the razor in the other. I pushed this warm buzzing creature in straight lines back from my forehead; it reminded me of the Greek barbershop of my childhood. I started in the center of my head and moved off to the right, the razor traversing my scalp like a sailor across rounded oceans. I could tell something was wrong, but it all happened so quickly. A small voice told me that the razor was overheating and that I must shut it off, but another voice equally strong said "just a few minutes more." As I envisioned what I'd look like half-shaved, the second voice won. I heard a tiny pop, everything went dark, and a sweet, acrid burning smell arose from my newly spiritless electrical device.

A few seconds passed before my eyes adjusted to the darkness, before I knew that not only had I blown the electrical circuits, but I also knew no one in the city who could help me. I stumbled around the apartment by the glow of the streetlamps outside. I found a candle and lit it. I found "electricians" in the phone book just in case. Then I found the fuse box in the kitchen. Much to my dismay, after fifteen or twenty minutes of every possible combination, nothing changed. I took a bath in the dark and worried and felt sorry for myself.

After much silence and waiting, I finally found the courage to call Thomas at his parents' home in Britain. Luckily, thankfully, he was home. "Oh, you've blown the circuits, have you? Well, look, you have to go down to the night store below the apartment, and ask them to let you into the basement to look at the circuits there."

Of course, it all worked out in the end. I covered my head with a bandanna, my American friend and I had a good night on the town, and the next day I sheepishly removed the cloth from my head at a hair salon and asked the woman if she could finish the job. She was more pleasant than the European boys here, who were shy and hard to approach. I was the only Asian in the bars that night, and to me it felt like I was moving backward in time, to the moments when the first immigrants arrived, to a place whose cultural homogeneity, unlike Canada's, had not truly been broken. We learn our lessons in one place, only to begin anew in the next.

Still, I figured that shaved would be the form in which I would stay in Europe. If I was to arrive in this world with a full head of hair, perhaps I could mystify the powers that be by turning into a bald child now, the round, smooth cranium glowing in the light of new days ahead, a retelling of my birth, my entry onto this harsh, strange planet. If only it wasn't so cold in the wintertime. If only it wasn't so cold.

Get a Lifestyle

Trevor Renado

When the editors of *Instinct* asked me to write a column for their new magazine, I was sure it was some kind of pickup attempt. Like at the gym when some guy comes up to me and asks me to show him my triceps routine because of my "awesome definition"? So I asked them, "Hey, magazine dudes, what makes you think I have anything important to say?"

They told me *everything* I had to say was important to them because I'm a young, successful, VGL guy, the kind of guy who reads magazines like this one and buys cool stuff like liquor and underpants. I thought about this for a long time, during my entire fifty-minute cardio workout at Crunch, and while I was in the sauna I came to two conclusions: (1) Those magazine dudes *are* trying to sleep with me; and (2) I do have important stuff to say.

Here's the 411: I'm twenty-six, six feet, blond/green, smooth, 170 (with twelve percent body fat), live smack-dab in the middle of West Hollywood (or "WeHo," as they say), have a great job, and drive a red Jeep. But it isn't all circuit parties and tanning beds (OK, maybe April is). I've got problems, secrets, hopes, and dreams. And I want to use this column to share them with you.

Which reminds me—I'm supposed to be writing about Valentine's Day, a holiday that's always been pretty special to me since I lost my virginity February 14, 1990, at Arizona State's Tri-Delt Cupid's Ball with the president (Duke) of their brother frat (Deke). Talk about getting pinned... Anyway, last February I thought I was majorly "all that." Some girl in that movie *Tales of the City* (which I guess was OK but seemed really, I dunno, dated) said you can never have a great

apartment, great job, and great boyfriend at the same time, which at
the time I remember thinking was such a lie. I had a wicked studio on
Westbourne Drive, my job managing Dr. Kaplan's office had never
been better, *and* I happened to be dating an incredible guy.

Sean and I met in Palm Springs. One of the discos was having a
Best Buns contest, and my friend Chet kept ragging on me to enter,
and I was like, "I'm so sure, dude!" Then the bitch shakes up her
Corona and sprays my new Raymond Dragon shorts so they're totally see-through and clinging to everything! Then Chet shoves me
toward the stage, where these drunks point me out to the drag
queen emceeing the show, and before I knew it, I was up there winning the contest. Then—and I'm sure this was against some state
law—the drag queen announced that, as Mr. Best Buns, I was that
night's door prize and would now be *spanked* by whoever was holding ticket number 78. I was so about to jump off that stage and beat
Chet up when Mr. #78 stepped forward. He was wearing hiking
boots and a Mighty Ducks cap, his muscle T casually swinging from
the back pocket of his 501 cutoffs, and looked like a cross between
Dermot Mulroney and Dylan McDermott. He said, "Hi, I'm Sean,"
then put me over his knee and paddled my beer-soaked butt.

Well, we continued to get closer, and Valentine's Day was coming
up and Sean told me what he's always wanted was to get flowers at
work. No problem, right? That's what I thought. When I called Casa
Bella Florist to order Sean a dozen roses, I realized I didn't know his
last name! And I couldn't just send them to "Sean" because I knew
for a fact there were two other Seans working with him at the Sparta
Travel Agency.

I looked through a few receipts and things left over from the long
weekend we spent in Cancun but only found this hysterical Polaroid
of Sean with a sombrero hanging off his you-know-what. Then an
idea occurred to me—I'd go to Sean's apartment and look at his
mail. Picking the lock on the mailbox was a little harder than I
thought, but half an hour with a piece of wire hanger did the trick
and also proved that on a doorstep on Flores Street in WeHo in
broad daylight, a twenty-six-year-old blond with twelve percent body

fat wearing Fila bike pants and a neon-green T-back can get away with pretty much anything.

Unfortunately, Sean's mail was no help. All catalogs—Neiman Marcus, Sanctuary, International Male, J. Crew, and Williams-Sonoma—all addressed to "Occupant." I'd barely shoved them all back into the box when Sean surprised me by coming home early. I had to think up an excuse for being there—and fast! Noticing the bulge of his Boy London wallet (I know, I know, *tres passé*), I told Sean I'd come for sex and pushed him into his apartment.

"Leave your jeans on. I want it rough," I said, eyeing the chain connecting said jeans to said wallet, which had to contain *something* with his last name on it, like his Abercrombie & Fitch credit card. I threw my legs up, massaging his buns with one hand and slipping the wallet out with the other. Aha! Sean's driver's license. I strained to get a better look at it over Sean's big, heaving shoulders but was distracted by the license photo. What was that haircut about? Bitch, please! He looked like Richard Simmons' cousin—then the wallet went flying out of my hand as Sean rolled me onto my washboard stomach. I realized I had the blocking all wrong—I should have had *him* bent over the Z Gallerie sofa. Dammit! Sometimes I hate being versatile.

After this (actually after this two more times), I decided to give up. Sean had his heart set on those flowers, so I had no choice but to cruise down to his office building, check out the list of names under "Sparta Travel," and guess. The Sean I picked was Sean Ellis (mostly because Perry Ellis is such a brilliant designer—I can never wait to see what he'll come up with next!). Well, on Valentine's Day I get a very pissy call from Sean Rodriguez. My boyfriend. Rodriguez?!? How was I supposed to know he was half Hispanic? He was circumcised, for God's sake. Anyway, Sean was furious I had spaced on his name and said he was breaking up with me, even resorting to abusive language like "airhead!"

I was fully prepared to spend a sad Valentine's night at the gym, alone, when my cell rang. I picked up on the first ring, so sure it was Sean calling to apologize and invite me to dinner at Café La

Boheme. And it *was* Sean. Sean Ellis! See, he'd loved the roses and asked me if I wanted to meet for coffee and, get this, turned out to be four times hotter than the first Sean.

Marianne Williamson is so right—give out caring energy and the universe completely rewards you. And if you give out energy like Sean Rodriguez, the universe punishes you with a citation for public lewdness behind Circus of Books three weeks after dumping me. Kinda makes you think!

☐   ☐   ☐

Everyone always assumes I'm an actor, and when I tell them no way, they look shocked and say, "But Trevor! You're so good-looking! And this is L.A. Why not?" First of all, I think stereotyping very attractive people as actors and models is really offensive, not to mention racist. I mean, would you just walk up to an obese person and ask which trailer park they live in? I'm not an actor because the three things I hate most are reading, memorizing, and waking up before 10.

My workout partner Reg spent like $100,000 getting an acting degree from NYU and is now a professional extra. Reg prefers the term "atmosphere work." Bitch, please! What is he, a meteorologist? He was in *As Good as it Gets* for like one second walking down a street, and his résumé says "Opposite Helen Hunt and Greg Kinnear." Mostly he works on TV shows like *NYPD Blue,* where he "costarred" as a corpse. As someone who's really grounded and not into all the Hollywood delusionalism, I find Reg pretty unbearable, but good gym buddies are hard to come by, so when he called me on my day off to ask if I'd fill in for him as "atmosphere" on this sitcom, I said sure.

I'd never seen this particular sitcom, but the star of the show, this middle-aged blond woman, was familiar to me from the tabloids. So I knew it was her when she came up to me and said in this weird, Elvis-y voice, "Extras ain't allowed at craft services."

I tried to think of some way out of it, but I was right in the middle of biting into this strawberry on a toothpick, so I gave her this really cute look I give my boss, Dr. Kaplan, whenever I screw up a patient's billing or forget to lock up the office or something. And it worked. This woman (*Instinct* told me not to mention any names) gave me a wink and said, "Don't worry, darlin'. I won't tell anybody. You must be new around here. My name's _____." She was being really nice and down-to-earth and told me how much she hated this week's script and all of her lines in it and that she couldn't believe someone as buff and handsome as me wasn't an actor and how much she hated all the writers and producers on the show and that she'd like me to come back to her dressing room and rehearse.

Can you believe I actually fell for this? Well, a minute later, we're in her dressing room.

"Wanna drink, hot pants?" she drawled. I shook my head politely, a little surprised after having read about her recurrent personal problems in the checkout line at Pavilions supermarket. I was relieved when she opened a can of Diet RC, but instead of drinking it, she poured it down the sink and began to refill the can with Bacardi, mumbling the whole time about how the writers were ruining her show. She reached right between my thighs into the couch cushion-crack and yanked out a Pez dispenser, popping several before tossing it aside. I tilted back Porky Pig's head and was stunned to discover the "Pez" were Percodans!

"So, um, excuse me, but since I don't have any lines, how are we going to rehearse?" I asked.

She sighed, picked up the phone, and told someone, "Bring a change of clothes in for Trent here."

"Trevor," I corrected her as she hung up. "And what's wrong with my clothes? They told me jeans and a tank top."

"Look, Trad. Just start shuckin' down so we can git this show on the road."

Who was I to argue with a Golden Globe nominee? I went over to the other side of the room and stripped. "Do you have a robe or something I could wear?" I asked.

She shook her head, a sleazy, stoned look in her eye. She pointed to my Calvins. "Them panties too." She reached out a drunken paw and started fondling my pumped pec! Then it hit me—this whole thing was a setup! I felt like Elizabeth Berkley at the boat expo in *Showgirls*.

"No way, lady!" I yelled.

"Come on, Teddy. I need to relax a little, baby. Five hundred bucks for a half hour." She moved toward the sofa.

"I eat with these hands!" I snapped, running out of the dressing room in my boxer briefs and smack-dab into the executive producer. He asked what was happening, and I said, "Three words. Sexual harassment."

"Oh, Jesus, _____, not again! What's wrong with you?" he groaned.

She lurched to the door with one breast hanging out. "If you'd fucked your wife as much as you've fucked with me this week, you'd still be married!" she roared like Dwight Yoakam in *Sling Blade*, then threw the soda can right at his head.

Well, they ended up shutting down production on the series and ordering her into rehab (again) so I never got to tape the scene or get my clothes back. But the production company felt so bad about it they offered me a guest lead on *Third Rock from the Sun* the next week. Reg was so jealous he threw a Tab at me.

Oh, well…that's showbiz.

☐   ☐   ☐

I knew I was reviewing a sexy flick for this erotica issue and was hoping for something classy like *Kiss Me Guido* or *White Squall*, but sure enough, what do I get but *Powertool: The Tenth Anniversary Edition*. The first thought that hit me—besides the fact that the tape was not sealed or shrink-wrapped, meaning the party pigs at *Instinct* had probably already had their way with it—was "How ironical" (you'll see why in a minute), and the second was how could it be the tenth anniversary when this is 1998 and *Powertool* came out in 1986?

You know, I've never really understood the point of porn. I mean, if you're hungry, you don't look at pictures of food, you eat something. So if you're horny, forget videos—go have sex. And if you're too shy or old or fat, you can always pay for it. In certain cities you can even hire the exact same guys from those videos.

But as far as actually dating porn actors goes, I don't recommend it. My relationship with Jeff Stryker (star of *Powertool*, in case you live in Utah or something) was a disaster. We went out for six months in 1995, and at first it was really great. We loved each other and had some really cool times. We did a lot of Rollerblading, and Jeff would make these incredible Chinese dinners from scratch, then spend the evening playing his guitar and singing U2 songs. Then I realized a certain male part of him was freakishly huge and always demanding attention—yup, his ego.

Jeff wasn't content to just be a famous porno star with his own production company and a best-selling dildo that's an exact replica of his cock. He wanted it all—a record deal, cosmetics line, even an action figure! Eventually our sex life became just market research for him. He would blindfold me to see if I could tell the difference between his dildo and the real thing (to be honest, I really couldn't). Also, Jeff was totally hung up on his macho image. All that nasty talk from the videos isn't just an act. You should hear him at the breakfast table: "Yeah, butter that toast! Pour that fuckin' cereal! You know you want it!"

But the last straw was when Jeff tried to recruit *me* into the jizz biz. He was about to get his first-ever on-screen enema in *The River Stryker,* this big blockbuster porno he was prepping, and he wanted me to be in it too. He'd even made up a stage name for me: Rock Bottom. Now I admit with my stunning all-American looks, buff build, and twelve percent body fat, I'd make a rad porn star. And I'm sure my boss, Dr. Kaplan, and his patients would be, like, delirious over it, so my day job would be safe. But wait…hello…*gross!*

Anyway, the point is, I still consider Jeff a friend, so I'm fully unprejudiced enough to review this *Powertool* "special edition," which is a total rip-off unless your idea of special is a bunch of filler from the Catalina preview vault (Beaver Alert: There are some horrifying seconds of straight intercourse), two extra segments of Jeff whacking off, and a few bloopers, including Jeff playing Señor

Wences with his urethra (don't ask).

Basically it's the same exact movie you remember beating off to when Honda scooters were hot. Jeff is sentenced to thirty days in jail for attempted murder or failing a smog check or something. After removing what look like Jordaches, Jeff bends over and spreads his legs for the cute but queeny Latino-type guard, sneering, "You like lookin' at that asshole, doncha?"—the answer, which sort of sums up why Jeff has a career, being "Well, duh!"

Jeff puts on a work shirt and Levi's and is led to his cell and strips again, only somehow on the walk down the hall white Jockeys have magically appeared between him and his jeans. Across the hall, Johnny Davenport for some reason gets really turned on by a letter from his girlfriend dumping him and jumps off his bunk and orders cellmate Michael Gere to service him.

This was Johnny's first video, and he must have been pretty nervous, since it's obviously Jeff drilling Michael in all the close-ups. Believe me, I'd know. And this had to have tuckered Jeff out, because when he screws the queeny guard later, someone else fills in for a lot of Jeff's close-ups.

The guard obviously doesn't mind being stunt-dicked, because next thing you know, Jeff's gotten an early release and goes back home where his hunky Puerto Rican–type boyfriend is fooling around with street trash (Brian Estevez). Jeff is devastated, packs his bags, and leaves, which seems slightly hypocritical considering we just watched Jeff screw not only the queeny guard but another jailhouse stud for two cartons of cigarettes.

But, as my friend Chet put it after Jeff and I broke up and Jeff refused to return my Real McCoy CD, when you inspire the world's best-selling dildo, you set your own rules.

□   □   □

Fags are such liars. Think about it: "I'll call you tomorrow." "I'm strictly a top." "Nicole and I are happily married." I, however, am one hundred percent honest and therefore a better person. For instance, if you're flirting with me in the grocery store and there's no way in hell I would ever, ever consider going out with your ugly ass, I'll come right out and tell you. Because lying hurts everyone. But, unlike many members of Crunch Gym think, I'm not perfect. I confess—I recently bent the truth a little. But if you had a chance to see Mitchell Anderson naked, I'm sure you'd lie too. But I'm getting ahead of myself...

My friend Chet has since told me that Mitchell Anderson starred in that play *Love! Valour! Party!* so thousands of people *have* seen him naked, but I only knew him as the hunky music teacher from that excellent TV show I don't watch. Mitchell came into Dr. Kaplan's, where I'm the receptionist/office manager, on a Friday afternoon. The doctor had decided to leave early for Palm Springs, and I'd rescheduled everyone. Except I must have gotten busy or sidetracked by the Celine Dion Web site or something because I forgot "M. Anderson—2:00." Of course I had no way of knowing M. stood for Mitchell, whose regular doctor was in Rio.

So I get back from moisturizing after lunch, and standing there in reception is Mitchell Anderson. "Hi, I'm Mitchell Anderson," he said, flashing me a smile that would melt Olestra. "You're pretty young to be an MD."

"Oh, I'm just—" I started to say, then all of a sudden, it hit me. *He thought I was Dr. Kaplan.* "...that smart," I quickly finished the sentence. "So, yes, I'm Stan Kaplan. That's me."

"I've been having a little trouble sleeping," Mitchell said. Hello, why not just look at your gorgeous self in the mirror and beat off? I very professionally had him step into the examining room then very smartly locked the front door.

"I'll just check you over," I told him and started looking for the stethoscope. When I turned around he was stripping! He sat down completely naked except for a pair of sweat socks. I was thinking doctors totally have it made, then remembered Dom DeLuise had been up on this very table last Tuesday. I pretended to take Mitchell's pulse, then checked his heartbeat. I couldn't help noticing how his nipple hardened right up when I placed the cold stethoscope on his smooth, pumped pec. I tried to keep my hand from shaking as I reached down to do the hernia test.

"When I push up, cough," I told him, totally freaked out to have actual TV star testicles in my hands but loving it!

"How can I cough when I'm groaning with pleasure," Mitchell joked, then he asked me out to dinner! Wanting to appear doctorly, I ignored the semi unfurling against his taut thigh and "prescribed" him Valium from Dr. Kaplan's secret stash for his insomnia. I told him I'd meet him at Marix Tex-Mex at 8.

(You may be wondering how I was planning to get away with it. The truth is, I was going to tell him at his place later, hoping my body [eleven percent fat] and what I could do with it [lots] would convince him to forgive me.)

That night we had just dipped into our first pitcher of Kick-Ass margaritas. Mitchell was spinning a guacamole-covered chip playfully toward my mouth when all of a sudden we heard some queen shriek, "Oh, my God! Emergency! Is there a doctor in the house?"

Mitchell immediately jumped up. "Over here! Stan is a doctor!" The host came running up and dragged us to the back of the restaurant while everyone stared.

I was shoved into the men's room and told by the host that Timmy, a waiter on break, had somehow inserted an entire tequila bottle up his ass. He couldn't get it out and everyone was terrified it might explode. "You must have handled lots of cases like this, Stan," Mitchell said, patting me.

"Uh, sure," I said. "Timmy, get your legs in the air and try to relax." Mitchell gave me a latex glove from his pocket. I had no choice. I had to go in. I'll spare you the details, let's just say twenty tense minutes later Timmy had pretty much given complete birth to Señor Sauza. I was about to give it a final yank when the bathroom door banged open and I heard my friend Danilo scream, "Girl, what the hell are you doing?!?"

"Do you mind? Stan here is a doctor and this is a medical emergency," Mitchell snapped as I freed the bottle.

"Her name is Trevor, and she is a doctor's receptionist. Omigod, you're Mitchell Anderson!"

"Hold on! You're not a doctor? You could have fucking killed me!" Timmy whined.

"If you want, I'll put it right back!" I snarled.

Mitchell gave me a hurt look, paid the check, and walked out of my life forever.

I haven't been able to drink tequila since, and that's no lie.

Fruit

Keith Ridgway

Five red apples. An afternoon's work for a normal mouth. Not I.

It wasn't always the case, apparently. Though my recollections, as far as this is concerned, are vague at best. I suspect that's because they're actually nonexistent. I've just been told that I used to eat the stuff as a child. I don't actually recall. Not definitely. Pictures present themselves to me of a plum-stained toddler perched in a happy high chair calling for more, apple butts abounding, a sticky mess of oranges webbed to his face. But if it's me, then it's imagined. Because it is not remembered. I have blocked it all out.

If I used to, then I stopped. I don't remember if I used to, but if I stopped, I remember why.

I don't know what age I was. About five, perhaps. Maybe a little younger. Not older. I remember the brown shed in the playground of the girls' school where I attended kindergarten. Not kindergarten. Older than that. Babies. That's what they called it. Babies. I was in Babies. I was a baby boy, in my first world past my mother. The brown shed and some kind of climbing frame and the railings and the road beyond. Sister Gerard with her great big gown and her paper face. The noise of kids. Running. Tripping. Washing my hands. Being caught in a lie. Spitting. Fruit.

There was a boy called Stephen, and I did not like him because he was big and grinding and his name made me think of poo. It was a brown name. He hung around the brown shed. He might have been in my class, I can't remember. I only remember him in the playground, a vicious little thug with snotty boys for friends and a girl with dirty knees always in the background. They ranged across the place, invisible to their elders, meting out a Barbary justice (he was big on pirates from what I recall), through slapping, pushing, tripping, and rubbing. This latter was done with some unpleasant substance, usually extracted from the nose, or by farting on the hand, which would then be clamped over the victim's face. Stephen always caught you. His coterie weren't as quick, as forceful. They could be shouldered away most of the time. One of them got me, in the beginning, in my first days. I had no idea what he was doing, arriving behind me and putting his hand across my mouth. I think I thought I had to guess who he was. I shrugged him off, baffled at the laughter that rippled through our age group.

"He farted on his hand," someone said. I made a face and felt sick. I hadn't smelled anything, though. Hadn't tasted anything. I comfort myself with the thought that it's not always possible to summon up a fart, even if you are under five and entirely devoted to that kind of thing. I suppose it's what made me think of poo whenever I thought of Stephen. Even as an adult I've had problems with people called Stephen, or Steven, or Steve. It is the sound of shitting. I can't help it. It is.

I learned about the gang and their mission—their playground voyages, roaming the seas, the lunchbox and skipping rope and chalk game and card swapping and lie telling seas, from one island of small heads to another. Planting time-delay nightmares wherever Stephen fancied that it might be fun. I was lucky he had sent a lieutenant after me, a minor creep. Stephen's buttocks bellowed each time of asking, with horrifying force, and he put his hand inside his shorts. And he was expert at avoiding the teacher's eye, genius of the innocent look, master of the sideways step that put some poor fool between him and his victim when the screaming started. In winter, during the time of Stephen's cold, as many as a dozen children might return to class with curious green traces mingling with the tears on their cheeks. It took a full year to end it. It took several false accusations, whisperings amongst the parents, the intimidation of stuttering witnesses, an increasing paranoia within the Barbary gang, leading to disillusionment in the ranks and a split in the organization, the turning of one on the other, a betrayal (the dirty-kneed girl, of course), a pointed finger, before finally the culprit was identified with certainty. And the tragic history of the five-year-olds' (or whatever we were) parallel playground universe found a calm space, a kind of childhood. Stephen disappeared. I believe psychiatry may have been involved. Five-year-olds (or whatever we were) have a limited capacity for understanding therapy. I think we were told that he had gone to a school for boys like him. Saint Shitty Hands School For Snotty Children. But all that was after my particular trauma. Long after. Too long after.

Following the first fart clamp, I escaped any interference as the Barbaries took stock of me. I was new to the school, and I was stupid. Perhaps this conveyed a confidence, a swagger even. I walked around with a dumb grin on my face. I'd talk to anyone—the outcasts, the popular girls, the boy with the port wine stain, the boy from France, the unpopular girls, the boy who knew everything, the poor brothers with the tight shoes and the cropped hair and the shared sandwich. I'd even talk to bullies. I believe I may have disarmed Stephen. I walked right up to him and said, "Hello." He stuck his head out and glared.

"What?"

"Hello."

"Who are you?"

Oh, it's useless. I can't remember what we said. I can't even imagine what language we might have used. Some kiddie cant unknown to grown-ups, long forgotten now. We talked. He sneered and looked me up and down and just as he was (I think, maybe, I don't know) about to ask me to join his gang, I turned and walked away, spun on my heel and trooped off, my little mind a blank, to discuss giraffes with the girls. He might have pounced then but didn't for some reason. It's probably wrong to ascribe human—sorry, I mean adult—adult emotion and reasoning to a five-year-old (the figure is approximate), but I think he was amused. You know, in that kind of arrogant, patronizing way we adults are amused by fools, subordinates, puppies, children. He thought I was a laugh. And maybe he was just a little bit impressed by the fact that though I'd talk to absolutely anyone, and did, eventually, I never, never, never ever talked to the boy who'd slapped his gas on my gob.

So I was regarded from a distance, and I was aware that I was watched, and for a long time it didn't scare me. I don't think I realized what Stephen was. I didn't quite see it. Even when I saw other children reduced to wetness—the mess on their face, tears, snot (theirs and others'), spittle (theirs and others'), bum sweat, and inevitably for a percentage, leg lengths of pee, sockfuls of pee, darkened shorts of pee—even then I didn't quite connect these horrors to any bubbling fears of my own. I was not struck by the random nature of the attacks. I didn't notice it was the boy next to me who ended up choking because he thought it might poison him to breathe Stephen's gritty handful, or that it was the little girl at my side who went palely back to class with her hair full of body fluids, foreign matter, and the detritus of flatulent five-(me judice)-year-olds. The potential for my own pollution did not dawn on me. I think that may have been why I was spared. The lack of fear might have made me seem unassailable, as if there was no point to such an attack because it would not have bothered me. Not true of course. I was just stupid. Innocent. Five (need I remind you). Any attempt to smear me with the effusion of other's orifices might have killed me. Can five-year-old (qu.) hearts fail? Considering what actually did happen, and the apparent (it now seems increasingly obvious—it's all becoming clearer as I go on), cause-and-effect result, one of the Barbary's usual sorties would probably have had me in therapy to this day.

But it didn't happen. I stood impassively by, with a lack of empathy for the assaulted that greatly impresses my adult self. We're born selfish and have it beaten out of us. I could do with it now. Anyway. A little girl accused me of heartlessness. I doubt she used the word. Perhaps she caught me in a half smile as she picked herself up off the ground. I remember her tone—tearful and shrill. She included me in her list of horrible things about life, after the Barbaries but before her older brother and peas. And she suggested (this is most important) in a vague and vaguely threatening way that I might be next. That I was not invulnerable. That they would come for me too, when they saw fit. And that when it happened, I was not to look to her for assistance. And it would be, it would, it would, it would be my own fault. Because I was horrid. Because I did nothing. Because I was neutral. Because I stood by.

I don't know why, but it felled me. It robbed me of something. Distance maybe, the notion that I was watching television, the idea that I was outside events, the hope that I would exist in the world only as an observer. Can all that have passed through the mind of a five-(you know)-year-old? In some undigested, elemental form I'm sure it can. Sure it did. Here was I. Living. I was alive. I could touch, not touch, talk, not talk, hurt, not hurt. Here, oh, God, were choices. If it had been in my vocabulary, I'm sure I would have whispered, spittled and lisped it, made it sound cute and funny. The awful adult word. Responsibility. Here it was. She pulled up her socks, that anonymous little girl, and scampered indignantly off, having changed my tiny life.

I'm not sure what paralyzed me initially. Sudden fear of Stephen or sudden fear of the shocking place I found myself. A world that expects. Ugh. But I froze for a while and grappled with my baby demons. I looked at the Barbaries in a new way. Critically. Weighing up their actions. I employed my baby judgment. They were bad. They were bold. They were bad bold boys, and what they did wasn't fair. And Stephen was the baddest boldest of them all. He was disgusting and naughty, and did things and said things that were so bold, I couldn't understand how I'd missed it. How I'd reneged for so long on my responsibilities, my duty as a, as an important and respected figure in Junior Babies. (Junior Babies? I think I'm making that up. We were probably called Pumas or Alligators or Sparrows. Giraffes, perhaps. Jellyfish.)

While I was engaged in my first and, to this day, most coherent bit of moral philosophizing, Stephen and his Barbary Apes were indulging in a much more basic and, for all I know, more honest bit of soul searching. They were wondering why they hadn't given me a proper going over since I got there. What turned their minds to this discrepancy I do not know. I imagine, though, that it was me. I attracted their attention. With my guilty slinking. My apparent loss of indifference. They sniffed my fear. Eyes were on me again, and this time malign, decisive eyes. They didn't like me. But before they could act (delayed perhaps by the extra significance an attack on me would have had after all that time of tolerance), before they could make a move, another scent came to them. They sniffed a threat. For I was beginning to fill with umbrage to balance my terror. A determination, a youthful, pre-youthful even, idealism seeped into my pint and a half of watery blood. Within days I had become a little time bomb of righteousness, increasingly flustered, on the verge of exploding in a pathetic puff of playground rage. I was getting close to being a voice for my people.

Then it happened. Forces collided. A conflagration. A moment only.

He approached me. Or I him. I do not recall. But before I knew what was happening I was standing near the climbing frame, the school at my back, telling Stephen the Barbary pirate, old Brown Hand himself, his apes by his side, the dirty-kneed girl gaping, I told him, loudly, that his name was like poo. That it sounded like it, looked like it, was the same as it. That he was a pooey boy. A toilet boy. A disgrace to his gender and his generation. An embarrassment to five-()-year-olds the world over. Oh, I was marvelous for a moment. So dignified, so eloquent, so small. I was conscious of a blur in the world, as if the fast-moving globe had come to a sudden, skidding stop. I sensed all eyes on me, all ears agape at my courage, my nobility, my resonant voice, my utter stupidity. He didn't react. Or at least I do not remember anything specific. He just looked at me. Looked and listened. I reached some kind of conclusion—I don't recall what, perhaps a reference to the children whom Jesus loved, or the purity of angels and the possibility of a vengeful God. Something to get his fetal conscience going.

Then I turned into the crowd, and the crowd, you'd imagine, would have welcomed me with open arms. No no no. Of course not. You imagined no such thing. We're adults, after all. We know now how these things work. The crowd parted. They created a space around me the width of which was considered prudent for safety, for security reasons. So as not to be in the way when I was torn limb from doll-like limb by the now-seething, psychopathic Barbary boys. My people offered me up. They stood back and called for me to be taken, consumed, by their own wrathful deity. Scared, they held up my now-trembling shape as a sacrifice. Stephen sniffed. He looked at the sky, put a finger to his lips. And as his men made a move toward me, he held up his hand. Stopped them. Stared at me. Smiled. Oh, God. He smiled. Called his soldiers to him, gathered them around him in a writhing pedestal, lowered his head to theirs, and whispered. God help us. Whispered. Within moments there uttered from the beast, from the band of arm-in-arm assassins, a chuckle, then another, and another. They uncoiled, relaxed, slapped their thighs, each other's backs, clutched at their pirate bellies, and guffawed a riotous, hearty laughter, pointing and nodding at me as if I was a circus clown in a circus car in the funniest circus in the whole wide world.

Terror. Dread. Think of it. At that age (circa, you might say), you have no experience, no knowledge, no sense of torture, of cruelty and revenge, of the things that might be done to you by a maddened monster. The only light you have to guide you is that multicolored, obscene fireworks display of your imagination. Even now I can only dimly recollect the extent of my fear, dulled as I am by years of being big and pragmatic and quiet in the world. I think of the contents of my little head then, and I quiver. My five-year-old life was to be dispensed with. I was to be murdered, I was certain of it. Shot after school, several times, several hundred times, and my bleeding body driven in a car boot through a foreign city, dismembered in a farmer's yard, dissolved in acid, and buried (alive of course—still horribly alive) in a hole full of rats, where I would writhe for all eternity. That was about the size of it. I think I cried. Rocked in my chair back in class, my mind filled with nostalgia for those happy, carefree, preschool years. Oh, how young I'd been, how innocent, how free. Now here I was, committed to martyrdom on behalf of an ungrateful rabble of finger painters and crayon tasters.

The time of my trauma crept up on me. It arrived before I noticed it. It began, my torment, quietly, softly, while I still waited for the violent clang of its assault. For Stephen, evil genius of that small world, had devised a revenge so devious, so insidious in execution, so perverse in conception, that it staggers me now. It astounds me. Could he have known? Did he guess that it would mold my life? Or was it an accident, a use of materials found close to hand? Perhaps he had had some other plan, never put into effect because of the startling results of that demonic stopgap measure.

Fruit.

After class we got our coats and put them on, ready to go out into the world and make the short trip to our waiting mothers. All afternoon I had fretted and feared, and by the time of leaving I was in a state resembling shell shock. Paranoid dementia. A kind of Pretraumatic Stress Disorder. I could barely walk. So when I put on my anorak, and put my little hand into the pocket, and felt a soft, giving wet mess, I think something snapped in my head. You can guess what I thought. What I assumed. I could not remove my petrified paw. Here it was. The ultimate handful from Stephen. I screamed, burst into tears, and threw up simultaneously. Sister Gerard came to my aid, sat me down, peered into my glassy eyes, and forcibly removed my clawed hand from the anorak pocket. It was covered in a gooey pale substance, a long way from brown. She sniffed. Mashed banana.

Sister Gerard, dear, innocent Sister Gerard, told me I must have put a half-eaten Fyffe in there and forgotten about it. Sure enough, she extracted some skin, little oval sticker still attached. I nodded. She cleaned me up. Said I was a silly boy. I think I believed her. Certainly I did not argue. Yes, my own fault. My own banana. Not the end of the world. But I was clammy and cold and shivered. My mother and Sister Gerard exchanged words, and I was taken home and put to bed. I slept with my hand in the air.

And there it began. The next day, passed fit by Mummy, I returned. There was chewed and spat out apple on my chair. I cleaned it up. Said nothing. In my lunch box later there was more masticated mulch, of what exact origin I wasn't sure. My sandwiches were ruined. My own orange (God—it must be true, I must have eaten it) went straight into the bin without a second thought. I was not hungry. I cowered in the playground, close to the wall. There were glances, but no one approached. An apple butt hit me on the head. We wore smocks for painting in the afternoon. In the generous pockets of mine there was a generous amount of banana, some orange segments, and what seemed like peach, squeezed to pulp, all of it swimming in juice and spit. People began to giggle. I kept on making trips to the bathroom.

It continued, covertly, quietly, for about three days. And I became aware that the eating habits of my entire class had changed. Fruit was de rigueur. They all joined in. All of them. Bits and pieces of fleshy produce found their way not just into the pockets of my anorak, unguarded most of the day, but also into the pockets of my shorts, onto whatever seat I headed for, whatever table I sat at. The floor seemed strewn. In the playground I was shunned, and a pile of ripened ovaries built up at my feet. Strawberries appeared, for God's sake, in my drink bottle. Cherries in my shoes. Plums, squashed purple plums in my schoolbag. Sister Gerard made a little speech about keeping the classroom tidier. I had grown pale, weak, thin. My mother talked ominously of the doctor. And gave me (I remember this—I do!) an apple as well as an orange.

Through all of it Stephen stayed in the background. Gleefully, I'd imagine. He watched my people poison me. Watched them delight in my obvious distress. Allowed the whole thing to distract them for a while from their own subservience. While I was the chief target it let them off the hook. A scapegoat had been found. A perpetual whipping boy. A receptacle for the peel and the stones and the hard-to-swallow stringy pieces of the fruits of their lives. My humiliation was almost complete. Almost. All it needed now, to crown it, to bring it full circle, was the personal touch. The hand of the creator. A little awesome intervention. I knew it would happen. My cup of misery was not yet full.

It was lunchtime, the playground, near the climbing frame—where else? I was lured there by a girl who was not one of Stephen's

gang. She said she wanted to show me something. She said she wanted to show me something. I could smell a rat, but that's about all I
could do. With resignation, in deep despair, I walked to my doom.
The girl disappeared, perhaps up onto a rung of the climber, where
a whole dark mass of children hung like bats, watching, waiting.
They were of all ages, younger, older. I imagined there were some
nuns as well. It's unlikely, I think. A silence expanded. A fluttering of
leathery wings. A shadow by the railings. A sweetish, tangy scent. I
stood and waited. Not for long.

He attacked from behind, of course, and his hop onto my shoulders was accompanied by a gusting roar from the crowd. Two hard
hands stabbed bananas into my cheeks, and then proceeded to massage my face with the stuff. I surprised him a little by dropping to my
knees, causing him to tumble over my head and land with his back
to me. The momentary advantage I had gained was lost as I wiped
at my soiled skin, already gagging, and the renewed roar told me that
the second assault was imminent. I was knocked backward by the
smack of an apple into my chest.

As I reclined, my legs folded painfully beneath me, Stephen loomed
with a half orange in each hand. He squeezed. Then he jammed one
of them into my hair and twisted it, as if I was a juicer, and left me
looking like a little Jewish boy with psychedelic yarmulke. Next (who
handed him his ammunition?) was another banana, smeared across my
mouth as I struggled to free my legs, and apple bits, stuffed into the
collar of my shirt. He pushed me over so that I lay and he knelt. With
the hands of a butcher he stuffed me. He pried open my mouth and
pushed it full of apple and plum mulch. He spat peaches on my shirt,
into my shirt, bits of wet peach against my skin. He tugged at my
shorts and loosened them, and forced handfuls of pulverized mango,
avocado, apricot (who can say?) into my underpants. Pounds of
crushed banana seemed to fill my clothes. A shoe was pried off, and
pushed on again, and I could feel a cold liveliness there, like the sand
under water. I became aware that Stephen had been joined by others
and that a kind of frenzy was developing. I began to choke. My ears
were stuffed with bloody cherries. My nostrils jammed with desiccated

pears. My shorts were pulled to my knees, and my spindly thighs were painted with the harvest of exotic lands—all the sickly colors blending into a bland and base confusion. From a height, children spat and hawked at me and dropped bombs of grape and peel. I lay fighting for breath, my eyes stinging, my stomach heaving, my skin crawling. In my mind I was a tiny seed, a new fruit, and I was being eaten by insects in the cold air. Ripped and torn. Sundered. I was peeled and swallowed. I passed through the bowels of cherubs and emerged steaming, soiled, awful.

I think I died. I lost consciousness. I may have stopped breathing. The next thing I knew I was sitting upright having my back pounded by a girl from the senior school, vomiting debris from my throat and mouth, gasping, ruined. The nuns were galloping toward us. Stephen was nowhere to be seen. The others returned to skipping and running and beaming. I was carried from my Calvary. My poor body was gently bathed by the heavenly sisters, and wrapped in warm towels, and driven home by the priest to my very own bed, my very own bed, my haven, my home.

I slept for a long time.

I don't know what age I was.

I'm sure there must have been some kind of investigation. But they told me nothing, or if they did, I have no memory of it. It was another few months, I think, before Stephen was removed, and in that time no one came near me. I was a broken child anyway. A shell. Brittle and sad. Childishly cracked. I was tearful. I slept in my bed as if I was hiding. I clung to my parents and refused to talk. I could not, would not, consider eating fruit of any description. Over time, I forgot about it, or pushed it into the background. I have never focused on it until now. Not really. But the aversion to fruit has persevered. Through the rest of my childhood and right through my adolescence, there were horrid little battles with my parents about it.

"Try a banana."

"NO!"

"An apple. You used to love them."

"No no no no no."

At times there was a scene. I would not be allowed to leave the table until I'd taken half a mouthful of some disgusting slimy substance, which inevitably ended up (if I got there in time) in the toilet, frequently accompanied by the rest of my meal. My parents understood, a little, I suppose, and the forceful approach was eventually dropped. My mother, bless her, sought to make up for the deficiency by encouraging an increased vegetable intake. Not that she had much luck with that either, the two food groups being linked in my deeply suspicious mind as somehow the same thing. That conviction has faded over the years, and I'm now quite good with veg. But fruit? Never. It's not the taste so much (I'll happily guzzle fruit-flavored drinks, chew fruity sweets, slurp exciting ice creams), but the texture. To feel it, any of it, in my mouth, is to return again to the playground and the shadow of Stephen and sense that it is all somehow connected with defecation and torture and death. My revulsion is so strong, on occasion so overpowering, that I wonder at those unfortunate people who, as children, endured abuses exponentially more horrific than the paltry ones I suffered. How do they keep going?

I had a happy childhood. I wanted for nothing. Not food, shelter, love. The trauma soon receded, to the point where I now doubt very much whether anyone else in my family remembers it. The only scar that remained, and remains still, is this peculiar dietary quirk. As personality disorders go, I'm quite happy with it. I get to have a whole bowl full of vitamin supplements every morning.

This fruit-a-phobia does have one ironic twist—the fact that I grew up to be one. A fruit, I mean. How's that for symmetry? Those of you who see a connection are commendable for the boldness of your psychological theorizing, but you're quite deranged. Unless...

Today my boyfriend took a train to Galway. He's gone to visit a friend. They'll swim in the sea, and he'll ring me tonight and tell me about it. About the cold of the Atlantic and the way the waves work and what he sees when he's underwater. He left after breakfast. Left me with all this on my mind.

He eats fruit. Loves it. The lot. Is sensitive to my aversion and is pretty good by now at not leaving peel around the place, or pips, or general fruity garbage of any kind. I think he buys stuff that doesn't smell, or smells less anyway. Thoughtful. But this morning, having seen him out the door, having run through the usual checklist, having kissed and waved and stood lovingly watching him recede, I returned to the kitchen and the definite odor of apples. A woody, thick scent that caught in my throat. The fool had bought five, for his train trip, and left them in a bag on the counter. Five no less, greedy man. I held my nose and picked them up and ran after him. But he was long gone, of course. I'd watched him go.

They haunted me, those apples, all morning. I showered and shaved and doused myself in smelly bathroom things. I opened all the windows. But still the apples, like a cloud that followed me. I thought about throwing them out, but I couldn't; I don't know why. Because he'd left them, forgotten them. They reminded me of him. They were him.

I put on my coat and put the apples into a second bag, and a third, then put them into my shoulder bag, and took them to my parents' house. It's just a bus trip away. They've never met my boyfriend. They don't want to know about that kind of thing.

I put my shoulder bag down in the hall and forgot about it, and sat and drank coffee and chatted with my mother and my father, and we listened to the lunchtime news and had a halfhearted argument about politics and drank some more coffee. On the way back from the bathroom I spotted my shoulder bag, remembered, retrieved the apples and went back into the kitchen. My parents washed dishes together, their backs to me, talking softly to each other, looking out of the window. I stood by the kitchen table and slowly, quietly, took the apples one by one out of their bags, and placed them gently into the fruit bowl on the table, on top of a couple of bananas and an orange. I was not furtive. I was open and deliberate, and if they'd turned around I'd have told them. I'd have told them that my boyfriend had left them in our home and I didn't like the smell and so I had brought them here, and here they were, a gift—enjoy. But my parents didn't turn around, and I said nothing. What could I say? Here are five red apples. They are here because...

It would be too long a story. A kid in a playground. His voice. Fruit. Silence. Boyfriend. Silence. Those things. Put together somehow. I don't know what way they go together, but they do. And there's a story in it. A long story. Too long a story.

He rang about an hour ago. The water in Galway is cold on the skin and salty on the lips and balmy on the soul. That's his news. I didn't mention the apples. I think I forgot, in all the talk of swimming. He's off out to eat in the city, to take food somewhere and then wander through the little streets. I'll eat by myself, some pasta maybe, something simple. Then I'll watch some television, read a bit, go to bed.

And in my parents' house now, there's five red apples—subversive little things, making me strangely happy.

The Last Innocence of Simeon

Frank Ronan

Exterior, garden, day. What more could you ask for? Well, granted there was sunshine through the high trees on the boundary and the hollowness of birdsong from within the hedges, and the lane away from the garden had never seemed longer or greener, or more as though it led somewhere and not just to the road to the town. And Mrs. Doyle, thinking herself alone, sat near some bearded irises she was tiring of and wept for a while.

No, she thought. Mourning, not weeping.

She laughed at herself then, for reaching the age that she had without losing an adolescent capacity for self-dramatization; and she told herself not to be such an old woman, and felt beside her for her secateurs and string, thinking, because she believed it to be so, that business might clear her mind; and she chanced, as her hand closed on the softness of the string ball, to glance down the longer, greener lane, down to where parts of the felled tree lay across it, still.

She thought of Simeon now, and smiled, and noticed the heat of the climbing sun on her face.

Not far away and well within walking distance, by field or the road depending on the weather, Simeon had other things on his mind, shaving cream over half his face, and a visitor at an unreasonable hour for visitors. To make matters worse, the visitor was screaming at him in a voice devoid entirely of reason, and shaking out her hair as if to emphasize that there was madness in her anger. Simeon (or Simmy, as those who had known him since childhood thought of him, though because he had made little progress beyond the geographical bounds of that childhood the diminutive maintained a currency at an age

when something a little more dignified might have been called for)
continued his shaving; his mirror propped on the kitchen dresser; his
hands, beautiful for their enormity alone, moving slowly to delay the
moment when he would have to turn and face the harridan who had
chosen to love him, whom he had once chosen to be loved by.

"Leave it so. Leave it so, will you? Don't be always shouting at me."

"I think," she said, "I have the right." Would it be unfair to suggest that she spoke with a certain coldness? Though not yet the mis-
tress of her art, she knew something of the craft of control.

She watched the mirror, hiding her love as his face was uncovered
from the shaving cream.

The more I think about it, the more I think it had something to
do with the curve of his mouth. In other respects he was immacu-
late, handsome beyond doubt; but it was the mouth that made you
think there was more to him, more than the cipher that any square-
chinned blue-eyed boy can be.

"This place is disgusting. A pig wouldn't live in it." She kicked at
the pile of hardened chicken crap on the tiles beneath the one chair.

"Clean it, so. If you're that worried about it."

He had turned, and was facing her, square on. Now that his jaw
was clean he felt an unwarranted courage in the face of her anger.

"Nobody asked you to come around at this hour of the morning
and I still above in the bed. Nobody asked you to folly me around
the house screaming like you have two heads on you. I was going to
be picking you up at the usual time tonight but, as it is, maybe I've
had enough of you for the day. Now, if you don't mind, I have work
to be going to."

It caught her unawares, to be spoken to, with authority, from a
quarter where authority had been so far dormant. It made her want
to explain herself, an impulse as alien to her as she had thought
authority to be to Simmy. She wanted to tell him how she had
woken up with such a happiness, and the freshness of early summer
and early morning outside the window, and she had thought of him,
and come along, late though it would make her for work, just to see
his face, maybe kiss him good morning, maybe tickle him as he lay

in the bed, maybe tell him of her happiness.

She would have told him all that except that she couldn't now pin-point the moment, between her entering the house and his opening his eyes, that her euphoria had changed to a black, uncontrollable anger; couldn't decide whether it had been caused by the filthy state of the place, or the smell of beer on his morning breath, or the slow, autistic complacency with which he woke. It might have been—it probably was—the sight of him alone in a big bed, apparently con-tented even though she was absent from it. It might have had some-thing to do with—and probably had—the big smile on his sleeping face, and her not knowing what or whom it was that he was dream-ing of. And, as had been intended, she was dumbfounded by the last thing he had said.

"Work?" she said. "Where?"

"That got you."

He was smiling, and though it could have been a smile of triumph, his smile was gentle on her. Now that she had stopped her scream-ing he had nothing against her at all.

"I'm felling a tree for Mrs. Doyle beyond. I have the back broke of it yesterday, and I'll finish clearing it today."

"How much is she giving you?" She could have bitten her tongue for the mean question as soon as she had asked it.

"Enough."

He turned his shoulder on her and left the house in his shirt-sleeves, with her looking after him; with her deciding she would get the morning off work and clean his house for him, and say nothing about it afterward; with her wondering how it was that she loved him most in his absence.

He went by the fields, through grass as thick and wet as seaweed, and before Mrs. Doyle came into view he could hear the scraping and clicking and swearing of her working her garden. He hung on the gate so as not to startle her, until she had seen him out of the corner of her eye.

"Is it breakfast time already?" she asked.

When he thought about it in the years to come, it seemed to him that she had said many extraordinary things that day, but he distrusted the memory, thinking that he had amalgamated in his mind things she must have said to him over the years, condensing them to one, significant, lengthy and broken conversation over the making of firewood and the tidying of a summer garden.

"How is Maggie keeping?" she asked.

"You know yourself."

"That bad?"

"As bad as that."

"The first one is always the greatest pain in the backside."

"The first what?"

"The first person you let fall in love with you. Let that be a lesson to you, when you find yourself in the same condition. It's no picnic."

She had a wry smile on her, and he was sniggering, and they felt, for some reason, that they understood each other.

"Mourning, not weeping," she said, at another time, snatching the phrase back from earlier in the morning, and muttering it as though she were alone, or as though they had taken drink, or as though she had nothing left to lose, or as though she were in no danger of losing it to him.

"Mourning?'

"Not the way you'd think. Not for the dead, any of them. For the things I can't have; thought I would surely have by now and know now I never will have. It's hard to reconcile being so selfish and hiding the selfishness with a lifetime of manners, and still not always getting your own way.

"I know."

"Times I want to bulldoze this garden. Will you look at it? All flowers and at the highest pitch of prettiness, and all it stands for is that it's the only thing I could do. Times I think it's pathetic, the delight I get. Do you know the most irritating thing anyone ever said to me?"

"That must have been a powerful one."

" 'You can't have everything.' I was six and it was a nun, and I remember thinking then, even then, and I've thought it all the time since, why not? No one has ever proved that you can't have everything. Just because something has never been done before does not make it impossible. There will, mark my words, be one day a happy member of this species who is still in possession of his sanity."

"Sounds good to me."

"Don't kid yourself," she said. "It won't happen by chance."

Sometime in the heat of the afternoon, with tea and melting chocolate-covered biscuits, and Simmy stripped to the waist, as though he were unconscious that it might be unfair to show such a body to someone who could not possess it, he asked Mrs. Doyle what had ended the bench.

To her, it was like changing the subject, because she had been looking at him so critically that he must have been aware of it. (She had been running her eye up and down the skin and the muscle and thinking: That is all he thinks there is to it; just that face and that body and he thinks there need be no more to him; as complacent as a bull in a field; as if there was something wrong with thinking and something worse with making a life for yourself.) She had, at the moment of his question, been about to say something irritable.

"Bench?" she said.

"It was there yesterday. We sat on it for the tea."

Marks were on the ground where the bench feet had stood for decades; there was a palpable absence in Simmy's line of sight. Mrs. Doyle kept looking, level, at him.

"A tinker offered me good money for it, and I took it."

"For God's sake."

"For God's sake, what?"

"You're paying me over the odds for cutting the wood as it is."

"I'll pay you whatever the notion takes me to pay you, and you won't pretend you don't want it."

"Wanting is one thing and fair is another, and besides, I liked the bench."

"You can save sentimentality for your old age, when you have nothing better to do with your mind." She made a grimace of self-mockery, perhaps because their talk had become too much like fighting, and she knew that if she made him angry, she would never get him to do what she wanted of him: it being easier to lead a bull than drive one.

The face she made reassured him, and while his guard was down she said, "I'm always surprised, when I think about it, to find you staying in this place, with nothing to keep you. If you're not careful, you'll wake up old one of these days. Or, at least, too old to do anything about it."

"About what?" He was looking at her with a discomfort that amounted to fear, and it wasn't just that the tone of their talk was more serious than anything between them might warrant.

When she saw how she had discomfited him she felt herself to be on the right track, and proceeded.

"I think you know. At least I'm not prepared to be the first of us to mention a word that describes it. That will have to be your own doing, in your own time. We are talking about the thing you least want us to be talking about. The thing that has you shivering in the heat now."

"There are some things you don't talk about." He said that with the outraged modesty of a child who has been surprised in the lavatory.

"If that is how you feel, perhaps you have to find a place where you're not afraid to talk about things."

Now there was a coldness between them, one that had been far from her intentions. He went back to what was left of the tree, where he worked with a savagery that made you think the muscles of his arms would explode.

She went into the house and watched him from a window, telling herself she should not be astonished by his anger. The animal you rescue is not to know you are trying to help it. From the back of her mind, at the same time, came the accusation that she was doing this thing more for herself than for him; that she was only salving her conscience for having let another man, and one she loved more, live and die, before she thought these things, let alone said them.

Thinking too that she had said, had assumed, too much; knowing at the same time that she had assumed correctly and not said enough.

Evening, and the wood stacked precisely, and the noise of the chain-saw finished with and the axes and wedges back in the shed, and only a scattering of sawdust by the stump of the tree, and bits of it lodged in Simeon's eyebrows and hair, and him smiling in the first crowd of midges, with satisfaction, you would think, for the work finished. Smiling, perhaps, in hopes of returning to a frame of mind he thought he had had earlier in the day; to conversations that were easy, knowing and bantering, and the subtexts of which were not his own, barely acknowledged, can of worms. (Best left unopened, he thought, pulling the smile tighter, until he was almost laughing with the effort of it.)

Mrs. Doyle was standing, with her head to one side, looking at him, and with a sudden shame he cast about him for his shirt, brushing wood dust from his nipples as if he were contaminated.

She smiled, able to read what was printed in lines across his forehead: She cannot know, she's only guessing, and even so there's no way she can have guessed that, the last thing anyone would guess of me, since I'm not convinced of it myself, since it isn't true, not really.

"That's lovely now," she said.

"I made it as tidy as I could."

"A work of art," she said. "You're very neat."

"Thanks." His smile now was one of genuine relief. The subject which had threatened earlier seemed firmly closed again. "I'd better be off home to the bath. I said I'd take Maggie out. She'll eat me if I'm late."

"Come in the house for your wages first."

He followed her, shambling, as though he suspected a trap. Once they were inside the kitchen he was aware of the pungent smell of himself, fresh enough to be more provocative than unpleasant. There were two envelopes lying on the long table. He picked at his fingernails.

She picked up both the envelopes and handed him one. The other she placed on the dresser, propped before a small pale yellow jug. It had his full name written on it.

"I'm leaving that there," she said, "and it's yours whenever you want it. You can, of course, do what you like with it, but it's enough for the boat and to see you through for a week or two until you find yourself a job. You could, I suppose, buy a gimcrack engagement ring for the Hanlon girl with it. She'd like that."

She saw that he was staring at the floor and that his body was rocking, unstable.

She said, "I'm sorry for the things I said earlier, but I had to do this, for my own sake. Eddie Doyle was like you and I watched him rot his life out married to me. The signs were there, but I never saw them till after he was dead. You can see nothing if you love someone enough. These days I see too much, including you for what you are. And you won't thank me for it. But the times are different now, and if you go away you'll find there's nothing wrong with what you are: It's only this place and others like it. Anyway, the money's yours and you're not to say anything. Not a word. The back door, as you know, is always open, whenever you're ready to take it."

He wished for the floor to open and swallow him; was surprised he had the strength to turn and leave the house.

She said, in his wake, "We'll all have to mourn, one of the days. But I'd rather see you mourning for a full life than an empty one."

He began to walk quickly, into the dew, trying to outpace the words that came after him, blind in his fear and thinking that this must be the end of everything, calling her a bitch, twice, to every pace he took.

2.

Interior, chateau. twilight. Thinking that, no matter how bad things got, one seemed to stumble from one idyll to another, in sensual terms at least. The milk-yellow stone of the fireplace deepening between one glance and the next; the distant ceiling fading, and then blacked out by the lighting of the lamps; the sparse conversation and elongated breathing of a kind of contentment that came with comfort and an indulged palate; the faint hope that the children would settle in strange surroundings and that the last had been seen of them until morning; the mixed scents of itea and cestrum groping a way through the open door, a conjunction of smells odd enough to be without association; the luxury of a clear subconscious; the occasional small cold breeze from the direction of the same doorway, just enough to keep you this side of dozing.

"What exactly is it that you do?"

There was a level on which Simeon enjoyed being asked that question. He liked to make a game of the answer, prevaricating as though he were being discreet and not ashamed. He was not, he told himself emphatically, ashamed. He was happy about what he did: his unhappiness lay in other people's perception of his job.

"I organize things."

"What sort of things?'"

There was something in the persistence of his interlocutor which had nothing to do with curiosity. Simeon raised a hand to shade his eyes from the pale orange cast of the nearest lamp, and had a proper look. The upper half of the face was in shade; the lower half a strong chin of some rotundity, and one of those inward-facing mouths. A long bony hand lay nearby, detached, by a trick of the light.

"Well, I suppose I'm a sort of enabler."

"What's that supposed to mean?"

He had been right about the tone of his questioner's voice. If it was provocative there was also an element of flirtatiousness. Simeon cast a quick, automatic, almost imperceptible glance in the direction of Jane. The mother of his children had the tip of her thumb in her mouth, her head bent over one of her hard-backed novels, in a daze of reading. At the other end of the sofa which she occupied, their host snoozed; layers of sleek dog in his lap.

"You could say that the parameters of my work are, loosely, perhaps ultimately, lifestyle investment."

"You could say that you were an estate agent." Their host, evidently, had not been asleep after all. Having spoken, he roused himself, sending rolls of dog tumbling to the floor. The cynical boom of his voice had caused Jane to look from her book to her watch.

"I'm for bed," she said. "Darling?" Simeon was aware, without looking, of the way in which the questioner must be smiling. This was no time to retreat; this was no taste to leave in the mouth of another.

"I'll be up soon," he said.

Soon enough, he thought. He set himself the task of remembering the other man's name. Christopher.

When the two men were alone, Christopher got up to close the door into the garden.

"I'm having another drink," he said. "I don't know about you."

Simeon said, "Whiskey." It was obvious now in which direction things were heading. He became aware of how he was sitting, that his legs were spread a little further than relaxation might call for.

Christopher handed him a glass that was a drip wet on the outside, the pads of their middle fingers touching as the handover was made. Simeon hoped that his shiver would not be taken for the nervousness it was.

"I don't blame you, really." Christopher looked him straight in the eye while speaking. "It must be bad enough to be an estate agent without having to tell people about it."

Christopher was leaning against the edge of a table, his arms over his chest. He had, Simeon noticed, the sort of thighs that would look good folded, knee to shoulder. Simeon pulled a cushion into his lap, as though to fiddle idly with the tassels. Meanwhile, he laughed at the last thing Christopher had said.

"And so what do you do?" Simeon thought he might as well get that one out of the way.

"I manage campaigns for Friends of the Earth."

Simeon said that that must be interesting, in a tone of voice which implied that they didn't have to talk about it.

The high windows were silvering. They became noticeable in the conversational hiatus, and served as a way out of it.

Simeon said, "The moon is up."

Christopher said, "Shall we go for a walk?"

The bench was surrounded on three sides by sharp-cornered yew, silver and blackened in the brightness of the moon. The change of light made a difference, it seemed, to everything: the garden monochromatically formalized, Christopher's face given a cast that made him familiar.

"You remind me of someone."

There seemed no point, once it was said, in having said it. The association faded as soon as it was confessed, as the memory of a dream will fade as soon as a breakfast companion has been bored by the telling of it.

"Who?"

"No one you'd know."

Simeon became aware of the smell of the other man and wondered for a moment why he had not noticed it before, and then realized how illogical it was to wonder such a thing, because it was only a minute or so since he had stretched himself out flat on his back the length of the bench and rested his head on Christopher's lap. It was a smell that was not entirely of man: There was an odd taint of aniseed in it, and Simeon wondered if it was the soap he used, or whether it was natural to him.

Christopher, playing with Simeon's fringe, said, "You don't sound very Irish."

"Don't I? Would you rather I did?" It was an effort to make the words come out in a discernible pattern, to make sounds that were anything more than the grunts of desperation that were lining up at his throat.

The noise, when it was released, was stifled because Christopher's mouth closed on his at the same moment that Christopher's hand went down the flat of his stomach and wound itself round his erection.

"That's some fucking monster you've got there."

For the first time Christopher's tone was not one of accusing banter, as though he had finally found something admirable in Simeon.

Simeon opened his eyes. The face was eight inches from his and smiling, and seemingly sinister viewed from below and in the half-light. Not knowing how to take the compliment, Simeon said, "It's not my fault."

"Do you always shake this much?"

"I don't know." Simeon had to stop himself and think about what to say next. This was not the moment to admit he had never done this before. "Yes," he said. "I suppose so." As if to change the subject he buried his face in the folds of the other man's flies.

The next words spoken were said by Christopher.

"That was an Irish groan if ever I heard one. You sound much more Irish when you're coming."

There were bats flashing overhead.

"Why do your balls smell of aniseed?" Simeon sniffed closer to reassure himself that his question was justified.

"Do they?"

From the corner of his eye Simeon became aware of the appearance of a yellow light. He looked toward the silhouette of the chateau and watched the lighted window until it became dark again. Someone using a bathroom, obviously. He worried that it was Jane; that she had woken, had missed him, had noticed how late it had become. He wondered idly, academically, what to do now about Jane: whether one night of felicity had canceled out eight years of fidelity; whether this was something he just needed to do every eight years, or whether he was debauched now, corrupted; whether there was no turning back once a lifetime's resolve had fissured.

He pulled himself closer, pushed his face into the smell of aniseed and the slick flaccid tangle, until breathing became mercifully difficult, until a new tumescence pushed him into renewed activity.

Like an unwilling and unbelieving parachutist clinging to the door jamb of an aeroplane, those of us who are genuinely innocent will cling to the last remnant of that innocence; will cling even to the memory of how that door jamb felt in our hand although we are already tumbling through the void, toward freedom.

It was mid-afternoon, after a morning of disconnection, before Simeon had the chance to be alone with Christopher. He hadn't gone to bed until nearly dawn, and Jane had sleepily wrapped herself around him, had sleepily asked him the time, had sleepily accepted his denial of knowledge of the time, had sleepily submitted to his ferocious lovemaking and, once aroused, had thrown herself open to him with an enthusiasm and a pleasure and an abandonment that only, somehow, made things worse. It had been a morning of responding to the children in the sort of snappish tones that let them know this was not a time for the sort of parent-child bonding recommended by the textbooks. It had been a morning of keeping tight hold of any inanimate object that came to hand, to stop his hands from shaking.

Jane appeared to be willing to accept his plea of a hangover as an explanation for his behavior, as she had not contested his claim that it was a drinking bout with Christopher which had kept him up all night. It was hard to know whether she was suspending her intelligence or being too clever by half.

It was hard to know how to phrase an opening remark to Christopher. He was lying, stocking-footed, on a sofa in the picture gallery which ran the length of the top floor of the chateau. There was a florilegium by his elbow which he appeared to be studying. He seemed smaller in the daylight, and more benign. It was Simeon's hope, as he walked the thirty-four paces from the door, that Christopher would be the first to speak. Christopher raised his head and smiled at him but not, perhaps, with the warmth he might have wished for. He shifted his feet a little as Simeon made to sit on the end of his sofa.

They were broad, rounded feet, the balls of which were almost spherical, the toes of which were blunt. It would have been hard for Simeon not to take one of them in his hands, and so he did, moving his fingers against the dry roughness of the cotton, folding his knuckles into the cavity below the toes. Alongside the fear and the excitement he felt a calm which he had never yet encountered as though, by holding this foot, he was absorbing opium through the palms of his hands.

When at last Christopher spoke, he did so without taking his eyes from the page beneath him. "D'you do this sort of thing much, then?" At the end of his sentence he shifted his eyes to the foot that was being manipulated and regarded it neutrally.

Simeon could not make sense of the question or of the tone in which it was spoken; could not think of a dignified reply, except to close the hollow of his hand around an ankle bone.

Christopher said, "I was having a chat with Jane this morning. She seems a very nice woman."

The accusing tone made Simeon answer with a note of impatience. "I wouldn't have married her if I hadn't thought so myself."

"Nice kids."

"We do our best."

"So what's all this about then?"

It was like being up before the headmaster. Simeon breathed deeper in an attempt at breathing more evenly and said, "I don't know. I honestly don't know. I honestly feel that this is outside my control. I don't know what to do next, if anything."

"Enabler, enable thyself."

"For Christ's sake. This isn't easy."

"I'm glad to hear it. I should hope it isn't."

Simeon looked as though he was in pain. He said, "What is all this; this morality all of a sudden? I felt something. I thought there was something going on. Now you're behaving more like someone who caught us at it than the person I was doing it with."

"Yeah. Perhaps I made a mistake. Maybe I misread things last night. You and Jane seemed hardly to know each other. I assumed you weren't getting on or something."

"We were tired. It was a long drive."

"Well, as I say: Now that I've spoken to her, properly, I like her. I think she's in love with you. Shagging men who like to think they're straight is one thing. Breaking up marriages isn't my idea of a kick. Last night seemed like a bit of harmless fun at the time.

Maybe we should leave it at that."

"I don't think I can."

"That's your problem, matey."

"Don't you feel anything?"

"Fucking Norah, you closets are beyond belief. Look at yourself. You're tall, you're gorgeous, you look as though you've got a big dick and you have. If you sit around with cow eyes and your legs splayed in front of any single gay man he's going to want to fuck your brains out. Well, those were my feelings on the matter anyway. If you want to create a retrospective justification of what went on by imagining we fell in love with each other, then you're on your own, matey. Personally, even if I wanted to get into a relationship, it wouldn't be with someone who lied about something as fundamental as his sexuality. My sympathies are with Jane. With those children."

"Harriet and James."

"Goodness me. You even know their names."

"That's not fair."

"I think I'd like to have my foot back now, if you've finished with it."

When Simeon reached the door of the gallery he turned to speak; to say the thing that had formed in thirty-four paces. The acoustics were extraordinary. and his voice was carried the length of the room without him having to raise it, over sofas and tables, between bookcases and fireplaces and outsized portraits of women with long noses. The smooth, neutral accent of the estate agent was cracked as he spoke.

"It's never felt like lying. It's always felt as though I was doing the right thing at the time. It isn't that I don't love her, that I don't want to."

Christopher's look could not have been more level, more knowing, more cynical.

"Maybe you need help. But not mine. Good luck." he said. The stairs, though broad and shallow, induced such a feeling of vertigo in Simeon that he held the banister with two hands, all the way down.

3.

Interior, bathroom, too bright for comfort. Thinking that if you tried to divide the world into those who were capable of falling in love and those who were not you'd have your work cut out for you. How would you tell? More often than not the subjects themselves, if they were honest, would have to tell you that they didn't know whether they had the propensity for falling in love or merely a desire for it. Thinking that if people realized how little they knew or could know about themselves they'd give up and go somewhere else. Perhaps that is what they do. Perhaps that is why, most of the time, when you attempt conversation with someone you get the feeling you are talking to their answering machine. What on Earth is making you think this way, at this hour of the morning? Love and life: You'll be contemplating death next. One of those mornings that happen often enough, when you step into the bathroom and the image reflected sets you thinking; when the face blearing back seems to have been sprayed with ugly in the night; when the tits are not quite as squared off as you'd like to think they are, considering the hours you work on them; when, let's face it, the frustration of not being able to admire yourself makes you philosophical. Now, you've caught yourself out, wallowing in the shallows. You catch your eye in the glass, as you would catch the eye of a conspirator, and it makes you grin.

Mourning not weeping. In his first love letter he said it was a smile that would turn pearls to cream. I can't see it myself, but then, even now, I don't think I am in love with myself to anywhere near the degree that Ewan was in love with me. And then, after all these years of studying this face and scowling at it and pouting at it and practicing handsomeness from all the angles, it wasn't until recently that I caught myself smiling. In his first love letter Ewan wrote a page and three quarters about the smile alone, in his flying handwriting. the tail of one letter splashing across the body of another; the cross of a t traveling the page, in his passion. Would this be the smile that Ewan had seen, or is there another dimension to a smile you'd turn on the beloved?

Smile you bugger, and get it right. In another ten years the handsomeness will be gone and you'll only have the smile to fall back on. Now you're laughing at yourself, in the mirror. That is a new development. Laughing loud enough to wake the trade, stretched in the bed beyond, through the open door, left open so I could glance at his flesh among the sheets, between strokes of the razor. Not a beauty perhaps, but sweet and tactile, and a dick you could exercise a horse on. Could it be I am becoming a size queen? Ewan wasn't exactly hung to his knees. In his first love letter he apologized for it, not knowing that as far as I was concerned everything on him and in him was perfect. He was so tentative in the beginning that I thought he must be backing off. I avoided him to save my dignity, and that was the occasion of the letter. He sent a typed version with the handwritten: a translation, afraid that any word might be misread, so precisely had he chosen the words he used: pearls to cream. Not Dear Simeon, but Simeon; not with love, but love; no date at the top, but the day of the week: Wednesday.

Do I think of him too much? Afraid that the memory might fade; that I might, one day, think a whole paragraph without a phrase of his mixed somewhere in it; that I might spend a whole night, some night, with another man without once feeling Evan's breath on the side of my face in a moment of distraction; that I might smell good coffee or K-Y and rubber or Chanel scent or burning milk on the stovetop and not think of him. He made me promise not to mourn him, and it is rare that I need to weep for him. There is little sadness in his haunting. Long ago he was forgiven for, having taught me to live, dying.

This one, on the bed, the sheets draped and undraped over him as if he had woken and taken the time to arrange them while my back was turned, who knows what this one is, beyond the fact that he is a sybarite, with the currency to earn his pleasures? We passed the same breath back and forth between our lungs until we were dizzy and high with the lack of oxygen. We flew and roared and coated ourselves in layers of sperm until our stomachs crackled when we moved and, now and then, we'd lean back and stare at

each other with frank admiration, and one of us would say something shamelessly jingoistic about the potency of our race, and
laugh at the ludicrousness of two paddies picking each other up in
preference to all the Action Men in the East Village. His name is
Eric. We met in the Crowbar, and I liked the way he smiled at me.
The paddock-sized dick was a bonus.

Inside myself, after all these decades. Inside myself for the first
time since infancy. I won't dramatize it. I won't say it was Ewan who
put me here, in my happiness. But it was Ewan who showed that the
happiness of an infant was possible, for someone who could be so
unself-conscious as an infant; that it is not a matter of being loved,
but of knowing you are lovable.

Sluice water over the scum of bristle that laces the basin. A beard
is such a disproportionately fecund thing. Think also of Eric's choking pleasure at the grating of that bristle on his rectum. Should I
brush my teeth, or would that be gaining an unfair advantage over
him when I poke him awake with coffee? Check by the ears and nostrils for stray wisps of Noxzema, and tweak the glass rod that opens
the blinds a fraction, the better to see. I love the light in this city. If
you say that to a native, he will look at you a little strangely for a
moment before agreeing with you. Plainly, you can become immune
to the light here. If that ever happens, it will be time to move on.
There are enough exciting places in the world and no excuse not to
be excited by the place you are standing in.

Brush the teeth for the comfort of a clean mouth. A twinge in the
gums, and a little panic at the possibility of a mouth ulcer, but there
is no sign of anything nasty. Not that it should make any difference,
but last night Eric made a confession of rare generosity. He was only
the second man I have ever known to have had the consideration to
do that and Ewan, of course, was the first. It was after we got back
here, at maybe one this morning, before we had done more than
kiss. There was no need for him to have told me, and he took a risk
by doing so. There are some, even in these days of putative enlight-
enment, who would have showed him the door in the light of that
knowledge.

"You don't mind?" he said, as I unbuttoned his flies.

"Why should I? The only difference between us is you know you're positive and I don't. If I'd had a test yesterday I still couldn't be sure. It isn't going to affect what we do or what we don't do. People like me are a bigger risk than you are."

I don't know if he heard half of what I was saying, muffled through the silken bulges of a mouthful of genitalia; trailed off toward the end as his tumescence took priority; punctuated in ungrammatical places by his grunts of encouragement. He pulled me to my feet and kissed me.

"My turn," he said, slithering down.

He has the sort of body that doesn't look much at first, and suddenly he is over you, a dick in each hand, both arms pumping, muscles bursting through his skin and a filthy expression on his face, and the sight of him alone could make you come, and did. I thought at first he was laughing at me, at the sight of me shuddering and squirting, until his own glutinous arc landed on my shoulder and I understood that his delight was his own. I've never before seen anyone laugh like that at a moment of crisis. It makes me wonder what sort of creature I have in my bed. I could stay here all day and watch the tempting way he sleeps, and wonder all those things that occur to you after a night with a man you like the smell and taste and smile of. Will he stay and will I want him to stay? I love this moment, before a man you hardly know wakes up, when you can think you might be in love with him, knowing in the back of your mind that you can impress him with a home-cooked breakfast and send him on his way.

Would he stay and would I love him? Why is it that as soon as you have decided you are happy to be single, have never, to your knowledge, been happier, you find yourself entertaining domestic fantasies, entertaining men with that store-cupboard glint in their eyes? Not in his, perhaps, but then I hardly know him. Or do I know as much as there is, as much as is significant? He seemed disarmingly honest. We talked, muttered confidences to each other as the sweat dried, our tongues loosened, perhaps, by being with someone who spoke our own form of this language. His mouth, full and lush in repose, became, in talking, wired; a hard, undulating line that curled and straightened about his teeth. I devoted at least as much concentration to watching his mouth as to hearing his words; flirted with alarmingly romantic ideas while watching it.

"You are," I said, "an extraordinary man."

"Being extraordinary," he said, "is relatively easy. I tried ordinary once, and it was a bitch."

While I was laughing I thought of all the years I had wasted in pursuit of ordinariness. Spent not wasted. You cannot accuse, even in your own mind, your children of having been a waste of part of your life.

I confessed my past to him.

"Where are they now?" he asked, in a voice too idle for accusation.

"Jersey. That's how come I'm here, originally. Jane, my ex, was offered a job over here, one that was too good to turn down, so I upped sticks and followed them. I know what it's like to be that age and not have a father. The only big problem at the moment is that they're beginning to get accents. It'll be a bit of a liability for them if they have to go through life sounding like Americans."

"A cruel and unusual punishment," he said. "So what do you do anyway?"

I love that. I love it when a man who has just been ferreting deliriously in your rudest bits has to ask you the most basic questions about yourself, things that people you wouldn't even undress in front of have known for years.

"I'm a hack. I write about property. I used to be an estate agent in the eighties, but then the crash happened and there was more money to be made by writing about houses not being sold than by not selling them. It took a while to break into it over here, but I had good credentials. Well, credentials that looked good from this distance. What are you at yourself?"

"Guess. Irishman abroad. It has to be navvy or novelist doesn't it?"

"So which is it?"

"Both, unfortunately. But so far I've only managed to gain recognition as a navvy. Luckily I look cute in sawn-offs with a layer of brick dust, so there's no problems on the entertainment front. Sometimes I feel like giving up on the novelist thing, and sometimes it's the only thing that keeps me going. I want to be published before I croak."

"Why?" I had asked the question before I realized how crass it was.

"I don't know. Because I want to find out how much of me is self-delusion and how much of me is worth anything. Because I'm promiscuous by nature and I want to fuck with the minds of complete strangers. Because I want to be less afraid of dying. Because, if nothing else, I think being a writer must be a complete blast. The ultimate fuck-off profession. I want to know what it's like to be as free as that. As shameless as that."

"And words? Don't they come into it?"

"This is not," he said, warily, "the sort of conversation I have with every shag."

"I have a little secondhand experience," I said. "I used to live with a writer."

"What happened there?"

"He died."

The question hung, and I let it hang for a moment, and answered it for him just before he had to ask it.

"No," I said. "Not the usual. He had a heart attack. He cheated the virus. He'd been positive for years, was positive when I met him. We were all worked up about how we were going to handle it when the count started to drop, and then the fucker goes and keels over on me with a heart attack. He was fit enough, or he seemed to be, and doing nothing strenuous at the time—hadn't touched the poppers for years, even when he was off his tits and screaming to be fucked, backing into me like a mare in season. No. He was just sitting at his computer. The last word he wrote was 'And.' Just that. 'And.' There was no other word on the screen, so it was obviously the beginning of something. It was his nightmare, that he would die with something unfinished, like the man with the sorrel filly in *La Peste*. 'And.' You couldn't have something more unfinished than that, if you tried.

"I wouldn't worry too much about getting yourself published if I was you. I've seen that racket at close quarters, and I'd rather be a navvy if I had the choice. Though Ewan always claimed that choice didn't come into it."

"Ewan?" he said. "Ewan who?"

"Ewan Strong."

"Fuck me pink," he said.

Then he did what a lot of them did when they found out Ewan Strong had been my lover. He looked down at my dick and closed his hand around it as though it was a talisman, the totem that had plugged the man who had described our lives. I tried not to react, to tell myself I would do the same in the same circumstances. To be honest, I was jealous, in a small way, as you are always jealous of the love of others for your lover, no matter what form that love takes.

To change the context of his action, I pushed his knees up either side of his face and gave him a big slap across the backside.

"You're into a bit of CP then?" he said.

"No," I said. "Proud to be vanilla."

"Good," he said. "It's the reluctant ones that squeal the loudest."

"No fucking way," I said.

"We'll see about that." He cast his eyes back toward the palm of his hand, where a vulcanization was betraying the excitement I had denied, and then, as if he was holding the erection at arm's length, he said, "What's it like fucking a woman?"

The question seemed stark in the circumstances.

"Fine," I said. "All right. Wonderful, sometimes. Easier, from a technical point of view, in some senses. Not all that different, in reality. I don't know. Why are you asking?"

He had dropped his hold of my dick and was looking at it in an odd way, as though it had been contaminated by encounters with women, when only moments before he had been revering it as though encounters with Ewan had sanctified it. I had the feeling he might have shuddered had I not been watching him so closely.

"I don't understand how anyone could. It doesn't seem natural somehow. A gay man doing that."

I'm afraid I got schoolmarmish with him at that point. "So? Fine. You, maybe, were always sure of what you were, maybe. I had to be certain, and perhaps I spent years codding myself, but I thought for a long time that I was doing the things that made me happy. I wasn't revolted by straight sex. I liked it. I thought sex was only about pleasure until the first time I fucked a man. And I was nearly thirty when that happened."

"And then?" he said, with a challenge in his tone that was not attractive. "What was so different then, in this catalytic fuck? I'm sorry, I find these conversion stories hard to swallow."

"What can I say?"

"What it was like? What happened? Explain to me, because I've never known anything else; explain the love of men."

I would have told him he was asking too much, but he knew that already. I had to remind myself that this inquisition would not be so pressing if he didn't want me to acquit myself.

"It's like drugs," I said, "or religion, or death, or fact. Once you've done it there's no substitute. There's no going back. It's like knowledge, and once you have it you can't cod yourself that you don't know. Times I find a last wisp of innocence somewhere about me, like going to a bar and, after half an hour of nonchalant cruising, seeing a bit of shaving cream by your ear when you glance in the mirror. Shreds of innocence are the hardest to live with, and the thing about innocence is that it's all or nothing. You can only be happy at either end of the process. Am I talking shite?"

"I like you talking shite," he said. "Naif philosophy is such a turn-on." He bent my head over and began to lick the back of my neck, arching his body tight until the end of his cock was banging on my nostril.

To see him now, seamless and breathing softly. He knows, I think, that I am watching him; knows it whether he is sleeping or not. He has that attitude of an animal that knows he is being admired. His skin is twitching to be touched. Who knows what he is, beyond what he has said he is? I remember more of what I told

him than of what he told me, but then my stories were the ones I
know more intimately.

Interior. bathroom, daylight. Shaved and teeth brushed and
almost fully awake now after nearly half an hour of grimacing in the
mirror and indulging his mind with a puddle of consciousness,
Simeon stepped into the shower and let the streams run between his
skin and the previous night's carapace of dried sperm; smiling at the
feel of the soap and the illusion of cleanliness.

The expression on his face would lead you to believe that he had
just fallen in love or, failing that, and very unlikely I grant you, that
he was happy in his own right.

Eric Hanlon in the bed, on hearing the beat of the shower, turned
himself over and arranged himself to be as enticing as possible, one
leg bent for a Caravaggian glimpse of the buttocks, lower arms hidden as if he might be tied, the manège of an organ stirring obliging-
ly, but no more than you would expect of a functioning young man
with a full bladder at that hour of the day. He liked that. He liked
being the slut in bed, reeking to heaven of two men; apparently
asleep, and the feel of a clean, slightly damp man, smelling of water,
climbing over him tentatively, gently playing with him as though not
to wake him. He liked to hear the first growl of satisfaction from one
who was trying to be silent, and feel the first flutter of a tongue that
couldn't help itself, on the head of his cock for preference. He liked,
above all, the idea that he was irresistible.

This one, whatever he called himself, was taking his time in the
bathroom. Perhaps it would not be a bad thing to devote this hiatus to an effort to remember his name. Sim Sim something.
Simeon. It could be worse. He had spent the night with a man
called Ashley once. The strain of not saying fiddledee had almost
overwhelmed him.

He could smell the water before he felt the first drip from
Simeon's wet hair. He waited to be touched but instead felt a slight
trembling in the bed. The filthy bugger was jerking off over him. It
was important not to wriggle at this stage; to maintain the illusion.

The first fleck splashed on his throat, the second slid down his hip-bone, the main consignment was delivered to his balls. It was hell not responding to it, and half the pleasure.

He woke officially when Simeon brought the coffee. He put his hand between his legs, brought it back beneath his nose, inhaled and grinned.

"What's been going on here then?"

"Sorry," Simeon said, without bothering to look too sorrowful. "I'll make it up to you."

"You betcha you will."

"How's the coffee?"

"Good. Spoiling the trade, you are."

"That means something else over here. Trade."

"I know. A lot of things do."

"They say 'trick.' I don't like that word. It sounds dishonest. It sounds as if you wouldn't look him in the eye after you'd fucked him."

Feeling it was a bit early in the morning for the semantics of gay slang, but not wanting to furrow the atmosphere, Eric said nothing.

"So," Simeon said, "let's get the ghoulish exile bit out of the way. Which tit of the Sainted Sow did you suck on? The only thing I can tell from your accent is that you probably went to UCD."

"Very good," Eric said. "Top marks. The only thing I can tell from yours is that you weren't long in losing it. You won't have heard of where I'm from. It's a place called Mowlinstown, in the middle of nowhere."

"Mowlinstown? Mowlinstown on the New Line? Beyond Pollick Cross? What's your second name?"

"Hanlon."

"Well fuck you pink and back again. What age are you?" The Hanlon boy was too stunned by Simeon's reaction and knowledge to do more than answer the questions he was given, and search the face in front of him for indications of its provenance.

"Twenty-six," he said.

"That's it, so. You look older. You would have been no more than a scrap when I left. What's Maggie doing with herself these days?"

"She got a job with Aer Lingus. Teaching the young wans to hand out boiled sweets while balancing half a pound of makeup on each eyelid. She married some tosser from Cavan with a chip on his shoulder about poofs, so I don't see much of her when I go home. Who the fuck are you anyway?"

"Simmy." The old form of his name almost creaked in the disinterment.

Eric went white and said something that sounded like "fffph."

"I know," Simeon said. "Fuck you pink."

Eric pulled the sheet over his midsection as if his nudity were suddenly immodest, at which Simeon smiled, at which Eric began to laugh. He laughed for ten minutes at a stretch and then again, in shorter bursts.

"I remember you, now that I think about it," Simeon said. "You were a disgusting child. A yard of snot in your nose and always trying to feck money out of my pockets."

"I was probably trying to get a feel of your dick."

"At that age?"

"Not all of us had to wait until we were thirty to work out what was what."

"So much for innocence."

An anger of some kind became evident when Eric next spoke. "There's more than one kind of innocence. And more than one way of being fucked up by whatever innocence afflicts you."

"What's wrong? What's the matter?"

"Don't say that like that. Don't ask me that as if you know me. I hate the way you're so complacent. Maggie still talks about you now and again and says you were a complacent cunt, when she has drink on her. You haven't changed much."

"I'm sorry. It seemed the thing to do at the time."

There was a time when Simeon's face could cave in sorrow and still be a thing to look at. Now, unhappiness made him look middle-aged, and would for years to come, until he gained the beauty of the old. "I don't understand," he said.

"Welcome to the human race." There was a kindness in Eric's voice when he said that, and a viciousness when he followed it with, "I knew Mrs. Doyle. I used to help her in the garden when she got frail."

"Knew?"

"She isn't dead yet, from what I've heard. She used to talk about you a lot, and speculate how you were getting on. The odd postcard wouldn't have hurt."

"I hardly knew the woman."

"She knew you. There was always an envelope on her dresser with your full name on it. I looked in it once and it was full of old money. I didn't like to ask her what was at the bottom of that one. Though we were close. She was my first fag hag. She knew what I was about, and she made things easier for me. She's the first I visit when I'm home."

"So that's why you're angry."

"No, I'm angry for all kinds of reasons. It doesn't take much to bring it out. I'm angry because I fancied you like fuck until I found out who you were."

"Now?"

"I don't know. Years ago I used to dream of you, and think you had everything. By coincidence you did. How many men could hope to have children and Ewan Strong in the same lifetime? When I let you jerk off over me this morning it was because you were a fantasy man, perversely enough, not unlike the fantasies I used to have in Mowlinstown when I'd think of you and masturbate. Now that I know what you are, this morning feels more like molestation than a game. Now I almost hate you, and it's too soon for me to explain it."

"I'm sorry."

"Don't say that."

Simmy reached out toward him, inhaling as he did so, and so becoming aware of the smell of the man before his fingertips lighted on his shoulder. Eric would have liked to flinch, but didn't. They kissed, like lovers; like a kiss of seduction.

Simeon spoke. He used only the one word, and it was the last word between them for some time.

"Stay," he said.

Excerpt from The Heather Blazing

Colm Tóibín

He woke during the night and went downstairs to his study. He had been dreaming, but now the dream escaped him. He went into the kitchen and took some cold water from a plastic bottle in the fridge. He sat at the kitchen table for a while, then went back into the study. It was a warm night.

He sat at his desk and looked down at the judgment he had written in longhand on foolscap pages. It was ready to be delivered. He wondered for a moment if he should have it typed, but he was worried about it being leaked. No one knew about it; even as he sat down to write it himself he did not know what he would say, what he would decide. There was so little to go on, no real precedent, no one obviously guilty. Neither of the protagonists in the case had broken the law. And that was all he knew: the law, its letter, its traditions, its ambiguities, its codes. Here, however, he was being asked to decide on something more fundamental, and now he realized he had failed and he felt afraid.

He took a biro from a drawer and began to make squiggles on a pad of paper. What was there beyond the law? *Law;* he wrote the word. There was natural justice. He wrote the two words down and put a question mark after them, And beyond that again there was the notion of right and wrong, the two principles which governed everything and came from God. *Right* and *wrong;* he wrote the two words down and then put brackets around them and the word *God* in capitals beside them.

Somehow here in the middle of the night with the moths and midges drawn to the window, the idea of God seemed more clearly absurd to him than ever; the idea of a being whose mind put order on the universe, who watched over things, and whose presence gave the world a morality that was not based on self-interest, seemed beyond belief. He wondered how people put their faith in such a thing, and yet he understood that the courts and the law ultimately depended for their power on such an idea. He crossed out the word *God*. He felt powerless and strange as he went back to read random passages of his judgment. He decided to go to bed and sleep some more: Maybe he would be more relaxed about his judgment in the morning.

Carmel did not stir in the bed when he came into the bedroom, but he knew she had woken. When he got into bed he put his arms around her. She kissed him gently on the neck, then turned away from him, letting him snuggle against her. She fell back asleep, and he lay there for a while holding her until he grew drowsy and fell asleep as well.

He was wakened by the alarm clock and reached across her to turn it off. They both lay there without moving or speaking, as though still asleep.

"Are you in court today?" she finally asked, almost whispering.

"Yes," he said.

"Do you have a full day?"

"There's a lot of work to get through."

Another last day of term; another year gone by. He hoped that all the urgent applications for injunctions would go elsewhere. He knew the press would be in his court today. This case was newsworthy. He hated the journalists' faces looking up at him, eager for something instant they could grasp and simplify. He snoozed for a while, and when he woke he found that Carmel had left the bed. He moved over to her side and lay in her heat until he knew it was time to get up.

It was a fine morning. Thin wisps of white cloud hung in the sky like smoke, and the sun was already strong. He realized as he tested the water in the shower that he would like to get into his car now and drive with Carmel to Cush and never set foot in the court again.

She was still in her dressing gown when he came downstairs. She poured tea for him.

"I think everything is ready now," she said. "Are you looking forward to getting away?"

"Yes, I am. I was just thinking that I'd be delighted never to set foot in the court again."

"You'll feel differently at the end of the summer."

He went into his study again and sat at the desk. He thought he should read the judgment over again before going into the court, but he could not face it. He felt unsure about it, but as he left the house and drove into the city the uncertainty became deep unease. It was not yet nine o'clock when he arrived at the Four Courts, and he was not due to deliver his judgment until eleven, or maybe later, depending on what injunctions were being sought.

The line of reasoning in his judgment was clear, he thought. It had not been written in a hurry; evening after evening he had sat in his study and drafted it, working out the possibilities, checking the evidence and going over the facts. Even so, he was still not sure.

He stood at the window of his chambers and looked out at the river which was low now because of the tide and because of the good summer. He watched a boy moving between lorries and cars on a horse, riding bareback with confidence. When the lights changed to green, the boy and his horse joined the flow of traffic toward Capel Street.

He had taken the judgment from his briefcase and placed it on the table. He went over and looked at it again. The case had happened in one of the border towns. A lot of people must live on the edge there, he thought, with strange upheavals, odd comings and goings. But this had nothing to do with the case, as far as he knew. The case was simple: A sixteen-year-old girl attending a convent school had become pregnant and been expelled. She was due to have the baby over the summer and wished to return to the school for her final year, but the school had made it clear she would not be readmitted. The girl and her mother sought a court order instructing the school to take her back.

The girl was clever, according to the school reports that had been produced in evidence. Her becoming pregnant had been a great trauma, and she had confided in no one until it became obvious. Both the girl and her mother had given evidence. The mother seemed surprisingly young, but had been very confident in the witness box as she told of her visits to the school to talk to the principal and her long discussions with her daughter about her pregnancy and her future. She seemed sincere and deeply upset about her daughter's expulsion.

It would have been easier for everyone, she said, if her daughter had had an abortion. But because they decided to have the child and bring it up in the town, her daughter was being made to suffer. She would have to go to the Vocational School or travel every day to another town. She was being victimized, stigmatized, her mother said. She told the court the principal had been more interested in keeping the pregnancy a secret than in her daughter's welfare or the welfare of the unborn child.

The daughter was a smaller, softer version of her mother, but just as articulate and just as sure that an injustice had been done to her. She liked the school, she said, she had a good relationship with all of her teachers, she expected to go to university after her final year. She told the court about her worry when she thought she might be pregnant, how she hoped she would have a miscarriage and wondered if she could get away and have an abortion without anyone discovering. When her mother found out, she said, she told her that all the family would support her. Her father had been upset for a few days, but he said nothing bad to her.

The principal was new, she said, she had replaced a nun who had run the school for years. She was young and everybody liked her. So she was not afraid when she was called into the office. But she was very surprised, the girl told the court, when she was informed that she could not come back that term. It was a few days later that the principal told her mother that the girl would not be allowed back to the school the following year. She was shocked by this and hurt, the girl said. She didn't want to go out and began to feel ashamed and depressed.

She told counsel for the school that she knew what she had done was wrong. And she agreed that it was a bad example for younger girls, especially in a Catholic school. She had told everyone she was sorry, she said. No one wanted to expel the boy, she said, although some people knew who he was. She felt being expelled from the school stigmatized her.

He had spent three days listening to the case. The principal could only have been in her late twenties. She, too, was calm, assured and articulate. She was employed to run a Catholic school, she said. It was an educational establishment, but with a very specific ethos. She was prepared to forgive anyone a transgression, she said, and it was for God, not her, to judge, but she had to protect the school's ethos. There were, she told the court, great pressures on the girls in a changing world, but some things were still not acceptable to her as principal, to her board of management or to the majority of the parents. She had the right to decide if a girl should be expelled, and she had decided to exercise that right.

Parents who had children in the school spoke for both sides. Some said the girl should be forgiven and treated as a normal student in her final year. Others said a teenage pregnancy should not be looked upon as normal or acceptable, and allowing the girl to return to school would have an abiding effect on her fellow students.

Eamon was aware as the case went on that the costs were rising, and if the girl and her family lost, it would be a great financial blow to them. He was disturbed by the case, which was widely reported on radio, television, and in the newspapers. He remembered how calm the young girl had been, how vulnerable. He realized this was one of the few cases he had heard where both sides were clearly telling the truth and were not afraid of the truth. All the witnesses were sincere; no one wished to hide anything.

He listened carefully to the counsel's submissions about various articles of the Constitution, but there was no argument about facts or truth, guilt or innocence. In the end he was not the legal arbiter, because there were so few legal issues at stake. Most of the issues raised in the case were moral: the right of an ethos to prevail over the right of an individual. Basically, he was being asked to decide how life should be conducted in a small town. He smiled to himself at the thought and shook his head.

As he worked on the judgment, he realized more than ever that he had no strong moral views, that he had ceased to believe in anything. But he was careful in writing the judgment not to make this clear. The judgment was the only one that he could have given: it was cogent, well argued and, above all, plausible.

He went to the window again and stood there looking out. How hard it was to be sure! It was not simply the case and the questions it raised about society and morality, it was the world in which these things happened that left him uneasy, a world in which opposite values lived so close to each other. Which could claim a right to be protected?

He went to his bookshelves and took down the sacred text: *Bunreacht na hEireann,* the Irish Constitution, which contained the governing principles to which the law was subject. The preamble was clear about the Christian nature of the State; it specifically referred to the Holy Trinity. He thought about it again, how the school had a duty to defend Christian principles, and indeed a right to do so, under its own articles of association and also under the general guidance of the Constitution.

Surely these rights and duties were greater than any rights a single individual, whose presence in the school might undermine the school's ethos and principles, could lay claim to?

His tipstaff came with tea. He began to think again. He wrote down three words on a notepad: *charity, mercy, forgiveness.* These words had no legal status—they belonged firmly to the language of religion—but they had a greater bearing on the case than any set of legal terms. Opposite them he wrote three other words: *transgression, sin, scandal.* He sighed.

One other matter began to preoccupy him. The family, according to the Constitution, was the basic unit in society. He read the words in the Constitution: "a moral institution possessing inalienable rights, antecedent and superior to all positive law." What was a family? The

Constitution did not define a family, and at the time it was written in 1937 the term was perfectly understood: a man, his wife, and their children. But the Constitution was written in the present tense; it was not his job to decide what certain terms—he wrote *certain terms* in his note-pad, underlined it and wrote uncertain terms below that—such as *the family* had meant in the past. It was his job to define and redefine these terms now. Could not a girl and her child be a family? And if they were, did the girl have rights arising from her becoming a mother, thus creating a family, greater than the rights of any institution?

He thought about it for a while and the consternation it would cause among his colleagues, a broadening of the concept of the family. The girl would have to win then, and the school lose. The idea seemed suddenly plausible, but it would need a great deal of thought and research. It had not been raised as a possibility by counsel for the girl and her mother. Lawyers, he thought, knew he was not the sort of judge who would entertain such far-fetched notions in his court.

If he were another person he could write the judgment, but as eleven o'clock grew near he knew the verdict he had written out on his foolscap pages was the one he would deliver, and it would be viewed by his colleagues as eminently sensible and well reasoned. But he was still unhappy about the case because he had been asked to interpret more than the law, and he was not equipped to be a moral arbiter. He was not certain about right and wrong, and he realized this was something he would have to keep hidden from the court.

The downstairs corridors of the Four Courts were like some vast marketplace. He had to push his way through the passage leading to the side door of his court.

"The courtroom is packed, my lord," his tipstaff said.

"Are we ready then?" he asked.

He tried to act as businesslike as possible when he came into the courtroom and everybody stood up. He sat down, arranged his papers in front of him, put on his reading glasses, and consulted with the clerk, learning that there were several barristers seeking injunctions. He tried to deal with them promptly, realizing that, if he hurried, he could be finished by one o'clock, which meant he could be in Cush by four, or half past four, and if the weather was warm enough he could have a swim. He told the clerk he was ready to begin the judgment. He surveyed the court for a moment: The press benches were full as he had expected, and the public benches were also full. He knew this judgment would be news. It would be carried on the radio, and there would probably be editorials in the newspapers. He would certainly be attacked in *The Irish Times*. As he settled down to read the judgment, sure now of his conclusions, he thought about how ill-informed and ignorant the comment would be, and how little of the processes of law the writers would understand.

He did not intend his judgment to be dramatic, but he wished to set out the facts first, clearly and exactly. The argument at times, he knew, was close and dense and it would be difficult for most people in the court to follow, but a great deal of it was clear. After half an hour, when he had set out the facts and paused for a drink of water, he was aware that no one in the Court knew which side he was about to come down on. He could feel the tension, and the few times he looked up he could see them watching him carefully. He caught the mother's eye only once: She had the resigned look, he felt, of someone who knew that she was going to lose. People would have warned her he was not a judge who would rule in her favor. He avoided eye contact with the girl.

As he read on and came near the passage that would make the result clear, he found he was enjoying the tension and noticed he had begun to speak more distinctly, but he stopped himself and went back to the rigorous monotone he had adopted at the beginning.

A murmur started in the court as soon as it became clear that he had decided in favor of the school; from the bench it sounded like the murmur in a film, and he felt he should bang the desk with a gavel and shout, "Order in the court," but he continued as though there had not been a sound.

When he had finished, counsel for the school was on his feet immediately, his face flushed with victory. He was looking for costs. There was no choice; he could delay it until the new term, but it would be pointless and he wanted to have done with the case. The costs would be high, he listened to the submission from the other side. When he looked over he saw the mother and father were holding each other, and both were looking up at him as though afraid.

"Costs follow the event, and I see no reason why it should be different on this occasion," he said. The mother began to cry. Although he had awarded costs against her, he thought she would probably not have to pay all of them. He wondered as he gathered up his papers if she would appeal, but he thought not; he had based a great deal of his judgment on matters of fact rather than law, and the Supreme Court could not dispute many of his findings. She would not have much chance of winning an appeal, he felt.

Back in his chambers he went to the telephone immediately.

"I'm ready now," he said as soon as Carmel answered.

"We're going to pick up Niamh in Rathmines. She's decided to come down with us today. She's taking the carry cot and all the things so we'll need to collect her," Carmel said.

"I thought she wasn't coming," he said.

"She's finding it very hard," Carmel said, as though he had complained about her coming.

"I'll be there in half an hour," he said. He sat down at his desk and put his head in his hands. He could feel the sweat pouring down his back and his heart beating fast. He tried to control his breathing, to breathe calmly through his nose. He tried to relax. He remembered Niamh best when she was fourteen or fifteen, when she was still growing; even then she was tall for her age and interested in sports: hockey, tennis, swimming. They had pushed her too hard, Carmel said, forced her to study when she did not want to. She had studied social science when she failed to get the points for entry to study medicine. She had become a statistician, working on opinion polls and surveys of social change. She had become independent and distant from them until she was pregnant, when she and Carmel became closer, but he did not believe she had felt any affection for him since she was in her early teens.

He sat at his desk as his heart kept pounding. He wondered if he was going to have a heart attack, and he waited for a dart of pain, or a sudden tightness, but none came and slowly the heartbeat eased.

Niamh was standing at the door of a small house down a side street in Rathmines. She waved when he beeped the horn and shouted that she would not be long.

"I thought she was living in a flat," he said.

"Yes," Carmel said, "but there are three flats in the house and she knows the other people, they're all friends. They're very good to her, they baby-sit and help out."

Niamh came out of the front door with the baby. He noticed she had lost weight and let her hair grow longer. She smiled at them.

"I hope there's loads of space in the boot because I have to take the computer as well as the baby, and that's not forgetting the go-car and the cot." She handed the baby to Carmel. Eamon went into the hall, brought out the cot and put it in the boot.

"The computer will have to go on the back seat," he said. "Are you sure you need it?"

She went past him without answering. He carried a suitcase and put it into the boot. He stood there then looking at the baby, who looked back at him sullenly and curiously, fixing on him as something new and strange. Suddenly the baby began to cry, and continued to roar as they arranged the go-car on the roof-rack and set off through Ranelagh and Donnybrook. "He's very big," he said after a while when the child had quieted down.. "He's much bigger than I expected him to be." He looked behind at the child, who began to cry again.

"It's better maybe if you don't look at him when he's like that," Niamh said.

He knew as they drove past Bray that if they turned on the radio they would get the 3 o'clock news, which would probably report on the judgment. Carmel would want to know about it, she would want to discuss his reasons for ruling in favor of the school, she would go away and think about it and want to discuss it further. With Niamh in the house it would be worse. He realized that he would prefer if they never found out about it. It would be difficult to explain.

"Who else is living in the house with you?" he asked Niamh. There had been silence in the car for some time. Both women told him to keep his voice down.

"The baby's asleep," Niamh said.

At Arkiow he took a detour to avoid the traffic in the town. It was close to four o'clock, and it was only now that he became relaxed enough to enjoy the good weather, the clear light over the fields, and the heat he knew would persist for at least two more hours, despite the clouds banked on the horizon. When they passed Gorey, the baby woke and began to make gurgling sounds.

"You should teach him 'The Croppy Boy,'" he said and laughed to himself as they passed a sign for Oulart. Niamh said she would have to change his nappy, so they stopped the car and got out. He walked up and down taking in the heat as the two women busied themselves around the child, who had begun to cry again.

When they reached Blackwater, Carmel said she wanted to stop to get some groceries and to order *The Irish Times* for the duration of their stay. The baby was asleep again, and he and Niamh sat in the seat without speaking. He closed his eyes and opened them again: In all the years there had been hardly any changes in the view from here up the hill. Each building was a separate entity, put up at a different time. Each roof was different, ran at a different angle, was made of different material: slate, tile, galvanized. He felt that he could be any age watching this scene, and experienced a sudden illusion that nothing in him had changed since he first saw these buildings.

They drove toward the sea at Ballyconnigar and then turned at the handball alley to Cush. There were potholes on the narrow road, and he had to drive carefully to avoid them.

"What's for dinner?" he asked.

"I'm not making any more dinners," Carmel said and laughed.

"I hope you can cook, Niamh," he said.

"Niamh is an excellent cook," Carmel said.

"It's time men pulled their weight," Niamh said dryly.

There was always that moment when he saw the sea clearly, when it took up the whole horizon, its blue and green colors frail in the afternoon light. The road was downhill from then on. He drove along the sandy road, saluting a few people as he passed.

"I want to unload really quickly," he said as he stopped the car beside the house, "because I want to go for a swim before the sun goes in."

"I'd love to go for a swim too," Niamh said.

"I'll take the baby if you both empty the car," Carmel said.

Niamh had gone to change, and he stood waiting for her. There was a sweet, moist smell from the high grass in front of the house. He was tired and felt the burden of the day in his back muscles and his eyes. Suddenly he looked up, and his eye caught the rusty red paint on the galvanized iron of the gate. He liked the color, and it seemed familiar as he stood there and took in the scene: the rutted lane, the tufts of grass clinging to the sandy soil of the ditch, and the sound of a tractor in the distance. He stood there for a moment fixing on nothing in particular, letting each thing in the landscape seep toward him, as he tried to rid himself of everything that had happened that day.

Down on the strand they could see as far as Curracloe. Niamh wore only a light dress over her swimming suit, so she was already in the water while he was still undressing. When he took off his shoes he felt an instant release as though a weight had been lifted from him. Most of the strand was in shadow. He left his clothes on a boulder of dried marl and walked toward the sunlight on the fore-shore, stepping gingerly over the small, sharp stones which studded the sand.

The water was cold; Niamh waved to him from way out. He watched her long, thin arms reach up from the water as she swam parallel to the shore. He was tempted, as usual, to turn back, but he waded in farther, jumping to avoid a wave, and then he dived in and swam hard out, gliding over each swell as it came. He turned and put his head back, letting it rest on the cold, blue water, and opening his eyes to stare up at the sky. He breathed in deeply and floated on the waves, relaxed now and quiet. He curled back toward the water after a while, and swam farther out, each movement half instinct, half choice.

He cast his eye down the coast and noticed as he turned that a family was moving slowly up the strand toward the gap, carrying rugs and babies, struggling as they reached the cliff. He watched Niamh wading out and drying herself. She waved to him. No one else would come until the morning, except maybe a tractor using the strand as a short cut. He was tired now; the swimming would be easier the next day and the day after that. He changed to a dog paddle, which consumed less energy than the breaststroke. A cloud passed over the sun and left him in shadow so that he could feel a cold edge to the wind on his face. He turned again and floated, keeping his eyes closed for as long as he could, not knowing whether the water was taking him in or out. For a few seconds he forgot himself, sustained by the rise and fall of the waves and the knowledge that it would carry him as long as he relaxed and remained at peace.

As soon as he arrived back at the house he knew that Carmel and Niamh had been listening to the six-thirty news.

"Well, you were busy this morning," Niamh said.

"Was it on the news?" he asked, as if it were a routine matter.

"Do you think I should be expelled as well?" she asked.

"Your father's on his holidays, Niamh," Carmel said.

"That's not what you said before he came in. My father thinks unmarried mothers shouldn't be allowed to go to school," she laughed bitterly.

"What exactly is biting you?" he asked.

"That poor girl. How could it be right to expel her and never let her back?"

"Read the judgment and find out," he said.

"Did you bring it with you?" she asked.

"Of course I didn't."

"I think it's a disgrace, that's what I think," Niamh said. "It's an outrage."

"But you would think that, wouldn't you?

"I know about it. I know what it's like to be a woman in this country, and I know what it's like to have a child here."

"And I suppose you're a legal expert as well."

They had supper in silence, which was broken only by the whimpering of the baby. He faced the window and noticed the first throbbing rays of the lighthouse glinting in the distance. He wanted to ask Carmel what she had said about him and his judgment before he came in, but he realized he could gain nothing by doing so.

"Do you want more tea?" Carmel asked him.

"Yes, please," he said. He tried to make his voice sound neutral, as though he was not annoyed with them. He was too tired now to want any further argument. He sat at the table as they cleared away the dishes.

"We're going to take Michael for a walk," Carmel said to him. "Are you staying here?"

"Yes," he said.

"Are you all right?" she put her hand on his shoulder.

"I'm tired," he said. "I'm glad to be here."

He stood up and walked into their bedroom and rummaged through the suitcases until he found a book. He lay down on the bed, but as soon as he opened the book he knew he was too tired to read. He knew he would sleep. He took off his jacket and his shoes and rested on his side, facing away from the window.

She woke him when she turned on the bedside lamp. He felt heavy and tired as he turned toward her.

"It's all quiet now," she said. "You were fast asleep."

"Is it late?"

"It's after ten. You were on the news again. Not you, but a report about you."

"Nothing they haven't said before."

"The Irish Council for Civil Liberties—Niamh says that Donal is a member—have issued a statement."

"Our son and our daughter," he said and laughed.

"They're fine people, both of them," Carmel said.

"I suppose I'm the one who's wrong?"

"No, you're all right too," she stood over him and smiled. "After a few days here you'll be fine, but I don't understand your judgment. It seems wrong to me."

She lay down beside him, not bothering to take off her shoes.

"I'm tired too," she said, as she turned toward him and put her arms around him. "I don't know why I'm so tired."

Couple kills

David Vernon

I wake up at 2 A.M. and my boyfriend, Herve, is gone. The place beside me, the spot we nestled into together at 11 that night, is still warm. We watched some cable movie about killer lizards, then the news just to hear the weather. More rain is coming this weekend, the newscaster promised. That song, "It Never Rains in California," a scratchy record, a pre–El Niño, destroyed-ozone-layer oddity. I wake up to tell Herve about my dream, a dream that is crumbling in my memory as seconds pass. All I can remember of it now is that God was angry about Happy Meals, so it rained for ten years. I wanted to tell Herve, but he's gone. I don't even have to look around the apartment. I know he's taking one of his mysterious late-night walks in the hills. Third time this week.

Herve and I have been together three years, two of which we've lived together. He likes to take walks in the middle of the night. I didn't know this about him until we moved in together. We'd had sleepovers before, so I don't know why it surprised me, when we moved into our sublet in the Hollywood Hills, to find out that he is a night person and I'm a morning person. He's creative and stirred by the mysteries of the night, the richness of darkness. He says the world makes sense to him when it is completely still.

I'm all logic. I exemplify the benefits of a dependable eight hours of sleep. Ten on Sundays. I have faith in maxims, the early bird catching the worm, early to bed, early to rise, those kinds of things. I feel most useful to the human race after a fruit smoothie and twenty minutes of the *Today* show.

I throw on a T-shirt because it's chilly, but can't find where I discarded my underwear because the room swims in darkness. So I walk downstairs half naked to make a cup of tea. I look out the windows as I enter the living room. It's not raining yet, but the wind is bullying all the trees outside. Just slapping the hell out of them. Wood wind chimes from some neighbor's house to the right and someone else's metal wind chimes from the left make it sound like the Los Angeles Philharmonic is getting slaughtered out there. Then, for a moment I think I hear my name being called. *Joshua. Joshua.* Then I realize it's the pig. A neighbor of ours has a pet pig. It's not legal, but the owner is one of those good-looking actors who has been playing a high school senior for the past eight years on some hit TV show. People tend to look the other way.

I sit down on the couch to wait for Herve, although I've never quite felt comfortable in this apartment by myself. It's a two-story house up in the Hollywood Hills. Near the actual Hollywood sign. In fact, just trees and hills separate us from the *H* in Hollywood elevated above our heads. Wobbling. We're subletting it from a German lesbian couple named Gretyl and Lissel. (The reference is lost on Herve. He's never seen *The Sound of Music*.) Gretyl and Lissel are traveling somewhere. I think Portugal this year. Lissel makes wood art. Art made out of wood. Based on how many pieces are on display in this house I'd say it's slightly more than a hobby, it's a bad habit. Twisty lacquered branches made into wall lamps. Wood candleholders. Wood frames for mirrors.

As I settle in on the couch I remember another part of my dream. Just before God decides to send the ten-year flood our way, I am asked my opinion.

"What do you think I should do?" God asks. When I don't reply, God adds, "You can stop this by giving me one good reason. One good reason why I shouldn't."

And it's not that I don't have a reason. Even given my limited level of awareness in the dream I still had plenty of reasons. The beach. Sex. (Rabid masculinity, but I wouldn't say this to God.) E.M. Forster. Coffee shop BLTs. The first few bars of "Rhapsody in Blue," the last episode of *The Mary Tyler Moore Show.* Monkeys.

Monkeys for crying out loud, who doesn't love monkeys?

But in the dream I couldn't speak to God because I'd lost my use of language. I opened my mouth, but nothing came out. I kept trying to heave out words but found myself only able to vomit out letters, letters that fell in a pool in front of me. Finally I noticed it had already started to rain, so I ran for shelter.

I wanted to wake Herve and tell him this. I wanted him to comfort me. I wanted him to hear my voice, to acknowledge I still had one. I wanted him to whisper to me in a voice full of recognition and belief, I hear you baby. I hear you.

It's 4 A.M. and Herve's still not here, so I retreat back to our bed. Later this night he will awaken me with ice-cold feet, the chill of his invigorated breath on my back. His morning beard, misted with dew that he will brush along my neck to mark his return home.

The next morning I'm bathing when Herve gets up to take a piss. His eyes are half open. He wants to do this without too much effort so he'll be able to go back to sleep.

"Late one," I say.

He looks around while holding his ground in front of the toilet. "Um-hmm."

"Want to join me?" I ask. The scent of eucalyptus from my bath parts for a moment and I take a whiff of Herve. He smells gamy and sour. "God, what were you doing last night?"

"Walking," he says as he flushes the toilet.

"Nowhere near that actor's house, I hope," I joke. There are all kinds of rumors about the actor, and Herve and I have seen him enter his house with plenty of young women as well as a string of hunky-looking guys. I expect Herve to jump in with a quick denial or sarcastic comeback, but instead there is a pause. I try to categorize it. Is it a pregnant pause? A Pinterarian one? A nervous silence?

Herve kneels down next to the cold porcelain bathtub. "What makes you say that?" There's an edge to his voice I've never heard before.

"Humor," I say. "Humor and a slight desire to know where you go to in the middle of the night. That's what made me say it."

Herve looks at me. "Want me to shave your neck?" he asks before picking up the razor. He picks up a snowball of foam and spreads it across the nape of my neck. "I just needed to go for a walk," Herve says, delicately brushing the razor against my skin. "Plus, if I even tried to show up at that actor's house, I'm sure I'd have to kick a few bimbos, a lifeguard or two, and that pig of his out of his bed before I could even get close to him." In five or six strokes of the razor, Herve is finished.

I find all this intimate grooming between couples very sensual. There's something primal about it, something very *National Geographic*. For Herve, though, this thorough grooming is essential. He detests body hair. Being a hirsute fellow, he shaves twice a day and gets himself body-waxed once a month. "Our ability to speak and body-wax," Herve has said, "is what distinguishes us from the beast."

"I'm having dinner with Sammy tonight after class," I say.

"My apologies," Herve says, standing up and turning his gaze to the mirror.

"I was going to ask if you wanted to join us, but I guess not. I don't understand why you don't get along."

"He doesn't like me." Herve's strong baritone voice echoes in the bathroom. "He barely even acknowledges me when I see him. I'm sure he thinks you could do better."

"He doesn't think that," I say a little too broadly. A little too definitively. I think back on all the conversations Sammy and I have had over the years about relationships. Sammy is part best friend, part historian. He remembers the name of every man I've dated and all the components of the relationship, the more ridiculous the better. For the record, he *doesn't* like Herve. He's unable to get past the brutishness of Herve's looks, to see the gentleness of this amazing man. Sammy is not just being a friend when he says I'm too good for Herve 'cause there are plenty of men I've dated that Sammy has thought were too good for me.

"Tell him I said hi," Herve says. He comes over and gives me a kiss. "I don't know why you're taking that class anyway. Why do you need to know Spanish?" Herve's family is from the Dominican

Republic, yet he claims not to know more than fifty words in Spanish. I tried to convince him to take this class with me, but he begged off, stating he's uninterested in learning the language. I have a difficult time comprehending this because if I had this other language, this inner language bursting about my DNA, I'd want to know everything about it. I'm only in my fourth week, but already I've pulled up words and phrases that I whisper to Herve in our bed once the lights are out. *Tu eres muy guapo. No dejes que los insectos de la cama te piquen.* (This last expression completely mystifies him, since he's never heard of a bedbug.) I talk to him in Spanish hoping to spark something within him. He usually answers back in English. *I love you too, Joshua.*

"I'm taking this class so I can understand the ways of your people," I say, joking.

"But dahlin'," Herve says in his best French accent, something between Louis Jourdan and Pepe Le Pew, "Ve both speek ze language ov loove." Then he goes back to bed.

The day at work is pretty mundane. (I work in retail; I'll leave it at that.) But the mood of the dream stayed with me, and I felt unsettled, foreshadowed somehow. The loss of language. That possibility terrifies me. It's happened to me twice in my life. Once when I was in sixth grade and was about to give a report in front of the class on the formation of volcanoes. I'd researched and practiced my report until I could recite it in my sleep. But as soon as I stood up, my ability to communicate vanished, disappeared like a debt-ridden tenant into the night. It wasn't that I had forgotten my report; I could hear the tape of it replaying shrilly in my mind. I just opened my mouth and nothing came out.

The second time this happened was five years ago after this guy I was dating abruptly broke off our relationship. Johan and I met shortly after he moved here from Belgium. Things were going great. We were talking about moving in together. We bought a painting together. Then in bed, after sex, he said, "That was great, I don't think we should do it again." After a brief, unrevealing conversation,

I left his house and walked home in a daze. It wasn't that I was upset about Johan. He was too tall and a horrible cook. But at this point in my life I was tired of dating, bored of these wonderful little wind-falls of men. All promising. All disappointing. I had started dating only foreign-born men, but found they too disappointed but in dif-ferent languages. Until Herve came along.

But that night, on the walk home from Johan's house, I went into a liquor store, preparing to buy a bottle of something cheap and nasty. When the clerk asked me what I wanted, again, there were no words in my head. At first I couldn't tell the man behind the count-er what I wanted to buy. Then I decided I needed to tell him some-thing, anything. My name, my address, my recipe for guacamole. To hear my voice. To unclutter my mind. But nothing would come. Not a single word.

That is one of the reasons I'm studying Spanish. Now, two lan-guages you can't lose. English is my day-to-day language. Spanish can be a spare. With two languages I'm covered. Three if you count the language of love.

My Spanish class meets Tuesday evenings at a nearby community college as part of their adult education program. There are ten other people in the class. Being in our early thirties, Sammy and I are eas-ily the youngest students in this group. The oldest is a couple in their late sixties who are planning a trip to Mexico later this year. The most interesting person in the group, though, is a woman in her early fifties known by a small circle of people as the Ring Toss Lady. The Ring Toss Lady is one of Los Angeles' more talked-about odd-ities. She's tall and thin and wears seven-inch platform shoes that give her the look of a mini skyscraper. She wears wraparound sheets of fabric that are folded around her, then pinned at the top. Her biggest selling point though is her hair. She greases it and wears it pointing straight in the air (hence her nickname). The Ring Toss Lady walks the side streets of the nicest neighborhoods in Hancock Park. It's rumored that she's a millionaire. It's rumored that she invented dental floss. Whatever the truth is, she's in my Spanish class, and even though she doesn't associate with anyone outside the class, I'm thrilled to get this close to her. I won't reveal her real name because it's nothing as interesting as her nickname.

The class is taught by Señora Bartlett, a gringa with big, frizzy auburn hair. Señora Bartlett's husband is having an affair. The class is not supposed to know this, but we do. In fact, we talk about it all the time before and after class. We speculate on what type of women would mess around with Señor Bartlett. We wonder whether Señor and Señora Bartlett are going to *divorsear*. The married couple in the class thinks they'll work it out. Sammy thinks they'll call it quits. The Ring Toss Lady keeps her opinions to herself and just hums when we're talking about it. I do know that Señora Bartlett must be making some progress. Last week she had us conjugating murderous verbs. (*Matar.* To kill. *Cortar.* To cut. *Destruir.* To destroy. *Decapitar.* To decapitate.) This week we're back to reading about the beach time adventures of young Juan y Delores.

The last fifteen minutes of class are open for discussion, either about the Spanish language or the Spanish culture.

"Señora Bartlett, who is Llorona?" asks a real estate agent named Joanne.

"It's pronounced LA-RONA," the Señora says. "Where did you hear this?"

"I was at a corner store and tried speaking Spanish to the man who works there. He asked me if I'd ever heard of this Llorona person. I couldn't really understand what he was talking about."

"Llorona is an old wives' tale. She's a ghost. She killed her children, and when the moon is full you're supposed to hear her crying out for them."

"Is it a cultural myth?" Luci, an Armenian woman in the class asks, taking notes.

"*Exactamente,*" the Señora exclaims. "It's what mothers tell their kids—if you don't go to sleep the Llorona will get you."

"Like the Chupacabra?" the Ring Toss Lady asks.

"Chupa-what?" the old married man asks, echoing my sentiments.

"ChupaCABRA," the Ring Toss Lady says, sounding irritated.

"He's a creature reported in Puerto Rico. He sucks the blood out of farm creatures, leaving their deflated carcasses behind."

"Another old wives' tale," Señora Bartlett says. "Like the Boogie Man. We all grew up with them. It's what our families used to keep us in line." The Señora looks around the room a little too earnestly and tries to open up the conversation to the class. "What was your family's version of the bogeyman?"

"Satan," the married man says.

"My family is from Norway," the man's wife answers. "My parents used to tell me about these malevolent little trolls that lived in the hills. They ate bad children."

The Señora looks at me and waits for an answer. This is one of those moments that I feel unbearably white. For as a kid I had an unexplainable terror of Ed McMahon. Just looking at him made me shake in terror. One day I saw a commercial with Ed McMahon walking up to someone's house with a Publishers Clearing House envelope and ringing their doorbell. The idea of it made me burst into tears. That puffy man with that scraggly gray hair and those desperate eyes. It still gives me shivers. All my family had to do to get me to listen was threaten to call the Publishers Clearing House phone number. "They'll send him right over," my mother promised. "Ed McMahon in person." Once my father got on the phone and pretended to have a full conversation with Ed McMahon until I relented and gave in to whatever it was they wanted me to do.

"No Ed, we've got it under control. You don't have to come over," my father spoke into the phone while staring at me. "Josh says he's going to be good. Don't worry, though. We'll call you if we have any more problems with him."

Señora Bartlett is staring at me, waiting to answer, and I just shrug my shoulders and she goes on to the next student.

After class, over dinner I tell Sammy about the weird moment with Herve in the bathroom. We're at Zankou Chicken, a Middle-Eastern dive on Normandie Boulevard. The smell of dead chicken flesh rubbed in garlic fills the air.

"So you accused him of having an affair, and what was his reaction?"

I try to replay the moment in my mind. "Startled," I say. "Almost angry."

"Something is absolutely up," Sammy says breathlessly. There are the kinds of people who find this kind of conversation embarrassing and degrading and others who find it invigorating. Sammy raises the bar as one of the latter. "Where there's smoke, there's fire."

"No fire. There's no fire here, you understand. Don't go around telling anyone there's fire."

"He's got those eyes, you know. *Ojos intensos.* I don't even like looking at Herve. I feel he's trying to seduce me or something. And I'm never wrong about eyes."

Sammy takes a huge bite of a chicken thigh, leaving his mouth masked with a ring of grease. Sammy is tall with shoulder-length blond, rock-star hair. He only eats messy like this when we're on the east side of town.

"I know you're always right about eyes. If eyes were the only thing you had to contend with in a man, you'd be in at least one successful relationship by now."

"Do you really think he's having an affair with that actor?" Sammy asks.

Sammy is totally starstruck, and I'm sure the thought of anyone, even my boyfriend, sleeping with a movie star just sends him. I don't say the name of the actor because I honestly can't keep up with all those syndie boys. Sammy doesn't say the name of the actor because frankly it would reveal his level of fascination. I don't want to even know what part of town he drives to, to buy his *Teen Beat* magazines.

"He does take a lot of walks in that area at night," I admit. "He even knows the name of the pig. Toulouse." By now I'm all worked up about this.

"Well, he's either sleeping with the boy or the pig," Sammy says.

"Thanks. As always, you've just made me feel so much better," I say, eyeing the front door.

Sammy looks into my eyes. He can sense I'm unsettled by all of this, and I'm hating him for all of his channeled cynicism. "Look,"

Sammy says, clearing his voice. His breath is flesh and garlic. "Who knows what, if anything, is going on. The main thing is that you two communicate. When I was having all those problems with Robbie, I found this book called *Couple Skills*. It's by this guy, Dr. Marver. It covers absolutely anything a gay couple might be dealing with."

I stop at my neighborhood bookstore. The clerk tells me they only have one used copy of *Couple Skills* by Dr. Louden Marver, which I purchase and plan on reading that evening, but as soon as I get home I find Herve sitting on our front stoop, his hands cradling his head.

"What's wrong, *mi amor?*"

"I talked to my mom."

He doesn't have to say much more than that. Herve's mother still lives in the Dominican Republic. As far as I know, he only talks to her every two or three months, but when he does it sends him into a dark mood.

"What is she upset about?"

"You wouldn't understand, Joshua."

"Is she upset because she hasn't seen you for a while? Is that it?" I sit next to Herve. "Why don't you have her come visit us? I'd love to meet her. We could chip in for a plane ticket."

The moon beams bright overhead. "It's so complicated," he tells me. "There's no way you could understand her. Or all of this...family stuff."

As I look at my boyfriend, I'm reminded how beautiful and how comfortable he looks outdoors. Some people look best in a well-lit living room, on a white couch, framed by a chenille throw. Herve looks at home outside, barefoot, his complexion favoring the moonlight and the lush greenery all around him. He grew up in the hills, he has told me. He grew up being connected to the land. "Or if she doesn't want to travel, we could go there," I suggest. "You haven't been back home since I've known you."

"There is a reason for that," Herve says. "I moved to Los Angeles to get away from all of that."

There is a pause, and then I realize that's all he's going to say about this.

At 3 in the morning I wake up and Herve is gone again. The space next to me in bed isn't even warm. I go downstairs, make myself a cup of tea, and settle into our easy chair. I find the book I purchased earlier in the evening and pull it out of the brown paper bag.

The clerk at the bookstore told me this was a used copy, but even that statement didn't prepare me for the sorry state this paperback was in. I would have checked it when I made the purchase, but I was in such a hurry to get home. The spine of the book is broken and held together by uneven pieces of gray tape and in the lower right hand corner of the book a chunk of the cover is missing, as if it had been bitten and chewed off. Someone had taken marker in hand and blacked out the first letter of the second word of the title, leaving it to read *Couple kills*. Passages of the book are underlined, and in some places comments are handwritten in the borders. Some of the comments are just words, like "**Ha!**" or "**Yeah, right!**" In a section titled, "Moving In. Is it time?" a sentence is underlined. "Before moving in together it is important to find out whether the two of you have mutual interests you both can enjoy over the years." Next to this sentence the previous owner wrote, "**Yes! Demolishing my already low self-esteem!**" A few chapters later another paragraph is underlined. "In your relationship, compromise should be your third willing partner." In the border someone wrote, "**No, that was Mitch.**"

I decide that it's *mas tarde* and put the book back in its brown paper wrapper and go to bed.

That weekend Herve and I attend a party hosted by our friends Leslie and Patrick. A buffet dinner is served at 7, so Herve and I arrive at 8. We're both vegetarians and don't want to complicate the situation for our friends. It's a game party, and various board games are spilled across the room. Leslie greets us and gets the attention of the room. "Everyone! This is Josh Blanchard and Herve Bustamente.

They're a couple, so hands off!" The other guests look up and make small acknowledgments, but they're all too involved in their games to pay us much attention. "You have your choice of Don't Spill the Beans, Mystery Date over there, and in that corner is Mousetrap. Leslie has every game from her childhood. She found boxes of them in her parents' garage when they moved to Arizona three years ago, and since then this party has become an annual event.

I take Herve by the hand and lead him to the couch. "We're just going to get comfortable for now," I say. Truth is, this room full of thirty- and forty-year-olds regressed into slumber-party mode is something I have to ease into. Gales of laughter come from the Mystery Date group, where one of the players opened the white plastic door and found herself face to face with "the dud." Herve looks at me and winces. He'd rather be just about anywhere but here. He's not a party person, and he didn't grow up playing board games. Sometimes I try to imagine his childhood in the Dominican Republic. Living on a farm. The middle child of a big family. Hard work during the day and big gleeful family dinners. Sort of like a Latin *Heidi* movie. But Herve has told me it was nothing like that at all.

A few beers later we get suckered into some games. I'm playing Clue while I see Herve across the room plodding his way through the game of Life. Every time I look his way I see that his plastic car is empty. Not a good sign.

"You're not paying attention," Patrick yells at me after I roll the dice and move my Mrs. White back into the Study. Patrick and Leslie have been together five years. He's British and works in the mayor's office, so you wouldn't think he'd be a stickler for rules, but he is. "You've been in the Study four times now."

"I like the Study," I tell him. "It's my favorite room. I mean, look at it, all those books and that fireplace. That's a room worth going back to."

"But you'll never figure out who did it if you keep going back to the same room," the Korean woman playing Colonel Mustard protests.

Mrs. White. Professor Plum. Miss Scarlett. Colonel Mustard.

They can all go to hell for all I care. I hate this game. Plus the point
of the game is lost on me because I don't care who did it in what
room, with what instrument of torture. I want to know why. Why,
why, why.

Why, for instance, would Herve be having an affair? Could he
be bored with our relationship? With me? Sex with me? Hey, come
on. I'm still speaking ze language ov loove here. No need to leave
so soon.

An hour later the party has thinned out. Herve and I are both silly
drunk and are enjoying ourselves. Patrick brings out another round
of desserts, and Leslie suggests we play a game of charades. I shoot
that possibility down right away. There's something unnerving to me
about a room full of adults gesticulating wildly with their hands.

"How about the Name Game?" I suggest.

The group hesitates until I describe the parameters of the game.
They're either enthusiastic or they sense I'm going to keep explaining the rules until they all finally give in.

"Maybe a quick round," someone says, glancing at his watch.

The Name Game is similar to charades, but it uses words instead
of distorted body movements. Everyone writes down the names of
ten historical figures or fictional characters on separate slips of paper,
then drops them into a baseball cap. Each round, a person from one
of the teams picks a name from the hat and tries to explain to the
team who the person is. We break into groups, and I end up on a
team with Herve, Patrick, a pastry chief from Whittier, and the
Korean Colonel Mustard.

As everyone writes names on slips of paper, I decide to avoid the
names of people in the news and obscure movie stars. (No Janet
Reno. No Vera Hruba Ralston.) I want to show off my knowledge
of the Latin culture, so I jot down the names of several poets,
painters, and writers. But when it's my turn up for our team, I seem
to consistently pick the names I wrote out of the baseball cap. It's up
to me to have them guess who I'm talking about, and they're all
looking at me with blank faces. Finally, I pick out an easy one. "OK,"
I say to my team. "Frida Kahlo's husband." My hand is in the hat to

pick out the next slip of paper, but my team still hasn't answered the first question. "Frida Kahlo's husband," I repeat.

"Fred Kahlo?" Patrick answers.

"Give us another clue!" the Korean Colonel Mustard lady screams out.

"He painted murals. *Allegory of California.*" I look at Herve with a forced glare. He doesn't have the slightest idea who I'm talking about. Finally, with the clock ticking, I take desperate measures. "Last name is the same as Geraldo's."

"Rivera," the pastry chief pipes in.

"Right! And the first name...the first name is the same as if I were in de Mafia and I wanted you to put down de frozen waffle. I'd say, 'Leggo...'"

"De eggo?" Herve says.

"Put them together!"

"De Eggo. De Eggo Rivera?"

I'm not proud of it, but our team still got the point. On our team's next turn, Herve looked at his slip of paper, shaking his head and narrowing his eyes. "I have no idea who this is."

"Act it out!" the Korean Colonel Mustard screams out.

"De Eggo Rivera," someone from the other team yells.

Herve puts his hands on his hips and keeps staring at the slip of paper. He starts to throw his body into motion, then freezes. His head lifts up. "I can't do this one."

"Why not?"

"You have to do it," Patrick says.

"It's impossible." Herve's voice is trembling. "It's fucking wrong." He balls up the clue and tosses it across the room.

"What was it?"

"The Chucapica," Herve says.

"Who?" Leslie asks.

"Who wrote that?"

"Who do you think?" Herve asks, looking dead at me.

"I can't believe you guys don't know this one. He's this monster from Latin America. He's a goat sucker and—"

"Goats?"

"—he's got beady eyes—"

"You mean the Chupacabra?" the Korean Colonel Mustard says.

"Is it the Chupacabra? I thought it was Chucapica. I just learned about it from my Spanish class—"

"Either way, it's offensive," Herve hisses at me.

Leslie pops up from her seat. "Does anyone want to take some rigatoni home with them?" She knows how to rescue a dying party. It's in her genes. Hostess CPR. "There's some garlic bread too if anyone wants a bag."

Herve and I arrive home drunk and quiet from our evening out. He scales up the staircase with effort like he's climbing a mountain. I follow him. Upstairs he flops down on our bed. He's sweaty, and his hair is swirled-up and out of control. Like a black tornado. I ask him if he wants to sleep in separate rooms tonight. "Do what you like," he answers.

"What are you so mad about?"

Herve closes his eyes. "You embarrass me with all those Latin names, trying to impress everyone. It makes you look like a fool."

"So this is about the Chucapica," I say.

"Don't make fun of me. It's about all of them. The pronunciation." His head peaks up to look at me. "Your pronunciation is just horrible."

"I thought you found it sexy. It's such a beautiful language."

"Not the way you speak it," Herve says, before he looks down at his stomach. "I think I drank too much."

"Even the names are sexy. Octavio Paz. Isabel Allende."

Herve pulls himself down the bed slowly until my mouth is up against his ear. "Tell me the name of that painter."

"José Maria Sert," I whisper. I don't often get such a view of Herve's ear as his long black hair usually hides it. It's enormous. Almost abnormally large. "Carlos Amezcua," I say lightly. Herve vibrates and grinds on the bed. He groans.

"More." Herve rolls in delight once or twice, then lies still. In a minute he is snoring. I kiss him on the neck to see if he's coming back or not, but his body has already loosened its grip on the day. He's gone for the night.

I walk downstairs to close up the apartment, moving quickly past all the wood art. I'm about to turn off the light in the kitchen when I notice a flash of motion coming from the linoleum floor. It's a thick, bushy trail of ants starting from somewhere under the sink and leading up to the garbage can. We have a problem with ants, so Herve and I have to be careful about leaving food in the trash. For a moment I consider turning off the kitchen light, returning to bed and acting surprised in the morning. But do I really want nightmares of those little insects crawling on the floor, up the stairs, in my bed?

I stand over the trash can and nearly gag. A foul odor floods my lungs. Holding my breath, I dig my hand inside the bag. There's a tickling sensation on my forearm, and I spot two ants on me. My hands dig deeper in the bag until I find the culprit: a heavy white baggie tied together at the top. The contents are soft and spongy, and it's hard to get a grip on the bag. I open it slightly. There's a flash of red, and that's enough for me to drop the bag. Poosh. Lands on the floor like a water balloon. Sends red liquid. Blood. On the floor. I can't breathe. Or express it. Breathe. Ants flee from this tsunami. But come back. And there's all this stuff on the floor. Meat. Raw. A bone. White. Marrow. On the floor. Smells foul. Everywhere. On me. A voice. In my head. Speaks English. We don't eat meat. *Carne. Carne* is meat. Deep. Breath. Meat and *carne* and blood in a bag. On the floor. Two bones. I'm leaving this room. Going to the study. Whodunit in the kitchen. Mrs. White with *carne* on the floor.

I leave the kitchen for the living room. Four steps in, I remember there's blood on my Keds, so I slip them off and send them flying. In the darkness I locate the couch and slide into it. Shadows of wood art. I feel like I'm in a forest.

Who would have left that bag in our house? No one has the keys. Except for Sammy, who does eat meat. But not in someone else's kitchen. I backtrack the evening. I was at the gym. Came home and picked up Herve. Went for dinner. He didn't eat much. So he ate the meat? But it disgusts him. Why wouldn't he tell me? I keep circling around these facts, but they don't add up to anything. Then a most bizarre, vastly implausible possibility comes to town. One so ludicrous, I scream with laughter. Still, I go to the computer in the corner of the living room and turn it on. Hook up to AOL. The main page greets me. The local news story, "Is a storm heading our way?" Time disintegrates as I surf the Web. The blare of the screen, the veracity of it burns my eyes. And then I find what I'm looking for.

I hear Herve's groggy voice calling from the bedroom. "Joshua, what's going on?"

"Go back to sleep. I'll be there soon." I don't even take my gaze away from the computer. I can't believe what I'm reading.

IS HE A MISSING LINK, A FLIGHT OF THE IMAGI-NATION OR IS HE THE NEW MILLENNIUM'S BIGGEST NIGHTMARE? HE'S BEEN SEEN EVERYWHERE FROM MEXICO AND PUERTO RICO TO MIAMI, SAN ANTO-NIO, AND EVEN SAN FRANCISCO. THE CHUPACABRA (PRONOUNCED CHEW-PAH-KAHB-RAH) IS THE LAT-EST MYSTERY THAT SEEMS TO HAVE EVERYONE TALKING. SO FAR THE REPORTS HAVE ONLY INCLUDED ATTACKS ON ANIMALS (GOATS, COWS, CATS, EVEN HORSES), SO KEEP YOUR PETS LOCKED UP. WOULD THIS CREATURE KILL A HUMAN? DON'T BE THE FIRST TO FIND OUT.

At the bottom of the page was a link saying, "If you enjoyed this page, click here to visit Astra's guide to the top thirty places to meet and socialize with aliens."

I sat at the computer and took all of this in. You see, I've experienced several times throughout my life moments where I've driven head-on and collided with the truth. Looking at a family portrait one afternoon and realizing that the people I knew as Mom and Dad weren't my biological parents. I just knew it. There was the time when I was a kid and my best friend and I went to see the movie *The*

Towering Inferno. In one scene Robert Wagner has just had sex with his secretary, Susan Flannery. Susan walks around the room just wearing his business shirt. My friend went crazy. "Look at that. Isn't that amazing!" He asked me what I thought. "Beautiful," I said, "I bet it's Yves St. Laurent." My friend just stared at me with his mouth open. At that moment I knew my friend and I were different; he liked women and I liked clothing. Another crash with reality came years ago when Johan and I were playing Scrabble. Johan made a few points with the word *love*. At that point I realized the word *love* didn't refer to how I felt about this man.

All of those collisions were painful and unlikely. I didn't want any of them to be true, but as soon as I knew it, I knew it.

My boyfriend is the Chupacabra. Wildly impossible. But every single piece of the puzzle fits in place. Every cell in my body agrees. Knowing this somehow relaxes me. I feel a flood of emotions let loose, flushing out of my system. My boyfriend. Chupacabra. Becomes a mantra to me. Chupa-Cabra. Chupa-Cabra. The sound of train tracks. I nod off to an untroubled night's sleep.

That night I dream that the trail of ants has left the kitchen and made a beeline for the front door. There are streaks of blood from where they've made their exodus across my carpet. I follow the trail, open the front door, and step outside. First I see the biggest, whitest moon I've ever seen. The kind Spielberg tries to get away with. Then I look to the hills and see the Hollywood sign. The letters seem wobbly. Elastic. They move ever so slightly. They stretch. Then they sway from side to side like a meandering hula dancer. In the dream I'm smiling. In the dream I think this is just beautiful.

I awake in the morning to find Herve standing over me. He is drying his hands on a plaid dishrag that hangs from his pants pocket. Sunlight has bypassed the drapes and is infiltrating the room. I sit up and notice that Herve smells of disinfectant.

"You're up early," I say.

"About noon," my boyfriend, the Chupacabra, says to me, squinting his left eye. He's trying to figure out how much I've seen.

"Doing something in the kitchen?"

He half-smiles. "A bit. It was kind of a mess."

I nod. "I know. The dishes in the sink are kind of piling up."

"I did them."

"Thanks," I say. Herve passes me and starts up the stairs. I can see how relieved he is just in the lightness of his footsteps. "By the way, did you happen to get any of that blood off the floor?" I ask politely.

He stops, then walks back over to me. "I was wondering if you saw that. I went to that awful Pioneer market, and there was a mix-up with the bags. Someone got my bag of baking stuff, and I got this bag full of meat scraps. I was going to..."

"Stop."

"...take the stuff back..."

"You're making it worse." Herve looks at me with a blank face. "I figured it out."

"That I'm eating meat again? It's only every once in a while..."

"No. That you're the freaking Chupacabra, dickhead."

Herve looks stunned. He starts to say something but stops himself even before the first syllable crosses his mouth. Before my eyes he is transformed from my boyfriend who is vibrant and alive, to someone who has that sad look that people in photographs seem to have. He looks like the past. "So I guess this means we're over, huh?" he finally whispers.

"Well, I'd certainly say it changes the parameters of things."

"It's not like I lied to you about some infidelity. Or my age. Or my political affiliation. Jesus, Joshua, it's only some family background I haven't gotten around to divulging yet."

"Haven't gotten around? Just when were you going to get around to telling me? The day before your picture pops up on the cover of the *Weekly World News*?" I leap from the couch and pick up my backpack.

"Baby, don't go," Herve pleads.

"We're just not speaking the same language right now. I have to think about this. So you just...you just be the Chupacabra and I'll think about it, OK?"

I drive around the city aimlessly for the next hour trying to get my bearings. Soon I'm having a hard time reading the road signs and the billboards. Language is starting to blur and blend. I stop the car, find a phone, and call Sammy.

"I was just thinking of calling you," Sammy says when he hears my voice. "I've had quite the day. It started with an Angelyne sighting on Sunset Boulevard. Her pink Corvette was right next to mine at the streetlight. I opened my window and said, 'All right, Angelyne! Rock on.' Then I saw that guy, Melrose Larry Green, on the corner of Highland and Melrose waving to everyone. *Then,* I go to Ralphs, and two people ahead of me in the checkout line, you're never going to believe this. Judge Judy! Arguing with the checkout guy about some expired coupons. This has been the perfect L.A. day."

I hate to interrupt Sammy when he's in such a good mood, but I need to talk to someone about Herve. I feel dizzy and my chest feels tight. I tell Sammy everything, from the blood in the kitchen to the revelation at hand. At the end I'm out of breath.

"You always do this, Joshua," Sammy says after a moment of silence. "You always have to top whatever I've said. I have an odd day, and you have to have an even odder one. I have a few celebrity sightings. You have to be dating one."

I ask Sammy to put it down and try to help me with this. "I need some...what's the word. It's...it's *consejo* in Spanish. Some help. Advice. That's the word. I need advice."

"Has anything really changed?" Sammy asks. "Deep down, isn't he still the same Herve?"

"Maybe not," I say guardedly. "So you don't think I should break up with him?"

"Actually I do. But I'd suggest you break up with him whether you found out he was the Chupacabra or he won the Nobel Peace Prize. I've just never found him all that attractive."

☐   ☐   ☐

Several days pass in which Herve and I manage to keep out of each other's way. I've made a bed for myself in the living room, and even though there are times when we're both in the house we rarely bump into each other. The whole process is exhausting and ultimately too sad for words. I decide this has to end. One of us will have to move. I go to leave a note for Herve on the refrigerator, but he's beaten me to it.

Josh!
I've been trying to give you space, but I give up! I can't do it anymore. I'm sure if we talk we can work this whole thing out. I'll be waiting for you here after your class.
Your boyfriend, Herve

I arrive at school early that night, so I hang out in the library. There's a small population of kids sitting at the desks, piles of books stacked beside them. I have forty minutes to kill, so I wander over to the Occult section. I turn a quick corner around Biography and almost run dead-on into the Ring Toss Lady. She's wearing a maroon-colored draping along with maroon straight-legged polyester pants. I think I've startled her. She's clutching a book on Muhammad Ali and one on gardening and starts taking deep breaths. I apologize for nearly running into her and move on. Two aisles away I turn back and find her, still poking around the Biography section.

"Are you going to class tonight?"

She's wearing long rectangular streaks of violet blush. "Si,"

"I was wondering...in class you talked about the Chupacabra. What do you know about it?"

She considers my question. "Part man, part beast. I pity it." This is the most I've ever heard her speak, and I'm surprised by the cadences of her voice. She possesses a high, tentative voice, almost the type that men have when they try to imitate a woman's voice.

"Why pity?"

"Caught in between worlds. Hard to live in human's world. Hard to live in animal kingdom."

Not to mention the gay community, I think to myself. I thank the Ring Toss Lady and tell her I'll see her in class. Before I leave she stops me.

"Why are you asking about El Chupacabra, Señor Blanchard?"

"Because I'm dating him," I blurt out. Two weeks ago I would have found this type of indiscretion on my part intolerable. But there's something about dating a creature from folklore that has made me throw discretion headfirst out the window. I've been telling strangers on the street. I told the teller at my bank the other day that I was in a hurry. "If I don't get home soon, my boyfriend, the Chupacabra, will kill me. *Kill me!*" When I returned a few minutes later because I'd forgotten to get a roll of quarters, I saw that her line was closed and she was talking to a circle of women in the back.

The Ring Toss Lady bows her head for a moment. She seems to hold the Chupacabra in some degree of reverence. I want to share the moment with her, but the spire on top of her head is now tickling my chin. "The Chupacabra is a beautiful creature. A proud one. He only kills when he must."

"Wow. Where'd you hear about that?"

"A&E," the Ring Toss Lady says. "I have cable."

"Herve is a proud creature," I admit to her, "but I'm not sure I'm ready for all the cultural differences."

The Ring Toss Lady nods. "It's a bitch. I won't deny it. But once I dated a gentleman fellow from Dusseldorf, which is in Germany. He cured his own pork. He introduced me to over forty types of sausages."

I wait to see where this story is going and how it relates to mine, but the Ring Toss Lady doesn't say anything else. Then her eyes get wide and she moves close to me.

"Something for you to think about."

I still have a few minutes to kill, so I wander over to the Occult section of the library and start pulling down books until I find a few that talk about the Chupacabra. I take a stack to a nearby desk where I proceed to read everything I can find on this creature. I'm so engrossed by what I'm reading, I miss my Spanish class completely.

Much of the same information is repeated throughout the books. Bloodsucker. Goats. Puncture Wounds. Small towns terrorized. But as I read I notice some things aren't making sense to me. The

Chupacabra is primarily a bloodsucker, yet there was an abundance
of blood in the plastic bag. The creature is supposed to be violent
and irritable, yet Herve cries during the pledge drives for PBS. There
is something mysterious and dark that I just don't see in Herve's personality—that he's keeping hidden.

I read everything I can about this creature until the library closes.
Then I head home.

"All of this is very different from what you think," Herve started,
cautiously. "Some of it's pretty technical, and I won't bore you with
that. But basically, there isn't just one Chupacabra. There are a lot of
them. Some of them are my relatives, and some of them I'm related
to as much as you are to any person you'd pass on the street. My
family still believes in the old ways, and they were pretty disappointed when I decided to move to L.A. Don't get me wrong, they're not
evil people, but they have a weird sense of humor. They like tor-
menting villagers. They like all the ghost stories. I just wanted to get
out of the limelight and meet a guy I could settle down with." Herve
lets this information sit for a moment.

"Have you ever killed anyone?" I ask.

"Never."

"Oh," I say. "Do you go out at night and suck the blood out of
wild animals?"

He laughs at me. "No-o-o! I just go for walks."

"What about that bag I found in the trash?"

"I was weak. I gave in. I bought a bag of doggie scraps at the market. I didn't even drink much of the blood."

"Don't you even get the urge to kill something?" I ask.
"Anything?"

"Sometimes, I guess. But I concentrate on other things. Recite
poetry. I get over it pretty fast."

"Poetry?"

"Sure! Poetry. Or sometimes I sing to myself. Like that Suzanne
Vega song. 'Luka.' It's a distraction. What's wrong, Joshua? You
look...something. Like you're disappointed?"

"No, really, I'm—"

"What is it?"

"It's just," I start, clearing my throat, "I thought that with you being the Chupacabra and all, you'd...you know, do some crazy stuff. What you're telling me sounds kind of boring."

"I do *some* crazy stuff," Herve said sitting up on the couch. "When you were in New York last year I didn't shave for the whole weekend. My hair got really long."

"And what did you do?" I ask, readying myself for a salacious story.

"I shaved it before you got back. Actually, I was in the shower shaving when you came home. I was so nervous you were going to open the shower curtain and see all that hair." Herve loses himself laughing until he sees me staring at him. "Maybe that's not what you mean by crazy."

"You're the goddamn Chupacabra, man, you're—"

"I told you. I'm not *the* Chupacabra—"

"—supposed to decimate villages. Kill cows. Dance underneath the full moon."

"Dance?"

"Yeah! I read in one article at the library that someone saw the Chupacabra dance under the full moon. The Chupacabra dance." Remembering the description given by the poor villager, I jump up from the couch and do an impromptu dance. It is part Agnes de Mille, part *In Living Color* Fly-Girl, and part *Million Dollar Movie* voodoo rhapsody. It is all sheer nonsense, but it feels grand doing it. Liberating and soulful. The thought of dancing under the moon. Capturing rays. Hugging the heavens. Thanking the universe for the gift of some wild animal. The gift of blood. THANK YOU, MOON. THANK YOU, FEET. THANK YOU, GROUND. THANK YOU, ANIMAL. THANK YOU, VILLAGERS. THANK YOU, BLOOD, OH, BLOOD, THANK YOU, BLOOD. THANK YOU...

Herve taps me on the shoulder. "You know," he says, cocking his head, "this is really not a culture I think you could understand. So I'd appreciate if you wouldn't mock it."

"I'm not mocking it! I'm celebrating it! I'm saying, it's OK. It's great that you're the Chupacabra. It's *sexy* that you're the

Chupacabra. You have my permission to be the Chupacabra."

Herve stands and grabs hold of my shoulders. His voice is stern but still loving. "Joshua, I'm living my life the way I want to, based on me, not you. If you were to leave, I'd still be living my life this way. I'm not living my life the way my parents want me to be, and I'm certainly not up to fulfilling your Internet-induced wet dream. Sorry."

"You're suppressing it," I say with some measure of desperation.

"Can we go to bed?"

"You feel shame," I tell him.

"I feel exhaustion," Herve says. "Can we move on now? Can we just continue with our life together?"

I tell him that of course we can. We go upstairs and go to bed, Herve falls asleep almost as quickly as we turn off the light. I try to act like all of this is fine, but deep down I know I'm disappointed. I ponder this in bed while Herve lies next to me, snoring like a caveman. This is just my luck. Always happens to me. I once met a porn star who, the day before we met, decided to become celibate and take up Buddhism. I dated a former millionaire who was now broke. I was hit on once by a former TV superhero two years after his show was canceled and his once-stunning body had gone to seed. In short, I've never dated anyone who was at the height of being who they are.

Flowers arrive the next day. "Now There Are No More Mysteries. No More Secrets. Just Us In Our Home Built From Love. Yours, Herve." The flowers are a dreary mix of white and red carnations. We don't have a vase, so I put them in an empty milk carton, place it on the living room table, and wait for them to die.

For the next few days Herve and I pretend that our lives are back to normal. We peck each other on the check once in the morning and once in the evening, and eat our meals together with cool detachment. One night, out of desperation, I even pick up Dr. Louden Marver's book again to see if there might be something to learn from it. But, in all honesty, by this time I'm reading the book more for the previous owner's comments than the doctor's. Under the chapter titled, "Communication: How to get it, how to keep it going," there is a section that states, "Think of what tools you might need to help your partner communicate better." In the margin the previous owner penciled in **"Sodium Pentathol."**

In the morning I put notices on the refrigerator for Herve to see. Things about the Chupacabra I've culled from various Web sites. When I get home the notices are gone. I find them balled up in the trash.

For two weeks this continues. We go to bed at night, say our "I love you's," then retreat to our separate sides of the bed. Herve is in San Francisco; I'm in Bangor, Maine. No plans on meeting in Michigan anytime soon. But then one night I wake up wistful and lonely. I feel alone on my side of the continent; I want to hug my boyfriend, find our differences healed. I am remorseful. I am forgiving. I am really, really horny.

I reach over to Herve's side of the bed and find only layers of unraveled sheets. Suddenly I'm awake. Awake in a way I haven't been in a long while. Feel like I've been sleepwalking through the days. Now the energy in the room feels electric. Now I need my boyfriend.

He's not in the house. I don't even have to look to know that. I throw on whatever clothes sit on a nearby chair. The house, the walls, the furniture, the wood art, the appliances, mirrors, all urge me to go. To find Herve.

I remember my dream from weeks ago about the trail of ants, and I head out the front door and once outside make a sharp turn. I turn away from the road. I head toward hills, toward the moon, and the Hollywood sign.

The night is pure power. Shadows stalk me. Dry leaves shriek underneath my feet. I am marching. Toward my partner. I've never been through these back hills before. They are wanton strangers. They flirt. Bony branches wave me over. But I keep marching. I have no choice. A chilled wind wraps around me, hugs me like a life vest. I can smell all of Los Angeles from here. It smells like a soup. A vichyssoise. And sounds. The snores of the city heightened, conducted like a concert at the Hollywood Bowl. All together now.

In a distance I see Herve. Actually, I feel him before I see him. His warmth. His blood percolating through his veins. His back is to me, but he doesn't turn as I approach. Still, he knows I'm here. His back flinches like I'm the crack of a whip. He is staring off at God knows what. When I'm behind him I see. There is a dog-house. There is a pig, sleeping in the dirt. We are at that TV actor's house. My Herve is looking at the pig like a kid marveling at the circus.

"He's sleeping outside tonight. Sometimes he gets to sleep inside." Herve shakes his head dismissively. "He's the dumbest crea-ture I've ever seen."

"Is this where you go?" I ask.

Herve just points at the pig. "I bet Toulouse is the best-fed pig in the world. He has the belly of a gourmand. Bet he gets porcini mushrooms and all the bruschetta he can eat."

I pull my arms around Herve. Light a fire with our warmth. "Let's go back," I say. I tug, but my boyfriend stays in place.

"Such a ridiculous creature. So unnecessary."

I slip my hands under Herve's sweater. He's sweating. I move my other hand down to his crotch and find that Herve has an erection the size of Delaware. "Have you ever touched him?" I ask. Herve shakes his head. There is only a fence that separates us from Toulouse. I climb over it.

"What are you doing? Josh, get back here. You're trespassing!"

"Touch the pig,"

"No—"

"I'm not going to be happy till you touch the pig. You're not going to—"

"We'll go home."

But I don't want to go home. I'm smashed. Fucked up. Overwhelmed by the beauty and compliance and energy of the night. I pick up a brick and hold it over Toulouse's head.

"Josh!" Herve climbs over the fence and stands next to me. "Put it down."

"Fat fucking pig," I say. "Fat fucking pig, fat fucking pig, fat fucking pig, fat fucking pig..." The pig stirs. But he's smiling. The stupid pig is smiling. Dreaming, no doubt, of chocolate orgies. I call in a few favors from my body and thrust the brick down on the pig's skull. The pig screams a monosyllable scream and looks up at me. This pig has probably only seen a silk pajama–clad white boy teasing him with slivers of Wolfgang Puck pizza. He's never seen a white boy clutching a brick. He gets up but falls back to the floor. His eyes are white terror. He keeps shrieking. I see Herve's eyes dart over to the actor's house.

"He's going to wake up. We're fucked," Herve says.

The pig keeps screaming. It's probably never heard its voice before. It keeps trying to stand. Herve grabs the brick from the ground and slams it against the pig's head with shocking magnitude. Even the sound is muted by the speed of the motion. Sounds like a baseball bat busting one out of the stadium. I look at Herve. "I had to put the poor thing out of its misery," he says. He starts crying. "I've never killed anything before," he says between sobs. He rests his head on the belly of the pig. "He's still warm."

"Not for long," I say.

Now this is the moment. The one that everything rests on. And we both know it. This moment crackles with potential. Herve caresses the carcass of this celebrity pig. A pig whose death could even make the papers in this town. A descendant of Arnold from *Green Acres*? A stand-in for Babe, perhaps.

"*El puerco es muerto*," I say.

Herve winces at my pronunciation, nods, finds a blood vessel then chows down.

An hour before sunrise we're back home and in bed. Herve is calm, but his body is moving in unusual little ways. Like he's one of those Disneyland robots that's been wired badly. He tells me a story about when he was a little...boy? And his...grandfather? took him out for a hunt.

"I'll never forget it. We saw this cow. He sped over and sucked the blood clean out of it before it even knew what hit it. Really, Josh, it was as quick as a flu shot. It was over that fast. I told him I found the whole thing repulsive. He laughed and said, 'Tssu, that will change.'"

"Tssu?"

"Short for Tschzymn. My real name."

"Your name's not Herve?"

"When I moved out to L.A.—"

"You mean you picked your own name? You had your choice of any name, like Andrew or David or Terrence, and you picked Herve?"

"I like my name."

I stroke Herve's beautiful mane of hair. Eventually we fall asleep holding each other.

Over the next few days Herve takes a stronger interest in the folklore of the Chupacabra. He sits with me at the computer as we look up information. Most of it makes him laugh uproariously. Some of it he reads and rereads. Prints up and puts in a folder. He is also flooded with memories. Words. Beautiful words. I write some of them down. *Wir-ra Perrute. Nyspooleen.*

One night Herve is too excited to sleep.

"I think there *was* a dance under the moon one night. After a kill. It was nothing like that mess you were doing. But there was a dance. Orz...something. Orztsay? No. Orz something. It scared me, but it was beautiful. There was a bonfire. I can't believe I didn't remember about that."

Then, as quickly as it started, it stops. Herve doesn't want to talk about it anymore. With me, at least. He becomes quiet and uncommunicative. He talks to one of his sisters one night on the phone. He brings the extension into the bathroom and shuts the door. "*Ries,*" I say to him one evening. It means perfect night. Herve just gives me a dirty look and walks away. He stops shaving every day. The hair in the shower drain gets so bad I have to call a plumber. Herve quits his job at the photo lab and starts working in an occult bookstore. All this happens the same week.

That weekend I return home and see Sammy's car in the driveway. I haven't been to Spanish class for a few weeks, so I imagine he's here to reprimand me. I don't see Herve's car outside so I wonder how Sammy got into our house.

I wander around inside the house until I find Sammy upstairs, lying on the bedroom carpet. Dead. Puncture wound on his upper neck.

I try to remain calm. I pick up *Couple Skills,* which is lying on the nightstand next to my bed. I search and search the book. Page after tattered page. The closest thing I can find is a section called "If your boyfriend has inappropriate contact with a friend." In the section Dr. Marver states, "Sometimes it is difficult to recover from this type of breach. You may find you have deep resentment toward your boyfriend. You may find yourself wanting to distance yourself from your friend. That is normal."

I do find that, as of now, I want to distance myself from Sammy. The stench is a little overwhelming. I go downstairs and wait for Herve to get home. He comes in a half hour later, in a jolly mood, with a big bag from Rite Aid.

"Where have you been?" I ask.

"Drugstore." Herve points to his stomach. "Tummy ache. So, how was your day, Josh?"

I don't answer him.

"Josh? Is something bothering you? Are you going to tell me or just pout about it?"

"It's about Sammy."

"I'm listening."

"He was a friend!" I yell.

"Was he?" Herve asks. "I thought you two had a falling-out."

"That doesn't mean you had to suck out all his blood! We weren't getting along that badly."

"You know, Josh, I understand your being upset. I do. I want to let you know I didn't plan this. Sammy came over, and it happened."

"I don't believe..."

"Hey, you can't be that upset with me. You're the one who's always telling me to follow my instincts. Leaving me those notes and articles on the fridge. Telling me to empower myself. That's what I was doing."

"But with my best friend? There's a million annoying people in this neighborhood. That woman…that woman who has a garage sale every weekend. Or that guy who's always playing show tunes at 2 in the morning. What about them?"

"You're really trying to make me feel bad about this, aren't you? This was a big step for me, you know."

"What you did is immoral!"

"You were raised Catholic, Josh. Don't talk 'immoral' to me. Blood of Christ, body of Christ. Eat your Gods? And I'm immoral?" Herve starts to go outside, and I follow him.

"Don't walk away from me. The difference here, Herve…"

"Tschzymn."

"Like I didn't see that coming," I say. "The difference here is that Jesus gave of himself willingly. Whatever you think about the religion, at least that's the story. I doubt Sammy came over and said 'Herve, pal, I'm lunch.' But correct me if I'm wrong."

Herve sneers at me. "Fesshah."

"Pardon?"

"It's an expression. You wouldn't understand."

"Ooh. Fesshah. I see. You eat my friend, now fesshah. You're getting all Chupacabra-y on me."

"This isn't working out," Herve says.

"What's next? You're only going to be able to date other urban legends? Don't forget, Tschzymn, I knew you when you were just Herve Bustamente. You didn't even know what gazpacho was when I met you."

"I have a migraine. Do you want to sleep on the couch, Josh, or should I?"

"I'm not sleeping on the couch. After you pick up Sammy's body, I'm locking myself in the bedroom. I don't want to wake up and find you biting into any of my limbs."

"You don't have to worry about that. I wouldn't eat you if you were the last living thing in Hollywood."

Herve starts going inside. "And another thing," I say. "If you're going to kill anything else tonight, don't bring it inside, OK? I'm going to have to get the carpets cleaned as it is. Now we're never going to get our cleaning deposit back."

"Fesshah,"

"Oh, Fesshah, yourself."

Chapter 28
Time To Call It Quits?

Many couples come to me to find out if there are ways to mend broken fences, broken relationships. For some, it is possible. Unfortunately, for many, the fat lady is already singing when they come in to my office. Some of these differences are philosophical. Some cultural. Some financial. But it does pose an essential question that you should ask yourself. How do I know my relationship is over?

When you know you'd rather kill him than eat dinner with him again at Boston Market.

Things happen fast from this point. Herve decides he needs space to fully explore the ramifications of his newfound identity as a postmodern folklore citizen. I wish him well and decide not to make a scene about it. We've had a good run. We stayed together longer than most. We did some traveling. We took a few gay ballroom dancing classes together. We killed a celebrity pig in the Hollywood Hills under a fierce moon. Maybe there is no place else for this relationship to go.

A week after Herve leaves, Gretyl and Lissel call me from Trinidad to tell me they're returning home to take advantage of the burgeoning wood-art market.

I start the process of looking for an apartment and pick the first one I look at: a depressing eighties stucco atrocity in Studio City, just around the corner from a fifties-style theme diner. I hear '50s music all through the night.

And the drought is finally over. It rains.

One day in Hancock Park I run into the Ring Toss Lady. She's dressed in red velvet drapes.

"You never came back to Señora Bartlett's class," she says.

"Yeah, life's been a little strange lately."

"We had a potluck. I brought some cured sausages."

"Maybe next year."

"Your friend, Sammy, didn't come back either."

"Well…my boyfriend killed him and buried him in the hills. I really didn't know who to notify at the school about that."

We walk at an even pace. A car slows down, stares at her and yells something out the window before speeding off. She takes no notice of it. "How is your boyfriend, the Chupacabra?"

"We broke up. It didn't…well, it was hard, you know…stressful, dating an urban legend."

The Ring Toss Lady stops and looks at me. She's balancing her stiff erection of hair that looms to the sky. "I see. That must be tough."

☐   ☐   ☐

It has been weeks since my last conversation with Herve, and it has gotten to the point where every time the phone rings I've stopped expecting that it's going to be him on the other line. I suppose I'd call that progress. That plus the fact that my number is only one digit away from an Italian restaurant, so several times a day I get wrong numbers. Rather than explain the situation to people who call it's become easier just to take the reservation. That's why I'm a little annoyed when I get a phone call at 8 P.M. on this Saturday night. They think they can get a reservation on such a short notice? I ask myself. Not in my restaurant. I AM NOT AN OLIVE GARDEN, GODDAMN IT!

"Buena Serra, this is Frankie's," I say, picking up the phone, feigning to be out of breath.

These are the kind of things that entertain me now that I'm single again.

"Oh, sorry, I must have the wrong…"

"Herve?" There is a silence on the other end of the phone. "Tschzymn, I mean."

"Josh, it's good to hear your voice. How are you?"

I don't want to admit it to myself, but hearing his voice is wonderful. It is an elixir. I imagine that he is still Herve. That we still live in the Hollywood Hills. That he's calling me on his way home. Do I need anything from the market?

"Keeping myself busy," I say. "It's been a while."

"Yeah, I was traveling around Northern California. Taking stock."

I think about how nice it would be to see him again. To hold him. "Do you want to stop over? I have plans, but I think I could break them." In the background there is a loud, echoed voice.

"Actually, I'm at the airport right now. I only have a minute."

"Oh. Where are you going?"

"The Dominican Republic to visit my family. Then Peru."

"Wow. That's pretty major." I try to sound as upbeat as possible.

"Yeah, well, a lot's happened since I've last seen you."

Then I hear someone else's voice from the other line. It is low and raspy.

"Sweetie," it says, "we're going to miss the plane."

"*Cocate*," my ex tells the voice, "I told you I need a minute here." Herve then addresses me again. "I have to go. I just wanted to thank you, Josh. You really helped me through some stuff. I know it wasn't easy on you."

"*Apurate!*" the other voice says, calling out to him."

"Guess I'll be reading about you," I say.

"Perhaps," he says. "So, take care. *No dejes que los insectos de la cama piquen.*"

"You too," I say. The phone clicks, and Herve is gone.

Later that evening I go to a bar because I have to get out of the house. The rain has become nearly torrential, but it's still better than staying home by myself. I need to be around people. Talking. Laughing. Ignoring me from across the room. I need to be around normalcy.

I find a place called the Alibi. It has everything a proper gay bar needs. Beer. Bad lighting and a pool table. The Alibi seems to attract an older clientele, but I don't even care. I buy a Corona, stick myself in a corner, and eavesdrop on conversations. Soon a group of younger guys come in and plant themselves at a table near mine. They're loud, a little drunk, and in a terrific mood. One of the guys starts telling the group a story he heard about a man stopped for drunk driving who sped off while the cop was writing him a ticket. The guy was caught the next morning because he'd mistakenly taken the police officer's car.

"That's not true," someone else at the table says. "That's one of those stories. The ones everyone tells. It's not even a new one."

"I heard a new one," someone else at the table says. "This guy finds out that his boyfriend is the Chupacabra."

"The Chupa-what?" someone says.

"He's a monster. From Puerto Rico."

"Anyway, this guy only finds out when his boyfriend eats his best friend. Then at Thanksgiving his boyfriend eats his entire family. He has to move out of the country just to break up with him."

I take another swig of my beer. Finish it off. The rain is banging at the windows. At the doors. Banging.

"That's bullshit. Where'd you hear that story?"

"At the gym. My trainer knows someone who knows someone who actually knows this guy."

It seems warm. The bar is...*caliente*...no, that's spicy. The bar is spicy. I brush my beer bottle across my temple, but it's hot too.

"So the Chupa—whatever, is queer?"

"What I'd like to know is whether the Chupacabra is a top or a bottom."

"I'd guess bottom," the guy telling the story says. "Bottom-feed-er, I mean."

They laugh.

I decide it's time to...go. I pick myself up and go to the entrance-way of the Alibi. Outside a man, a mustached man, stands under the doorframe. It's raining so hard that you can't even see the street.

"I'm waiting for a lull, but there hasn't been one. Can't even make a run for my car. Can't even see it."

"It'll pass," I say, looking to locate my car.

"I hate this fucking city," the guy says. "Moved here from Dallas."

"It's not so bad," I say.

"You like living here?" he asks. A cold breeze hits us. I feel like I'm going to pass out.

"I don't really think about it that much. But there are a lot of good reasons to live here."

"Betcha can't name one," he tells me.

I look into this man's eyes. They are impatient eyes. They seem to be communicating with me, but I don't know what they're saying.

"Name one thing," the man repeats.

I look out toward the rain. In the background I see a billboard. I attempt to read it, but I can't make out the words. The letters. The letters on the…the letters in my mind, scampering away like roaches when the light is turned on. My mind is empty, and I am left groping. Pull them back. Letters and words and sentences and phrases and emotions and boyfriends who return home and parents who are truly yours. To a language that is….mine. I start to cry and speak. Gibberish. The man stares. I'm speaking. Louder. Till I hear myself. It is not English or Spanish or any other language I've studied or learned or loved or stolen. It is mine. It's not even the language of love. The rain hits the pavement sounding apologetic. Forgiving.

What I realize now is that I have nothing. What I'm speaking here, the only language I have, is a language of loss. That is what I have to work with. That will have to do for now.

Contributors

Eitan Alexander, born October 6, 1962, resides in Los Angeles and sometimes, in a free moment, plots to insinuate himself into the lexicon of the future by pimping the past. He lives with two cats—brothers, named Lyle and Erik.

M. Shayne Bell is the author of the novel *Nicoji* and editor of the anthology *Washed by a Wave of Wind: Science Fiction From the Corridor.* His short fiction has been published in Asimov's *Fantasy and Science Fiction, Amazing Stories, Tomorrow, Gothic.Net,* and *Realms of Fantasy,* and in ten anthologies, including *Starlight 2, Future Earths: Under African Skies, Simulations: Fifteen Tales of Virtual Reality,* and *War of the Worlds: Global Dispatches.* His stories have appeared in each of the *Star Wars* short story anthologies. His story "Mrs. Lincoln's China" was a 1995 Hugo Award finalist.

Bernard Cooper is the recipient of a PEN/Hemingway Award, the O. Henry Award, and a 1999 Guggenheim Fellowship. His most recent book is *Truth Serum.* "Hunters and Gatherers" is from *Guess Again,* a collection of short stories forthcoming from Simon and Schuster.

Mitch Cullin's short fiction has appeared in *The Santa Fe Literary Review, The Gilasolo, CTC Chronicle, The Bayou Review, Austin Flux, Christopher Street,* and *Flux* (Houston). Mr. Cullin's prose can be found in *Best Gay Erotica 1996* (Cleis Press), and one of his modern fairy tales appears in the anthology *Happily Ever After* (Richard Kasak Books). His short story "Sifting Through" is in *Best American Gay Fiction 2* (Little, Brown). His novels *Whompyjawed* and *Branches* are forthcoming from The Permanent Press.

Jameson Currier is the author of a novel, *Where the Rainbow Ends;* a collection of short stories, *Dancing on the Moon;* and a documentary film, *Living Proof.* He resides in Manhattan.

Robert Drake: See "About the Editors."

David Ebershoff is the author of the novel *The Danish Girl* and a forthcoming collection, *The Dress and Other Stories*. Originally from Pasadena, Calif., he now lives in New York, where he works at Random House and is the publishing director of the Modern Library.

About his story he writes: "I have begun to set most of my fiction in Pasadena, and I wrote 'The Rose City' to examine the type of man who has no place in that society. I imagine that gay fiction in the 21st century, along with all thoughtful fiction, will continue to tell the stories of people whom we often, and sometimes for good reason, overlook."

Thomas Glave's collection *Whose Song? and Other Stories* will be published by City Lights in fall 2000. A 1998-99 Fulbright Scholar and recipient of a 1997 O. Henry Award, he is an assistant professor of English at the State University of New York, Binghamton.

Scott Heim is the author of *In Awe* (a novel), *Mysterious Skin* (both novel and screenplay), and *Saved From Drowning* (poetry). In 1998 he taught classes in the United Kingdom as the London Arts Board's International Writer-in-Residence. He lives in Brooklyn, N.Y., where he is finishing a third novel, *We Disappear*.

David Leavitt is the author of *Family Dancing*, a finalist for both the PEN/Faulkner Award and the National Book Critics Circle Award; *The Lost Language of Cranes*, which was made into a BBC film; the short story collection *Arkansas*; and, most recently, *The Page Turner*. With Mark Mitchell, he is a coeditor of *The Penguin Book of Gay Short Stories*, *Pages Passed From Hand to Hand: The Hidden Tradition of Homosexual Literature in English From 1748 to 1914* and coauthor of *Italian Pleasures*. A recipient of fellowships from both the John Simon Guggenheim Foundation and the National Endowment for the Arts, he lives in Italy.

Russell Leong's book of poems *The Country of Dreams and Dust* received the PEN Josephine Miles Literature Award. His forthcoming book of short stories, *Phoenix Eyes,* will be published by the University of Washington Press in 2000. Leong edited *Asian American Sexualities: Dimensions of the Gay and Lesbian Experience* (Routledge).

Michael Lowenthal, born in 1969, is the author of a novel, *The Same Embrace,* and editor of *Gay Men at the Millennium, Obsessed, Flesh and the Word 4,* and other books. His stories and essays have appeared in periodicals such as *The New York Times Magazine* and *The Kenyon Review* and in anthologies including *Best American Gay Fiction, Men on Men 5, Queer 13,* and *Wrestling with the Angel.* A graduate of Dartmouth College and a former university press editor, he now lives and writes full-time in Boston.

William J. Mann is the author of the novels *The Biograph Girl* and *The Men From the Boys* as well as *Wisecracker: The Life and Times of William Haines,* soon to be a cable television film. His new book on the gay experience in the Hollywood studio system, *Behind the Scenes, Behind the Lines,* will be published by Viking next year.

This story, "Say Goodbye to Middletown," was originally conceived as—and may eventually still turn up as—part of a collection of interrelated short stories in homage to Sherwood Anderson's *Winesburg, Ohio.*

Jaime Manrique was born in Colombia. His first volume of poetry received his country's National Poetry Award. In English he has published the poetry collection *My Night with Federico García Lorca* and the novels *Colombian Gold, Latin Moon in Manhattan,* and *Twilight at the Equator.* The recipient of many awards, Manrique has taught in the MFA Program at Columbia University and at New York University, Mount Holyoke College, and the New School for Social Research. Forthcoming in July 1999 is his autobiography *Eminent Maricones: Arenas, Lorca, Puig, and Me.* He has just completed a new novel.

Christian McLaughlin is the author of *Glamourpuss* and *Sex Toys of the Gods*. He lives and works in Los Angeles, where, in addition to cranking out many, many episodes of disreputable television sitcoms, he is currently collaborating with Robert Rodi on a sure-to-be-offensive new novel. For the record, he has never met Mitchell Anderson, nor does he want to.

David A. Newman grew up in Michigan and is a graduate of the University of Notre Dame. An award winner in the Hemingway Short Story Competition, his stories have appeared in *His* (Volumes I and II) and in *Men on Men 7*. Newman lives in Los Angeles, where he is at work on a novel and a collection of stories. Of his story here, he writes: "When I was little, there was a well-advertised Mystery Spot somewhere in Northern Michigan. It was deemed a worthless tourist trap by my parents, who drove right by no matter how loud I screamed. Now I'm grateful they kept Mystery Spot a mystery. I would like to dedicate this story to Bunny-J, Pops Pud, K-Bun, and to the memory of Leigh Hudgins."

Andy Quan, born in Vancouver, B.C., is a third-generation Chinese-Canadian and fifth-generation Chinese-American writer and singer-songwriter. His short fiction and poetry have appeared in Canada, the United States, and the United Kingdom, including in *Take Out: Queer Writing from Asian Pacific America* and the gay men's anthologies *Contra/Diction*, *Queeries*, and *Best Gay Erotica 1999* and *2000*. He is coeditor of *Swallowing Clouds: An Anthology of Chinese Canadian Poetry* (Arsenal Pulp Press). He has lived in Toronto, Brussels, and London, and is currently in Sydney working as the international policy officer for the Australian Federation of AIDS Organizations.

Keith Ridgway is a novelist and short story writer from Dublin. He has had stories published in various anthologies in the United Kingdom and Ireland. His novel, *The Long Falling,* was published by Houghton Mifflin in 1998 and was nominated for a Lambda Literary Award. He

lives in a state of disarray between Dublin, London, and Florence but
has no money.

Frank Ronan was born in Ireland in 1963. He has written four
novels, *The Men Who Loved Evelyn Cotton,* which won the *Irish
Times*/Aer Lingus Prize; *A Picnic in Eden; The Better Angel;* and
Dixie Chicken. His first collection of short stories, *Handsome Men
Are Slightly Sunburnt,* contains work published in the anthologies
Best Short Stories and *The Best of Cosmo Fiction* as well as in the
Daily Telegraph and various magazines, and broadcast on BBC
Radio 4.

Colm Tóibín was born in Ireland in 1955 and now lives in Dublin.
He is the author of *Walking Along the Border, Homage to Barcelona,
The Sign of the Cross: Travels in Catholic Europe,* and *The South,* his
first novel. *The Heather Blazing* won the Encore Award for best second novel in 1992.

David Vernon says of his story here: "I am pleased to say that
'Couple kills' actually began its life around a campfire. A short
while back I was on a camping trip with my partner's family, and
over the evening campfire someone starting talking about the
Chupacabra. Since the Chupacabra is a relatively new myth, I was
delighted to hear all about this new folk legend. After that, the conversation shifted toward family gossip, and I saw how, in a way,
through the mysteries of our own lives, loves, and actions, we all
become urban legends. After I wrote 'Love Is Thin Ice,' I thought
I purged myself of weird Los Angeles stories, but luckily, a few
nights later in my Wednesday writing group, this story just spilled
out of me.

"I need to thank my partner, Crespin Rosas, for his wonderful
feedback and support, my astute and talented writing group,
Precious and Few, particularly David Newman, who went above and
beyond the call of duty. I especially need to thank Lydia Rameriez,
campfire storyteller extraordinaire."

Other stories by David Vernon can be found in: *His* (Volumes 1 and 2), *Men on Men* (Volumes 4 and 6), and *Blood Whispers* (Volumes 1 and 2).

About the Editors

Robert Drake is the author of *The Gay Canon: Great Books Every Gay Man Should Read* and the novel *The Man: A Hero for Our Time.* He is coeditor of the anthologies *Indivisible: New Short Fiction by West Coast Gay and Lesbian Writers* and the Lambda Literary Award–winning series *His: Brilliant New Fiction by Gay Men* and *Hers: Brilliant New Fiction by Lesbians.* From 1986 to 1998 he earned his living as a literary agent, finding time to serve from 1993 to 1998 as book review editor for the *Baltimore Alternative* and teach writing at community colleges in the city of Philadelphia and Anne Arundel County, Maryland, as well as the American University and St. John's College, where he received his master's degree in 1993. Born in Portland, Maine, and raised in Charleston, W. Va., he was living in Ireland when, in January 1999, he was beaten unconscious in a gay-bashing attack, sustaining severe trauma to the head. He is currently undergoing rehabilitation in Philadelphia.

Terry Wolverton is the author of the novel *Bailey's Beads* and two collections of poetry, *Black Slip* and *Mystery Bruise.* Her fiction, poetry, essays, and dramatic texts have appeared in numerous literary publications, including *ZYZZYVA, Calyx,* and *Glimmer Train Stories,* and have been widely anthologized. She has also edited several acclaimed literary compilations, including *Blood Whispers: L.A. Writers on AIDS* and, with Robert Drake, *Indivisible: New Short Fiction by West Coast Gay and Lesbian Writers* and the Lambda Literary Award-winning series *His: Brilliant New Fiction by Gay Men* and *Hers: Brilliant New Fiction by Lesbians.* Since 1976, Terry has lived in Los Angeles where she's been active in the feminist, gay and lesbian, and art communities. In 1997 she founded Writers At Work, a center for writing workshops and individual creative consultations. She is currently at work on two books: *Embers,* a novel in poems, and *Insurgent Muse,* a memoir to be published by City Lights Publishers.

Acknowledgments

The editors wish to thank Gwin Wheatley for incalculable editorial assistance and so much more, and to Elaine Howell and Robin Podolsky for additional editorial assistance. Thanks to Scott Pretorius and Ciaran Slevin for making Robert's files accessible during his incapacity. We gratefully thank the authors, publishers, and agents who gave permission for the works to appear in this book. Finally, deep appreciation to John Talbot, and to Scott Brassart and Angela Brown for patience and support.

Credits

EITAN ALEXANDER: "Beneath the Planet of the Compulsives." Reprinted by permission of the author.

M. SHAYNE BELL: "Mrs. Lincoln's China." Reprinted by permission of the author.

BERNARD COOPER: "Hunters and Gatherers." Reprinted by permission of the author.

MITCH CULLIN: from "The Cosmology of Bing." © 2000 by Mitch Cullin.

JAMESON CURRIER: "Pasta Night." © 2000 by Jameson Currier.

ROBERT DRAKE: "Power." Copyright © 2000 by Robert Drake.

DAVID EBERSHOFF: "The Rose City." Reprinted by permission of the author.

THOMAS GLAVE: "Whose Song?" Reprinted by permission of the author.

SCOTT HEIM: "Deep Green, Pale Purple." Reprinted by permission of the author.

DAVID LEAVITT: "The Term Paper Artist" from *Arkansas*. © 1997 by David Leavitt. Reprinted by permission of Houghton Mifflin Company. All rights reserved.

RUSSELL LEONG: "Virgins and Buddhas." Reprinted by permission of the author.

MICHAEL LOWENTHAL: "Into the Mirror" from *The Same*

"Novel excerpts bump up against short stories; science fiction jostles beside literary fiction; punk sensibility elbows its way next to high camp and classically constructed stories. The end of the 20th century has been about the breaking down of fixed categories—of art forms, of culture, of gender, of sexual orientation—the blurring of borders to allow an infinite variety of options for identity and expression. What this anthology aims to do is introduce you to, or remind you about, a selection of writers whose intelligence, style, and heart may ease our passage into the next millennium." —from the introduction by Terry Wolverton

Contributors include:
Andy Quan
David Vernon
Frank Ronan
Scott Heim
Russell Leong
Jameson Currier
William J. Mann
Mitch Cullin
Christian McLaughlin
Eitan Alexander
M. Shayne Bell
Keith Ridgway
Michael Lowenthal
David A. Newman
David Ebershoff
Thomas Glave
David Leavitt
Jaime Manrique
Bernard Cooper
Colm Tóibín

About the Editors:
Robert Drake has worked as a literary agent since 1986. His pop-culture novel THE MAN rapidly developed a cult following after it was released in 1995. Terry Wolverton is the author of the novel BAILEY'S BEADS as well as two collections of poetry, BLACK SLIP and MYSTERY BRUISE. She is the founder of Writers at Work, where she teaches workshops in creative writing. The two editors have also worked together on the acclaimed HIS and HERS anthologies, and have garnered nine Lambda Literary Award nominations between them.

alyson publications
printed in usa
www.alyson.com
$14.95 USA
£9.99 UK

ISBN 1-55583-517-1

51495

9 781555 835170